# YRARTZ!

## Do not be alarmed!

By

BA Eytcheson

BA Eytcheson Publishing

2017

This book is dedicated to Louis Ramey. His comedy inspired me to this madness.

# Prolog

Should you someday find yourself in Northern Wisconsin near the Bibon Swamp, enjoy the beauty and variety there. If you are adventurous enough, brave enough, to go into the swamp you may hear some strange sights and see some strange sounds.

Ask the locals about West Falls and most will say they never heard of it. Some will stare off into the swamp, terror in their eyes. Others will simply walk away without a word.

# Chapter 1

Earl Stinnett looked the part of the typical farmer he was, bib overalls, slightly greasy and very dusty, red bandana hanging lifelessly from a back pocket. His feet held inside down-at-heel engineer boots that hadn't seen shoe polish since they were born. And always the John Deere hat perched atop his head hiding the line between the sunburn and the sunless.

He was of average height and thin. The wrinkles on his face were permanent now. Arthritis was creeping up on him but hadn't yet caused any deformity.

Earl Stinnett still lived on the small farm he grew up on. He lived there alone most of his life. The place was located on the edge of the Bibon Swamp just a few miles from the town of West Falls, Wisconsin.

His father was killed in a tractor rollover when Earl was seventeen. Once he took over the farming duties full time his mother moved to Ashland. He lived alone until a pretty, young school bus driver pulled into his yard one sunny morning.

"Excuse me sir," she began then thought better of it and shut off the bus engine. Earl climbed up onto the bus. "Sir I'm new on this route. Could you tell me do you have any school age children here?"

Earl shrugged and said, "Not that I've seen. I live alone." It was obvious to Earl she was lost and he smiled at that. She was truly beautiful at least to him. He noticed things like that and quickly too.

"Oh, I must be lost," Belinda blushed.

"Yep, afraid so," Earl said. He stood on the lower step and asked her where she was supposed to go, then gave directions. As he stepped off the bus to let her finish her route he was wishing she might get lost up this way again sometime.

Earl found himself wistfully thinking of the lost girl throughout the day. He smiled when he remembered her long auburn hair and green eyes. She looked like a slightly sad, lost puppy. He couldn't tell at the time but she had long, slender legs that helped her attain a height just over five feet.

Since her last stop of the day was near his farm Belinda returned that afternoon. She brought him a homemade apple pie she made in between morning and afternoon routes. He thanked her and they talked a while. Earl had to milk cows at five so the conversation was shorter than either wished for.

Belinda visited often after that and Earl asked her out on a date during one of their chats. They got on well and six months later he asked her to marry him. He was twenty-five and she was twenty-four.

They married in the spring. For a man who lived alone since he was seventeen this was a happy change. The pair enjoyed several years together but were never able to have children.

Twelve years after they married Belinda caught a bad cold. The cold developed into pneumonia. Earl took his wife to the hospital where she was given IVs including antibiotics. She seemed to get better and after a few days was discharged. Earl took her home.

The next day, after morning milking, Earl found Belinda lying on the kitchen floor unconscious and breathing shallowly. She was rushed to the hospital where she passed away a few days later. Earl was alone again.

Earl Stinnett was sixty-nine on the heaviest night of the Draconid meteor shower. He didn't usually stay up late and had rarely seen meteors streaking across the night sky. But that particular night he could not sleep.

Russell, Earl's Jack Russell terrier couldn't sleep either. Finally Earl got up to let the dog out. The farmer was standing at his back door awestruck by the intensity of the falling stars. The numbers and how bright they were thrilled him.

"Wow they are beautiful," Earl said aloud to his dog. He watched silently as lights flashed across his view. They all seemed to be landing in the Bibon he thought. "Hey that's not a falling star. That things flying." He wondered if he was seeing it clearly or was he hallucinating? But there were lots of them zeroing in on the Bibon.

"Russell, get in here," Earl called in a near panicked whisper as he opened the screen door. Dutifully the dog trotted into the house ignorant of the vivid display above his head.

Russell was fourteen in human years. He had one blind eye, his hips were arthritic and he couldn't hear well. He didn't hear Earl call him, he only went in the house because the door was open, he had done his business and it was cold outside.

Earl noticed Russell did not bark at the lights. The dog was not concerned with the unusual display. Just the same the old man grabbed the shotgun he kept next to the kitchen door.

It was an old, slide action Remington, but it would do the trick. If those falling stars or meteors or UFOs, whatever they were turned out to be hostile, he was ready. He checked the action to make sure it was still smooth and well oiled. He glanced at the chamber to see if it was loaded for bear. Keeping the gun in his hand he opened a cabinet door and took down the box of double aught he had stashed there.

# Chapter 2

The star shower was spectacular but scientists were baffled. The numbers, size, location and timing of the meteorite shower was unusual. Of these, the quantity was of least concern.

The Draconid meteor shower was sometimes a sleeper, sometimes fair in number. So, many star gazers and astronomers were amazed at the number that fell. The count was in the thousands. The dragon awoke and gave a truly spectacular show. They came hurtling down as if some giant somewhere was throwing snowballs of light.

What was most peculiar about the event was all the meteors seemed to be the exact same size and brightness. They all seemed to be of fireball status. Odd. And they all appeared in telescopes only minutes before they hit the atmosphere.

Unpredictable. However most baffling of all was the location of the fall.

Nearly every meteorite fell into the Bibon Swamp in Bayfield County of Northern Wisconsin. Oh a few fell into Lake Superior and other far flung places. But 98% fell in the swamp or the farms and forests surrounding it.

Farmer Earl was far from the only one to witness the multiple fireballs. Astrophysicists at the Spring Brook Observatory in Stone Lake, Wisconsin were closely monitoring the sky when this event occurred. They photographed hundreds of the objects whirling thru the atmosphere.

Many ordinary citizens noticed the spectacular light show out their windows too. Most just thought it a completely natural event and went back to bed. No one deemed it as anything but slightly unusual.

Scientists, instructors and students at the Shell Lake Institute of Astrophysics recorded the event. Many were awed by the sheer numbers of falling stars and plans were made to run up to the impact area in search of debris. However the meteor shower did not end the toga party.

Initially only Earl Stinnett felt the need to arm himself. Everyone else who saw the lights believed it just a spectacular natural happening. No one was alarmed by the meteors.

Even Granny Hayward went to bed without a second thought to the potential danger thousands of falling objects might create. She still had her loaded shotgun leaning against the wall near the front door.  But that was standard practice for her. Unwanted guests sometimes entered the chicken coop and needed a forcible escort out.

# Chapter 3

Dan Bury was driving his USFS pickup truck along a forest road parallel to the swamp. This was a finger of forest that dug its way into the Bibon. It was an edge area where forest met swamp.

Edges such as this were perfect places to find wildlife. Wildlife attracted wolves. Wolves were Dan's area of expertise. Hence Dan worked this section often.

The forest in this area was made up of spruce, balsam, hemlock and aspen. It was thick but not impenetrable. Little undergrowth existed further in as the forest canopy let no light reach the ground.

The day started normally with Dan talking with some of the guys at the office, making small talk. His buddy Stan asked, "How did that blind date go the other night?"

"It was okay."

"Tell me about it."

"Nothing to tell."

"You could tell me what you did, where you went, you know things like that."

"Why the sudden interest? Your feminine side acting up again?"

"Hey if you don't want to talk about it just say so."

"Okay, I don't want to talk about it."

"Went that bad huh?"

Dan was getting his gear together and preparing to head off into the forest. What he and his date did was none of anybody else's business. Besides most of the guys would think it was boring. They sat outside, talked and watched last night's meteor shower. He really did not want to spend any more time on the subject of his latest date. So he ignored further attempts to dig out information and continued out the door.

One good thing happened recently. The guys at work finally stopped making jokes about Stan and Dan being brothers. Stan's last name was Berry. Dan Bury and Stan Berry. Well they sound the same but they aren't spelled the same and after a few years the joke gets old. However maybe the jokes were the reason Stan and Dan were best friends.

Dan had been checking a large alpha male he radio collared a year ago. The wolf roamed this section of forest and was seen near here. Most people didn't see the tracking device but some observant logger called about it a few days earlier. Charlie or Carl or some such. Vue was the last name.

He checked the map on his tablet and scrolled down a little. Dan zoomed in on the area ahead. He often worked on his computer while driving, knowing full well the trouble he would be in if he hit something. So when he looked up at the road the adrenalin surge slammed his foot on the brake and skyrocketed his blood pressure. What in the world he wondered?

Dan put the truck in park and sat for a while to calm down before he climbed out. He donned nitrile gloves as he slowly walked forward. There in the middle of the forest road was what appeared to be the headless carcass of a recently deceased male wolf.

His head on a swivel looking for the culprit, Dan slowly approached the animal. He crouched down next to the wolf his hand reaching out to touch the fur. It was still warm, an indication of a very recent death. But what could have killed it?

The thought came to him, cougar. But Dan hadn't seen tracks of a cougar in six months or more. No one in the area had reported one lately except that old farmer. What was his name? Earl, he thought.

Earl Stinnett reported a cougar roaming his farm just two weeks ago. This was only a mile or so from Earl's place, however no tracks had been found or any other evidence of the lion. But what bothered Dan most were the bite marks.

It appeared as if something with a much smaller mouth had torn pieces from the wolf. It was more the size of a fox or a cat. These marks did not look at all like cougar bites but no small animal could take down a wolf.

Dan stood up and backed a few feet away. He studied the ground around the site. He looked carefully along the edge of the road. He scanned the trees for no logical reason.

He took some pictures with his tablet, checking every angle, making a large circle around the carcass. Suddenly he heard something in the brush behind him. He turned around and waited scanning the brush and trees along the road edge.

He was about to head back to the truck when he heard it again. Sounded like someone giving a warning. Out of the forest came this thing. It looked like a three foot high green cone with a head on top. The head reminded Dan of an oversized Chihuahuas head, maybe ten times as large. A Chihuahua headed Christmas tree, Dan snickered silently.

The thing rolled up onto the road. Yes that's right, rolled, on wheels even. In a metallic, monotone it began, "We are Yrartz from the planet Yrartz. Do not be alarmed! We are here to take over your planet." Dan chuckled at that. His buddy Len Root must have come up with this. It was an elaborate practical joke, the kind Len would dream up.

"Hey Len, where are you?" Dan shouted at the forest. "This is pretty good. What is it some kind of remote control deal? You get Stan Berry and some of the other guys to help?"

He knelt down to get a better look as the Yrartz approached. "Come on Lenny. Come out, come out wherever you are." Just then the Yrartz shot out a wireless stunner, a taser type dart.

# Chapter 4

Earl came out of the old, faded white, wooden barn with a bucket of corn in one hand. His other held a red handkerchief to his nose. He felt he might be coming down with something as he wiped his face and stuffed the rag into a back pocket.

He walked over to the pasture fence. Neither of his heifers were standing nearby as they usually were. That seemed odd since Earl usually hand fed them grain this time of day.

He had been a dairy farmer for many years but Earl decided to sell the cows. Milking was getting hard on his knees and just too much of a chore.

He still had cows on the place, well heifers anyway. He was raising young stock for a dairy farmer up the road a piece. But Earl also had two heifers of his own.

The old farmer was raising the dairy-beef cross heifers for himself. He planned to breed them and raise beef for his table and for sale to the locals. He would sell the heifer calves to the dairyman and keep the bulls for steers.

As he stood by the fence Earl wondered where his animals had got to. Bessie number 5 was missing. He named her that because he was a dairyman so long he ran out of new names and just started adding numbers to the old names. His other heifer, Lizzy number 6 was gone too.

The pasture they were in was only ten acres and its entire length ran along the road. Earl could see the whole paddock from where he stood. He knew the fences weren't in the best shape especially next to the road.

Last year Tracy number 3, Bessie number 5s mom, got out and got stuck in the swamp. Earl had to pull her out with the tractor. After that he set to work fixing the fences on the swamp side but he never got to the road side.

The farmer set the bucket down and went to his old pickup truck. He climbed in and settled before starting the engine. Russell was moving too slowly and oldly to get a ride. The motor ground a bit before coughing to life and Earl shoved it into gear and took off in a cloud of dust and blue smoke.

The truck was ancient and left a trail of fog behind it but Earl had neither the money nor inclination to replace it. He didn't need much of anything new. He didn't need a cell phone because he had no one to call. He didn't like music enough to need any device for that. He didn't need GPS because he never went farther than Ashland and he knew how to get there and back. An old deck of cards was a cheaper way to play solitaire than a computer or a smart phone.

Oh sure Earl had been to the big city, Superior. But he had no interest in massive cities like that. West Falls, with its hundred and some people was plenty large enough. He could find everything he needed there and plenty of stuff he didn't need.

Earl's attention was divided between these thoughts and searching for the heifers as he pulled out onto the road. He peered intently at the fence line when BAM! He saw it and hit it at the same time.

Earl hit the brakes hard almost standing on them. Something underneath the truck was screaming like a little child. Earl Stinnett was scared. Had he actually hit someone and what was he or she doing way out here?

He jumped out of the truck as fast as his old body would take him. He rushed around the front of the vehicle and got down on those tired old knees and looked under. What he noticed first was the powerful smell. His nose could not remember a more vicious odor. He knew children sometimes smelled bad but didn't recall any that reeked quite that much.

A few weeks ago someone hit a family of skunks near here. Earl drove past the spot days later and the smell was overpowering. This stench made the rotten dead skunks smell like finest perfume by comparison.

Earl couldn't make out what it was under his truck. Whatever it was it was still alive and screaming. "Hang on little fella. I'll try getting you out from under there," he told it. He tried reaching in but it was near the middle, much too far for his short arms. He heard voices behind him. He thumped his head on the truck bumper as he straightened up, still on his knees.

First he couldn't make out what it, they were saying. But then he heard it clearly. The voices sounded odd, monotone and tinny.

"We are Yrartz from the planet Yrartz. Do not be alarmed! We are here to take over your planet."

He half turned and saw them coming toward him. The last thing Earl Stinnett heard were many voices saying the same thing. Then he was hit by something small, like a pinprick electrical charge. It wasn't just one, but rather a dozen of them. His arms and legs went limp.

The day started out clear just as the night before had been. It was cold and a slight breeze was blowing in from the northwest. Only an occasional wispy white cloud smeared the azure sky.

Corn stalks had dried to yellow-brown above the dusty soil. The least breeze rattled the leaves drowning out all other sounds. The field was flanked in part by irregular formations of trees. The forest was a thin shield between the farm and the swamp.

The swamp covered thousands of acres in the basin of an extinct glacial lake. Bibon Swamp contained varied species of plants and animals. The finger of swamp bordering Grandma Hayward's farm ran mostly to white cedar with tamarack, hemlock and tag alders mixed in. Good cover for the whitetail deer that lived there.

Tom, covered head to toe in camouflage, stepped out of the woods and spotted Nathan near the edge of the cornfield. Nate was similarly dressed in camo from head to waist. Both men started toward each other. "Did you see anything?" Tom asked as they came close.

"No deer. A porcupine walked under my treestand about an hour ago," Nate replied.

"Well you did better than I did. I didn't see any deer or porcupines." Tom sniffed the air then wrinkled his nose. "Nate what did you have for breakfast?"

"Why do you ask bro?"

Tom decided to state the obvious. "Did you cut loose?"

"No bro that isn't me."

"You sure?"

Bob came out of the woods then wearing his newest camouflage jacket and pants. He pulled off his facemask and he too sniffed the air and made a face. Tom and Nathan watched his progress across the dried and dead field.

"You guys see any deer?" Bob asked as he approached them.

"No," Nate answered. Tom shook his head.

"I didn't see anything either," Bob said in answer to the unspoken question.

"I'm not surprised you two didn't see deer the way you were talking the whole time." Tom shook his head in disgust. "You probably hold hands when it gets dark too don't you?"

"Hey that's wrong. Well anyway we weren't holding hands," Nathan protested. "That was yesterday. Today we were in different tree stands."

Tom looked at Nathan to see if he was serious. But Nate had that innocent, childlike expression he often wore. One could never tell for certain if Nathan Minong was making it all up. He had a stony face look that was impossible to read. If he knew how to play poker he would win. Nate always won at Go Fish.

"Actually I did see three bucks run past my stand early on. Two were small but one was a shooter. The thing is, they were running so fast it was like something was after them or scared them. I didn't see wolves or anything chasing them," Bob told them. He wrinkled his nose again. "You guys smell that?"

"Yep. It's Nate. He won't admit he let loose a gas bomb," Tom stated as he started walking toward the truck. Bob and Nate fell in with him.

"Hey I told you bro it's not me." Both Bob and Tom looked at him in a way that said they did not believe him. "I'm telling you it must be swamp gas or something."

"Well then," Tom started. "The swamp must be eating beans or skunks or something else nasty."

Changing the subject Nathan excitedly asked, "Did you guys see the big star shower last night?"

"No we went to bed early last night so we could get up and go hunting this morning," Bob replied.

"Well I couldn't sleep so anyway I looked out the window and there was just a lot of falling stars. It was big."

"So that's what you were doing instead of hunting," Tom suggested.

"Huh?"

Bob turned to Tom with understanding, "So he was sleeping in his tree."

Nate took a candy bar from his pocket and began unwrapping it. Tom smiled. "No he wasn't sleeping he was eating."

"Hey I wasn't eating the whole time."

"You're right, he was eating," Bob agreed.

"Hey bro you saying I'm fat or something?" Nate looked hurt.

"No we're not saying that," Bob defended.

"I'm not fat," Nathan told them. "I'm just big boned." He expected that to end the conversation.

"You got bones in your stomach?" Bob asked looking innocently at Nate's belly.

"Only if he ate some," Tom laughed.

"Hey did you guys feel like you were being watched?" Bob asked. "It feels spooky in there, more than normal. Like someone was watching and listening."

"I know what you mean," Tom admitted. "I had the same feeling. Even walking across the cornfield it definitely was like someone was there, listening."

"I see what you guys are saying," Nate added enthusiastically, eyes wide. "It's like, the corn has ears."

The trio approached Bob's truck. "Man what's that smell?" Bob asked again. Both he and Tom turned in Nate's direction, questioning looks on their faces.

"The swamp," he said again.

"The Bibon doesn't smell that bad even in August."

"True," Tom admitted. "Got to be something dead in there."

"Maybe old man Stinnett is dumping his dead cows in there again," Bob suggested.

Nate shook his head. "No, okay you got me. I spilled a bottle of doe-in-heat urine on me. It's all over my hunting outfit."

Bob and Tom leaned in toward him. "Oh that stinks alright, but that ain't what we're talking about."

"No it's as if the whole swamp reeks." Tom pondered that. "I suppose it could be some really nasty swamp gas."

"I still think its Nate gas."

"Bro I told you in ain't me," Nathan insisted.

"Well let's get out of here before we choke to death. Bob let me have the keys. I'll drive."

"Keys are in the ignition and why are you driving? It's my truck."

"I always drive. I'm gonna drop you guys off. I have something to do," Tom answered.

Bob and Nate exchanged glances. Both had ideas neither would say aloud in front of Tom. As they started out Nate suggested, "Why don't you buy a new truck?"

"He's right we should buy a new truck," Bob added.

"New trucks are expensive. Why not buy a late model used one instead," Tom suggested.

"Hey that's a good idea," Nathan agreed. "Where do they make used trucks?"

"At the used truck factory, silly," Bob advised.

"Oh yeah," Nate said. "Where is that at?"

"Probably Detroit," Bob figured.

"Detroit's in Michigan. That's not too far away," Nate added.

"Well let's go anyway. You want to come too, Tom?" Tom looked at them to see if they were serious. As they bounced onto the road he was thinking there were days when he wanted to call them Dumb and Dumber but he was too nice a guy for that.


Grandma Hayward's back forty bordered Earl Stinnett's farm on one side. The boys waved out the windows as they passed Earl's house in case he should see them. But a short distance past the driveway Tom hit the brakes.

"What do you suppose Earl's truck is doing in the middle of the road?" Tom asked.

"Maybe he ran out of gas?" Bob suggested.

"You would think we would see him walking here somewhere. It isn't that far from his house."

Nate opened the door saying, "Well let's find out." The three got out of the truck and walked forward. They looked the truck over and scanned the surrounding ditches and fields. No sign of the old farmer or his dog.

They came close to the farmer's truck. Nate asked, "You remember Pastor Gordon's sermon Sunday? When he said you can't fix a you broken with a broken you? You can't fix something that's broken with a broken tool. Only Jesus can fix a broken you, remember that?"

"Yes I remember that. What made you think of that now?"

"Well judging by the smell, something under Earl's truck is broken."

Tom remembered what else the pastor said. "It's like we are made of glass and we fall. Most often we break off an arm or a leg or a hand. We pick ourselves up and Jesus puts us back together. But other times we fall and like glass we shatter. We can't pick ourselves up. We can't put ourselves back together. God, Jesus picks us up piece by piece and puts us back together."

"Tom," his train of thought broke. "What do you make of this?" Bob was pointing under the truck.

Tom crouched down and looked under. He got up and went to the open driver's door. He climbed in and since the keys were in it Tom started the truck and backed up. He stopped as soon as he could see what had been under the vehicle.

Tom got out of the truck and joined the others. Bob and Nate were kneeling next to the thing on the ground their hands over their noses. "Bob what are you looking for?"

Bob had a stick and was poking the thing. "I wouldn't do that if I were you," Nate told him.

"I'm just checking to see if it's dead."

"Dude you can smell that can't you? Its dead, believe me its dead. Nothing alive smells that bad." As usual Nathan was wrong.

Rising Bob asked, "Why do you suppose Earl left his truck here? Not like him to leave it in the middle of the road like this and we know it runs. You backed it up off that thing."

"I don't know but we should check out the house. Maybe he got hurt when he ran that thing over."

Looking around Nathan asked, "Hey bro why are there tire tracks all over the ditch?" He pointed. Bob and Tom put their heads together and studied the situation.

"Those aren't tire tracks, at least not from truck or car tires. Look," Bob pointed. "They are more like wide bicycle tires but with different tread."

"Lot of strange things around here," Tom commented.

"You talking about my eating habits again?" Nate asked. Tom snorted. "Hey I told you I was big boned."

Tom smiled, "My friend, there are no bones in your stomach."

Tom went back to Earl's house and looked around inside and out. He checked the barn and out buildings too. He found some shovels and a rake and went back.

Bob and Nate went along the ditches and checked for anything unusual. They found nothing but the odd tire tracks. The three men came back to the thing in the road.

"Hey I just realized something. Not only didn't I find Earl but I didn't find Russell either."

"Who's Russell? Earl have some other old guy living with him now?" Nate asked.

"Naw, Russell is Earl's dog," Bob answered for Tom.

"Oh yeah I forgot about the dog. What do you suppose became of him?"

"Probably with Earl most likely," Tom said as he looked at the thing in the road again.

"What do you suppose it is and where did it come from?" Bob wondered aloud.

"It looks like something from the Black Lagoon got mangled," Nate commented.

"Mangled alright. Looks like it could have come from one of those Saw movies," Bob added.

"But it doesn't look like it came from around here." Tom continued, "I mean it looks alien to me."

"So it don't look like it came from the Black Lagoon or the Blue Lagoon either. Comes from the Outer Limits maybe?" Nate speculated. "Way outer limits. Like Plan Nine or Ten."

"Naw more like Independence Day creatures or Invasion from somewhere. Maybe even a Star Trek or War movie," Bob suggested.

Nathan moved around to the side and cocked his head. "Almost looks like something from a nightmare on some street type of thing." He looked at Tom, "So what do you think it is?"

Tom stood there thinking with his left arm across his chest and his right hand under his chin. Finally, shaking his head he said, "I really don't have any idea. It could be some exotic animal someone brought in and it got loose. It is pretty beat up and run over so it surely doesn't look like it used to.

Shrugging he added, "I just don't know. But we better get it off the road so people can drive around here. I don't think we want to run it over again."

"Well I don't know what it is either but it surely stinks. Skunks smell better and that's for sure." Nate started to pick up part of the creature with a shovel and move it to the edge of the road.

Bob and Tom began helping move the dead thing. Bob turned his head, "Wow that thing sure stinks. I've never smelt anything that bad."

"Hey bro maybe it's the Creature from the Black Garbage Dump," Nathan suggested.

"Or the Creature from the Seriously Polluted Cesspool?" Bob added.

"Or maybe it's the creature from the Tom wants you two clowns to help him move it off the road so we can get moving film."

"Really bro? Was that a good one?" Nate asked innocently.

He rolled his eyes and shook his head at that. "I tried my cell and couldn't get a signal," Tom said. "Either of your phones work?"

Bob had a sheepish look on his face. Nate answered, "I left mine at home."

"Bob?"

"Ah well ya see I sort of lost it in the swamp," Bob admitted. Tom merely shook his head again.

Finally back in the truck the trio were on the road to town again. For no good reason Bob was in the middle seat. He turned the radio on and started looking for a station he liked.

Nate reached out and stopped Bob's hand. "Hey I like that song. Turn it up."

*"I look at you with such love in my heart*

*I caress your sides and touch you everywhere*

*I'd lay with you at night if I dared*

*I oil you up and you know I care"*

Tom looked at the radio then at Nate. "What is this song about?"

"This guy must have been in the Army or something 'cause he is talking about a mini-gun." At their blank stares Nate added, "You know those machineguns they put on Blackhawks and other helicopters." Still no recognition so Nate continued, "They put them on gunships."

Both brothers nodded understanding. Tom asked, "Could we have more explanation please."

"The guy is talking about his baby, his weapon. He tells how he takes real good care of her so when he needs her she will fire and work the way he wants her to." Nathan pauses thinking, "Wish we had one. They're fun to shoot."

"Hey sure and why not a case of grenades and some rocket launchers too?" Bob added snidely.

"Hey come on a mini-gun would be the bomb," Nate protested.

"A bomb would be the bomb," Bob said. Tom just shook his head yet again.

"So what else do these guys sing?" Tom asked.

"They are the same band that sings the song, 'My trucks got three-wheel-drive."

"Huh? Three-wheel-drive? What?" Tom asked.

"Yep," Nate nodded. "It's a song about an old truck that's a piece of junk and one axle is not working or something or maybe a wheel fell off," he shrugged, then shook his head. "I'm not really sure.

"So what's the name of the group?" Bob asked.

"They call themselves Manfred and the Aliens." Nate looked at the brothers, "Kind of a weird name for a rock group, don't you think?" Neither brother answered but both agreed.

# Chapter 5

Sleepy was too active a term for West Falls, Wisconsin. Located on a peninsula jutting out into the Bibon, the town had a population of 121. In the summer it jumped to over 140.

A man named Adam Gilbert West founded the town in 1851. There never was a falls since it is a swamp after all. There are falls at River Falls and Chippewa Falls. There are falls at Black River Falls too but none ever existed at West Falls.

Some say there never was a West Falls, Wisconsin either. However there are many people who would disagree. You won't find the place on any map these days.

The only way to get to West Falls was Cumberland Road. Just north of Grand View a ways take Bibon Road off U.S. Highway 63. Where Bibon turns there used to be a road going off along the White River.

Cumberland Road meandered next to the river and crossed Telemark creek a little over two miles from West Falls. Telemark Creek is one of those muddy, little streams zigzagging painfully through the raggedy brush-land eventually draining into the river. Normally the creek causes no trouble.

When he first arrived Adam West built a small house and later a barn. He claimed forty acres of land from the government and started his farm there. Plenty of cedar for fence posts grew in the swamp and there were white pine nearby for building homes.

The land was good enough for some crops but the weather sometimes failed. Often crops would freeze. Dairy farming seemed to be a way around that since the cows could pasture much of the year.

Mr. West had a number of visitors early on. He decided to try bringing in dry goods to sell. He opened a small store in one corner of his house. His wife Loretta did most of the selling while Adam farmed.

In 1861 President Lincoln invited Mr. West to join the Union cause in the War Between the States. A confederate musket ball invited Adam West to make the ultimate sacrifice. His body never made it back home. He was buried at Antietam.

Loretta West took back her maiden name of Draper but stayed in West Falls the rest of her life. She sold the farm to a man named Hudson Hayward. The dry goods business she sold to one Glen Flora. Hudson later sold the farm and bought another just north of town. Glen's son lost the business during the Depression.

The original West farm became the nucleus of the town of West Falls. In addition to the old farm house and the dry goods store several other homes went in. Hudson Hayward parceled the land into lots and sold these to families interested in settling there.

By 1920 the town of West Falls had a population of 250 or so. That was as large as it would ever get. The decline began in part, as a result of the depression.

At the time Bob, Tom and Nate walked out of the woods West Falls was standing at 121 souls. She had a Lutheran church, an auto repair shop, a farm machine repair shop, a Food-n-Fuel and a bar. The bar was the Yellow Rose or more commonly, The Rose.

The Yellow Rose started as an ordinary home. The first owners began taking in occasional travelers and turned the place into an inn. Later the rooms upstairs became a single family dwelling. The rooms downstairs became the bar and kitchen.

No one had seen a yellow rose in West Falls in at least fifty years. The name came with the latest owner. Bill Webster was from Texas, born and raised.

It was rumored Bill ran into a little trouble down San Antonio way. He escaped to northern Wisconsin figuring no self-respecting Texas lawman would come looking for him in a place this cold. So he bought the bar, moved in and changed the name.

Like most bars in northern Wisconsin, The Rose had good food. It was the only eating establishment in West Falls. So, sooner or later everyone ended up at the place, even the preacher.

Pastor Gordon Washburn loved the Friday night fish fry. He wasn't Catholic he was Lutheran but that didn't stop him. Nearly every Friday he and his wife Sarona made the trip to The Rose for the fresh whitefish and perch from Lake Superior.

The Yellow Rose was at the southwest end of town. It sat on a small hill just above and overlooking the swamp. The bar had an expansive deck on the two sides bordering the Bibon.

The deck saw little use during the summer because the swamp stank and the mosquitoes were fierce. But like most hardy Wisconsinites the folks of West Falls enjoyed being outdoors. So the deck was heavily employed from September thru early May.

During those months the weather was the only thing that would close down the deck. Thunderstorms, bad snow storms or seriously below zero temperatures closed it for a few hours or a day or two. With cold weather the party often moved to the pot-bellied stove that still warmed the bar in winter.

Such a small community as West Falls was also a close community. Everyone knew everyone else. You might not think someone from Texas would fit in, but Bill did. The only exception was he couldn't handle the cold.

Being a close knit town, the loss of one was felt by all. But since funeral homes weren't as popular in Wisconsin as bars people had to go to Ashland for funerals. The reception after was usually held at The Rose. That way people did not have to clean house and make food while grieving a loss.

Bill was good about keeping the place family friendly. He served alcohol but kept loud obnoxious behavior to a minimum. Most drunks found an out of the way corner or went outside to puke their guts up. Probably added to the stench from the swamp.

There were three reasons people came to The Rose. Food, drink and Kelly. Kelly Minong was an American Indian waitress at The Rose. She kept her long black hair in a single braid down the back. She was the youngest of the wait staff at the bar.

American Indians, like all peoples, come in two kinds, attractive and not so fortunate. Kelly was of the stunning, knock-out, drop dead gorgeous kind. Her long legs, pretty face and otherwise fantastic body made her very popular with the men of West Falls.

Kelly had a friendly personality and good sense of humor that helped her in her job. But she also had a hard edge that kept drunks from getting too fresh. The men of West Falls had a healthy respect for Kelly.

She invariably wore a T-shirt and jeans everywhere. Fall, spring and winter this was her outfit. In summer she might wear shorts and in winter she often added a flannel shirt. Actually T-shirt and jeans was a likely outfit for the majority of West Fall's residents, both male and female.

Kelly wore her clothes semi-tight to loose and baggy. She did not like tight fitting garments. But even baggy outfits couldn't hide her beauty. She had the face of an angel and her body would turn Venus way beyond green with envy.

Tom drove to Kelly and Nate's place first. He planned to leave his brother and Nate there and head for home. "Hey bro I only need to change clothes. Won't take a minute so just wait, okay?" Nate asked.

"Okay," Tom answered impatiently.

Nathan lumbered up the steps and inside as fast as he could. Seconds later he came out chewing on something. Tom and Bob looked at each other. "So why did we stop here?" Bob asked.

"I took off my camouflage shirt and grabbed a sweatshirt."

"Looks like you grabbed some food too. I thought we were going to The Rose for lunch," Tom said.

"We are," Nate agreed. "I just needed a little snack to tide me over."

Bob noticed Nathan's sweatshirt had the letters RBI on the front. "Nate what do those letters mean?"

"Really Big Indian," he stated matter-of-factly. "I think it fits." Bob started giggling and Tom barely controlled his laughter. "You guys are cutting on me aren't you?"

"You know Nate if you didn't open your mouth…"

"I know I would be a lot smaller."

"Well, that too," Tom admitted. "But what I was going to say is if you didn't open your mouth we wouldn't have anything to cut on you for."


They stopped at Bob and Tom's and all piled out. Tom felt he needed a shower before going. That left Bob and Nate unsupervised. The pair went to the basement to watch TV.

Bob asked, "Nate want something to drink?"

"Sure." Bob got two water bottles from the fridge.

"Ouch, what the heck," Bob reached around and took hold of the plastic arrow Nate shot him with. "What are you doing? Dude you shot me with a plastic arrow."

"Yep and I can do it again."

"Where did you find that kids bow and do you really want to be a stereotypical Native American?"

"How's that?" Nathan asked, looking around the bow. "Oh you mean shoot white man and drink firewater?"

"Well, something like that."

"Hey I thought shooting you with a rubber tipped arrow was funny. I don't know about firewater but I'd go for some of the Cajun's fiery hot chili and a root beer at The Rose. Plus I would even let you pay for it."

"You're on as long as you quit shooting me with the arrows."

# Chapter 6

Doctor Nehemiah Roswell hated his first name and his title for that matter. His middle name was Michael but he didn't like using that either. He much preferred people call him NM. Even Corona, his wife of forty-two years, referred to him by NM.

NM looked years younger than he was. His face was long and angular with a large nose and thin lips. He wore his medium length gray hair parted on the left. Maybe the full head of hair was why he looked younger.

Doctor NM Roswell was a most pleasant man of mid-seventies who happened to have one really annoying habit. He believed he was always right. However since he was among the smartest one hundred people on the planet he probably was always right.

Mensa wanted him as a member but Doctor Roswell refused believing they were too pedestrian for him. Later an organization made up of some of the top one hundred coerced him into joining. This exclusive group met once a year to share ideas. NM quit going to these meetings finding them tedious.

NM and wife Corona owned a cabin in West Falls that they used in summer and occasionally other times. Doctor NM was usually accompanied by his wife. This visit however, he was merely closing up the cabin for the winter so she stayed home.

Corona and NM lived in South Range these days. Doctor Roswell was semi-retired and still taught a class or two at the Shell Lake Institute of Astrophysics. He also made rare appearances to the Springbrook Observatory at Stone Lake.

Most of NMs work now centered on interpreting data gathered by others. He analyzed the data and built theories based on this. He consulted by phone or computer, rarely face to face.

As was his custom NM stopped at The Rose both when coming into town and before heading home. Kelly Minong came to his table with a smiling face and a pot of black coffee. "Good morning NM," she said as she poured the coffee and handed him a menu. "What can I get for you today?"

"Kelly I still don't understand why you stay here. You seem like the brightest and most attractive girl around. Why not move out of here and make something of yourself?"

"If I did that you wouldn't have me as your waitress. Now what was it you wanted?" the smile a little strained.

The brothers Hayward, Bob and Tom, trooped into The Rose followed by Nate. Nathan Minong was two years older, two inches shorter and two hundred pounds heavier than his sister Kelly. The trio took the table next to Professor NM.

Tom ignored the conversation between his brother and Nate. He was busy studying Kelly and trying not to show it. Besides odds were whatever they were arguing about wasn't worth it.

"When I fill out one of those survey things I put I'm a Native American because they don't have a space for American Indian," Nate told him.

"Fine then I'm a Northern European American."

"A what?"

"A Northern European American," Bob repeated. "N-E-A for short."

"You're a Neah?" Nate asked confused.

"No I'm a Northern-European-American," Bob stated slowly. "N-E-A for short."

"Yeah a Neah."

"So what are you two little boys squabbling over now?" Kelly asked as she approached the table and gave them glasses of water. She caught Tom looking at her out of the corner of her eye and smiled warmly at him.

Pointing at Nate, Bob answered, "He shot me in the butt with a plastic arrow."

"Again? Shame on you Nathan," Kelly said feigning anger.

"Well he called me an Indian," Nathan protested.

"That was after he shot me," Bob pointed at Nate again.

"Oh such violence," Kelly shivered, smiling at Tom once more. Their eyes met and held a moment.

"Then," Nate pointed back. "When I corrected him and said I was a Native American or American Indian he called himself a Northern European American."

"Oh my, the escalation," Kelly put her hands to her face with a shocked expression. "Anything else?"

"Well I said I was that and then I said it was N-E-A for short."

Kelly noticed Tom mouthing a word as he stood up. Understanding she looked back at Bob, "Neah?"

"No, N-E-A. Nate called me a Neah."

"Yes Neah."

"So what's happening?" Tom asked as if he wasn't any part of this. His hand rested on Kelly's back.

"Why is your hand on my back?" Kelly asked as she turned toward him. "No touchy, no feely. Got it buster?"

Tom immediately drew back, a surprised expression on his face. "I thought we had a date tonight."

"We did. But Bill needs me to work tonight so I'm pulling a double. I tried texting you."

"So we can get together later?" Tom suggested.

"I work till midnight," she answered. "So no, I don't think so. I will be tired and crabby." Kelly left in a huff. *And you're not crabby now*, Tom thought but did not say.

Pastor Gordon Washburn came into The Rose for lunch. He loved the Cajun's chili and often ate that on these colder days of fall. As he entered he noticed NM and went over to talk to him.

"NM how are you today?"

"Pastor Gordon good to see you sir," NM smiled and reached out his hand. They shook hands. "I'm good. How are you?"

"I'm well. Say NM the other day I was driving past your cabin and I saw that birch tree that died last year finally fell. It landed in your driveway so I got my chain saw and cut it up. Piled the wood next to the driveway. I threw the branches into the woods."

"Well thanks pastor. I sure appreciate it." NM paused, "You know it's preachers like you give Christianity a good name."

"Well thanks. Will I see you in church Sunday?" Gordon asked.

"Probably not. I plan to finish by tomorrow and head home. Corona has plans for us on Sunday." With that Gordon moved to the bar to pick up his chili to go.

"Hey pastor here's your chili," Bill handed it to him. "Say pastor I heard the Belknap girls had a fright this morning. Heard you was involved. What happened?"

"Oh that," Gordon smiled. "Well it seems the Belknap ladies did indeed have a terrible fright real early this morning." Pastor Gordon paused. "They heard or saw something and it scared them so bad they came running down the street screaming about aliens attacking. Of course two women in their eighties can't really run all that fast.

"Anyway I got a call from Deputy Hawkins and came as quick as I could. Loretta and Donna were very upset and frightened. I did my best to calm them down and offered to drive them home. They said no they didn't want to go home and insisted I take them to the church.

"So I dropped them off at the church and went up to their place with Ted to see what was what. I did not see any aliens or spaceships or anything out of the ordinary. But after going back to the church and telling them I found nothing they continued to insist we were under attack.

"They decided to stay with Loretta's son Mitch for now. I know they were scared but I can't figure what scared them. There was just nothing amiss at their house.

"After I dropped them off at Mitch's I went back and Ted and I did a more thorough search. The house was still okay but we went out to the garage. That's where it all happened.

"The Belknap sisters shot at something in their garage. When Ted and I looked it over we couldn't tell what they shot at but they hit it. We found blood and a trail leading out the door. But we lost the trail.

"It seems the local dog population licked up the evidence so we couldn't follow the trail. Ted thinks it was a coyote or something. All we know for sure is they shot something and it left in a hurry."

"They didn't happen to smell like blackberry brandy did they?" Bill asked with a smile.

"No I did not smell alcohol on either of them."

"Well this isn't the first time something like this has happened. Usually no one pays them no mind. They are known to enjoy their homemade blackberry brandy that they cook up on the stove.

"They are always trying to pay some of the local kids to pick blackberries for them and they aren't particular about a few sticks and bugs in the pail. It was good money."

"Truly Bill I do not think they were hitting the bottle. They seemed genuinely afraid. And I just can't believe a coyote would scare them that bad."

"Why didn't Ted check things out a little more or call in the sheriff? He's a deputy after all."

"He was up all night and he didn't think they were telling the truth about aliens. He thought like most people that they had been drinking and they just got scared after they shot the coyote. Well I have to get going. I'll see you later Bill."

The *coyote* would be found a week later by a U.S. Army ranger.

Being highly intelligent didn't mean one was imaginative with food. NM invariably ordered chili or a ham and cheese omelet with potato pancakes depending on the weather and time of day. Kelly brought the bowl of chili and a couple bags of crackers.

"Anything else I can get you?" Kelly asked.

"I'm good," NM answered.

Kelly turned toward her brother's table ready to take orders. "Okay guys what are you having today?"

"What's good here?" Nate asked trying to be funny.

Kelly bent down nose to nose with her brother. "I will ask you once more and only once more," she straightened. "So what do you guys want?"

"Chili," Tom answered handing his menu to his brother.

"Chili," Bob answered handing the menus to Nate.

"Chili," Nate whispered seemingly unable to find his voice. He handed the menus to Kelly with a nervous smile. She did not return the smile but instead gave him a look that said, "Do not mess with me Mister or I will take you out," in that unfriendly kind of World of Warcraft way.

Kelly went away to put in the order. Nate stood up and told the guys, "I gotta hit the john."


If one entered The Rose through the front door, directly in front of you was the bar. To the right was the dining area. Past the bar on the far side of the room were the restrooms. The kitchen was immediately behind the bar with the restrooms off to the side.

As is often the case with northern Wisconsin bars The Rose's restrooms were designated "Bucks" and "Does". Naturally there were wood cutouts of an antlered buck and an antlerless doe on the doors. The doors, like nearly everything else in The Rose, were made of stained wood.

The bar itself was made of oak stained dark, almost black from years of use. Behind the bar were shelves on either side of a large mirror. The shelves held bottles of various kinds of booze, some nearly empty, others dusty from lack of use.

The wood floor was some type of badly gouged and scratched maple recently waxed. Like most old wood floors it creaked with every footstep. It served its purpose well and was easy enough to clean now that the grooves between the boards were filled with ancient wax.

The tables were wood as well and old enough to be wobbly and warped. They were painted a mustard color to hide at least some of the daily grime and grease. Each held salt and pepper shakers and a napkin holder.

The north wall of the room had only one window as it faced the parking lot and the street. The west and south walls were lined with windows with a single door in each. The door to the west was centered and the door in the south was at the end near the bathrooms. Both doors opened onto the deck overlooking the swamp.

Nathan returned to the table to find Tom talking with Ted Hawkins. "So you were out to Earl's and his truck was in the road but no Earl?"

"Yep, so we looked around a bit and parked his truck in the driveway," Tom answered. "His dog, Russell wasn't around either."

"That's a bit odd. Earl never goes anywhere without Russell."

"I was going to call the sheriff or someone," Tom said.

"Well I'm going out there now. Earl wants me to look at his old H. Seems it's making some odd noise so I will find him and see what's up."

"Okay and thanks," Tom said relieved. Deputy Hawkins was a good man and a good deputy sheriff. Technically he was a reserve deputy which means he did not have any regular duties. He would be called in when the county needed to bolster its forces. Even though he was not required to he would call in to the department office every Saturday just to update them on happenings in West Falls and the surrounding area.

Ted also owned the local farm machine repair shop. The shop was where he spent much of his time and could usually be found. He knew how to repair almost any tractor or piece of farm machinery or logging equipment. He was just plain a handy man to have around.

On his way out Ted stopped at the bar and set his empty mug down. It was early for most people to be drinking but Ted Hawkins did not follow other people's rules. When off duty he often had a beer with lunch and sometimes with breakfast. But today he only drank coffee.

Looking up at the wall above the bar he commented, "Bill it don't look like you added any mounts lately. I see that one there is a spike I shot when I was only thirteen. Don't you hunt anymore?"

"Nope I give it up a couple of years ago. But I still fish. I just haven't got anything worth mounting. No one seems to want to leave their mounts here anymore either."

"Well that spike would be embarrassing if it wasn't for the fact that it was my first deer." Ted took the final sip of his coffee, set the mug on the bar and said, "See ya for fish fry."

"Say Ted I heard something about Loretta and Donna. They woke up half the town yelling about aliens or some such. Pastor Gordon said they weren't drinking. He felt they really were scared."

"Oh yup. I don't know what they had going on. Most people around here pay no attention to their rants. I don't know what happened but they have calmed down now." Ted paused to catch his breath. "See you tonight," Bill waved him out the door.

# Chapter 7

Every galaxy in the universe has a species of humanoid creatures that is superior to all other species in that galaxy. The Yrartz were just such a species. They came from a galaxy they called Yrartzway. If you look at the sky at night Yrartzway is approximately right here and the planet Yrartz is left of center.

The Yrartz were not the brightest beings in the universe. In fact they were the dumbest superior race in the universe. However they were also the most numerous and the luckiest. These facts made them dangerous.

They looked a bit like someone's idea of an alien joke. The Yrartz were roughly three feet tall including the wheels, giant's maybe forty inches. They wore a cone shaped composite suit, wide at the bottom pointed at top, in forest green. The only things showing were the head and the arms.

The whole being rested on a chassis with multiple wheels capable of a zero turn radius. It seems the Yrartz had weak legs and so overcame that with a leg support structure inside the cone. If the cone and supports were removed the beings would be crawling and very vulnerable.

The little aliens had an oval shaped face, wide and short. They invariably wore a stupid expression often with mouth open. The ears stood up and curved in like the horns on a pronghorn antelope.

All Yrartz carried a laser on their right side and a stun wand on their left. The laser had a maximum range of thirty feet. The stun gun or wand was wireless and had a range of just fifteen feet. The Yrartz accidently figured out how to make stunners wireless but they never figured out how to make them powerful. The weapons were short range and a single hit by the stunners would not slow a man. The Yrartz had to rely on numbers and one other factor.

The Yrartz attacked thirteen other planets before arriving at Earth. They conquered the only other two planets in their galaxy with life on them in the space of a few years. They moved on to another galaxy.

It only took Yrartz fifty years to take and destroy twelve of the thirteen planets they struck. The first six planets they approached, landed on and then ate every speck of protein on them. Then they came to the solar system containing the planet Mmyra.

A small Mmyrian military/science craft approached the Yrartz ships. They were five thousand kilometers apart. "Sir the approaching ships are silent. We have been hailing them but there has been no answer, no communication."

"No communication?"

"None sir."

"You are on all frequencies?"

"Yes sir. We are hailing them on all frequencies in all known languages."

"Very well lieutenant. Keep trying." Turning to the helmsman the captain said, "Steady as she goes Shenda. Get us within a thousand kilometers then hold your position."

Almost immediately Shenda told him, "We are at one thousand kilometers and holding sir."

"Very well," the captain said. "Half shields lieutenant Dagga. Prepare weapons but keep them silent and unaimed. We don't want to provoke a war." Turning back forward the captain added, "Shenda put them on screen. Let's see what they look like."

The holoview came up. The captain stood up and squinted as he peered at it. "There are approximately one hundred and fifty of those ships sir. Each appears to be made up of a loosely held matrix of balls with tails streaming from the back.

"There seems to be some sort of command ship attached to the front of the matrix. Apparently the lead ship or command ship powers the whole system. We are only sensing a power source in the command ship which must be feeding the rest of the ships through the matrix."

"Fascinating. They look like metal balls held together by a lattice work structure. The command ship or module must be a tow vehicle."

"It would seem so sir. No other power sources are coming from anywhere else on the ships."

"Sir I'm picking up a signal from the ships. It seems to be repeating every twenty-five seconds or so."

"Lieutenant Dagga bring up the audio."

Nasally voices came out. "We are Yrartz from the planet Yrartz. Do not be alarmed! We are here to take over your planet."

The captain reached down and flipped a switch. "This is Captain Merrill of the Mmyrian ship UMS-Baldwin. We come in peace. What are your intentions?"

"We are Yrartz from the planet Yrartz. Do not be alarmed! We are here to take over your planet."

"Shenda shields up full," looking at Lieutenant Dagga Captain Merrill continued. "Lieutenant aim all weapons at the lead command ship. Fire on my mark. Shenda on my mark drop shields.

"Yeoman Herter send an SOS to all Mmyrian military vessels in this quadrant. Tell them we are under attack." The captain heard the Yrartz saying not to be alarmed as he commanded, "Three, two, one shields down, fire all."

The ship shuddered violently, the lead Yrartz ship disappeared in a brilliant flash of white light quickly fading to magenta. Several of the ball ships disappeared as well and many more were damaged. The magnetic connection holding them together failed and the ships began to break apart.

The Mmyrians fired several more volleys as the remaining Yrartz ships retreated. The UMS-Baldwin followed the enemy until the Yrartz exited the galaxy. Other Mmyrian ships kept track for a few billion kilometers finally called off by the powers that be.

The Yrartz moved on to easier prey. They assaulted six more planets with unqualified success. Finally they arrived at Earth.

Since the Yrartz were not that bright their first few hundred space flights ended in death and disaster. Short on intelligence but long on perseverance and good fortune they finally made it into space and survived. With twelve successes and one utter failure they believed they could conquer any foe.

The invasion of Earth began May 18, 1980. The first Yrartz ship was a single man unit sent to scope out the planet. It landed on the side of a mountain. Unfortunately for the occupant his ship had a tripod landing gear. As it touched down on the slope it tumbled and rolled until the ship reached the bottom.

The ship landed on its top. Small Yrartz ships have a hatch on the top and an escape hatch on the bottom. Unfortunately while tumbling the spacecraft started an avalanche. Several tons of rock sat on top of the escape hatch.

The pilot of the ship began emergency evacuation procedures. He also sent a signal to orbiting craft to send help. That was at 7:30 A.M. At 8:32 A.M. Mount St Helens erupted covering the craft with two hundred feet of rock. First attempt at invasion a resounding failure.

The second landing occurred late in the evening of December 31, 1996. Again a single ship, this time a midsized unit, landed with three crew aboard. The tripod landing gear worked to perfection as the craft came to rest atop a building in Las Vegas.

The building chosen for this landing was the Hacienda Hotel and Casino. While the Yrartz crew were preparing to disembark from their ship fireworks began going off. The Yrartz thought they were under attack and sent an immediate call for help.

When midnight came the section of hotel the ship was on imploded. The spacecraft was buried under tons of rubble, the crew killed from concussion. Later, demolition crews would find the craft and thinking it had been part of the décor of the hotel sent it off to a salvage yard. The ship was melted down and became new automobiles. Try number two again a colossal failure.

In a slow, monotone voice that sounded metallic, computer generated, "But commander we have lost two ships already. Both of our early probes were destroyed." He paused to catch his breath. "Perhaps we should move on to another planet that is less prepared," the Yrartz lieutenant suggested.

"No matter," another lieutenant's squeaky, slow monotone answered. "The first probe was destroyed in a volcano blast. The second appeared to be a similar if smaller eruption."

"Yes," began the Supreme Commander in a voice that sounded funny even to his aides and generals. "I realize what both of you say. The probes were lost by accident not by design. We have watched this planet for years now. There seems to be no intelligent life here. We invade," he slammed his fist toward the console and missed. "Tomorrow."

"Hey NM did you see the star shower last night?" Nate asked.

Doctor NM Roswell nodded his head and swallowed a mouthful of chili. "Yes Nathan I surely did see it, but not while it was happening. I watched it on my computer this morning. I did not expect much and that is why I didn't watch it last night. I was truly surprised how many fell as the Draconid doesn't always put on such a show. I counted into the thousands."

"Yeah me too," Nate said thinking he should have kept his mouth shut like Tom suggested earlier. "So what do you think it means all them stars falling like that?" Nathan Minong couldn't help himself.

"Well," NM paused pondering. "It either means a large amount of debris came off the latest comet to come near Earth or we are being invaded by aliens," he smiled as he answered. Nehemiah thought this was a good joke.

"Just remember Nathan," NM continued. "If they are invading they are coming as a conquering force. We are the ones they intend to conquer and make slaves of...or lunch." NM smiled, almost laughed again as he shrugged into his coat and put the fedora on his head. "See you later gentlemen," he addressed the trio.

"Bye, sir," Nathan came close to saluting. He turned to his friends and asked, "What do you think he meant by that?"

For a change Tom was listening. "I think he was just pulling your chain," Bob answered. "What do you think Tom?"

"I think he is right, about the alien thing anyway. If some aliens invade Earth we are the ones they will try to destroy or make slaves of."

"You don't think they would eat us or something do you?" Nate asked, a tremble in his voice. "I mean what if they wanted us for supper? You ever see that one Twilight Zone episode?" Naturally Nate would think of food.

"What's the matter Nate? You afraid you might be the first one they ask to dinner?" Bob wondered aloud.

"Hey you know if they want food I would be the first one," Nathan had a worried look on his face as he scanned the room and peered through the windows.

Tom felt it was time to let his friend off the hook. "Nate first off we wouldn't let any aliens take you without a fight. You're our bud. We take care of our friends, you know that." He let that sink in a bit. "Besides we can use you as a shield," he smiled.

"You're all heart bro."

Kelly brought their food and waited for the prayer. Everyone bowed their heads and closed their eyes. "Lord Jesus, thank you for this food we are about to eat," Tom began. "We praise you and thank you for all the good things you give us. Lord we also thank you for the tough times and problems you allow in our lives that help us build character. Thank you and bless this food to our bodies."

"Amen."

Tom took a bite of his chili and almost gagged. He looked at Kelly. "Who made this?" he asked putting down his spoon. Bob nearly spit out the chili as he looked over at Kelly waiting for her answer.

"I did," called Bill Webster. "Why do you ask?" he asked as he came close to their table.

Tom didn't answer. "It tastes like crap," Bob volunteered.

"Why isn't the Cajun cooking?" Tom inquired.

"I fired him," Bill answered.

"Why did you do that?" Bob asked as Nathan slurped loudly.

"He tried to scalp one of the waitresses."

Nate looked at him. "Is that an Indian joke?" he asked.

"It's no joke. He tried to scalp a waitress with his meat cleaver."

"Not my sister?" Nate wondered aloud as he pulled Bob's bowl closer and started eating again.

"No not Kelly. It was that redhead."

"She's hot," Nathan offered between slurps.

"Yes she is," Tom admitted.

"Hey I thought you liked my sister?"

"I do. Doesn't mean I can't notice a hot woman when I see one," Tom said looking around to see if Kelly was still within earshot.

"I guess," Nate agreed.

"Hey where's my chili?" Bob asked looking at the two now empty bowls in front of Nathan.

He smiled at Bob and said, "Not as good as Baloney-Os but it did the trick."

Looking down at his bowl Tom added, "It does look a lot like Baloney-Os. What are those little circle things in the chili?"

Bill was still standing behind them. He reached for the empty bowls. "Something for you?" he asked Bob.

Bob looked up at him. "Do you know how to make a cheese sandwich?"

# Chapter 8

Granny Hayward, real name Hilda Hayward, had lived on the farm since she married. Archibald Hayward was a good man and a good husband. He passed away twenty years ago and Hilda remained on the place choosing to live alone.

He was only five feet and seven inches tall and most would call him skinny. But Archie could work harder and longer than most men. He had a never give up style and believed in God, his family and hard work.

Hilda was shorter by three inches but made up for it in spunk. She could never be called anything but thin even when pregnant. She was a woman that worked alongside her man every step of the way.

After Archie's death her children all left the area except for son Edward. He moved into the old farm house with his wife and kept the farm going. Their sons Bob and Tom were too young to help at first but Tom followed along on his two-year-old legs. Baby Bob just cried a lot.

Granny started life out as the oldest girl and second child of a farm family. She went to work around the house and farm early on and never knew anything but hard labor. She grew up believing a good life could be had through hard work and perseverance.

Hilda went to church with her family every Sunday but had never noticed the young man before. Oh she saw him every week but this time she really saw him. He had changed she thought. In truth she was the one who had changed.

Granny was fifteen when she set her cap, as they used to say, for Archie. Archibald Hayward saw her and thought about her but he was a bit too shy to ask her. He, for his part, noticed her the year before. His big brothers gave him guff telling him if he wanted her, he should do something about it before some other guy did. Archie decided to do just that.

One Sunday after service the church had its monthly summer time church picnic. Archie walked over to where Hilda's family was preparing a place to sit. They spread blankets on the grass and began getting plates and such out.

Just as Archie approached Harold Philbin stepped up to Hilda. "Hilly would you like to come sit with me at lunch?" the boy asked.

Hilda looked over at Archie and smiled, taking Harold's arm she said, "Why yes I would love to." As the pair walked away she looked back at Archie and winked.

Dejected he went back to his family. His brothers watched it all but his parents were busy with preparations. The oldest, Fred said, "Don't worry Archie. She wants to be with you and not that Harold Philbin. He may be taller and better looking than you but he isn't the brightest and you are the one she is interested in."

"Yeah," Ben added. "You see the way she looked at you just now? She will come around soon. You just wait. And she don't care if you are ugly either."

Archie's brothers were not stupid but they sure didn't know how to cheer him up. He felt even worse after what they said. So he walked off down to the creek behind the church and sat down on a rock to eat his lunch alone. That is where she found him.

He heard someone approaching and sat up and looked behind him. "Hi Archie," Hilda smiled a deep, pleasurable smile, the kind that comes close on the border of love. She reached out a hand and put it on his shoulder as she stood beside the boulder he sat on.

"I thought you were with Harold."

"It took me a while to get rid of him," she answered.

He really looked at her then. His eyes piercing to her soul. It was then he realized she was the one and only one for him. She stood beside him and their hands found each other and held. They stood together from that day on.

They married a year later and she moved to the farm. He was eighteen, she was sixteen. The big white house was large enough for two families and then some. They shared the upstairs with his brothers and sister. Archie's parents and grandparents shared the first floor, nine people in all.

During the war the house burned to the ground and in 1943 the family built a new ranch style home. It was spread out and not nearly as big but by then the brothers were off at the front and the grandparents both passed away.

Archie's sister got married and left and his mom and dad decided to stay in the shed they converted into a house. That left Archie, Hilda and their two children in the home. They added three more children to complete the family.

Mary, Edward's wife, and Hilda got on well. It was almost as if she were the daughter and he was the son-in-law. They worked together to keep the house clean and neat. Both helped with farm chores too.

The day came when Mary discovered a lump on her breast. First she kept it to herself. She was afraid of doctors and hospitals. But finally she had to admit there was a problem.

The doctors did what they could for her. She chose to go home and die there rather than in a hospital bed. After her passing Edward decided he had to leave. He could not deal with so many memories in the home they had shared. He moved to Arizona.

Edward called his mother almost every day and sent cards at Mother's Day and on her birthday. He came home for visits twice a year. But he would never call West Falls home again.

Bob and Tom moved to a house in town just a few months before their mother's death. They offered to come back and live with Granny after dad left but she said no. She actually laughed at them saying she felt she was old enough to take care of herself.

Granny Hayward was only five four and a hundred and eleven pounds. She seemed frail and helpless but many a coon, coyote and fox could attest to the fallacy of that idea. Stealing one of her chickens wasn't a good plan. Granny had a big, thirty-six inch long, double-barreled, ten gauge goose gun and knew how to use it.

Her age and size belied a strength and fortitude that could rain death and destruction on anyone and anything that sought to harm her livestock. She kept the shotgun beside the front door to her house and always had it loaded with double aught.

The front of the house looked onto the farm yard and all its buildings.

But the gun wasn't Grannies only defense. Buster was a very large mongrel that wasn't particularly impressed by the local bear population. He was as big as most wolves and had a temper that flared at the same things that bothered Granny. He seemed never to sleep and was always up for a fight of any kind.

Buster wasn't so much a pet, more a one dog army. Built like a tank and faster than a rabbit he could kill anything he couldn't scare off. He treated the local deer the same way he treated the livestock, like family.

Before Buster, Granny fought off a bear with a pitch fork and a loud voice. She took on a pack of wolves with a handful of rocks and won. After Buster came, Granny had an easy time with varmints. With her trusty double-barrel and Buster, Granny was unafraid to live alone. Animal, human or alien, the smart ones left her be.

Carl Vue was twenty-six and single. He wasn't worried. He knew he could always return home and snag a wife any time he wanted to. But for now he was content to live alone.

He had a plan. Carl was saving up to buy a business. He worked and then he worked. Then he worked some more.

Carl was always working at a job or in his garden. When he wasn't working he was sleeping or hunting. He did not feel he had the time for a wife and family just now. Someday, but not now.

Vue's place was almost a mile north of the church. Gordon Washburn's Lutheran church was the last building at the edge of town. Cumberland Road was the only way into West Falls and Carl lived just east off Cumberland.

The house was small, only two bedrooms and one bath. It was sided with green vinyl. Vinyl to save Vue time and maintenance costs, green to fit into the forest. It was nearly surrounded by forest with little lawn to mow. This suited Vue just fine. He hated mowing and had no time for unnecessary items.

Out back of the house was a garden and shooting range. Carl was a hunter and especially loved archery. He had a target set up year round at the far end of his garden. He wasn't opposed to shooting at varmints that tried to eat his vegetables either. He practiced enough to bag errant squirrels and rabbits and enjoy them for dinner.

Like Earl Stinnett's and Granny Hayward's, Vue's place was isolated. There were no neighbors within shouting distance. In fact a gunshot was likely to go unnoticed. Just not many people around.

Carl kept his home and land neat and clean. He was a logger by vocation. He spent his free time shooting, hunting, gardening and reading. He also spent some time hanging around The Rose talking with his friends. Among the friends he counted Nathan and the brothers Hayward.

Since he was an independent logger, Carl decided to take that Friday off to go hunting. His preferred stand was just a few hundred feet from the end of his garden. There was an old game trail that led down to Telemark Creek. He had a tree stand in a large white pine that overlooked the trail and the creek.

All the hunting gear was laid out on the counter in the laundry room at the back of Carl's house. He kept his archery equipment ready in case he had the urge to hunt. The room also housed his guns and ammo in a cabinet in the corner.

He knew it was unlikely he would see anything this early in the afternoon but Carl couldn't resist. He loved the outdoors and especially loved hunting. So he left the house an hour after lunch and headed down the path. On his way out the door Carl grabbed an apple, his only food for the hunt.

He climbed into the tree and settled in. It would be a long wait but at least he was outside and enjoying his favorite activity. Breathing the fresh crisp air of Northern Wisconsin while scanning the spectacular view, how could it get any better? For Carl this was the life.

He leaned his back against the tree and prepared himself. It could be some time before Carl saw anything but it could be a big deer might wander by real soon. One never knew and that was just an added benefit. That was the reason they called it hunting.

The excitement at seeing big deer walk close to the stand was part of the fun. But for him there was no boredom in the long wait. He would scan the area, keeping his eyes moving, roving over every square foot he could see.

# Chapter 9

"What are you guys going to do while I go feed the livestock?" Tom asked his brother and Nate.

Bob was nearly finished with his grilled cheese sandwiches. Nathan reached out and picked up a handful of bread crusts. He began placing them in his mouth one at a time.

Bob looked at him. "Hey bro no sense letting perfectly good food go to waste," Nate answered the unasked question.

Turning back to his brother Bob finally answered, "I guess we will hang out at our house until you get back." He shrugged. "We don't have any other plans do we Nate?" he nudged his friend.

Caught off guard he mumbled, "No bro. I got nothing."

Tom got up stepped back and pushed his chair in. Bob followed suit. Nate was slower to move but he did push his chair in too. The trio walked over to the cash register to pay their bill.

Tom paid and went out the door. He climbed into the driver's seat of his brother's truck and tried to start it. The engine clicked a few times and then started. He didn't notice a problem, his thoughts were elsewhere.

Nate went to the bulletin board next to the front door of the bar. As he scanned the items he noticed several were old and out of date. "Hey we should clean this up Bill. Some of this stuff has been up a long time." He pointed. "This has been up here for nine or ten months now. Kinda getting old."

"Leave it alone," Bill barked. "It's a calendar."


Kelly took her break right after she served her brother and friends. She sat down at a small table in the kitchen behind the bar. She needed to get off her feet for a bit.

She felt bad that she had been a little rude and standoffish with Tom especially after she told him she had to work late. Now Kelly was feeling like she should apologize. It wasn't his fault she had to work another shift and she shouldn't take it out on him.

It was only recently they began seeing each other. She thought back just a few months. Kelly had a lively banter going with her brother and his friends. Well they had been around so long she guessed they were her friends now too.

She remembered leaning in close to Tom as she swished the bar rag across the table. It didn't clean anything but it did wipe some crumbs off onto the floor. Tom said something to her and she smiled and moved on to the vacant table next over.

Kelly turned back toward him, "What did you say?"

"I said you're the most beautiful girl I've ever seen," he repeated in a whisper.

She looked at him then said, "You live in West Falls, Wisconsin. How many girls could you possibly have seen?" Kelly went back to wiping the table.

"I've watched television and I've seen some movies and magazine covers."

Kelly half turned toward him again, a quizzical look on her face. Was he for real? The thought jolted her like an electric shock. She knew he liked her but he had never been so forthcoming.

Too bad he doesn't have the guts to ask me for a date. He's the oldest, the smartest and the most mature of the three of them. But he is also the least bold.

The three blind mice, that's how she thought of them. She giggled at that. No maybe the two blind mice and the toothless cat that protects them. No but that was unkind Kelly felt. The three blind mice and she could be their seeing eye dog.

To her complete surprise Tom came over to her and took her hands in his. He had an odd look in his eyes but she knew he hadn't been drinking and she was fairly sure he wasn't crazy. He had something to say.

It was slow going at first but he finally blurted out would she go out with him. She was so shocked she couldn't immediately answer. This made Tom even more nervous. But she found her voice and they had been seeing each other ever since.

Kelly ended her muse and got up. She would go out and talk to Tom. She would apologize and suggest another date night. But by the time she got out of the kitchen the boys were gone.


Tom dropped Nate and his brother off at their house. Apprehensive at leaving that pair alone he headed north out of town. Granny Hayward's place was on Hawthorne Road. Hawthorne went west or left off Cumberland Road past the Food-N-Fuel and the farm machinery repair shop. It looped around coming back to Cumberland about a mile or so north of town.

Granny's farm lay on the west side of Hawthorne. At the south end of Hawthorne around the bend from the machine shop was a road going west toward Earl Stinnett's farm. That road had no official name but locals called it Earl's Road. It curved north past Earl's and finally dead ended at the cornfield Nate and the Hayward boys hunted near.

Tom turned the truck in to Grannies driveway. He parked the truck in front of Granny Hayward's house and got out. Granny opened the door and stepped out on the porch.

"Hey Sonny," she called all her grandsons Sonny.

"Hi Grandma. I came out to feed the livestock early so Bob and I can go hunting tonight."

"Yer going hunting?"

"Yes."

"I thought you had a date?"

"Apparently not. Kelly has to work tonight."

"Why don't you marry that Injun gal?" she asked. Tom's eyebrows raised. "Oh I know," she waved him off. "Calling someone an Injun ain't politically correct, but I'm an old woman so I'll say what I want how I want."

"It's okay grandma."

"Well Sonny?" Granny asked.

"Well what?" Tom asked, a bewildered look on his face.

"Why don't you marry that gal? She's the cutest thing around, she's hard working too. And she likes you."

Tom snickered and shook his head, "I don't know about that."

"Well I do," Granny nodded her head once to emphasize the fact. "She likes you and you can see it in her face when she talks to you or talks to someone about you.

"Tommy boy you better snatch her while you got the chance. She's liable to run off to the city and if that happens you won't stand any chance at all."

Tom wanted to ask her why that was but kept his peace. "She ain't gonna wait forever. If you're worried about me or your dad, don't. We will welcome her into the family. It don't make no difference that she's an Injun. We don't care what her skin color is or her background either. She could be an alien from outer space and if you loved her so would we."

"Can we change the subject?" Tom whined.

"Sure," she held the door open, "Come on inside. You had lunch but I bet you didn't have dessert."

Granny didn't wait for an answer and it wouldn't have made a difference. She started gathering up plates, forks and coffee cups. She put them on the kitchen table then grabbed the coffee pot. After pouring coffee she returned to the table with a fresh apple pie.

"Pastor Gordon was here this morning helping me gather eggs," Granny offered.

"I didn't know he got up that early."

"Shoot Sonny except for when you go hunting he's up before you every day. That man never seems to sleep.

"I was talking to Sarona at the market the other day. She said he prays for a couple hours before bed every night," Granny told him.

"Really? What does he pray for?"

"Oh his family for sure, but he also prays for everyone in his congregation by name. I guess he prays for the government too. Heaven knows the government needs it what with that man this country elected President."

Once again Tom kept his peace. Granny Hayward could get wound up and it was best to let her rant unimpeded. She seemed to have a full head of steam.

"I give Pastor some steaks from that steer we butchered. He didn't want to take them but I insisted. I told him it was a part of my tithe to the Lord and His church. Besides I always thought it was best to make sure the pastor has plenty to eat and enough money for clothes and such.

"The Bible says we are supposed to take care of them that preaches and teaches us. Your grandpa always felt that way too. He made sure the pastor had beef and venison, vegetables and even picked blackberries for them."

Tom talked with Granny for most of an hour then went to feed the animals. He fed the cows and horse and checked the stock tank. He made sure the rest of the animals had food and water too. Finally he stepped up to the door of the house to let his grandmother know he was finished.

Tom looked up at the sky and noticed it was a cloudy, mottled steel color. "Looks like the weatherman was right," he said more to himself than to Granny.

She stepped out the door. "Yep it looks like rain."

Tom reached out and gave her a hug. "All finished Gram. I'll see you tomorrow."

"Good-bye," she said to his back as he went down the steps.

He climbed into the truck and turned the key. Tom heard a clicking sound at first so he let off the key. He checked to make sure the lights, the radio, the wipers and the heater blower were off. He tried it again and after a few clicks the starter caught and the engine did too.

"What in the world?" Tom said aloud to himself. "I better tell Bob to take this truck in and get the charging system checked out." He wondered if the battery was going bad. Note to self, he thought, start driving my truck instead of Bob's.

Tom headed back into town to find his brother. On the way he glanced at his cell phone. There was still no service. Odd he thought. Must be something with the towers or who knew what else?

Since he couldn't call Bob, Tom decided to try the house first. Bob might still be there but if not he would try The Rose. Kelly would know where their brothers were.

At 3:01 AM that morning the cell tower directly across the road from Earl Stinnett's farm came tumbling down. The noise woke Earl and his dog Russell. Earl lay in bed for some time but couldn't fall back asleep. He decided to get up and start the last day of his life a little early.

Yrartz a-1197 and his partner m-1236 were tasked with destroying cell tower number 1. Actually m-1236 was to take out the tower and a-1197 was there as security and backup. If m-1236 was unsuccessful in his mission a-1197 would continue on and destroy the tower.

The plan was simple because, let's face it so were the Yrartz. M-1236 would dive on Earth and land appropriately close to cell tower 1. He would then proceed to place explosives at the base of the structure and then detonate. The tower would fall and Earthling communications from West Falls would cease.

That was the basic plan. A-1197 would land close to m-1236 and provide security. If anything went wrong he would blow the tower. If things went according to plan the pair of saboteurs would simply join the invasion squads.

M-1236 turned his ship toward Earth at 2:59 AM. He was an inexperienced and poor driver. He put the craft into a steep dive and entered the atmosphere. A-1197 watched in horror as m-1236's ship went into a flaming spiral dive.

Yrartz a-1197 followed as closely as he could. His partner was heading in the right direction but appeared to have control issues. "This is Yrartz a-1197. Do not be alarmed! M-1236 are you having flight difficulties?"

"This is 1236. I cannot control the ship. I cannot come out of this spiral dive. I am alarmed."

"A-1197 to 1236, try pulling back on the sticks. Pull one harder than the other."

Yrartz m-1236 pulled hard on the left control stick which came apart in his hands. He scream-screeched as he looked at the now severed control lever. A-1197 watched as his partner's spiraling ship went completely out of control in a flat spin, still falling fast.

The spin increased rapidly. 1236 was thrown violently back against his seat now unable to do anything with his arms. His face a mask of horror, the new screams no longer leaving his throat.

"Yrartz m-1236 do not be alarmed! Pull on the other stick and let go of the one you are holding now."

Too late. M-1236 was blacking out but he managed to let go of the broken left stick and reach the right lever. No amount of pulling and reefing on that control stick changed anything. The left control was full on and the handle lay useless on the floor.

M-1236 lost consciousness as the ship spun ever faster. 1197, now terrified for his partner, saw m-1236's ship collide with and explode cell tower 1. There was a brilliant flash and then nothing.

A-1197 landed safely in the woods near cell tower 1 and immediately began a search for m-1236. He soon found the mingled and mangled parts of m-1236's ship and cell tower 1. Half the tower was gone with only smoking ruins on the ground around it.

In an electronic, monotone voice, "A-1197 to commander. Mission accomplished. Cell tower 1 destroyed."


On any normal days hunt Carl Vue wouldn't have any trouble staying awake. But last night there was such a spectacular show in the skies that he was up much later than usual. He was up and about at his regular time this morning and so he had less sleep.

Carl was dressed in his regular camouflage hunting outfit with extra layers underneath. He had on a pair of bib overalls and insulated hunting pacs. He was warm and toasty as he headed to his tree stand. He would not feel the cold this evening.

He went out earlier than normal for an afternoon hunt. But he had the day off and he didn't get up early enough for the morning hunt. So Carl was on his way to his stand before two. He would be up there all afternoon and evening.

His short stature meant the climbing spikes were close together and he had to use more of them. But Carl's height never mattered when it came time to shoot. The deer didn't care how tall he was either.

Sitting in his tree stand Carl's head drooped. He came awake with a start, smiled to himself. Moments later his head drooped again. The third time his head nodded he did not wake immediately. After a few minutes he began snoring. Good thing he had his harness on.

As he slept Carl had a dream, a good dream. The smile crept across his face. Lost in his fantasy he never saw the small trees and brush sway in the dark, windless swamp.

Z-123 was running late. He and his squad were tasked with taking out the bridge over Telemark creek. The mission was supposed to be complete within minutes of the cell towers coming down.

But the best plans of mice and Yrartz often go astray. So it was that z-123 and his unit barely made it to the bridge before daylight. First it was z-123's ship wouldn't start. Then after transferring to another ship the mechanics forgot to fuel it up.

He finally got a ship ready and took off for Earth. After landing, z-123 had to wait over two hours for his Yrartz to assemble. Then they discovered they landed at the wrong bridge. They had to fly three kilometers to find Telemark creek.

The group finally assembled around the bridge with security units out. Now z-123 was fuming. He stomped up and down the road near the target. In his scratchy monotone he shout-screamed-belched, "How is it possible you came here without the explosives entrusted to your care? Are you really that stupid? Do I have to do everything myself? Have I command of a bunch of blithering idiots?"

L-1313, second in command addressed z-123. "Sir do not be alarmed! I have sent three Yrartz back to the mother ship to retrieve the explosives. They shall return in a matter of minutes."

"You fool! They cannot return!"

"Why is that sir?"

"It is daylight. We are not allowed to fly in daylight. Our orders are very strict. We are to remain as covert as possible until we gain a foothold. Do you not understand?" z-123 fumed and raged some more and then attempted to kick l-1313.

Upon picking himself off the ground z-123 snarled at his lieutenant, "You will be in big trouble for this fiasco. Now go and find something we can use to blow up this infernal bridge. Go now!"

L-1313 sauntered off in search of explosives. Z-123 continued to rant and rave about the immense stupidity of his subordinates. The rest of the squad began settling in to their positions and looking for food.

Fred and June Seeley managed an early start on their trip to Ashland. They were going for groceries and sundry other items. It seems Fred was having problems that June felt some bran and perhaps a laxative might help.

The Seeley's lived next to the auto repair shop in West Falls. The shop was located in what could be called the industrial section of town. The auto shop shared a backyard with the farm machinery shop owned by Deputy Hawkins. Next to the farm machine shop was the Food-N-Fuel and across the street was the church. All of the major businesses in the village were clustered here except The Rose.

Fred was owner and head mechanic of the auto shop for many years. He could fix the transmission on a 1941 Willys coupe or rebuild a 225 slant six engine on a '65 Dodge Coronet. But when the new cars sported computers instead of breaker points Fred gave the keys to the shop to his son.

The Seeley's were arguing, some would say bickering, on their way north. For this reason Fred did not see the thing in the road and so did not swerve to avoid it. But both he and his wife heard the scream and they felt the thump as too late he slammed on his brakes.

They sat in the car a moment, stunned and unmoving. Fred checked the rearview mirror and was horrified to see what he thought was a young child lying in the road. "I killed some little kid," he managed to mumble with tears in his eyes.

Both got out of the car and walked the few yards back to the thing in the road. They could not tell whether it was a boy or a girl. First they noticed the incredible stench. Looking down at it June stated factually, "It's dead for sure but what is it?"

"Not sure mother but it isn't a child. It looks like some kind of animal someone dressed up in a costume," Fred added.

"Why would anyone dress up an animal in a costume?" June asked.

"Well it is getting close to Halloween. Maybe they were trying it on to see if it fit."

"Maybe, but what kind of animal is it? I have never seen anything like it before."

"Well it is probably a monkey of some kind. They have all sorts of species of them things," Fred told her. "Anyway it's dead so I'm just going to kick it off the road and we can get going again."

The Seeley's got back in their Ram 3500 and headed north again not looking back. Both continued to wonder what it was they ran over. But by the time they made Ashland Fred was thinking about his bowels and June was snoring a short nap away.

L-1313's bad day came to an end as did his life. He was feebly breathing when Fred kicked him into the ditch. He felt intense pain as he rolled down the embankment. At the bottom he splashed into a foot of putrid water stagnating there. Shortly thereafter 1313 drowned and was never heard from again.

Z-123 tired of waiting for l-1313 and began a search of his own for explosives. Here success finally caught up with him. He found some material brought by a platoon of Yrartz who were supposed to provide security farther north on Cumberland Road.

It seems this platoon got lost in the drop from space. Most of them ended up in a ditch and field near the bridge at Telemark Creek. They had no officer to command them and had no real idea where to go or what to do.

This played into the hands or claws of z-123. He immediately saw the need for them to provide security for his unit and his mission. He made them give over their supplies of explosives. Now he could accomplish his objective without further delay.


Tom pulled into the driveway and shut off the engine. He climbed out and went up the steps into the house. "How's Granny?" Bob asked as Tom entered.

"She is fine. She told me Pastor Gordon was out there early today. Gram gave him some steaks from that steer we butchered the other day."

"Steaks! Did someone say steaks?" Nate asked enthusiastically.

"Hold on Nate. I didn't bring any and I didn't cook any and we don't have any steaks here," Tom informed him. "Hey did you change your shirt again?"

"Yep, I spilled chili on my other one."

"That's my shirt you're stretching out," Tom said matter-of-factly. "I thought I recognized it." He sniffed the air. "Nate are you wearing your sister's perfume again?"

"I figured that odor was coming from him," Bob agreed. "What is that, Angel Spit perfume, right?"

Nate sniffed the shirt. "No that's from the last time I wore this shirt. It's called Angel Tears not Angel Spit. It's put out by Bodwar. Surprised you didn't know that."

"You mean I haven't washed that shirt since the last time you stole it and wore it?" Tom asked flabbergasted.

"Guess not," Nate answered innocently. "Now how about those steaks?"

"All he ever thinks about is food," Bob began again.

"True and if we had a cow or steer here he probably would start eating it before it stopped mooing," Tom added.

"Ha-ha, you guys are regular comedians. You should be on TV or something." Nate's face brightened. "Hey you could have a radio talk show. We could call it the Bob, Tom and Nate show."

"You crazy?" Bob asked. "The Bob, Tom and Nate show? Nobody would watch it."

"No because it's on the radio silly," Nate retorted.

"You know Tom now that we started talking about food..." Nate's eyes lit up.

"I thought we were talking about a radio show," Tom said looking confused.

"That was before," Nate interjected. "Go ahead Bob."

"Well as I was saying I really didn't eat that much for lunch and it's been a couple hours. I could go for something else."

"Yeah me too," Nathan added enthusiastically.

"Well granny gave me some apple pie when I was at her place so I'm not hungry. However because I can see you both are hungry let's go down to The Rose and have a quick sandwich." Tom grabbed his camo coat and started for the door. Bob followed taking his hunting jacket too.

Nate rubbed his hands together in anticipation and with a big smile on his face picked up his hunting coat too. By the time the others were to the truck Nate was already seated and waiting.

"How does he do that?" Bob asked wondering.

"Do what?"

"How does he move that fast?"

"We are going for food," Tom answered as if it should be obvious.

Once again the trio entered The Rose preparing to consume something good. However since the Cajun had been fired they anticipated something not so good. Perhaps cheese sandwiches all around or maybe just toast.

Kelly looked up and smiled as she saw them come in. She was clearing a table at the time and turned toward them. Her smile widened as Tom came close. She touched his arm and reached up, kissed him lightly on the cheek.

"The Cajun's back so you can order anything you want," she informed them. Kelly didn't bother asking them why they were back so soon. She knew her brother was always hungry and could eat anywhere, any time.

While the guys found a table and sat down, Kelly dropped off the dirty plates and dish rag. She washed her hands, picked up her order book and headed for the table. Before she could say anything Tom looked up at her, "I'm sorry."

She leaned close, "I'm the one that should be sorry and I am. I was a little upset. I had no call to be angry with you." Standing up straight she asked, "What can I get for you boys?"

"We just want something light to hold us while we hunt tonight," Tom said.

"I'll have a big bowl of chili and a sandwich," Nate answered.

There was a loud roar and everyone in the bar looked toward the kitchen door. The clatter of pots and pans hitting against each other and the floor could be heard. Muffled voices. Unidentifiable noises were heard too.

Bill Webster, owner of The Rose, was a big man. He stood six foot, five inches tall. If he chose to step on a scale the instrument would groan out a number significantly over three hundred. He could have been a bouncer in any bar in America.

The Cajun was somewhat shorter and a few pounds lighter. But he was also stronger. He could have made a serious contribution as a lineman on any NFL team. He was also a great cook.

The Cajun slammed thru the kitchen door carrying the chili pot in his huge arms, face bright red and if possible, steam coming out his ears. Bill was stomping right behind yelling at the Cajun's back. Both men headed for the deck door closest to the kitchen.

Without a word the Cajun wrapped one beefy arm around the chili pot and used the other hand to open the door. He took two steps out onto the deck and heaved the pot over the railing, turned and headed back to the kitchen.

Bill stood looking over the railing then he too turned and went back toward the kitchen. He reached one arm out to the door, thought better of it and went to the bar. There he poured himself a stiff root beer and sat down on a stool. "What are you all looking at?" he demanded. Everyone turned back to whatever it was they had been doing.

"I think, ah do you still have that hot beef? I'll have one of those," Bob said.

"Me too," Nate added. "Make that a double."

Tom smiled, "Kelly could you bring me coffee and a single hot beef?"

She smiled at him again, "Sure I can do that. I'll put your order in and be right back with your drinks." Kelly turned away and headed for the kitchen.

"I didn't even tell her what I wanted to drink," Nathan pouted, arms folded.

"Would it be any different?" Tom asked.

"No but I still like to be asked."

The boys ate quickly and headed for the cash register to pay up. After paying, Kelly kissed Tom and said, "I don't work tomorrow. How about we go to Ashland and have dinner someplace. Maybe take in a movie." She smiled coyly, head tilted.

Even if he had wanted to Tom couldn't have said no to that look. "Sure I think I can find time from my busy schedule." He took an imaginary pen and tablet from his pockets, "Let me see, what time should I pencil you in for?"

Kelly punched him lightly on the shoulder and with a big grin answered, "Remember I work til close. Don't call before ten."

The guys left and Kelly went back to her work. She moved from table to table wiping them down and removing any dirty dishes. One of the locals grabbed her arm as she passed.

"Kelly honey, bring me another beer."

"It's three o'clock. Isn't it a little early in the day for you to be drunk?" she asked him.

"I'm not drunk," he answered.

"Ben, you're calling me honey and you aren't being polite and saying please any more when you ask for a beer. You know my policy. You've had enough.

"You want coffee I'll get you coffee. You want more alcohol, get it yourself. You know I don't serve drunks."

He blinked and looked at her. Slowly the obvious became obvious to him. "Aww I'm sorry Kelly. Could you get me some coffee please?"

"Sure Ben. Be right back."

"Thanks."

Orrin Hurley watched all this from his seat at the bar. "Boy Kelly don't take no guff from nobody, does she Bill?"

"No she doesn't," Bill paused. "I'm lucky to have her. She is tough and strong and really knows how to handle every kind of customer."

"Yup I see that. She must be close on six feet tall too. Good looking gal."

"Yes she is and she really draws in the customers. She is cute and has a body that won't quit. She works hard too. If she ever quit I'd have to work twice as hard and probably still go broke and have to sell out."

"Probably right. She's strong too. I've seen her move those kegs around. Does she work out?" Orrin asked.

"Nope, she doesn't have time to. No she just works really hard here and at home. Why she lets that lazy brother of hers live there is beyond me. I mean I like the guy but I don't think he's ever had a job."

"I thought he worked for Bob and Tom on the farm."

"Naw he hangs out with Bob and Tom but I don't think he ever does any work out there."

"So, what? He eats their food and keeps them company?"

"I guess so. Nathan is a nice guy, just lazy. He's friendly and will talk to anybody. But I've asked him to help out around here and he always gets real busy somewhere else."

"Too bad. He could use a little hard work and exercise."


Bob, Tom and Nathan were loaded up and ready to go. They stopped by Bob and Tom's so they could get their gear and then stopped at Nate and Kelly's. The trio always put their bows and other gear in the truck bed because there simply wasn't room in the cab for all of that.

It was Bob's truck but Tom almost always drove if the two of them were together. He climbed into the driver's seat and turned the key. There was a whirring sound but the engine didn't fire. He released the key then tried it again.

"I've been meaning to talk to you about this Bob."

"What is it?" Bob asked.

"I think the starter is going," Tom replied. "Jump out and check it. See if the cables are tight. That might be what's wrong."

Bob and Nate got out of the truck and Bob popped the hood open. He was about to check the battery cables when the engine roared to life. Tom stuck his head out the driver's side window and said, "It's working."

Bob slammed the hood down and the pair got back in the truck. "Hey brother thanks for almost chopping off my hand."

"Aww you were in no danger Bob. I could see your hands weren't anywhere near the fan or any other moving parts." Tom smiled at his brother then put the truck in gear. He backed out of the driveway and started out of town.

Nate leaned over and turned the radio on. He put it on his favorite station and turned the volume up. It happened to be playing one of Nate's favorite songs so he turned the volume knob even more. Tom reached over to turn it down.

At that moment there was a loud explosion. Most of the residents of West Falls heard the sound. Some came outside to see if they could place it. The rest just went about their business as usual thinking it was nothing important.

Bob, Tom and Nate didn't hear the sound. They were too busy fighting over the volume control. Finally the song ended and Tom won. He turned the sound down to a reasonable deafening level.

Up the road z-123 had finally succeeded in destroying the bridge over Telemark Creek. He also took out three of his troops. The explosion was sufficient to remove the bridge and drop it in the creek.

Z-123 and the rest of the Yrartz prepared defensive positions on both sides of the creek. They were ready for anything the people of Earth had to throw at them. At least that is what z-123 told his trusting troops.

Fred and June Seeley were on their way back from Ashland. They still knew nothing about the Yrartz invasion. Both had completely forgotten the little green monkey they ran over on the way north earlier that day.

Fred was driving and daydreaming. June was talking and getting no response as usual. "I think we should have gone to another store. I'm sure we could have saved money. You know Fred we just can't throw money around like we used to when we were both still working."

That brought Fred back to consciousness. "What?" he said bewildered. He could not remember a time when either he or his wife had squandered any of their income. He looked at her at the exact wrong time.

Their vehicle went off the end of the road where the bridge should have been. It sailed and sank and hit the concrete abutment on the far side of the creek. Neither Fred nor June had time even to be frightened as the truck back flipped and landed on its top.

The Yrartz closest to the upside down truck stood up in awe. They had never seen a vehicle do a back flip before. They were on the verge of giving a cheer but the surprise lasted only until their leaders started yelling at them.

The Yrartz troops moved in unison converging on the overturned truck from three sides. They were as curious as they were defensive. None of them had ever seen a human up close and personal. Were they dangerous? Were they edible? What did they taste like?

Fred and June looked with dazed eyes at the Yrartz coming toward them. They still had no idea what they were seeing or that these were aliens from another planet come to take over the Earth. The husband and wife were trapped in their truck hanging from the seatbelts. The Yrartz would eat them where they hung.

# Chapter 10

Bob, Tom and Nate were taking a left past the Food-N-Fuel when the Yrartz closed in on Fred and June. They roared up the road and took the first left onto the dead end toward Earl Stinnett's. The road narrowed and curved left then right then left again. Trees of the forest marched alongside for a quarter mile or so.

Once past the trees farm fields extended out from both sides of the road. On the right was a slight rise and on the left the land dropped away toward the Bibon. Both sides were used for pasture now.

They rounded the corner and Tom peered thru the windshield, squinting. "Isn't that Ted Hawkins truck?"

"Where?" Bob asked.

"Right there," Tom pointed. "In the ditch, well half in and half out."

"It sure is," Nathan answered. "It looks like it's in the same place Earl's truck was."

"Sure enough," Bob agreed. "But what's it doing there?"

"Maybe Ted found Earl and they are trying to get the heifers back in the pen," Tom hoped aloud.

"Could be. Well we can't get around Ted's truck so I guess we stop and find out," Bob suggested.

Without comment Tom pulled alongside Ted's truck and stopped. He put the vehicle in park and shut off the engine. He got out of the truck as the other two exited and walked toward the truck.

The first thing Tom noticed was the driver's side door was open as if someone were in too much of a hurry to bother closing it. The second thing he noticed was blood on the

92

ground as he approached the vehicle. He saw blood on the seat and steering wheel as well.

Many thoughts raced through Tom's mind. What had happened? How come the truck was parked like this? What was the big hurry? What happened to Ted? Where was Earl and what happened to him?

Bob opened the passenger's side door and was staring at the blood on the seat and wheel. Some had splattered on the windshield across the seat to the right hand door. Nate came up behind him and tried to see inside too.

"What is it guys?" Nate asked.

"What do you suppose happened?" Bob asked as he stepped aside to let Nate see. Tom didn't answer. He had glanced quickly at the interior then turned and went up to the road again.

"Holy crab cakes on wheat toast!" Nathan exclaimed. He looked at Bob and Bob returned the look with a shrug. Both men were thinking this was the oddest and scariest thing they had ever seen.

The two looked things over a little more closely. Bob stepped around the truck to the driver's side and leaned in for a better look. Nate pulled a candy bar out of his pocket and began unwrapping it.

Bob looked at Nate then at the candy bar. The tragedy before them temporarily forgotten. "How many of those things you eat a day?"

Nate held up the candy. "These? I'm not sure."

"Well how many do you eat at lunch?" Bob inquired.

"I don't usually eat candy bars for lunch."

"When do you eat them?"

"Various times," Nathan answered vaguely.

"Okay let's make it easy. How many do you eat for a snack?"

"Which snack?" Nate asked. "Before breakfast, after breakfast, before lunch, after lunch, before supper, after supper or before bed time?"

"You have seven snacks a day?" Bob asked flabbergasted, shaking his head. "Well of course you do."


Carl Vue woke with a start. He was sure he heard something very loud but could not make out what it was. He wondered if the rumble he heard and felt was just a dream. As he looked out over the swamp he couldn't see anything unusual.

He sat up and stretched then leaned back again. Carl shifted a bit to try and get comfortable. He told himself he would stay awake now. That lasted but a short time as his head started to nod once more.

Within minutes Carl was leaning back eyes closed. Soon he was sleeping. Shortly he was snoring loudly enough that no self-respecting deer would come near.

Granny Hayward was just about to sit down in her rocker with a hot cocoa and a good book when Buster started a low growl. He leaped to his feet and let out an I'm going to murder you if I get my teeth in you roar. His bark was deafening in the small house.

"What is it Buster?" Granny asked as she set her book on the end table and headed for her shotgun. Usually when Buster let loose like this there was an intruder out in the yard somewhere.

Granny snatched up the double barrel and broke it open. As always it was loaded for bear. She snapped it shut and reached for the door. When she opened it Buster nearly knocked her over trying to get out. He stopped on the porch and barked.

"What is it?" she asked again. She couldn't see anything that the dog might be alarmed about. But she knew him well enough to know he didn't bark at leaves blowing in the wind. Buster raced down the steps and out into the farm yard.

Granny noticed the skies had darkened and a slight drizzle was falling. She saw that the chickens had disappeared into their coop. The horse, the goats and the cows all with ears twitching, were looking toward the swamp.

Buster's growl turned nasty. He too, was facing the swamp. He took a few steps forward and held his ground, hackles up. This was a dog that was angry and bold and most certainly ready for a fight.

The cows went back to eating the hay in their manger. The dumb bovines were unconcerned with anything but food for the moment. Eat, chew their cud, and sleep. This was a cow's life.

Granny peered through the mist at the swamp. Still she could see nothing amiss. There was almost no breeze at all and few leaves remained on the trees anyway. No movement anywhere.

The animals continued to stare, yes that's what it was, a stare. They were looking into the swamp and the tall grasses and cedars down there. Buster stopped growling and seemed to listen intently.

Grandma Hayward heard them coming. How could she not? She turned and grabbed a coat from off a chair in the kitchen and quickly put it on against the wet and cold.

She stepped further out on the porch and watched, waiting. Suddenly some of the grasses and brush began moving. Something was coming up out of the swamp on a wide front. Her hands tightened their grip on the big shotgun and she reached into a pocket of the coat. Her fingers touched some more shells and reassured she stood ready.

They came slowly, menacingly. First the horn-like ears appeared, then the tops of their green heads. Granny waited wondering what these things were and what their intention was. She realized what that sound she had been hearing was.

"We are Yrartz from the Planet Yrartz. Do not be alarmed! We are here to take over your planet," they said in unison. The loud chorus blended with Buster's renewed growls. The goats started in as well.

One kid standing close to the single wire electric pasture fence reached out its neck to sniff the nearest Yrartz. The alien sent a wireless taser at the animal. The little goat jumped and tried to run as several other Yrartz zapped it too.

The Yrartz rumbled thru the pasture attacking anything that moved or appeared to move. Hundreds of blades of grass and small trees were fried. Numerous weeds bought the farm so to speak. A couple unlucky fence posts burst into flames from the lasers. One Yrartz bumped into an old wooden wagon. A wheel fell off and six Yrartz lasered it into smoking ruin.

Grandma Hayward stepped forward on the porch, double-barrels aimed. "Git yer stinkin' little green goobers outta here!" she shouted.

That stopped them in their tracks, but only for a moment. They rolled forward again. Now they were attacking the helpless goats cornered against the fence.

Granny's next words came from the end of the double barrels. BOOM! BOOM! Loud and clear the shots rang out. Two Yrartz disintegrated and others were wounded. Many more were splattered by Yrartz particles. Surprisingly the green aliens had red blood.

Grandma's double-barrel shotgun spoke mostly in double-aught. She still had some ancient 00 buckshot that Archie used to down geese with. There were boxes of these and they worked just as good as new.

She reloaded and fired off both barrels again. Then she quickly went inside and opened a cupboard door. Granny had a possibles bag in there with the equivalent of three boxes of ammo in it. She grabbed this and went back outside.

The buckshot made big, mean holes in things like Yrartz and Granny wasn't afraid to use it. The weapon was a ten gauge with thirty-six inch barrels and one hefty piece of metal. Some said it weighed more than Grandma Hayward did. No matter, she could handle it and knew how.

The gun spoke again and again as she fired at one group of Yrartz after another. They seemed to come on in never ending waves. But Granny had been a widow for twenty years now. She defended the chickens from many a marauding coon or fox. She ended the life of more than one skunk. She feared no enemy, not even little green ones from out beyond.

BOOM! BOOM! The big gun roared and after each shot the old woman cackled like a hen. She broke open the shotgun, pulled out the empties and replaced new shells. BOOM! BOOM! Then the maniacal laughter.


Tom stood in the middle of the road and looked first north then south. He glanced down and saw something glint in low light. He scanned the road edge and saw it again. Bending over he reached down and picked up an object. It was an empty shell casing in 9 mm. There were several more lying about.

Tom realized then that Ted Hawkins had reloaded at least once. Some of the blood in and on Ted's truck probably wasn't his. He turned his attention to the trees that grew close to the road just a few yards north and west of where he was. He glanced back at the guys then thought he heard something.

He couldn't quite place the sound. Tom shook his head to clear it. It was vague but there was something. The noise was just out of his range of perception. He listened intently trying to filter out the boys talk and any normal natural sounds.

Suddenly he heard the two sounds simultaneously. The one he recognized as the roar of a big gun fired a long way off. The other was much closer and as he listened he thought there were several noises.

One sound seemed to be a rustling of grasses and small brush. The other was like words spoken by many voices all at once. Tom was confused and could not make out what it was he was hearing. But something, some inner voice warned him.

Tom started backing toward the vehicle. Without turning to look he said, "Guys get in the truck." His words made little impression on Bob and Nate. He repeated, "Hey guys I think we better get in the truck." He turned his head and saw they were not moving. "HEY! GET IN THE TRUCK!" he shouted.

That got their attention. Nate's head poked up from Ted's truck. Bob turned and looked at his brother. Both men felt the tension in Tom and they turned and scrambled up the bank. Whatever the problem was they believed him and moved accordingly.

Tom stopped a few feet from the truck, listened and watched to the west. Bob opened the door, climbed in and reaching across opened the driver side door. Nate stood next to the truck holding his door open and asked, "What is it Tom?"

Tom irritated, waved his hand in back of him and said, "Shush." Nate shook his head and frowned, wondering he climbed in beside Bob. Finally Tom heard it clearly.

"We are Yrartz from the Planet Yrartz. Do not be alarmed! We are here to take over your planet."

Tom tilted his head, "What in the world?" A smile crossed his lips. He thought what kind of joke is this. Then he saw them.

The Yrartz came up out of the swamp to his left front. Others moved out of the trees farther to his right. The smile forming on Tom's face turned into a hard, determined line. He realized at that moment these were the things that destroyed his friends and neighbors.

They all carried a laser in one hand or claw. They all carried another item he couldn't immediately identify in the other. The lasers were lit up and ready. The Yrartz, for now they had identified themselves, were intent on destruction.

Nate, mouth full of candy bar pointed forward excitedly trying to mumble something. Bob had been preoccupied with his seatbelt. "What is it?" he asked. Then he looked out the window, his eyes getting big.

Tom rushed to the truck took hold of the door and swung inside. He didn't wait for the door to close before turning the key. Nothing happened. Without thinking he stomped on the gas pedal and tried the key again. Still nothing.

Peering thru the windshield he could see the Yrartz closing in. Looking like solid ranks of plastic Christmas trees with heads on top the Yrartz would have been comical. But they repeated their mission with every step. The plan was clear, take over and destroy.

They were coming down the road faster than they were coming up out of the swamp. Soon dozens of them would surround the truck and the guys would be in serious trouble. Nathan was choking on his candy bar and Bob was ready to bail out and run.

He tried the key again and nothing. Opening his door Tom called, "You guys get out and push."

Nate jumped out followed by Bob. "Push where?" Bob asked.

"Get in front," Tom answered as he piled out turned and took hold of the door post. "Push it down to that field entrance."

"But that's a field. We'll be trapped by these things," Bob protested.

Nate spit out the last of the candy bar and yelled, "What are these things?"

"Apparently they are called Yrartz and they are the things that killed and maybe ate our friends. And I think they want to do the same to us. We have to get this truck started. If we push it down that driveway into the field I may be able to jump start it. Now push."

Neither man needed any further incentive. Bob and Nathan gave a mighty shove and the truck began to move. Just then a wireless taser dart hit the hood of the truck and bounced off. It narrowly missed Bob's hand. The guys pushed harder and faster.

When the front of the vehicle came even with the field road Tom hit the brakes. Bob and Nate rushed around to the back and began pushing again. The truck started to roll ever so slowly.

Tom turned the truck sharply into the driveway. The vehicle began to pick up speed and when he thought the time right Tom slid into the driver's seat and let out the clutch. The truck jumped and bounced. The engine sputtered but did not come to life and continued to roll down into the field.

Tom got out and started pushing again. Bob and Nate caught up and pushed from behind. There was still a small incline in this end of the field so once more the truck picked up speed.

Yrartz were coming up from the far side of the field now. The men were trapped between the two groups as they tried to start the truck. Yrartz were coming down the ditches and the drive into the field. They were only a few yards away in every direction and the ground seemed to be spewing them up.

The truck engine sputtered. It coughed. Finally it caught and roared to life. Tom gave it some gas and yelled for the guys to get in. Bob leaped in as the vehicle slowly rolled past. Nate, already heaving from the exertion tried to run to catch it.

"Hey don't leave me," he waved. Nate looked behind him. The closest Yrartz fired a wireless taser directly at his face. He stood paralyzed as the dart arched toward the ground and landed at his feet.

Tom backed the truck up and Bob pushed open the door. "Get in," Bob encouraged.

Nate jumped in the truck and Tom threw it in first and slammed on the gas pedal. The truck leaped forward just as three Yrartz climbed into the bed and held on. Tom saw them in the rear view mirror and spun around in a tight circle to try and throw them.

"Bob is that shotgun in the back loaded," Tom asked pointing his thumb at the gun rack in the back window while twisting the wheel as hard over as he could.

"Nope," Bob answered as he leaned forward and opened the glove box. "But it will be," he added as he checked to make sure the safety was on. He took some shells and began loading the gun.

"Good. You want to shoot those," Tom looked in the mirror again. "You want to shoot that Yrartz in the bed back there?" again pointing with his thumb.

"Oh sure, gladly," Bob said as he turned in the seat. Nate reached up and opened the window. Bob placed the gun between them and leveled it at the Yrartz.

The Yrartz expression changed from an angry, snarling, victory grin at the chance for his next meal to one of surprise then terror. Bob touched off the shotgun. The Yrartz head exploded in a pink mist. The momentum threw the body into a back flip over the tailgate.

Tom put the truck up the driveway knocking down a couple Yrartz on the way to the road. He spun the wheel over and the vehicle screeched as it swerved onto Earl's road kicking a few more Yrartz into the ditch. He slammed his foot to the floor and the old truck responded. Bob and Nate hung on best they could.

BOOM! BOOM! And then the cackle from Granny. She had plenty of ammo and she was determined. The Yrartz might win here but they would surely pay a dear price for victory.

The aliens were closing in on the farm yard now. The oddly named Billy, the goat, gave no ground. He attacked them furiously. He knocked over the first Yrartz and then tangled with another. Hitting one to his right then one to his left. A shake of Billy's horns launched a Yrartz ten feet or so.

He was fuming and fighting. His horns taking down one alien after another. Billy roared in fury. Finally one Yrartz caught on Billy's horn. It started zapping him which sent the goat into a rage.

Buster joined the fight. The big dog went roaring in like a hundred car freight train out of control. He snapped off the head of the first Yrartz he came to, shook it and let fly. He turned left and bit one then turned right and bit another.

Billy ran thru the barn yard in a wild attempt to dislodge the alien creature hanging on his horn. The Yrartz taser had its effect though. Finally the brave goat dropped to his knees as other Yrartz hit him from all sides. He rolled onto his back and died.

Hilda, Granny Hayward, never saw Billy go down. She turned back into the house for more shells. She dumped them in her bag and returned to the porch.

The gun roared and took out a Yrartz. Another one standing nearby lost a horn or ear, whatever. He cried out with a low moan that made his mouth into an O. The look of surprise was comical but Granny had no time to laugh.

Once again Buster drove into a herd of aliens and attacked. He chomped on one and let go then hit another. The stink of Yrartz didn't bother him. Dogs enjoy a good smell. But the stings of the tasers began to take their toll.

Like a crazed Cujo, Buster went wild. He ripped arms and heads from bodies. He knocked over cones and pawed at the wheels. He turned and bit at every stinging taser fired at him.

The dog killed a dozen Yrartz and injured as many more before they closed in on him. Buster's rage deepened. He tore ears and other pieces off. He crushed lasers and tasers. He jumped on bodies and sent them sprawling.

Granny kept up a barrage of buckshot. Reloading and shooting as she came down the steps and out into the yard, and reloading again. Her hysterical laughter disconcerted the enemy. Yrartz had never seen such insane fury before.

"I'll put some whuppin' on your butts baby. That Battle for Los Angeles ain't got nothing on what we doing here. Come on, yeah baby let me give you a little o' this." BOOM! BOOM! The gun spoke yet again.

Buster the one dog army rampaged thru the masses destroying Yrartz after Yrartz. What he couldn't bite he bulldozed. All the while Granny continued shooting. She was protecting her dog and her farm. He was protecting humanity.

The big furry shoulders continued to bull over the enemy as the stings became more painful and more frequent. Buster smashed and grabbed and tore and bit in a frenzy of power and anger. This was his farm and Granny was his owner. He would defend to the death.

The great dog killed or scattered the first few rows of Yrartz. But there were just too many of them. They kept coming moving in as a tidal wave taking out any animal that got in their way. Buster was the only thing that slowed them down.

The lines crept closer to Granny as she retreated toward the house. Yrartz surrounded the angry Buster and began attacking him from all sides. The stings enraged him all the more.

"Buster get over here. Come on dog!" Granny shouted hoping to save the dog from his own fury.

There was no thought of retreat for the big canine. Even as he grew weaker Buster went on biting and clawing. First it was a hind leg that gave out. Then the other stopped working too. He couldn't feel his hips but he kept pulling himself with his massive front shoulders and legs. Finally even these gave out on him.

As he lay there the head came up and he bit a Yrartz on what passed for a hand, crushing and destroying it. Before the dog was fully paralyzed the Yrartz began feeding. Buster was Yrartz food.

Granny Hayward saw this and it sickened her. She stepped forward, reloaded and fired faster. She would save Buster if she could or at least keep them from eating his remains.

But as she stepped closer she suddenly realized they were forming on both sides. They planned to surround her too. Granny turned and blasted a Yrartz out of her way and ran as fast as a ninety-two-year-old can. She gained the front porch turned and fired.

She slammed open the front door. Granny was down to her last three shells. She had to get ammunition now. Once inside she closed the door and went rummaging thru the cabinets.

That's when she heard something in the back of the house. Hilda Hayward turned toward the bedrooms in time to take a taser dart to the ribs. She let go with both barrels knocking the Yrartz backward and peeling paint and wall board.

Bob, Tom and Nathan careened around Earl's road, up the hill and into the forest. Tom brought the truck to a stop, his hands shaking. It had been a tense few minutes and he needed to calm down.

In shock Bob asked, "What happened to Ted?" His eyes stared straight ahead unbelieving. Tom just looked over at his brother as if to say you already know the answer.

"And Earl," Nate added. "What about Earl?" None of the men wanted to believe what they all realized was the truth. None wanted to believe that this nightmare had taken the lives of people they knew and considered friends.

Several moments passed then Nate asked, "Who are they? What are they? Where did they come from?"

"I don't know for sure," Tom answered. "They say they are Yrartz. Well I don't know what that is but you've seen them, little green men and women too maybe?

"They look to be three feet tall or so. They all have some kind of lasers and maybe tasers too. And they've apparently come here to eat us. That's who they are.

"Where they came from is a mystery. Out there somewhere," Tom waved at the sky. "I'm guessing they got here in that meteor shower you marveled at last night. That would be the easiest way to come in undetected I think."

Nate's eyes grew big. "So that meteor shower wasn't a meteor shower." He looked at Bob. In unison they exclaimed, "It was an invasion!"

They heard the shots coming from Granny's farm. "We better get to Granny's and rescue her and get out of town."

"Let's go," Tom said as he put the truck in gear. "We need a plan."

"We don't know what to expect when we get there," Bob said.

"Bob can you climb thru the window?"

"Sure," Bob answered. "What do you have in mind?"

Granny's farm was only half a mile as the crow flies from where the guys had engine trouble. By road it was closer to a mile and a half. Tom floored the truck in hopes they wouldn't be too late.

The taser had put Granny down but only for a moment. She dropped the shotgun and pulled herself erect with both arms out stretched. She reached down and took hold of the gun in time to blow two more Yrartz out of the hallway.

Weakly Granny fumbled for more ammunition, finding some in a drawer. She dumped the shells into her possibles bag and reloaded the gun. Next she prepared to clear the house of intruders. After that she hoped to find a way out of there.

She moved through the house using the shotgun as a cane. The Yrartz that got in had climbed thru a broken window in the spare bedroom. Hilda closed the door and hooked a chair under the knob thinking that might keep them out.

She continued her search coming up empty. The house was clear but now Yrartz were everywhere outside. Granny knew she had no chance unless someone came to help her. She couldn't run fast enough to escape or to get to the old pickup truck. She wasn't sure she could get the truck started or drive it either. Neither had happened in several years.

Hilda sat down at the kitchen table to think. She tried the land line earlier and discovered it dead. She never bothered to acquire a cell phone. She had no way to call for help and no immediate way to escape. Most folks would sit back and wait for the inevitable.

Hilda Hayward pushed herself off the chair and began rummaging through the cupboards. She collected shotgun shells and a few water bottles. She grabbed the makings and made a sandwich that she ate while preparing. This was one old lady that wasn't giving up so easily.

Bob, Tom and Nate drove wildly through the forest and up the road. Bob was hanging on best he could in the back of the truck. Nate held Bob's shotgun, ready to fire at any Yrartz that made their presence known. Tom gripped the steering wheel with white knuckle force.

The twenty-two rifle that was in Bob's gun rack now lay fully loaded between Tom and Nate. Bob had his forty-four magnum stuck in his waist band. The plan had been hastily made and all three were ready or so they hoped. Would they make it in time? The thought pushed Tom's right foot harder down on the gas pedal.

The old truck roared down the road sending dust and blue smoke into the air. The three camouflaged men had no intention of sneaking up on the Yrartz. They planned on slashing thru them with all the stealth of a Sherman tank.

They came over the rise and got their first glimpse of the farm yard. All of them peered ahead at the seemingly endless army of Yrartz surrounding the buildings, as Tom slowed the vehicle. It looked as if they were much too late.

"I don't think she's still alive," Bob shouted from the back of the truck.

"Doesn't matter," Tom replied. "We're going in and we're going to find out for sure."

"Maybe we should pray before we go down there," Bob suggested. "I mean it couldn't hurt and we all believe in God."

"I have been praying silently ever since we found the blood in Ted's truck. But you are right little brother, it wouldn't hurt to pray." He looked at Nate and nodded.

"From here they look a lot like smooth, shiny green, metal Christmas trees with heads and arms."

"Okay?" Tom said slowly. "Nate you with me?"

"Sure Tom, only I wish I had some of that fish sausage I ate the other day. The taste was incredible, indescribable."

"That bad huh?"

"Yep, in fact the smell coming from these Yrartz kind of reminds me of it."

"Good to know Nate, good to know." Tom put the truck in gear and stomped on the gas pedal again.

Bob started, "Our Father, who art in heaven..." Tom and Nathan joined in. The three friends recited The Lord's prayer as they raced down the road ready to fight and hopefully rescue Granny.

# Chapter 11

Hilda Hayward worked hard all her life. She was never one to give up easily on any project once started. So it was this day. She had everything she felt she needed as she reached for the door knob.

Granny had no real plan lined up. She was just going to go out the front door and start shooting, walking forward as she went. Her only hopes that perhaps someone would come to her rescue or the Yrartz would realize taking her was too dear a price.

Bob, Tom and Nate hit a solid wall of stink as they closed in on Granny's farm yard. The odor was overpowering. The stench choked them and Bob almost lost his lunch. Nate put away his candy bar. Tom just gagged.

The smell nearly blinded them but they pushed on. If Granny was still alive she needed rescuing. If she was gone then this was probably a suicide mission. None of the trio gave it much thought as they rolled in.

BOOM! BOOM! Granny touched off both barrels again. She cackled once more as she reloaded. "She's still alive," Tom shouted as he turned the truck into the farm yard.

Bob jumped from the back of the truck before it came to a stop. He ran up to Granny and grabbed her arm. "Granny are you okay?" he shouted.

"I'm fine," she laughed toothlessly. "The little stinky-doos didn't even get close. Too bad 'cause I coulda used birdshot. Woulda got a lot more of them," she cackled again.

"Come on. Let's go," Tom shouted from the truck. Bob led Granny to the back of the truck and helped her in while Nate fired off three rounds from Bob's shotgun. Tom began picking off individual Yrartz with carefully aimed shots from the twenty-two rifle.

Tom waited for Granny Hayward to take a seat on a hay bale in the back then he floored the gas pedal again. Bob put out a hand to hold the old woman in place as the vehicle accelerated. Nathan fired off another series of shots from the shotgun.

Tom ran over several Yrartz on the way out of the driveway. The tires, greasy with Yrartz blood, slid sideways as they hit the highway. Granny let loose two more rounds and laughed uncontrollably.

Nate turned to Tom as they sped away. "That was easy. Like pulling a genie out of a barrel."

"You mean a bottle," Tom smiled.

"No I mean a barrel. He's a big genie."

Bob held onto Granny with one hand and the truck with the other. Hilda set the bag of shells on the floor between her legs and reached in to grab more ammo. She reloaded and turned to Bob. "Don't get in my way sonny," she said and laughed again.

Granny's dress was one that might have been stylish in the '50s. It had been white with small, blue flowers, possibly flax? Now it was faded and gray from too much wearing and washing. But it wasn't the faded gray Bob noticed, it was the red. The front of the dress was covered in blood.

"Tom! Granny's been hit!" Bob yelled. "We got to get her to the hospital immediately."

The truck swerved as Tom looked back at Granny. He saw the same thing Bob had. "Alright, we should get Granny checked out anyway. She's had a lot of trauma."

"So we take her to Ashland?" Nathan asked.

"Have to. There are no doctors or nurses in West Falls."

"You would think a town this size would have a hospital or at least a doctor or two," Nate commented.

Tom looked over at him. "It's a hundred and twenty people."

"Exactly."

"Anyway we will go to Ashland. Everybody hang on."

Tom hit the brakes hard and flipped the wheel over. He pulled into an old logging road, slammed it into reverse and backed onto the road again. Once more he pushed the pedal to the limits.

"Tom we're going back towards the farm!" Nate shouted excitedly.

"I know. It's the fastest way." Tom caught his breath. "We will just have to chance going past them again. This will save us a mile or so."

"Everybody reload!" Nate announced needlessly.

The truck roared down the gravel road headed back the way they had come. Yrartz were in the path in numbers. But Tom had no intention of stopping. He figured the grill guard Bob had put on the front would take out anyone that failed to move.

Most of the Yrartz left the road in time but a few were splattered. Granny let loose with the double-barrel. Nate fired off a couple rounds too and even Bob joined in with the twenty-two.

The Yrartz closest to the road launched both tasers and lasers to no effect. Many suffered wounds for their efforts. None of them was killed simply because it is impossible to aim and hit anything from a vehicle bouncing over the pothole infested surface.

The humans took no casualties but the truck received some minor dents from the darts.

Tom swung the pickup onto Cumberland Road and headed north. They quickly passed the road Dan Bury died on when once again Tom hit the brakes. He crept slowly forward staring ahead. Nate gave him a questioning look.

Bob stood up in the back. "What's going on?" he asked as he looked over the top of the cab. "Oh!" He sat back down. "Granny we can't go this way. The bridge is out. We will have to find another route to get you to the hospital."

"What are you taking me to the hospital for?"

"You're hurt," Bob replied motioning to the blood covering her dress.

"I ain't hurt sonny. That's Yrartz blood," she cackled again slapping her knee. The cackling made Bob think Granny really was hurt, possibly hit in the head or something.

The pickup came to a halt and Tom shifted it into neutral. He thought about it, trying to come up with a way across Telemark Creek. There had to be a ford somewhere. The bridge had not always been here and people still crossed.

"Ah, Tom," Nate nudged him. "Something moving in the grass over here." The warning received no response. Nate nudged Tom again a little harder. "Tom there's something moving over here and it ain't water buffalo," he said a little louder.

Bob and Granny were sitting waiting, both keeping a wary eye on their surroundings. They, too saw the grass and weeds moving and shifting in unusual ways. Bob stood up to see better and Granny held her gun tighter, flipping the safety off.

Unpredictably the grass stopped moving. There were no sounds except the truck engine. Nothing moved within sight. The eerie stillness gave them over to thoughts of horror movies they had seen. It was as if the world was waiting, silently waiting.

Tom could not come up with a safe place to cross. Finally he sat back exhausted. Somehow he had to get Granny to a doctor. He was very worried about her. If she was bleeding that bad she might not make it anyway but he had to try.

Suddenly Yrartz appeared in front and to the sides. The group were hemmed in and nearly surrounded. Nate's shotgun roared, a pitiful sound next to the BOOMS of Granny's double-barrel. That was all Tom needed to hear. He shifted into reverse and turned his head around to the right in order to see behind them and realized Bob and Granny were in the way.

"Tom! Let's get out of here!" Nate shouted, dire urgency in his voice.

He put his head out the window and stepped on the gas. Tom learned over the years on the farm. He was fairly good at driving backwards. The Yrartz were coming on as fast as they could but losing ground to the much faster moving truck.

Bob laid the twenty-two on the roof for support and fired as fast as he could. Nathan kept up a steady barrage with the twelve gauge. Granny had no targets so she wisely set the stock of the gun down between her legs and held onto the weapon by the barrels.

Tom found a wide spot in the road, turned the truck around and headed for town. He was worried about Kelly and the rest of the residents of West Falls. Bob and Nate were worried about them too. Nate was wondering if Yrartz liked candy bars.

"Tom, I've known Granny Hayward almost as long as you guys. I never knew how tough, how murderous she was," Nate exclaimed. "I sure would hate to have her mad at me."

"Me too. You know Nate, I knew she took out 'coons and skunks and foxes. But I never saw her do it with such enthusiasm."

"Exactly."

"You know she never had any trouble spanking us when she thought we needed it," Tom said.

"Probably still could," Nate added.

Bob looked hard at Granny and noticed she was missing her teeth. Great he thought, now we are going to have to go back and get them. Almost as if she could read his thoughts, Hilda leaned forward. Still holding onto the shotgun with one hand she rummaged around in her bag. Reaching in, she took out her dentures and put them in her mouth. She turned to Bob and laughed.

He wondered again about her sanity as anyone surely would. These thoughts quickly left him as they passed Carl Vue's driveway. He began to think about Carl and whether he was safe or not. Where was he and did he have an encounter with Yrartz yet?

"Hey Tom," Bob shouted over the truck noise.

Tom half turned his head. "Yes?"

"We just passed Carl's place. Wonder if we should check it out and see if he is okay."

"We should. When we get to town we can organize something."

Moments later they entered the town. Tom pulled into the Food-N-Fuel and came to a stop next to a pump. He and Nate got out of the truck. As he was lifting the nozzle Tom began outlining his plan.

"Bob, you and Nate take the truck and go up to Carl's place. Find him and bring him back here with all his guns. I'm going to get Granny settled and then get together some of the town folk. We need to alert everyone."

"What if Carl is already in trouble?" Bob asked.

"Then get him out of trouble and get him back here." Tom thought a moment. "If he is gone already then see if you can get inside his house and get his guns and ammo. Maybe even his bows and arrows. Those should work too."

"Okay but we are going to need more ammo and another shotgun. Maybe some handguns too."

"Right."

Bob took the forty-four and tried to hand it to his brother. Tom held up his hands. "No you keep it. I will go to our house and get our guns."

"Hey guys we need another vehicle. Why don't we go get my car and Bob and I can get my guns too?"

"Good idea Nate," Bob agreed.

"Nate when was the last time you had that car running?" Tom asked.

"This year," Nathan answered defensively.

"When this year? How do you know it will even start?" Tom continued.

"I had it running in August," Nate said proudly. Bob looked at his brother and nodded as if to say see, there you go.

"Okay let's pay for the gas and get some supplies. Water bottles, maybe some sandwiches." He paused, "Just in case."

"Another good idea," Bob agreed again since he had no good ideas of his own at the moment.

"Here's what we will do," Tom added. "We get some supplies. We take Granny over to the church and leave her with pastor. I take you guys to Nate and Kelly's and make sure the car starts. Then you guys get together some guns and ammo while I find Kelly and organize some of the town's folk. Sound like a plan?"

"Sounds good to me," Bob said.

Nathan leaned in close to the other two and put his hand in. "All for one and one for…" He let it drop. Neither brother was having any of that.

Bob helped Granny Hayward into the passenger's seat while Nate rolled onto the tailgate and pushed himself up. Tom jumped in and fired it up. Bob climbed in back and they were off.

The church was just across the road from the Food-N-Fuel. Tom parked the pickup near the church office and got out. He went to the church and tried the door. It was open so he went to the truck and helped Granny get out.

Pastor Gordon Washburn was still working on his sermon for Sunday when they walked in. He heard them and went out to see who was there. "Welcome Hilda and Tom," he said smiling as he reached out his hands to take hold of Hilda's. "What brings you here today and at this hour?"

Tom went into detail telling Gordon all they had encountered. Granny interrupted occasionally with a comment or laughter. Tom summed it up with, "So I think we should get the town together and plan some sort of defense. We don't know if this is the only place hit or if the entire country is overrun." He caught his breath. "What do you think pastor?"

"Well Tom it all sounds so incredible. If it was someone else I would wonder if they were crazy or had been drinking. But I see the blood on Granny's dress and the look in your eyes and I absolutely have to believe you.

"I think you are right, we must get the town together and soon. I believe we need a defensive perimeter. We have to do this now before dark if we can. We don't have much time.

"First, before we do anything I think we should pray and ask the Lord's help and blessings on our efforts."

"Yep it always is a good idea to pray in any situation, good or bad," Granny agreed.

Tom looked at Gordon and nodded in agreement. The three bowed their heads and closed their eyes. "Lord, we ask your guidance in this matter," Pastor Gordon began. "We believe these are your creation too but we believe they are not listening to your will. We ask that you help us to defeat these invaders. In Jesus precious name, amen."

Granny Hayward and Tom said amen in unison. They raised their heads and opened their eyes.

"Tom do you have some evidence, something you can show people? Say a weapon or body armor. Maybe a sizable body part of one of these things or something like that. It would be a lot easier to get folks to believe and it would speed things up a bit."

"No pastor I don't have anything. I never even thought about it. I figured people would believe me." Tom looked about helplessly, shrugged, "Nothing."

Granny cackled and leaned over rummaging in her bag again. She pulled something out and held it up. "How about this?" she asked as she handed the arm over to Tom.

Tom was apprehensive at taking the arm. He had yet to touch a Yrartz with any part of his skin. However since Granny held it and seemed to have no ill effects he took it from her.

The arm was badly mangled up near the shoulder as if ripped or torn from the body. Granny shot it off the Yrartz during the fight at the farm. The arm still held onto the taser with a dart still loaded.

Tom looked it over then handed it to Gordon. "Yes I think this will do just fine. I do believe people will find this is good evidence." Pastor Gordon looked at Tom. "So okay what's your plan?"

# Chapter 12

Bob and Nate were anxious to get going. They wanted to get Carl and get back to town before dark. So when Tom finally appeared they were ready. Both were once again seated in the cab of the truck. Nate had a candy bar unwrapped and on its way to his mouth.

Tom drove the block and a half to Nate and Kelly's. He waited while Nate tried the car. It ground for a while and looked as if it would die but finally fired. With the engine running somewhat smoothly Tom left.

Bob knew where pretty much everything was so the two began grabbing guns and ammo. Nate added a case of water bottles and two boxes of candy bars. "Just in case, bro," he answered Bob's questioning look.

Tom left the double-barrel shotgun with Granny and Pastor Gordon. The good pastor had a forty-five automatic in his glove box and a twelve gauge in the trunk. He occasionally went grouse hunting after a day in the office. The handgun was for self-defense and target practice.

Heading for home, Tom forced himself to stop rather than continue on to The Rose. He really wanted to see Kelly but first things first. He got out of Bob's truck and went to his own. It started almost immediately. He would use it instead of Bob's.

Next Tom went in the house and found guns and ammo. He put together some extra clothes, blankets, jackets, and then went to the pantry. He loaded guns, ammo, food and clothes in the truck. Whereas Bob's pickup was a single bench seat three passenger affair, Tom's was a crew cab with a locking bed cover.

Carl Vue awoke to unusual sounds coming at him from nearby. He shook his head to clear it. Yes, there it was again. Something rustling in the brush close on.

Vue yawned and stretched as his eyes began searching. But the noise suddenly stopped. Something made him look down. There at the bottom of his tree was?

"What the…?" Carl wondered aloud. He had never seen anything quite like it, them before.

As if in answer to his question they chorused, "We are Yrartz from the planet Yrartz. Do not be alarmed! We are here to take over your planet."

His first thought was these things are ridiculous, funny looking. Then a cold finger of fear began creeping up his spine. There were dozens, maybe fifty or more of these things surrounding his tree. And those were just the ones he could see.

They looked funny, stupid to him. He said, "Hello how are you? What can I do for you all?"

They repeated, "We are Yrartz from the planet Yrartz. Do not be alarmed! We are here to take over your planet."

They looked up at him in childlike wonder. Carl considered climbing down to greet them but decided against it. They were circling the tree and one or two of them seemed to be trying to climb up.

He was trying to decide exactly what to do when a Yrartz taser dart came at him. It landed harmlessly in a branch a few feet below. There wasn't enough power to get it all the way to him.

Suddenly a barrage of darts came flying. Only a very few hit close and two actually stuck in Carl's boots. He lifted his boot and pulled the darts out. "What's this then?" He threw a dart at one of them. "You all don't seem very friendly," he shouted. More darts came.

One taser dart hit Carl's ankle and stung him. But there wasn't sufficient power to cause more than a momentary sting. It did not cause his nerves to spasm. He jumped in surprise and decided it was time to move.

Carl loosened his climbing harness and got up. He stood on the treestand seat. He could climb higher if need be but he might have to abandon his bow and arrows if he did. What to do?

While he was making up his mind about actions to take a dart would fly up near him. Every now and then the Yrartz would go into their spiel about not being alarmed. Now Carl was clearly alarmed. How was he to get out of this tree? How was he to get away from these aliens?

Yes they were aliens. He understood that now. His mind was clear and he was thinking hard. Carl reached out and grabbed his bow. He notched an arrow, aimed and let fly.

Carl Vue was a good shot so his arrow went true. One Yrartz let out a cry as it fell, an arrow stuck in its body. "Well I guess you guys aren't invulnerable anyway," he said aloud. That action brought another series of darts winging their way toward him with little effect.

He only had six arrows to start with. But Carl always carried a twenty-two revolver in case squirrels or chipmunks got too friendly. It might be loud enough to scare away the occasional black bear too. Now with wolves in the area he was thinking of upgrading to a forty-four or something similar. He really wished he had done so already.


Stan Berry began to wonder what happened to his friend Dan. The biologist should have been back hours ago. He was starting to get worried. He knew that Dan loved his job but he was never this late getting back.

Dan Bury always carried his cell phone in case he needed to contact someone. Stan decided to call his friend and make sure everything was alright. This time on a Friday night the office was dead, everyone went home long ago.

Stan punched up the number and waited for a reply. A voice came on saying the call couldn't be completed and that the phone was out of range. He looked at his own phone to make sure he had the right number. He shrugged and cancelled the call, put the phone in his pocket. He would try later. He figured Dan was someplace in the swamp where the signal couldn't reach.

Tom had everything he felt he needed packed and ready. He had his deer hunting rifle, a shotgun and two handguns up front in the cab. The rest of the gear, including Bob's rifle, was stowed in the bed under the cover. He made sure the truck had plenty of fuel as he started it up. His next stop was The Rose.

He knew Pastor Gordon was trying to get a hold of people in the town. The good reverend agreed to call if the phones worked. If not he would walk around alerting folks. He needed to find Loretta and Donna Belknap and assure them they were not crazy and that the aliens they had seen were indeed real.

Tom's priority was to find Kelly. He would alert everyone at The Rose to the danger and try to convince them of the need for a town meeting at the church. There they could plan the town's defense and then give out assignments and supplies.

This was serious business. An invasion by Yrartz could overpower the town. They needed all hands on deck and every available gun or other weapon.

Tom was wishing they had one of those machine guns Nate had been talking about. They could mount it on a truck and let her rip. It would blow out a whole lot of Yrartz.

The land lines were down too. Pastor Gordon desperately wanted to check on his wife and children first. But his responsibility was to the whole town and not just his own family. He started out heading south from the church. He would stop at the houses along this end of town then weave slowly toward the west. His home would be the last stop unless Tom or some other person got there ahead of him.

No one was home at Fred and June Seeley's, the first house on Gordon's route. Next was Nate and Kelly's but he didn't need to go there. The pastor's apprehension grew with every place he came to. Was his family still safe?

Nathan tossed the keys to Bob. "You drive, okay?"

"Sure okay," Bob answered. "First we're going to our house so we can get more guns and ammo."

"Okay, fine with me. The more guns and ammo we have the better."

Tom was already gone when the pair arrived at Tom and Bob's. Bob jumped out of Nate's car and ran to the house. Nathan waddled up a little slower. Once inside they quickly gathered up what they needed.

"Hey Bob, can I have that thirty-thirty of yours?"

"Sure Nate. You got a newer rifle already so sure, take it. It's always been a good gun. I killed a lot of deer with it."

With all the gear rounded up they began packing the car. The need for speed drove them. Their friend might be in danger and they had to get there soon.

They got in the car and Bob drove slowly up Cumberland road and out of town. They wanted to find Carl but both were afraid of running into a herd of Yrartz. They now knew what the little greenies could do. Neither man wanted to become Yrartz food.

They knew they were limited as to time. The sun would set before 6:30. It was after four now but the sky was clearing so daylight would last. Still neither wanted to be out in the woods after dark. They had no idea whether the Yrartz had night vision capabilities and didn't want to find out by trial and error.

Carl had to make a move and soon. He realized he had maybe two hours before dark. He knew his way around the swamp even at night but maybe these things did too.

He had a short drag rope and a long, heavy string he used to pull his bow up to the stand with. He figured he could make a usable rope out of these and maybe swing to another tree. Perhaps then he could drop to the ground and make good his escape.

It was iffy but he had to try something. Staying here was not an option. He would starve or freeze to death if the Yrartz didn't find a way to get him first. He had no clue as to their abilities or their plans. Carl had to get away and warn the people in West Falls.

Tom stopped his truck in front of The Rose. He climbed out and strapped on the holster with his forty-four. He pulled the gun out and checked again that it was loaded. Then he reached in the truck and grabbed the Yrartz arm.

There were only five or six people in sight as he walked inside. Tom strode up to the bar and motioned to the owner, Bill Webster. Bill came over and listened as Tom quietly told him why he was there and showed him the arm.

"Hey everybody," Bill yelled. "Everybody come on over here please," he gestured toward the bar. "Come on everyone. Tom here has something he needs to tell you all."

Kelly came out of the kitchen and saw Tom. She smiled at him then saw the look on his face. Rushing over to him she asked, "What is it Tom? Is Nathan alright? Is Bob?"

"Nathan and Bob are fine. Just hang on a minute. I will tell my story to everyone."

Kelly waited at his side as the others gathered around. Tom looked over the crowd. "What I have to tell you is going to sound fantastic but it's true. Every word of it." He paused a beat. "Many of you saw that meteor shower last night. Well it wasn't a meteor shower. It was an alien invasion."

A murmur swept through the group. Some smiled thinking this was a joke. "I know what you're thinking," Tom continued. "This is no joke. This is no wild story. I fought these aliens myself. I just got back from rescuing my grandmother."

He could see he wasn't getting anywhere. Tom held up the arm. "This is an arm from one of the aliens. Take a good look at it. Touch it, feel it. My grandma shot it off one of the aliens."

Tom passed the arm to one of the men standing nearest. He marveled at it and passed it on. "What's this thing?" one of them asked.

"It's a taser-like weapon. My grandma got hit by one of these. They all carry them in one hand and a laser device in the other."

"It's a fake, a good one but a fake. You been drinking the same hooch Donna and Loretta Belknap drink."

"None of you ever seen Tom drink and you know it," Bill defended.

"Don't believe me if you don't want to. But come to the church right now. We are having a town meeting there as soon as possible. You can see my grandmother and ask her about all this.

"Nate and my brother are going up to get Carl Vue. When they get back you can ask them. You can ask them about Earl Stinnett's truck. You can ask them about the blood in and on Ted Hawkins truck. Then ask yourself what happened to them.

"I'm getting in my truck and heading back to the church. I suggest you warn your friends and family and join me. Bring food, blankets and guns. If you don't believe me come anyway. See for yourself. Ask questions of the four of us that have seen and fought these things."

With that Tom turned to Kelly, his speech to the crowd over. "Kelly come with me now. Nate and Bob went to your house to get guns and ammo. Now they should be on their way to find Carl.

"I stopped at my place and grabbed supplies. Come with me to the church. We need to set up a defensive perimeter soon and I sure want you with me. I want to know you are safe."

Kelly did not know what to believe. She had never seen Tom this agitated before. She knew he was telling the truth and he was both scared and ready to fight. She took off her apron and turned to Bill, "I'm going with Tom."

Bill nodded an okay. "Guys let's do what Tom says. Get home and get your guns and ammo. Pick up some food, maybe water bottles too. Meet at the church."

"Thanks," Tom said as he shook Bills hand. He left with Kelly in tow.

"Cajun, you in there?" Bill roared.

The Cajun came out, meat cleaver in hand. "Whatta?" he demanded gruffly.

As The Rose cleared out Bill went upstairs to his apartment and claimed his guns. He gave one to the Cajun and told the man he should come with. The Cajun shrugged and said he would stay and defend The Rose to the death. He meant it too.

"Cajun if you change your mind lock up then come to the church. I'll be there at least until the meeting is over." Bill left with an uneasy thought in his brain. He wondered if he would ever see the Cajun alive again.

As he closed the door behind him and started for his car Bill noticed people out on the street. It seemed everyone in town was on their way to the church for the meeting. He climbed in with the rest of his gear safely stowed in the backseat.

Just a block from The Rose bill saw Pastor Gordon. He stopped. "Hey pastor, you need a ride?"

Startled, Gordon looked at him. "Yes Bill I do indeed." He climbed in the car. "Say Bill could we make a quick swing by my house? I want to check on Sarona and the kids. Give her an update on what's going on."

"Sure pastor, we can do that."

Carl tied the end of his makeshift rope to a large branch above his head. He tested it to make sure it was secure and would hold him. In the interest of speed he decided to abandon his bow. He only had five more arrows anyway.

Before he tried to swing from the trees like a monkey he fired off his arrows. He did this to use them rather than waste them and as a distraction. Carl figured if he took out a few Yrartz it would help in his escape and just maybe scare the little green men a might.

He left the bow hanging from a branch and swung out. The rope held and Carl was able to reach a tree a few yards away. He got his balance and jumped to another, smaller tree. This one was not big enough to hold his weight and it bent over landing him safely on the ground a good twenty yards from his treestand tree.

The Yrartz were amazed and surprised. This was all Carl could hope for. He ran into the woods along a path next to the swamp. When he gained some distance he turned onto a game trail heading in the general direction of his house.

Carl ran up the trail like a gazelle. He needed to get to the house and fast. There were guns, ammo and food enough to let him hold off a siege for days maybe weeks. He believed he could outrun the little aliens. He was right but…

Bob stopped at the end of Carl's driveway. "What you stopping for?" Nate asked.

"Check your guns and make sure they're loaded, and listen for any sounds of fighting or Yrartz coming."

"Okay," Nate said nervously. He looked around anxiously as he got out of the car.

Bob came around to his side and the pair began slowly walking along the driveway. It was more of a road than a driveway. It was about five hundred yards from Cumberland Road to Carl's house. The drive was lined on both sides with trees, mostly pine and spruce.

Both men were worried. They were jumpy, expecting Yrartz to be behind every rock and tree. Any bird flitting away or small animal scurrying in the brush startled them.

"You ever read the book, *Pond Scum*?" Nathan asked.

"What? No why?"

"It's about a mad ichthyologist who crossbreeds piranhas with flying Asian carp. You think that's possible?"

"Huh? What?"

"You know, to breed piranhas with Asian carp."

"I don't know," he shook his head, irritated.

"You wouldn't even have to get in the water to get bitten," Nate paused. "You think these Yrartz are something like that? Maybe somebody crossbred Chihuahuas with some kind of monkey?"

"Nate, could you keep the talking to a minimum so we can hear if there are any Yrartz around?" Bob entreated.

"Oh sure Bob," Nate answered. The talking calmed him down and helped keep his mind off the nightmares swirling around in his head. But he complied with the request. It did not matter. The young man was as quiet as a Sherman tank in a cymbal factory when he walked through the woods.

Bob did not want to offend his friend. "Hey Nate why don't you follow directly in my footsteps? It might be quieter that way." He thought a moment. "You're not afraid are you?"

"Ah, no bro. I'm not afraid. I'll boldly follow right behind you."

Tom and Kelly were seated near the front of the church. Singly and in small groups the town residents came in and sat down. Low murmuring came from the crowd as they waited for the meeting to begin.

By the time Bill and Pastor Gordon arrived there were sixty people in the sanctuary. A few more trickled in but most that were coming were already there. It was a good crowd and many came armed. They had guilt feelings coming into a church that way but they wouldn't leave their weapons at the door.

Gordon walked to the front, motioning. "Folks please move up to the front here. We are all friends and neighbors. There is no need to be shy or hold back."

Many moved forward to fill in the seats up front. "Folks we all know why we are here. You have all been told. Well I'm going to ask Tom Hayward to come forward and tell you what has happened to him. Then we can talk about what we need to do." Gordon held his hand out toward Tom.

Tom stood up. "Friends and neighbors you all know me. You know that I don't drink and I don't tell wild stories. I don't panic easily either. You have already been told some of what has happened.

"Well Nathan Minong and my brother and I found Ted Hawkins and Earl Stinnett's trucks abandoned. There was blood on Ted's truck. While we were examining this vehicle a gang of aliens attacked us."

Tom went on to tell of the battles they fought and the rescue of Granny Hayward. He told of his brother and Nate going to rescue Carl Vue. Finally he turned the meeting over to Bill and Gordon.

Gordon stood at the front and began, "Okay you've heard what Tom has seen and experienced. Most of you have seen the alien's arm we have. Granny Hayward is here to confirm what he said if you need that confirmation.

"Now we need to decide what we can do and what we need to do to defend ourselves. Bill here has some experience at that. He was in the Army and learned some about defense. Bill," Pastor Gordon motioned to him.

Bill stood up and nodded acknowledgement to Pastor Gordon. "First I'll take any quick questions anybody has," he looked over the crowd. Seeing a hand raised he said, "John what's your question?"

"What do they look like? I want to be able to recognize them."

Tom rose to his feet again. "Okay they are about three feet tall. Their bodies are protected by some sort of plastic cone. All you can really see is this cone and their arms and head sticking out of it.

"Their heads look a lot like a very large Chihuahua's."

"Oh so they're cute," one lady said.

"Ah, not exactly," Tom continued. "I misspoke. Actually when we first saw them we thought they all looked the same. But they don't. Some have heads like a Chihuahua. But some have heads that are more flat, oval shaped and their ears are different.

"Their heads look more wide and short. The ears look more like horns rather than the Chihuahua triangular shape. They look a little like a pronghorn antelopes horns.

"They remind me of a fake Christmas tree with one of the two types of heads. The cone is about the same color as a balsam fir. On one hand they have a laser with a blue light. On the other hand they have some kind of wireless taser-like device with blinking red and yellow lights. They have something on their heads that has green lights on it that I think may be a tracking or aiming device."

"So we're looking for little Christmas trees dancing around in the forest and fields?"

"Rolling," Tom added.

"Huh?"

"They appear to be riding on some sort of carriage. They have wheels."

"We should be able to do something with that. They ride on wheels. We can use the Bibon. We can use the swamp to stop them. We can't get across it on an ATV most places."

"No!" Tom cut him off. "They came out of the swamp."

"How did they do that?" someone asked.

"I don't know. All I know is they can travel in the swamp. Unfortunately they can get across the Bibon. They came out of the swamp and we think they landed in the swamp in the first place."

"How do they travel?" N. M. Roswell asked.

"Like I said, I don't know."

"Wait Tom. I'm not asking you to tell me exactly what they do or how they do it. Describe how they travel.

"You said they have wheels. Are the wheels large or small?"

"Small. They appear to be smaller than ATV wheels. More the size of a kids wagon wheels."

"Are they wide or narrow?" NM continued.

"Couldn't say for sure. I wasn't able to get a good look at them," Tom answered a little frustrated.

"Did you hear anything that might indicate they have some sort of air assist system?" At Tom's quizzical look Dr. Roswell added, "Like a hovercraft. Was there a whooshing sound, the rushing of air?"

"I guess I really didn't notice. I can't remember anything like that but it could have been." Tom wished he could remember for certain.

"Okay so we don't know for certain by what means they travel the swamp," he paused to collect his thoughts. NM continued questioning. "How powerful were their lasers and tasers?"

"Not very. Grandma got hit by a wireless taser and it put her down but did not stop her. As for the lasers I really don't know. They didn't seem to have much effect on us and not much range either."

"The wireless tasers had some sort of dart that they fired?"

"Yes, and the range was less than twenty feet."

"The lasers didn't burn you or your vehicle?"

"Well NM they didn't hurt us but we didn't stick around long either. I think they might have put a few marks on the trucks paint but that's all."

"One last line of inquiry," NM went on. "How effective were your weapons? Your guns, did they kill the Yrartz or just maim them?"

"Yeah I want to know that too," someone in the crowd agreed. There were nods and me too's.

"I believe our guns were very effective. I saw several Yrartz explode. They blew. They splattered everywhere. We used shotguns mostly and they just disintegrated.

"Now my brother used a twenty-two and I think he killed some with that. But I know we killed them with birdshot and buckshot. Yes I'd say the shotguns were very effective."

Bill looked at Tom. "Son one thing I want to know. Why do you think they ride on wheels? I mean what would they need them for? Clearly they haven't penetrated far out of the Bibon."

"Okay I'm not completely sure. But we did see their mangled bodies after Earl ran one of them over and after we shot some of them. I think their legs are weak. They have spindly legs and I don't think they can walk very far."

"That would explain the wheels," Gordon mused. "But can we use that to stop them?" he asked turning to NM.

"That is a good question," NM said without offering an answer. "Another good question is has anyone had any communication with anyone outside this area?"

There were only no answers from the crowd. One woman held up her cell phone and said she had no signal. Others nodded in agreement. No one had a signal and no one had any communication outside since late last night.

"So we know they hit the cell towers and apparently the land lines as well," Dr. Roswell continued. "Is there anything else you can tell us Tom?"

Sarona, Gordon's wife spoke up. "You say the bridge at Telemark Creek is out and we can't get out by road?" the worry in her voice readily noticeable.

"Yes that's right," Tom confirmed.

"Hey has anybody seen Fred and June Seeley?" someone asked.

"Fred and June went up to Ashland early this morning," someone else answered.

"Maybe they called the authorities and we will be rescued," a hopeful voice offered.

"Or maybe they's dead and eaten by now."

"Tom how many people did these things kill so far?" Gordon asked.

"Well as I said we found Earl's truck abandoned on the road and later Ted's truck near the same spot. I didn't see any livestock at Earl's and they killed and started eating all of Granny's livestock.

"They killed two people I'm pretty sure of. Fred and June are missing. Are there any others missing?" Tom asked.

Bill and Gordon looked around the room. "Donna and Loretta are still at Mitch's," Pastor Gordon said. "Some folks decided to stay in their homes. I think everyone is accounted for except Carl Vue."

NM stood up, a worried look on his face. "We don't know for sure if the attack here is an isolated one or if the Yrartz have taken over the country or the world." Most of the gathering had not thought of it that way. Murmuring swept the crowd. What if the Yrartz had taken over the world? The fear spread.

# Chapter 13

Carl opened the back door and entered as quietly as he could. He quickly closed the door and turned toward the kitchen sink. His thirst from the running and the excitement choked him.

He drank deeply of the water and refilled. Glass in hand Carl moved to the hallway just as a Yrartz hidden in the shadows fired a taser. The dart was coming at his face.

Carl instinctively threw up his hand and the dart struck the back. Yrartz tasers are weak and the young man's adrenalin level was high. He threw the glass at the Yrartz and quickly pulled the dart from his hand. A spasm went through the hand and arm followed by numbing all the way to the elbow. But Carl had broken his left arm once and learned how to get along with one arm.

He went into combat mode. He kicked the Yrartz in the head. Carl was short, just a few inches over five feet. But he was built strong from years of hard work so his kicks and punches had power behind them.

Carl followed his kick with a punch to the stomach, smashing right through the protective cone. He grabbed a kitchen chair and slammed it down on the things head.

The Yrartz crashed into the floor and seemed to melt. Carl didn't wait to see if it was dead. He leaped over it and pulled his twenty-two. He quickly moved down the hall hearing sounds from the back bedroom.

Slowly a Yrartz crept out into the hall. Carl crouched in a shooting stance and fired three times. The little green man went splat. Three more shots made certain the alien would never move again.

Carl locked the front door of the house and cleared the place making sure there were no more Yrartz. Next he began putting together some supplies. He moved rapidly from room to room not knowing how much time he had.

Back in the kitchen Carl began looking through the cupboards. He needed food and water in case things got extreme. He had no idea what he was up against yet. Better to be prepared than to want for something.

Outside Carl's place half a dozen Yrartz gathered waiting for their leader. They were the first of the troops to arrive. More straggled in every few minutes.

Bob and Nate walked slowly along the road to Carl's. Every twig that broke and every leaf that fell made the intrepid pair jump with fright. The only comfort each had was in knowing the other man was just as scared.

Finally Bob stopped and turned to Nate. "You doing okay?"

"Yep, sure am. You know I figure if I wake up breathing, I get plenty to eat and nothing gets caught in my zipper I'm good," he stated seriously.

"I meant are you as scared as I am?"

"Oh," Nate answered sheepishly. He looked down then at Bob. "Well I haven't wet myself yet if that's what you mean."

"Well let's keep going then." Bob started out again, Nathan following closely behind.

"You know this kind of reminds me of a movie I saw once. You ever see 'Midnight at the Concrete Plant?' before?"

"No I don't believe I have."

"Well there's this guy named Frank and he drives a forklift. He loads trucks and anyway he works at night. One night this alien ship flies over him and lands near the plant.

"Frank tries to convince everyone that there are aliens outside. Nobody believes him and they all tell him to go back to work. So he does but he sees the aliens attack his friends and he runs one of the aliens over. He finds a ray gun the alien dropped, I guess because he got run over. So he picks up the ray gun and attacks back."

"Nate!" Bob hissed. "Will you be quiet? How are we supposed to sneak up on Yrartz with you talking?"

"Hey bro sorry but I don't think it's a problem. We get close we should be able to smell the Yrartz. I mean you know how bad their odor is."

"So what do you think they want?" one of the towns folk asked.

"I think it's obvious. They want us for lunch. They want to make dinner out of us," Bill said.

"That is what all the evidence points to," NM spoke up. "We need to defend ourselves. We need to prepare the town and we need to find out if the invasion is localized or on a wider scale."

"Our cell phones and land lines are out. The bridge is gone. How are we going to find out how big this thing is?"

"We will send out someone through the swamp. It's the only way I know of since we have no communications with the outside," NM suggested.

"So we should elect someone as our leader," Bill added. "We need someone in charge, someone to give us direction."

"Who?" someone asked.

Bill looked at NM. "How about NM?"

"Oh no. I can be your science advisor. But I cannot be your leader. I'm not even a full time resident." NM looked over at Gordon. "I think Pastor Gordon would be a good choice."

"I am your spiritual advisor. I would be honored to lead you, however, I don't have any military experience. But Bill does have military training."

Bill looked up at Pastor Gordon. "Who told you I had military training?"

"You did."

"Oh yeah, that's right."

"Bill is a business owner, an upstanding citizen and he was in the military. I think we should vote," Gordon said. NM nodded in agreement. "All those in favor of Bill raise your hand." Hands went up all over the sanctuary. Gordon motioned to Bill as he sat down.

Bill stood to address the group. "Okay if you really want a Texan to lead you I guess I'm your man. So let's get down to it. First we need to organize.

"We need to take stock of our resources and make a plan. However since we are already under attack we need to get people out there now." Bill looked out over the crowd. "How many of you brought a gun?"

Several hands went up. "John you were in the military too, right?" John nodded affirmative. "Okay John, I want you and," he looked over the group. "You two," Bill pointed. "You join John and take up a position on the Cumberland Road. John you're in charge for now. I want you guys to get two vehicles and park one on Cumberland just north of here. Block the road as best you can. Use the other vehicle to block Hawthorne the other side of the machine shop. When I can I will send help. Now go."

Bill turned his attention to the rest of the people as John and his crew went out the door. "Okay now everyone else go home and prepare. Anyone who has a gun find it and get ready to defend the town.

"Get guns, ammunition, some food and if you have them some water bottles or filled canteens. Meet back here as soon as you can but no later than two hours from now.

"We will use the Food-N-Fuel as a supply depot. The church will be our hospital, kitchen and rest stop. Hawkins machine repair will be our command center. Bring everything to the command center and we will distribute it from there. Now is everyone clear on what to do and where to go?"

One of the ladies stood up. "Should we bring blankets? And should we bring sheets for bandages too?"

"Yes, those are good ideas. Everyone bring any sheets and blankets you aren't currently using. We need them. Also any coats and other warm gear you don't need or is extra.

"If you have a truck or four-wheel drive vehicle bring it. ATVs would be useful. We need every item that will help us defend our town. Mostly we need you people.

"Many of you have military experience, most of you have hunted. Almost all of you know how to use a gun. We need that right here, right now. Come back prepared to fight." Bill took a much needed breath. "Any more questions?"

There were none. The town folk filed out, most with determined looks on their faces. These were people who could truly trace their ancestry back over two hundred years, perhaps not biologically but in spirit. They were like those other Americans whose can do attitude and inventiveness won countless battles.

Bob and Nate were closing in on Carl Vue's place. "Look," Nate pointed. "I can see the light at the end of the rainbow."

Bob made a silent hissing sound with his mouth and a slicing motion across his neck. He was exasperated by Nate's never ending dialogue. The large man's noisy footfalls didn't help either.

Both men stopped and peered into the gloom that the overhanging trees caused. They made Carl's driveway dark and foreboding even on bright sunny summer days. With the October sun slipping under the horizon the path was much less inviting.

The brave pair heard an unusual noise in the gathering darkness. They looked at each other and shrugged. Neither had any idea what the sound was or where it came from.

The noise came again, louder, lower, more menacing. It sounded like someone or something caught in a meat grinder. They listened, ears cocked toward Vue's house.

Suddenly a genuine scream came at them loud and clear. Their eyes got big, they looked at each other again and both turned toward Cumberland Road and Nate's car. Slowly one step, second step a little faster then into a full out sprint. Nate was surprisingly fast for such a heavy man.

The friends reached the car, grabbed door handles and pulled open the doors. They jumped in, knocking their heads together. As they rubbed their foreheads Bob started the motor and gunned the engine. He threw it into reverse and backed out of the driveway, slamming the car into a forward gear before it stopped moving.

He opened the back door hoping to escape before the Yrartz could surround the place. But a Yrartz pushed its foot into the crack before Carl had the door more than an inch wide. He slammed it shut on the foot eliciting a moan/scream from the injured alien.

Carl pushed harder on the door and the Yrartz made louder noises. Finally Carl opened the door wider and slammed it shut with greater force. The little alien screamed loud, long and enough to scare the fur ball out of a cats gut.

Vue opened the door slightly and kicked the foot out, then shut it again. Now he had to find a way out and fast. The Yrartz were everywhere. Carl knew he had very little time. It was make a run for it now or make a stand in a house that had already been breached once.

The smashing of the sliding glass door in the living room made the decision for him. Carl thrust his arms through his backpack straps, grabbed his shotgun, a rifle and dashed for the back bedroom. He closed the bedroom door then crossed the room, opened the window and slipped outside.

Yrartz were coming around the corners from both ends. Carl ran to the trees and into the woods as fast as he could. He kept to game trails knowing he could outrun the Yrartz. Later he would hit thick brush to discourage the invaders but for now he needed distance.

Branches tugged at his clothes and scratched his face and arms. But he continued running as if on fire. He knew his life was forfeit if he stopped even for a moment.

Several hundred yards from the house Carl turned south heading for the driveway. He figured to run on that giving him more speed in the open. However as he neared the road he slowed to listen. The pounding in his ears from running made it impossible so he stopped, bent over trying to catch his breath.

One Yrartz heard him coming and hid behind a tree. As Carl went by the alien zapped him with the taser. The man's right leg went numb and he tumbled to the ground rolling. His side smacked into a tree, the backpack and shotgun skidding across the forest floor.

The Yrartz came at Carl intending to finish him off. But Carl pulled his twenty-two pistol and shot the Yrartz three times. He got up and limped to his guns, picked them up and checked to make sure the barrels were clear. Next he got his pack.

Carl's leg was completely numb. He couldn't use it at all and he knew he had to find someplace to hold up. But he knew this area well and there simply was no good place to make a stand. He did the only thing he could do. He found the largest tree he could and sat with his back against it. If this was Carl's last stand then he would take out as many of the little green vermin as he could.

Jimmy drove up to the cell tower and parked his truck. The cell phone company had received complaints about cell service being out. He had confirmed the lack of service in the area as soon as he arrived. He checked several things and found them all in working order. Now he planned on checking the tower to see if the problem lie there.

It was getting late but he would see what was up. Jim got out of the truck and noticed a series of small tire tracks in the sand all around the tower. He considered that rather odd. He went in and checked the tower and immediately saw the cable had been severed.

Jim thought about calling the sheriff but remembered no service. He could call later. He was tired and it was getting dark. He wanted to wait to fix the cable but knew he would never hear the end of that. So he went back to the truck and started putting gear together. Splicing the cable in the dark and alone would take some time.

# Chapter 14

The meeting over, Kelly held Tom's arm more tightly as they got up and prepared to leave. He sensed something in her touch and stopped. He looked into her eyes and saw the apprehension, perhaps fear there.

Her eyes searched his for answers before the questions. "Are we going to be all right? Are we going to come through this alive?" Tom understood the trepidation, the worry. He knew her as well as any man alive.

They had been friends forever. Kelly first started crushing on him when she was eight and he was twelve. She never really stopped crushing on him. But it wasn't until recently they began dating.

Why was that she wondered? I guess it's because we only recently stepped out of the friend zone. Kelly was really glad they did. She needed him now as she never needed anyone before.

Kelly was a strong woman but this situation was beyond any she, or any woman had ever known before. You read books and see movies about alien invasions. But this was real. They really were under attack. One wrong move and you were dead.

She wanted the man she loved at her side in this place. No other would do. For one of the few times in her adult life she needed the protection of a man and Tom was the only person that fit that bill.

Tom put his arm around her and smiled. "We will be just fine. We have a great group of people here in this town. We will defend ourselves and we will win. We will knock out the invaders and take back our home."

The confidence Tom exuded was the direct opposite of what he was feeling. He was glad Kelly was with him. She gave him a strength he did not otherwise possess. He needed her as much as she needed him.

They walked hand in hand down the aisle of the church and out into the coming night. Tom went to his truck to retrieve his shotgun and get ready to defend the town. Kelly walked with him. She took the gun he gave her and began the process of preparing to fight.

John and his group moved off toward their road block. Most of the other town folk went home to prepare. The church parking lot was an ant hill of activity.

Nathan was rethinking his decision to let Bob drive. He was hanging on to the hand strap with his right hand. His left was white knuckling the shoulder strap. His right foot kept stomping the imaginary brake on the passenger's side of the car.

The road from Vue's place to town wasn't perfectly straight. Bob was scared and he was taking the turns as fast as he could. He wanted the dubious protection of West Falls and its people.

Bob rounded the last curve and saw the road block. He slammed on the brakes and swerved nearly hitting the parked vehicles there. Then he drove past slowly and stopped in the church parking lot.

"Oh good our brothers are back with Carl," Tom said to Kelly. "I'll go check on them."

"Okay. I'm going to the store and get some coffee." They parted and Tom trotted over to the church.

Bob and Nate were just getting out of the car as Tom approached. He stooped down and looked inside the vehicle expecting to see Carl. "What happened? Where's Carl?"

"We tried to get to him but it was no use. There were too many of them. We had to turn back," Bob explained.

"So is Carl dead?" Tom asked.

"We don't know for sure," Nathan answered.

Tom looked from one to the other. "So what are you saying? You just left him there? You don't know what happened to him? Did you even see him?"

"Well no we didn't see him. We heard shooting and a scream. We figured they got him," Bob added.

"So you got scared and chickened out. You didn't even try," that last was a statement not a question.

"Hey bro we went there and there was just too many of them," Nate began. "We had to strategically fall back man."

Tom turned from his brother and Nate and headed for his truck. They followed him. "What are you going to do bro?" Nate asked.

Tom didn't answer, he kept walking. Kelly ran up to him. "Tom what's going on? What are you doing?"

He turned to her and pointed his thumb over his shoulder. "Sir Scaredy cat and Baron von Chicken liver here were approaching Vue's place and the Yrartz scared them off before they confirmed whether Carl was alive or dead. I'm going to find him if I can and try to rescue him."

"I'm going with you," Kelly said firmly. Tom looked at her and nodded knowing he couldn't stop her.

"We're coming too," Bob said.

"Yeah both of us," Nate confirmed pointing back and forth at Bob and himself.

Tom turned from his truck. "Okay, but you come with me you stay with me. You chicken out I'll shoot you in the back as you run away." Bob was fairly certain his brother was kidding about shooting them. Nate wasn't quite so sure. "We will take Nate's car. Too many of us for my truck. Kelly will you drive?"

Carl, his back against a tree, fired round after round at the Yrartz as they came in waves. The fourth attack they tried to flank him but had no better results. He was too good a shot and he still had plenty of ammunition.

Vue believed he was in this alone. He expected no help and wasn't even sure anyone yet knew these things were here. However he held hope that someone would come. Either way he was going to fight to the last bullet and maybe use his knife on a few too.

With these thoughts in mind he fired slowly and carefully. Conserving ammo, taking only sure shots. He was determined to keep up the fight as long as possible and take as many of them as he could.

The rescuers drove out of town as Tom outlined his plan of attack. Nathan interrupted. "Ah Tom, instead of going in Carl's driveway which we know is full of Yrartz why not take that old logging road?"

"I don't remember any logging road," Tom answered.

"It's on the other side of Carl's and it goes real close to his driveway. Comes in from the north," Nate added.

"Really? I didn't know that," Bob said.

"Where exactly?"

"You go past Carl's and then just past the eagle's nest there's a rock."

"You sure?" Tom asked.

"Yep, my uncle took me down that road. It goes all the way to Telemark Creek. We fished for trout there and got our limit."

"Oh now I remember," Tom admitted. "I've never been down it but they put that road in when they logged the red pine plantation there."

"That's right," Bob agreed.

"How bad is it grown over?" Tom asked.

"Don't know but I was there just a few years ago." Nate continued, "It's between the eagles nest and the highline."

"We passed Carl's," Kelly said.

"Okay there's the eagles nest. It's just past the rock," Nate informed them.

"I don't see any rock," Kelly tensed.

"Well, it's really more of a pebble," Nathan told her as she scanned the gravel shoulder.

The old logging road was grown over in places and Kelly was forced to leave it. She drove down the lanes between the trees of the plantation dodging rocks and fallen branches. It was slow going but she guided the car skillfully until Nate ordered a stop.

"This is where the road gets close to Carl's drive."

"Okay you guys get out. Kelly stay here and wait for us. Give us three hours in case we run into trouble. If we're not back by then you get out of here, understand?"

Kelly couldn't speak, she just nodded her head. She quickly wiped away a tear before anyone noticed. Tom kissed her and held her a moment before exiting the car.

"You'll be safe here." As an afterthought, Tom said, "Don't worry. I will be back and I will bring our brothers back too. I love you." With that he led off, Bob and Nate following.

Jimmy finally had the cable spliced. He put his tools back in the box and carried them to the truck. He stowed everything, shut the doors and gave the area a once over.

He climbed into his truck, shut the door and put on his seatbelt. Jim started the engine while dialing his cell phone. He put the phone to his ear as he put the truck in gear.

Jim could hear the phone ringing as the vehicle lurched. He heard something like a scream. "What the…?" he said aloud. He put the vehicle in park and unhooked his seatbelt. He opened the door and climbed out.

Perplexed, Jim scratched his head as he kneeled down. On his hands and knees he looked under the truck. Pulling a flashlight from his pocket he shined the beam at a dark object near the rear.

Just then Jimmy heard what sounded like an old-fashioned monotone computer voice. He could barely make out the words. "Do not be alarmed! We are Yrartz from the planet Yrartz. We are here to take over your planet. Do not be alarmed!"

Before Jim could back out from under the truck he was hit by several darts. "Ouch! What the..?" His words were cut off as the tasers zapped him. Several more darts bounced off the fearsome truck as the Yrartz tried to immobilize it as well.

This time when Stan Berry called his friend's phone someone answered. "Hello Dan, this is Stan. I've been worried about you," he paused. "Dan are you there?"

"We are Yrartz from the planet Yrartz," said a monotone voice over the phone.

"What?" Stan asked dumbfounded. The voice continued and a smile crossed Stan's face. "Hey that's very funny Dan. Where are you and why aren't you back yet?" The voice at the other end stopped abruptly.

The Yrartz dropped Dan's cell phone on the ground and ran over it. He continued on following his leader never looking back or thinking about the device he tossed.

Stan was frustrated. His pal Dan was acting strange, at least stranger than normal. He put his phone away and prepared to head home. Let Dan be that way, he would talk to him Monday morning. At least now he knew Dan was alive and well. After all he answered his phone even if it was in some weird made up alien voice. He was probably just getting back at him for asking about his date the other night.

The sun had set and darkness was settling over the land. Birds stopped singing and went to sleep. Soon travel in the forest would became difficult if not impossible without lights. Bob and Tom each had a pocket flashlight. Not much distance and not a very wide circle of light but they would keep the brothers from tripping over things.

Nate had a flashlight that flickered frequently. It was old, beaten up, rusty and not very good. The bulb had dimmed and the batteries were never ready. The light was one of those you had to hold a certain way or it would just go out completely.

The guys barely got in the woods before they heard shots. Tom turned to Bob and Nate. "He' still alive," he whispered. "Let's move it. Keep your ears open and see if you can tell what direction he is from here." With that Tom began moving faster. He realized it was only a matter of time before Carl was over run.

Bob and Nate picked up the pace trying to stay with Tom. Nate was having a tough time unwrapping a candy bar, stumbled and nearly fell. Bob let go of a branch he was holding. The branch snapped back and hit Nathan's hand sending the candy bar flying into the brush.

Nate decided it would be impossible to find in the dark so he reached into his pocket for another. He vowed this one would find its way into his mouth. With determination he unwrapped this candy bar and held it with both hands as he began to eat.

The Yrartz had him surrounded and were moving in from all directions at the same time. Carl figured this was it but there was still no give, no surrender in him. His shots became fewer and fewer but better aimed.

There were dozens of dead and dying Yrartz lying about. The aliens were starting to have trouble climbing over the bodies. It helped slow the advance and gave Carl a glimmer of hope.

Carl had been hit by some of the many darts fired at him. His right leg was still numb and he was having problems with his arm. He felt lucky in that at least the Yrartz tasers and lasers were incredibly ineffective. He knew they had far less power than the ones people made.

Tom heard the change in Carl's shooting. He realized what was going on and broke into a run. Bob had all he could do to try and keep up. Nathan stuffed the rest of the candy bar into his mouth and trotted after the brothers.

The sound of shooting mingled with the moans of wounded and dying Yrartz. This spurred Tom on to greater speed. Bob tried to keep up but he kept getting hit with branches.

Nate was doing his version of running when the flashlight went out again. He couldn't tell how close the trees were. "Bob," Nathan whispered loudly. No answer. "Bob," he said aloud. Still no answer. "BOB!" he yelled.

Bob skidded to a halt. "What is it Nate?" he asked turning back to see.

"I'm stuck," Nathan replied.

"Where are you?" Bob asked peering into the darkness with his penlight.

"Over here," a worried voice answered.

Finally Bob saw his friend and walked toward him. "Wow your camouflage is really good. I couldn't see you at all. Now what's the problem?"

"I'm stuck between these two trees."
"How did that happen?"

"I was running trying to keep up with you guys when my light went out. Next thing I know I'm stuck here."

"You must have been running very fast to get stuck like this," Bob said doing his best to hold his laughter. "Let me help you."


"Pastor I'm going to go over to Ted Hawkins place and see if he had a radio or any weapons we can use. You want to join me?"

"Sure Bill I'll come with you. But what if Ted isn't dead? What if he is still alive and can't get back here just now?"

"Well pastor I figure if he was still alive he'd find a way to get back here. So I'm pretty sure he is gone. However if he is alive and comes back I think he will understand. I think he will figure it was okay for us to get any weapons or other gear of his and use it for our defense."

"Yes you are probably right. So okay let's go."


Carl was using his left hand to reload and fire the guns now. His right hand was completely numb so he used it only to hold the gun up. It was cumbersome but it was the one way he could continue the fight.

Vue had switched to his shotgun. It had greater impact than the rifle or handguns he had. Carl was loading it with the last of his number four steel goose loads.

He thought he heard someone shouting. Carl held his fire for a moment to listen but the Yrartz kept moving in like the blowing of a steady wind. So he began shooting again.


Bill Webster and Pastor Washburn, with two other towns folk entered Ted Hawkins house. As always, Ted left the front door unlocked. Most people in West Falls left their front doors unlocked. They trusted their neighbors, figured they would inform them of strangers coming to town and knew bears couldn't turn the door knob. If a bear wanted in he would smash the door down or climb in an open window.

They came in quietly, almost reverently as if afraid of waking the dead. Bill and Gordon scanned the living room then moved to the kitchen. The other two went directly to the back of the house searching the bedrooms. They found nothing in the way of radios except a police scanner. They could listen but not call out. Bill decided to take it with in case there were reports of the Yrartz elsewhere in the county.

Everyone in town knew Ted had a gun cabinet. Most knew what guns he kept there. So Bill and Gordon went to the den and checked it out. In the cabinet they found the two weapons they sought. There were other guns also and they grabbed them all.

The basement was dusty and musty. It contained the furnace and an old wood stove. There was a wood box next to the stove. An ancient freezer stood against one wall and when opened yielded meat, mostly venison and vegetables. Bill made a mental note of this should they need more food.

There were several boxes containing papers and a steel cabinet. The cabinet held paint cans and supplies. The work bench along one wall had some tools lying on it but little else.

The group went out to the attached garage. Three cabinets covered the back wall. A snow blower and a lawn mower sat along another wall. On the far side of the room sat Ted's other vehicle, a 500cc ATV. Bill would use that if they needed it too.

Of the three cabinets two held tools, automotive supplies, and other odds and ends. One was locked. Bill and Gordon began looking for keys. They knew Ted carried several keys on his keychain and they had no idea what some of them unlocked but they hoped he left one for this door.

After a fruitless search Bill stopped and stood in the center of the garage, arms crossed, thinking. He scanned the room, "Where would I hide a key to something important enough to lock up?"

Gordon remembered an incident from his interactions with the deputy. "I think I know where it is," he announced. He moved to the electrical panel next to the kitchen door. He opened the access door and there taped to the inside was the key.

By way of explanation Gordon said, "I came here one time and saw Ted putting something in here. I didn't know what it was and he didn't explain. But the way he acted, like a kid caught with his hand in the pickle jar, I just figured it was a prime place to check."

"Good call," Bill admitted.

Gordon handed the key to Bill. He felt the man in charge should be the one to open the cabinet. It just seemed more official and the proper thing to do.

Bill stepped to the cabinet and inserted the key. He turned it and grasped the door handle and opened the door. His eyes lit up like a gasoline soaked bonfire when the burning match hits.

Carl was certain he heard someone coming. "Over here!" he shouted. "Over here!"

"We're coming Carl. We brought extra ammo too," Tom shouted back.

Looking over his shoulder Carl saw Tom's pocket light. He turned on the flashlight he had giving Tom a better fix on his position. The older Hayward brother slid to a stop beside the tree Vue leaned against.

"We're here. We can fight off the Yrartz and help you get out of here," Tom told him.

Carl looked around. "Who's we? I don't see anyone else."

Tom looked about. "I had my brother and Nate with me." He turned back the way he came. "BOB, NATE!" he shouted. "Hey you guys, where are you?"

Tom and Carl heard crashing in the brush. It sounded like a herd of buffalo and the men got ready for a fight. Thinking the Yrartz had regrouped, they prepared to shoot. Nate's flashlight came on suddenly and close by.

"What happened to you guys?" Tom demanded as the pair approached.

"Nothing man. I'm just a little slower than you are," Nate offered.

"Nate got stuck between two trees. I had to help him get out."

Carl started laughing. As much as he hurt and worried that they wouldn't get out safely he couldn't stop the laughter. Nate and the brothers stared amazed in the dim light.

"What's with him?" Bob asked.

"Donno," Nate replied as he unwrapped another candy bar. He checked his pockets and realized he was running out. "It's time to go."

"He is right," Tom agreed, surprised that Nathan did not want to rest for an hour or a day. "Carl that's a twelve gauge right?"

He stopped laughing long enough to answer. "Yep."

"Here are six rounds," Tom said as he handed the shells to Carl. Reaching into his other pocket he added, "I have…a hole in my pocket." Looking at the other men he continued, "I don't have any more shotgun shells. What about you guys?"

"I'm out of shotgun shells but I have plenty of twenty-twos," Bob said.

"I'm out of candy bars and I lost the box of shells I was carrying when I got stuck in those trees." Nathan looked behind him. "It's back there some where's. Think we should go find it?"

"No. We will never find it in the dark," Bob answered. "I only have twenty-two ammo myself." He smiled diabolically. "But I got over three hundred rounds."

"Okay Bob, you lead off. Carl how much ammo you got?"

"The six you gave me and some twenty-twos. I ran out of shotgun shells just as you got here and my rifle was empty a while ago."

"Great," Tom said sarcastically. "Bob get going. Nate and I will hold Carl up. Don't go too fast. I don't think we will be moving very rapidly."

"We might be alright," Carl said. "I'm getting feeling back in my right leg and arm. I think I will be able to walk on my own soon." Using the tree for support he pulled himself up.

Bob took a couple steps when the woods in front of him lit up like Broadway in New York City. Well that's a slight exaggeration. Red, blue, green and yellow lights blinked on in a phalanx of Yrartz.

Tom quickly realized the enemy had regrouped and were attacking in force. "Bob," he grabbed his brothers shoulder, turning him. "Let's go this way."

Bob needed no encouragement. He started off in the opposite direction the Yrartz were coming from. Tom helped Carl move out. Nathan trailed behind, keeping watch for enemies getting too close.

Bob carried Carl's empty rifle on a sling over one shoulder. He held his own Twenty-two rifle at the ready. He walked faster than planned now that they knew the Yrartz were rolling along in a larger, organized force.

Carl was able to hobble on one good and one bad leg. He carried his shotgun in his left hand, waiting for a target. His right hand, still a bit numb, held the flashlight.

Nate moved into the third spot now that Carl could walk reasonably well. His shotgun held only three rounds since he lost the box. He had no other gun with him.

Tom brought up the rear hoping they could outrun the enemy. He worried about getting back to town since they were headed in the wrong direction from Kelly and the car. He hoped she was doing okay waiting alone in the dark.

# Chapter 15

The car radio was too loud so Kelly turned it down. She needed the comfort of the music and occasional voices coming from it but did not want it overpowering. Waiting was difficult under the best circumstances. This was nearly unbearable.

She had been alone and waiting for over an hour now. Kelly wished she had insisted on coming with them. She would rather be doing something than just sitting and wondering. Too bad they had no way to communicate, then at least she would know what was going on.

The moon wasn't up yet and no stars shone through the thick clouds. It looked and smelled like rain. The only light came from the dashboard. Kelly occasionally looked out the windows but really couldn't see much.

There was a bit of a breeze and it made what shadows there were move about eerily. She was thinking it makes for a good horror story especially because of the Yrartz out there somewhere. Kelly smiled as a chill crept up her spine. It's fun to be scared as long as it isn't real.

Kelly suddenly realized she had been hearing a strange sound for a while now. She reached out and turned the radio off, listening more closely. She heard it again but could not quite place it.

Voices! The boys were back! She let out a sigh and relaxed as she looked out the window. She drew back quickly. There staring at her stood a Yrartz. She scanned the outside and noticed they were all around the vehicle. Kelly was surrounded!

She ducked down in the seat hoping they hadn't seen her yet. Kelly reached over and hit the door lock button. The loud click alerted the Yrartz and they began to creep up and look in the car windows.

Kelly let out a scream which scared the Yrartz almost as bad as they scared her. She turned the ignition key and heard a grinding clicking sound. *Oh don't tell me the battery is dead* she thought. But the engine caught and she put it in gear slipping into her seatbelt.

They knew she was here so Kelly didn't hesitate. She flipped on the lights and slammed down on the accelerator. The car jumped forward. She took several Yrartz by surprise, mowing them down as she sped off.

She had never been down this road before tonight. Kelly was going all of thirty when a curve on a hill came into view. She spun the wheel over and almost made the turn. The car smashed into a couple small trees before hitting a hump of dirt and rock. The vehicle became airborne for a few feet then landed on the right front tire first.

The tire blew and caused the vehicle to slide and jerk. Kelly hung on as best she could but could not keep from piling into a large pine tree. The car stopped abruptly, the front end wrinkled and smoking.

In tears Kelly released her seatbelt and pushed open the door. She knew she wasn't far from the squad of Yrartz who had surrounded her. She needed to get out of there and fast.

Kelly grabbed the backpack from the backseat and a flashlight from the glove box. She picked up her deer rifle and slung it over one shoulder. She took the shotgun and checked to make sure it was loaded. There were extra boxes of both rifle and shotgun shells in the pack as well as water and something Nate added.

Without a backward glance she strode off into the woods. Kelly decided not to use the flashlight until she felt she was safely away from the aliens. She didn't know this section of forest but was confident she could find her way.

Kelly heard the Yrartz attack the car with their darts and lasers. By then she was fifty yards away but she started running anyway. Soon she was at the edge of the swamp and committed to continuing on.

The tree branches tore at her clothes and the occasional spider web in her face gave her that yucky, creepy feeling. But then so did the Yrartz. Fear kept her going further and further into the swamp.

She knew that eventually she would come upon Telemark Creek. This gave her confidence as she trudged through the muddy bogs. The biggest fear here wasn't the Yrartz, it was sinking into the mud between hummocks and not being able to get out.

Bill smiled as he held up the Thompson machinegun. He addressed his unit commanders, "Gentlemen, I knew Ted had some good weapons but I had no idea he had this." He paused a beat. "As most of you know it is a Thompson. This one is in forty-five caliber and the drum holds fifty rounds. Ted wisely kept four hundred rounds of ammunition for it. These slugs should do a job on those aliens out there.

"Now Ted also had this," Bill held up an M-16A1 rifle. "I don't know where he got it or what he used it for but I'm glad he had it. The little five point five six bullet will also do a job on those little Yrartz."

"So who gets to use them?" one of the men asked.

Bill smiled and said, "Well I'm a lousy shot so I will use the Thompson." He shook his head. "Actually I am a lousy shot so I'm using a shotgun. I know Pastor Gordon is a former soldier so I think he should use the M-16. The Thompson goes to my second in command, John. He fired one of these years back and knows something about them. Is that okay with everyone?" Bill asked expecting no resistance.

"I don't have a problem with that," the man who asked about the guns said. No one else had a problem with it either.

Bill continued, "So far we haven't seen any Yrartz in the town. Other than the Hayward's and Nate the only people to see these aliens and live are John and Pete. They drove up Hawthorne as far as the turnoff to Earl's road.

"I was going to have them set up an LPOP but the Yrartz are already set up near there. We had to pull back to just the other side of Hawkins garage. That is where we have our forward position as of now.

"As much as possible I plan to have pastor and John rotate through that position during darkness. In daylight we will have two of you with semi-auto rifles in there. The idea is to have as much firepower as possible in that position at all times." Bill paused again, thinking.

"Okay you all have your assignments. Get your gear together and get your people. Check them to make sure they are properly equipped. I realize we don't have all the stuff we need like the military does but make sure they have guns, ammo, water and reasonably warm clothes.

"Let's get out there and defend our town. Dismissed." The group sat waiting for something more. "When I say dismissed it means get out there and get going. Now go."


Tom heard rather than saw the aliens moving along behind them. He stopped every now and then to listen. At first he felt they were getting farther away with each step the men took. But after half an hour it sounded to him as if the Yrartz were directly ahead.

He rushed past Carl and Nate and grabbed Bob by the shoulder. "Where are you taking us?"

Bob shrugged, "I think I'm heading south. But soon we should turn west. Why?"

"I think you took us in a circle." Tom pointed toward the front. "I can hear someone."

"You sure it isn't someone on the road?"
Nate and Carl came up to them. "What is it?" Nate asked.

Before Tom or Bob could reply Carl inquired, "Why are you taking us in circles?"

"Didn't know I was," Bob protested.

"How do you know we are going in circles?" Tom asked.

"Because that's my driveway right over there," he pointed. "And my house is just about a hundred yards from here that way. If it was daylight you could see it." Tom gave his brother a nasty look but in the darkness Bob didn't see it.

Tom turned his attention to the tactical situation. "What are the odds of us sneaking across the road? If we go straight north we will hit the old logging road and get back to Kelly and the car."

"I don't know but it's worth a try," Carl said looking at his watch. "It's two fifteen. We have several hours before daylight."

"Don't see as how we have much choice," Nathan commented. The trio turned to him with the unspoken question. "There are Yrartz right behind us," he pointed. Just then the guys could hear voices.

"Some of them are still telling us not to be afraid," Nate said.

"Remember what it says in Joshua, chapter one, verse nine?" Carl asked.

Tom answered, "Something like have I not told you do not be afraid?"

"Yep, and I think they are the ones who should be afraid." Carl continued, "I don't know about you guys but I have been praying. In fact you guys are an answer to one of my prayers. I asked God to help me out because I knew He was the only one that could. He sent you. BTY thank you all."

Bob touched Tom's arm. "We are surrounded."

Tom looked the direction his brother was looking. Then he turned and looked the other way. "Yes and they are back there too. We are indeed surrounded.

"What was it that French general in World War I said, General Ferdinand Foch? My center is giving way, my right is retreating. Situation excellent. I am attacking." Without another word Tom moved toward Carl's driveway firing his twenty-two pistol. The other three moved up on line with him and started forward in a skirmish line.

The closer they came to the driveway the faster they moved. When the boys crossed the drive they started running. Carl fired off the six rounds he had and dropped his shotgun, pulled a pistol and continued firing.

Nate fired the three rounds he had in his shotgun then grabbed hold of the barrel. He would use it as a club if he got close to any Yrartz. With no other weapon handy he figured his two hundred pounds, okay maybe three hundred, well three fifty or so would be enough weight behind the swing to do some damage.

Tom slung his pistol under one arm and fired wildly behind him hoping to discourage the enemy from following. Bob stopped, turned and fired occasionally. He had to run fast to catch up each time.

Kelly gratefully climbed out of the swamp onto dry ground. She thought she was on an island in the swamp. The good news was that it was relatively dry and not spongy like the rest of the territory she covered so far.

When she stepped between two birch trees she became entangled in a large spider web. "Yuck," she gagged. Kelly spit out a thread of web and quickly checked herself for loose spiders. She brushed her face and hair off several times to make sure it was all gone.

She was dead tired and dearly wished she could lie down and go to sleep. The rain turned out to be more of a mist or heavy fog, but it still chilled her and got her wet. To top it off she was really hungry.

That's when Kelly remembered her brother put something in the backpack. She stopped and leaned the guns against a tree. Pulling off the pack she rummaged around in it looking for the candy bars she knew had to be there.

Sure enough there were several Snickers and Milkyways. These were Nate's favorites. He likely had at least a dozen of each on him right now she mused. Her brother surely liked his candy.

The dart came flying at her head and the only thing that saved her was she leaned forward to check for more candy. Kelly grabbed the shotgun, flipped off the safety, aimed and fired all in one smooth motion. The Yrartz head exploded in a mist quickly dissipated by the rain.

The sound of the shot helped other Yrartz zero in on her position. Kelly, hunger forgotten, straightened up picking up the pack as she did. They were coming from the east, she turned west.

There were Yrartz to her left as well as behind her. She ran as fast as she could hoping to reach the road to town. But as Kelly neared Cumberland Road she saw they were already there waiting for her.

She had to make a decision now. The two guns she was carrying were getting heavy and awkward and the backpack wasn't helping either. Kelly did not want to drop her deer rifle and run but she knew the shotgun was more immediately useful. The problem was she didn't have time to sort out the ammunition in the pack.

Kelly quickly pulled off the pack and crisscrossed the slings on her guns. She grabbed up the pack again and started running. She ran right for a small group of Yrartz that seemed to be waiting for her. As she came close she took the backpack in both hands and swung left then right bowling over several aliens.

The Yrartz were temporarily stunned into inaction. Kelly reached the road, ran across it, down into the ditch on the other side and kept running. She ran out into the open field and continued on looking back once in a while to see if they were still coming. She stumbled on a gopher hole and nearly took a dive.

The Yrartz followed but could not go as fast as Kelly's long legs carried her. She made it to the swamp on the other end of the field and dove into the brush there. Once in the swamp she slowed down to catch her breath and try to orient herself. But she had never been in this area of the Bibon before. She bent over, hands on her knees breathing hard.

Kelly wasn't waiting for the aliens to catch up. She started off further into the swamp. She trotted forward between some cedar trees and once more her face smashed into a large cobweb. Wiping her face again she picked pieces from her hair. "Don't spiders hibernate," she asked the forest. She opened her mouth and spit hoping no Yrartz were near.

Bill was manning the roadblock on Cumberland near the church. He couldn't sleep so he decided to take a watch for a few hours. He could hear occasional shots off in the distance but couldn't tell what was happening.

He turned to the two men with him. "You guys be ready. Someone is having a running fight with the Yrartz and we may need to give them some assistance." Bill paused in thought. "If that's Tom's group God help them. It sounds like they are having a tough time."

One of the men suggested, "Maybe we should go out there and find out who it is and help them."

"No not a good idea. It's dark and we have no way to communicate with them. Someone would be sure to get shot. We don't want that."

"No we don't want anyone hurt. I really hadn't thought about that."

The three men went silent, listening to the gunfight. The shots were more spaced now. Bill worried that whoever it was might be running out of ammunition.

Tom was the first to reach Telemark Creek. He came upon it so quickly that he nearly fell in. "Hold it guys. The cricks here."

"Whoa, good thing you said something. I almost fell in," Nate told him.

"We need to turn back toward the road and try to get to Kelly," Tom said with alarm in his voice.

Carl looked at him. "Tom if she is still on the logging road she may be surrounded too or..." He let it drop.

186

Tom had been thinking the same thing. He was doubly worried now. He was the one that let her come along and he was also the one that left her behind in the car. If anything happened to her he would never forgive himself.

Without a word he headed toward the place he thought the car should be. The others followed along in single file. Each alone with his thoughts, they moved swiftly and silently.

The foursome went through the ritual of checking their gear and reloading. They were all relying on twenty-two's now. The little bullets might not kill with one shot but they could carry a lot more rounds and if they took the time to aim, kills still happened.

Kelly thought she would be alright in the swamp. She heard Tom tell how the little aliens came from the swamp but she took that to mean they were along the edge and not actually in the Bibon.

She found a hummock up out of the water and next to a cedar tree. She set the pack down and sat on it, back against the tree. She unslung the guns and checked to be sure they were fully loaded. Exhausted she had to do something to stay awake.

Kelly checked the time on her cell phone. 3:32 A.M. It would be some time before dawn and she so wanted to sleep. But to sleep was to die and so she tried very hard to keep her eyes open and her mind occupied.

Tom was still in the lead when he came upon the logging road again. This time fortunately there were no Yrartz within smelling distance. But the car wasn't there either. Panicked, he shone his light up and down the road looking for any sign of the vehicle.

"What's up Tom?" Bob asked.

"The car. It's not here."

"What's happening? Where's the car?" Nathan asked.

"It's gone!" Tom squeaked. Just then he noticed something shine in the light. He looked more closely at the ground where he thought it was. "Here," he stooped and picked something up.

"What is it?"

"Darts. Some of those taser darts. They must have come upon her here while we were gone." If Tom had been worried now he was frantic.

"So where's the car?" Bob asked again.

"Kelly must have gotten away. Let's go guys," Tom said and started off toward Cumberland Road.

Kelly nodded off just for a moment. Her head jerked and she opened her eyes again. But shortly her chin dropped to her chest and she was asleep. Soon she was dreaming and then a nightmare. She was running away from some terrible aliens and she was alone. Somehow no matter how fast she ran she couldn't get away from them.

With a start she woke. There was rustling in the brush nearby. The rain had stopped and the clouds were gone. The moon was up and there was enough light to see the shadows of movement. Quietly, quickly Kelly picked up the shotgun and prepared to fight.

One of the Yrartz looked her way and cut loose. The dart never got close but it alerted the others. Kelly fired the shotgun and took out that alien and wounded the one behind him. That's when she realized they had been going through the swamp looking for her and had her surrounded again.

Tom was running down the logging road as fast as he dared. He saw the car and slid to a stop next to it. He bent down and looked inside. Nothing! He could see better now that the moon was up and the clouds were gone.

Nate was next. "It looks like she hit a tree. Do you think she got hurt?" he asked, concern in his voice.

"I think she was alright when she left here," Tom said hopefully. "I don't see any blood or anything like that. The tracks leading away look as if she was walking normally and not staggering or having trouble."

"Hey Tom isn't that your phone ringing?" Bob pointed.

The ring tone had been going for several seconds before anyone noticed. Tom looked down at his pants pocket. He reached into the pocket and pulled his phone out. Holding it to his ear he said, "Hello?" No one thought about the fact cell phones were working again.

"Tom I'm lost in the swamp over near Granny Hayward's. I've got Yrartz on my tail and I'm running trying to keep ahead of them," Kelly said breathlessly.

"Is that my sister?" Nate asked reaching for Tom's phone.

"Yes," Tom hissed. "So Kelly do you know what direction you are heading?"

Nate snatched the phone from Tom and when he tried to retrieve it he pushed him back. "Kelly is that you?"

"Yes Nathan."

He put the phone on speaker. "What's up? Where are you sis," he asked.

"I'm lost in the Bibon up near Granny Hayward's." Kelly stopped to catch her breath and talk to her brother. "I was in a running fight with some Yrartz but I got away. But I think they are still coming so I have to move."

"Can you tell us anything about where you are at? Do you have any idea how far you went into the swamp or what direction you were going at the time?" Tom asked impatiently.

He wanted to get started looking for her, find her and get her safely back to town.

"I was travelling west when I went into the swamp but I have no idea how far I went or if I changed directions. It was raining when I went in."

"Hey sis don't worry. Now just follow the sound of my voice and I will get you out of there," Nate promised her.

"Man, that's not going to work. Nate, you're on a cell phone," Bob groaned.

"Dude, I got it on speaker."

"Nathan, Kelly is not going to be able to follow the sound of your voice whether you have it on speaker or not," Tom informed him.

Nate looked at the device in his hand. "Oh. Yeah I guess you're right. Ah Kelly we are going to have to come up with something else. I guess you can't follow the sound of my voice on a cell phone."

Kelly rolled her eyes as if to say thanks big brother I knew you would figure it out eventually. "Okay but come up with something quick. I don't know how far back they are or where I am. I have to keep going and I just hope I'm not going in circles."

Pastor Gordon left the church and walked to the roadblock. He had his shotgun in one hand and flashlight in the other. He was surprised to find Bill Webster leaning over the hood of one of the cars used at the block.

"Bill, have you been here all night?"

"Yep," Bill replied tiredly.

"Why? You have been manning this post?" Gordon asked incredulous.

"Well, actually no. I have been here all night, yes. But I am not on duty."

The pastor leaned on the hood next to Bill. "Couldn't sleep either. I been in the church praying for those kids. Whenever one of my parishioners is ill, injured or in danger I will be praying for them."

"I know that pastor." Bill looked out into the dark again. "Pastor I know I'm not one of your parishioners."

"True, you don't come to the church."

"But could you pray for me?"

"Sure Bill. Anything specific?"

"No, well maybe safety and help in leading this town."

"Okay. You know Bill you could come to church," Pastor Gordon added.

"But pastor I'm a bar owner," Bill protested.

"So?"

"I serve liquor."

"So?"

"People get drunk at my place. It happens almost every night in fact," Bill told him.

"Yes and some of those drunks come to church," he paused. "You know Bill, I've never been a judge and I'm not about to become one. You are always welcome in our little church.

"You know Bill, I don't recall anywhere in the Bible that Jesus told anyone to change jobs before He would accept them. He never told people they had to change their habits or their friends or their clothes or take a bath before they came to Him. In fact many times Jesus went to them.

"He might someday tell you to sell your bar or change jobs. He might not. But right now He is just asking you to come to Him."

Pastor Gordon was quiet then. He thought he saw a tear dribble down Bill's cheek but he let it pass. He looked out into the blackness again praying for this man beside him.

"I'm praying that they find Carl alive and that they all get back safely."

"Me too," Bill said. "I've been out here praying, watching and hoping." He turned to him. "I wish we had found those walkie-talkies at Ted's before they left. At least we would know what was going on now."

"True, and that surely would help," Gordon mused. He put his head in his hands as he leaned on his elbows.

"I heard gunshots several times tonight. Faint, very faint, but gunshots for sure. For a while there it sounded like someone was having a running fight. "

Pastor stood up straight and looked at him. "That's encouraging. It must be them." He shrugged, "Who else could it be?"

"That's what I figure. We pretty much know Ted is gone and Earl is gone. No one else up there. No one else it could be." Bill gazed out into the dark. "Only others unaccounted for are the Seeley's. Fred never carried a gun along to go shopping far as I know."

Gordon nodded. "We're pretty sure we know what happened to Ted and Earl. But I still have hope for the Seeley's. Maybe they stayed in Ashland. Maybe they saw the bridge was out. Maybe they turned back."

Bill huffed at that. "Tom said they saw a car or at least part of a car in the creek. I realize they didn't stop to identify it but the color was right. Odds are."

Once again Gordon nodded, his hopes for Fred and June Seeley wilted. "I guess." He cocked his ear toward the forest, then pointed. "You hear that?"

Kelly still had some ammo for the shotgun and when she saw an opportunity she cut loose. Two Yrartz died and two others were wounded in the shot. She didn't wait around to see the outcome. There were too many of them so she took off at a fast pace.

The Yrartz seemed to be everywhere in this part of the swamp. Kelly was dodging trees and low hanging branches. She tripped over a root and nearly tumbled again. She was getting tired but knew she must keep going, she must find the guys or get back to town.

Her foot snagged a tree root and she went flying. The shotgun fell several feet away and she heard a loud crack as her rifle hit something solid. Kelly landed hard and stayed down for a moment.

She listened closely for sounds of the enemy. Nothing. She slowly took inventory of her body starting with her arms and legs. Nothing seemed to be broken or badly hurt. Finally she stood up, brushed herself off and picked up her equipment.

She confirmed the shotgun barrel was clear and the gun loaded. Next Kelly checked the rifle. The scope was broken and therefore useless. She would have to rely on the open sights.

Not a problem for her. She used the scope primarily for long range shots and these Yrartz were never that far away. Someday she would replace the scope but for now her problems revolved around finding a safe place.

Kelly stumbled and pushed her way through the thick brush. Just as she broke through into an opening a sider web attached itself to her face. She fell to her knees and cried, "Not again!" She wiped the silky stuff off her face and continued rubbing it off in a panicked frenzy.

She was so angry and frustrated that she almost started blasting cobwebs with her shotgun. Kelly was afraid of and disgusted by spiders. If one did land on her she would shriek.

She thought as she went, trying to remember where the moon usually set. *It rises in the east and sets in the west just like the sun. Duh!* She chided herself. All this running and fighting must have slowed her thought processes she felt.


The guys left the car and headed toward Cumberland Road. Tom led off going as fast as he could in the half light from the moon. None of them worried much about making noise since they believed they could outrun the enemy or fight them off.

"This reminds me of an episode of Real Housewives of Escanaba," Nathan told Bob. "You know the one where Bertha is surrounded by wolves."

Tom turned around and looked at him. "How does this remind you of a TV show?"

"You know, Bertha is surrounded by wolves and only has an axe to fight them with. We are surrounded by Yrartz and only have twenty-twos. Kind of the same thing."

"Well if we could find Kelly we would have ammo for the shotguns," Tom said.

"And we would have something even more important," Nate added.

"Oh? What's that?" Bob inquired.

"More candy bars."

"Nathan are you out of candy?" Tom asked with mock concern.

"Oh my, Nate may suffer a sugar deficit. This could be tragic," Bob chimed in.

"Over twenty years of sugar and a sudden shortage. This could be very serious," Tom smirked.

"Do you feel faint? Are you hallucinating? Any ill effects?" Carl threw in his two cents worth.

"I'm fine," Nathan grinned and held up a candy bar. "I still got some left. I'll be okay until we find Kelly."

"Speaking of Kelly. Nate, where's my cell phone?"

Nate's grin exchanged places with a frown. He patted down his jacket and pants pockets, then he began again. "You lost my phone?" Tom asked.

"No he gave it me," Bob informed them. "Well actually it fell out of his pocket and I picked it up."

"Fell out of my pocket? Which pocket?"

"The one with the hole in it."

"Oh yeah, that one. I forgot about it."


Kelly's phone rang. She forgot to set it on vibrate. She looked around the swamp to see if any Yrartz were close. "Hello?"

"Kelly you have any idea where you are now?"

In answer they heard a shotgun blast over the speaker. "Kelly! Kelly! Are you alright?" Tom shouted into the cell phone. Another shot.

"I really don't have a lot of time to talk just now." BOOM! "I'm multitasking right now." BOOM! "Come and get me if you can and hurry!" She hung up and another shot rang out.

Tom was beside himself with worry. "What are we going to do?"

"Tom don't worry. Listen for a minute."
"Huh?"

"Hear that?" Carl asked him. "You listen close you can hear Kelly's shotgun."

"Let's go," Tom said and started off at a fast trot. They were getting close to Cumberland Road and they spread out a little, became more wary.

Tom stopped within sight of the road. Turning to the others he said, "We are close to Cumberland. I don't see any Yrartz but they are small and dark, hard to see in this light."

Carl moved up beside him. "I think we should keep going across the road and down Hawthorne. Kelly either went south and is near Earl's road or she went west and is near Earl's farm."

"You may be right but what if she is just going in circles? She could be right where she started," Tom suggested.

"Could be but I think we should assume that since she is being chased she is going in a relatively straight line," Carl answered.

"If that's true she could be anywhere from Granny's cornfield to Earl's Road. So where do we start looking?" Bob asked.

"We can't split up. We don't have the firepower to go alone," Nate said. "We don't even have enough to separate into two groups."

"True, we should stay together," Tom agreed. "If we split up we have a greater chance of accidently shooting each other too."

"I think we should follow Carl's plan."

"Okay," Tom said. "Let's get going." He jumped up and started moving again. Bob ran alongside stride for stride. Carl was shorter than the brothers but in good shape. He had no trouble keeping up. Nate dragged along behind, out of breath.

The Yrartz temporarily backed off to regroup. They realized they were fighting people who knew how to shoot and weren't afraid to. They had been surprised by the extraordinary resistance these folks put up. It tended to confuse them especially in light of how easy the first few were taken.

Even one person could inflict untold casualties on their forces. The Yrartz had only studied Earth for a short time but they believed the early successes were the norm. Now they were finding out that was not the case.

The Yrartz usually landed on a planet encountering very little resistance. They would quickly mop up whatever enemies they found. Then they would start eating every morsel of protein they could gather. Yrartz have poorly developed taste buds and anything and everything tasted good to them.

The one exception to this had been Mmyra. They hadn't even landed on that planet. Many of their fellow Yrartz died in that conflict against a single enemy ship. It was their only disaster to date.

The Yrartz landed unopposed on planet Earth and began wandering around looking for food. The fact they encountered no defenses in space as they approached made them believe they had nothing to worry about. However, by now every Yrartz unit involved in a fight had sustained numerous casualties and some units were severely decimated.

The Yrartz did not realize the reason for their earlier success was simply because no one knew they were here. One Yrartz accidently hit an HBO satellite and forced over a hundred-thousand viewers to watch network television for a few hours. Otherwise, the invasion went unheralded.

# Chapter 16

Bill rounded up four people to send out as scouts. He decided he needed to know what was out there and figured they might encounter Tom and his group too. They left before daylight planning to sneak up Cumberland Road all the way to the bridge if possible.

"You all be careful. We don't know what's out there or how many of them. We think they only have tasers and lasers but we don't know for sure," Bill told them.

"Ed, I'm putting you in charge. You have the most knowledge of the terrain and you were in the Army. I'm depending on you to get us some intel and to get your people all safely back here."

Bill looked them over making sure they were dressed appropriately in dark colors. He didn't want anything showing that would make them easy targets. He had them do the rattle test to see if any of their equipment made noise. Finally, satisfied he gave the group a few tips and wished them luck.

They left then, walking slowly, two on either side of the road. No one spoke and all had their eyes and ears wide open to any sound or movement. They were tense, alert and everyone had his or her finger on the trigger.

Ed Madison led off walking on the left side of the road. Clem Appleton was slightly behind on the other side. Behind Clem was Slim Monroe. Nobody could remember Slim's real name any more and he didn't seem like the type you would want to ask. Behind Ed walked Greta Dells, the only female in the group.

Mr. Madison at fifty-two was the youngest in the group. He had two bad knees from milking cows most of his life. He sold the farm and the cows a few years back and moved to town.

Clem was in his early seventies and had one bad knee. Some undefined injury, probably from an auto accident. He lived his entire life in West Falls and the surrounding area.

Slim Monroe turned sixty-eight on his last birthday. He moved into town ten years ago after a logging accident put his left arm out of commission. The bones shattered and the doctors set it with a slight crook in the elbow so he could use the arm for some everyday tasks. Arthritis pained him most days but he wasn't a complainer.

Greta was born and raised in Chicago. She met a man named Dells from the UP, got married and moved up there. When she became a widow she decided to move close to her only remaining relatives, cousins Donna and Loretta Belknap. She was the other scout in her sixties.

The unit crept quietly along the road until they came close to Carl Vue's driveway. There they saw some shadows that might be the enemy. The four made themselves small and held close to the ground. They kept silent and waited.

They were afraid yet brave. All had accepted the mission without hesitation. They knew that someone had to do this job and each felt he or she could manage the part they played. Four pairs of nervous eyes watched the enemy.

The Yrartz seemed completely unaware of the threat. They went about their business as if nothing were amiss. One separated from the unit and came close to where the humans were hiding. He or she squatted down with its back to the scouts.

Ed rose up from his position and pulled his knife. He crept silently up to the Yrartz and plunged the blade into its neck. The alien squealed like a terrified pig and went rolling as fast as it could toward the center of their camp.

Ed turned and whispered for the others to get moving. He led off at what for him was a fast trot. The group followed as quickly as they could looking over their shoulders as they ran. Ed would have to find a knife to replace the one stuck in the Yrartz.

The eastern sky was sliding from black to gray to blue as the scouts made the roadblock. Bill was the first to greet them going beyond the barricade to meet them. He had a thank you, a smile and a handshake for each member of the group.

Bill took Ed aside to debrief him while the others went to the church to find breakfast. The pair talked for several minutes before Bill let him go to find food and bed. The town commander went to his command post and stood over the table making marks on the map there.

"Tom, the shooting has stopped. How are we going to tell where she is?" Bob wondered.

"I'm pretty sure I know where she is or at least close to where she is. I think she is south of Granny's near Earl's road."

"Why do you think that?" Nate asked.

"When she was shooting it sounded like it came from over that way. Now you know as well as I that sound travels around or over objects. But if you think about the terrain over that way it makes sense. She said she was still in the swamp so where else could she be?"

"Good point. She is still in swamp, so she either has to be there or she has to be the other side of Granny's cornfield," Carl agreed.

"Let's keep going," Tom pushed them. "We will be close to her if she starts shooting again." He didn't wait for an answer. He continued on toward the place he believed she would be.

Deep in NSA headquarters, the real headquarters, a low level scanner operator picked up a super-ultra- high frequency Yrartz transmission. First he thought it was just space noise coming off some as yet unknown quasar. But further investigation told him it was close, just above the Earth's atmosphere. Then he found the transmission was aimed at something or someone on Earth.

The NSA can move at the speed of a sluggish snail at times. Perhaps if some senior analyst had seen the report earlier things would have happened. As it was a tired, nearly retired analyst read the document and passed it off as a malfunctioning Russian satellite.

So it was that the government response to the first real alien invasion came much later than it should have. Possibly if the Yrartz had attacked Manhattan by sea or Dallas by land the military would have pounced on them within the hour.

Conversely if they had attacked LA nothing would have happened. People would believe it was just another alien invasion movie or an ordinary protest march.

The four men ran past Granny Hayward's farm and on down to Earl's Road. They turned and ran along it until they came to where the road entered the forest. There was a thin band of trees between the road and the Bibon. Tom took off into the trees headed for the end of a finger of the Bibon.

Coming close to the swamp, Tom stopped to listen. The others gathered next to him. No sounds of fighting came to them. Even the animals were silent. The only thing they heard was the wind in the trees.

"What do you think?" Bob asked. "We haven't heard anything for a few minutes."

Tom answered without looking at him. "I think she is moving and there aren't any Yrartz close to her. Spread out guys. We can cover more ground that way but stay in sight. We don't want to lose anybody."

"Call out. We don't want Kelly shooting any of us either," Carl added.

"Good point," Tom admitted. "So let's go." He started moving into the swamp. "KELLY," he yelled. Each of the other men began walking, calling more softly. They did not want to alert every Yrartz in the neighborhood.

Kelly heard them calling and relief draped over her like a warm blanket. She was only a hundred yards or so away. She started moving toward them staying silent for the moment. She wasn't sure if there were any enemies about but she wasn't going to take a chance.

Daylight was slowly penetrating the bare branches of the forest trees. Even in the swamp the black gave way to gray. Soon the sun would rise above the horizon and shadows would turn into trees and brush.

Tom heard a twig snap and halted. He crouched down and peered under the trees and brush as best he could. Kelly called out then. "Tom, Nate, Bob, can you hear me?"

"Over here," Tom called quietly.

Kelly turned when she heard him. She moved as rapidly as she could jumping from one hummock to another. A smile creased her face as a sweet release from the dark and danger flowed over her.

They came together and she fell into his arms. He held her and they kissed. She had never hugged anyone so tightly before. Kelly spent a fearful night alone in the swamp and now the exhaustion overwhelmed her.

Carl saw her meet up with Tom and he quickly came over keeping an eye out for danger. Tom called to his brother and Nathan. When the five were together they headed back to the road.

They were all ready for food and sleep but it was over a mile back to town. "Boy sis' we were really worried about you. We didn't know if we would ever see you again," Nate told her.

Kelly smiled at him, "I'm glad you all came for me." She let go of Tom's arm and stood in front of Nate and put her arms around him and hugged him. "Thank you bro, thank you all."

"You are welcome Kelly. I sure appreciate you guys coming to get me too," Carl added.

"No problem friend." Tom continued, "We have a little walk ahead of us and then breakfast and several hours of sleep."

"What is that in dog years?" Nathan asked.

"Why, you planning on changing species?" Bob asked. The others grinned at that.

Nate ignored his comment. "You think they will have breakfast waiting for us?" he asked rubbing his tummy.

"I sure hope so," Bob said. Kelly and Tom just looked at each other and smiled. They were so happy to be reunited that everything else faded away. Their hunger went unnoticed and Kelly's exhaustion was a distant memory.

Carl took the position of rear guard since he was the only one still paying attention. His eyes scanned across the road and into the tree line on either side. He was walking with a limp but his leg was showing signs of improvement. He was ready to fight or run as needed.

Shadows shortened and the sky turned pale blue as the four turned onto Hawthorne Road. Finally they could see the edge of town, a most welcome sight. Safety, food and rest were just ahead. West Falls never looked so good to them.

Bill heard a shout from one of the roadblock sentry's and came running. They were shouting to Tom and the group, as excited as school children at recess. He ran past the guards and kept going until he reached the five adventurers.

His smile was almost too big for his face as Bill shook hands all around and greeted each of them. "Man it sure is good to see you all back here safe and sound. I wasn't too sure when or if you would make it. Praise God."

"Hey it's good to be back," Tom told him. "We've had enough escapades for one night."

"I'm sure you have. Well I am glad to see all of you. Come on in and let's get you some food and rest." Bill led them through the roadblock. "You guys get some sleep. I've got a mission for you later."

"What kind of mission?" Bob asked, curious.

"I'll tell you about it later but for now let's just say I need some reconnaissance. See I sent out Ed Madison with a group up Cumberland Road. They met up with the enemy and Ed stabbed one of them."

In a quieter voice Bill continued, "He thinks they are planning an assault on the town. He figures they will come down Cumberland and the woods on either side. If that happens we may have some trouble stopping them.

"We don't have any big guns. No mortars or cannon. Plus everyone has had some watch duties last night so we are all a little tired. I'm concerned about our ability to defend the town."

"I have some ideas on that," Tom informed him.

Bill opened the church door and held it for the team. "We will talk later. You get food and rest. This will keep."

Ed, Slim, Clem and Greta were just finishing up at breakfast when Toms' group came in. Ed Madison stood as the gang came over. He thrust out his hand to Tom. "It's good to see you back Tom." He nodded to the others.

"I heard you had your own encounter with the Yrartz," Tom said as a question.

"Yep, sure did. Bill tell you about it?"

"Just that he sent you out and you stabbed a Yrartz."
"Durn thing squealed like a stuck pig," Clem snickered. "We

didn't wait to see if he died or not. Woke the whole neighborhood."

"Yep, made the awfulest noise you ever heard. I sure hope it died," Slim commented. "I figure the only good Yrartz is a dead Yrartz and even then they ain't no good."

"So what did you think of them?" Nate asked as he sat down at the table.

"Well it was dark yet and we couldn't see them real well," Ed said. "But what I did see both frightened me and gave me courage."

"How do you mean that?" Carl asked.

"Well they is a lot of them and that frightens me. But judging from the one I attacked I think they is easy to kill. From what Tom and Bob said we can kill them with most any gun.

"Who knows maybe we can just hit them with baseball bats or sticks. They seem to go down easy enough. I'm confident we can take them and make ourselves safe here."

"I hate to burst your bubble but there are a lot of them out there. We have no idea how many either. And they can see at night. They have some kind of night vision device," Bob told him.

"Well then maybe at night they have an advantage but in daylight we have," Slim stated as fact.

Ed picked up his plate and cup. "Well we are going to get some shuteye. See you all later."

Everyone said their goodbyes. Nathan was already scooping up fried potatoes and eyeing the bacon. He wasn't about to let any conversation get in the way of stuffing his face and filling his stomach.

The group of five ate mostly in silence. Each lost in their own thoughts. They had survived a scary night in the swamp with enemies all around and now they were as safe as they could be. They could let down their guard and relax if only for a short time.

"I'm not sure Bill should be sending out patrols," Nathan announced between bites.

"Why not?" Bob asked.

"Well what if they are attacked? We don't have anyone available for an immediate reaction force. I mean there are no reserve troops in this town."

"I see what you mean. But if we don't send out patrols how are we going to know how many they have and where they are?" Bob asked.

"Well that's a good point. I guess we need someone out there." Nate thought a moment. "However, if we send out people who don't know what they're doing all sorts of problems could happen. They could get lost or come up to the barricade and get shot by one of our own.

"You just can't have them out there like that. Next thing you know people will be walking around in the woods talking to trees, eating rocks and smoking fish. That's not a pretty picture, believe me. It's just something you don't want to see happen."

Kelly looked at her brother and wondered what brought these thoughts on. Tom shook his head and continued eating. Bob wasn't sure what his friend really meant but he nodded his head affirmatively. Carl wisely ignored him.

In the woods at the side of Cumberland Road the Yrartz commander spoke to his unit leaders. In his annoying monotone squeal he told them of his plans and gave out orders. This was no longer about finding food. This was about getting revenge.

"We will assault the town they call West Falls. We will kill every living thing in the town. We will do this before anyone takes any spoils. I do not wish to see anyone eating until all is conquered. Is that clear?"

"Yes my liege," each of them said together. They would carry out his orders to the letter and without question. To do less was unheard of in the Yrartz community. This was a strict, militaristic species.

"This is my plan. General 145, you will move along the west side of this road and into the town. General 323, you will take your forces and move along the east side of the road and stop at the edge of town. You are to stay out of sight. Make them believe they have a way to escape.

"General 516, you go along behind 145 until you reach this road," he used his pointer. The commander gave each unit leader the instructions they needed. He was prepared to move just before dusk. He came to realize the humans could not see in the dark but all his troops had night vision devices.

The people of West Falls were tired and worried. Anxiety and fear darkened the faces of the town's folk. A pervasive tension rode in with the sun. Rumors spread of the Yrartz massing for an attack. Everyone had heard the report from Ed Madison and his scouts.

Bill was dog tired and dearly wanted sleep. But he knew he had to appear strong and brave and all the other things a leader had to. So he stayed awake the best he could and continued making plans and giving orders.

There were few children in this town but they were put to work along with the adults. Every able-bodied person in West Falls was expected to do their fair share. So even the kids were working on the road block and the berm that Bill hoped would stop or at least slow the Yrartz. At their request, three elderly, wheel chair bound individuals stood guard duty. Everyone wanted to help defend the village.

Several automobiles had been placed across Cumberland Road and in the ditches next to it. Wood pallets, old furniture, logs, almost anything was used to build the barricade. It now stretched from the swamp on the west side of Hawthorne Road to the swamp east of the church.

The barrier would not stop the enemy if they chose to enter the town. However, it would stop them from coming down the road and straight into West Falls. The Yrartz had to go into the Bibon to get around the road block but they seemed capable of doing just that.

Bill knew the barricade would only slow the Yrartz for a short time. But he also knew that the citizens of West Falls felt safer with it in place. What if he was wrong and the enemy just gave up and went after another town? Well he could dream.

The residents of West Falls elected Bill as their leader and he took that seriously. He brought together some of the towns leading citizens in an advisory council. They decided to put up barricades using Pine Street. Pine was the first street in town on the right side.

The council wanted to greatly reduce the amount of land they needed to defend. Only six houses, the church, the Food-N-Fuel, the auto repair and farm machinery repair shops would be inside the perimeter. This was to be the fall back position. Out of necessity the rest would be sacrificed.

Some of the people stayed in their homes rather than sleep in the church. But most slept at the church at night and went home during the day. They believed they were safe in daylight, that the Yrartz would not attack then. What they failed to realize was so far, all the people who fell to the little aliens died during the day.

With the meal finished, Bob, Tom, Carl, Kelly and Nate decided to sack out in a couple of the Sunday school classrooms. They were all dog tired and ready for a few hours of much needed rest.

Some of the rooms in the church were set up specifically for sleeping. All other activities were banned from those rooms. With people going on or coming off guard duty at all hours of the day and night this was no place for talking, eating or anything else.

It was to these rooms the five retired. Kelly went to the women's room and found a spot along one wall. The guys all crowded into another room a few doors down. None brought sleeping bags or blankets but they were welcomed to use any vacant bed.

Four of them quickly fell asleep and left their cares and worries behind as they entered dreamland. But Tom, though tired, couldn't sleep. It wasn't worry about the enemy aliens at the door. It wasn't that they had no real army to fight with. It wasn't even that they were surrounded. It was the loud snoring

216

and occasional gas expulsion that kept him from dreamless sleep.

Eventually pure exhaustion worked its magic and Tom drifted off. He had no dreams or nightmares. He slept the sleep of the dead. Hence not one of the five heard the shotgun and rifle shots.

# Chapter 17

The enemy generals sent out scouts as any good commander is want to do. The men at the barricade noticed some unusual activity in the brush along the west side of Cumberland Road. Greg, one of the guards, lifted the binoculars to his eyes and focused in. "John, Bill said if we see anything suspicious we should get him."

"What do you see?" John asked.

Handing the binoculars over he said, "Take a look."

Peering through the glasses John told him, "I see three of them little green guys. Maybe four." Handing the binoculars back he added, "It looks to me like a scouting party. Like they are trying to stay out of sight but still see what we are doing."

"I think you're right." Greg agreed. "I think we should shoot them and let them know we are here and capable of defending ourselves." Without waiting for a reply he lifted his gun to his shoulder and took aim. John did the same. They fired so close together it sounded like a single shot.

All the Yrartz disappeared immediately. "Did we hit any of them?" John asked.

In answer they heard screaming from the brush. "For sure one of us did."

"So what do we do?"

"One of us needs to go find Bill. The other should stay here and keep watch in case that wasn't just a scouting party," Greg answered. "You go find Bill okay?"

Bill Webster was sleeping when they woke him. "Whaaa?" he tried to ask as he rolled over to see who was bothering him. When John told him what happened his eyes flew open and his head cleared. "Get some more men up and ready in case of an attack," he commanded as he pulled on his boots. "We will check on the Yrartz you guys shot at and see if they are still there or not. If so we may have a prisoner or a body. Either way find NM and get him to the roadblock too." Bill slipped into his jacket and grabbed his rifle as he headed out the door.

The roadblock was a beehive by the time Bill arrived. More than a dozen men and women milled about as he approached. Greg handed him the glasses and pointed. "They was over there in the brush by the edge of the road. John and me both shot at them. We hit one sure and scared the rest away." He paused to catch his breath. "Did we do alright?"

Bill smiled and patted him on the back. "You two did fine. You were alert and you took action. Good job," he shook Greg's hand. "If we find one of them alive I'm going to give each of you a hug and a kiss," he laughed at Greg's sudden frown.

Turning to the people standing near he said, "Okay I need some volunteers to go check it out. If possible bring me a live Yrartz. But if he or they are dead bring them back anyway. Even a body can help us understand what we're up against."

Turning to the guards he said, "Greg, I want you and John to lead them. You know where you were shooting and you deserve some of the glory. Is that okay with you?"

"Yep," John answered.

"Yes sir," Greg confirmed. "We will lead them and recover what bodies we can."

Bill chose six men to accompany Greg and John. He believed that would be enough to get them there and back safely. He figured they could carry two Yrartz bodies if there were bodies and still have an effective covering force.

The men gathered behind the roadblock in single file. Greg made sure each man was armed and ready. Silently he raised his hand and motioned for them to move out the way he had seen on so many war movies.

Greg led off followed by two of the men. John was fourth then the others. The rear guard held a double-barrel, sawed off shotgun. If the Yrartz tried anything he planned to change their minds and quickly.

The men ran across the road and entered the trees on the far side without incident. Greg found blood almost immediately. The trail was shorter than the enemy.

They gathered around the body of the alien and stared at it until Greg realized they were all bunched up. Pointing he said, "You two pick it up and head back. John go with them. I'll take the rest and scout around a bit. It looks like we hit another one and I want to see if we can find it."

"Okay but you be careful. They may just be hiding, waiting for you," John warned.

"I will," he nodded. "You get going," Greg waved him off. "Okay guys lets go see if we can find the wounded one." Reluctantly the four men followed. None of them wanted to go stumbling around in the brush after an enemy they knew so little about. They kept their own counsel but wondered how many aliens were out there and how close.

The two men carried the dead Yrartz in an old blanket brought for the purpose. John followed close behind frequently checking their back trail. Bill greeted them as they returned. "Where's the rest of you?" he asked.

"There was a wounded one. We found a blood trail and Greg decided to check it out," John answered.

"No!" Bill bellowed. "You guys were just supposed to recover bodies and get back here. I didn't want anyone out there hunting these things. We don't have enough manpower and weapons to chance losing anyone." Bill shook his head disgusted.

Yrartz 1839-L couldn't keep up. He was in a lot of pain and his shoulder was still bleeding. The sergeant thought about leaving him behind but decided against it. Instead he called a halt in a small clearing and told the men to set up a perimeter.

The sergeant started out with twenty men but two got lost somewhere along the way. Another got killed and now this one was bleeding and slowing down the unit. The mission was simple enough. Go to the edge of the Earthlings town and scout them out. They weren't supposed to be seen and he wasn't supposed to lose men in the process.

Greg took the lead on the blood trail. He wanted to capture a live alien to bring back to town. In his haste he threw out all the rules of safely following an armed enemy. It didn't help that the five of them moved through the forest with the silence and finesse of a herd of buffalo.

He stopped suddenly. Turning toward the men he whispered, "Any of you hear anything just now? I thought I heard something up the trail a little ways." None of them heard any sounds so Greg continued on.

The sergeant had two men help 1839-L to his feet and sent them ahead of the column. He was about to pick up and move out when he thought he heard something. He turned to face the sound.

Greg stepped out into the clearing and came face to face with the sergeant, well face to top of the head. The sergeant screamed in terror, turned and ran up the trail with the rest of the unit in close pursuit. Greg screamed and turned back so quickly he stumbled over the man behind him. Both humans and aliens ran away as fast as they could.


NM was overjoyed to see the body. He immediately took charge of the Yrartz remains. The dead alien was carried into the farm machinery repair facility. Space was cleared and it was laid on the workbench. The scientist took a screwdriver and a pair of pliers and prepared to work on removing the armor.

Shirley Richmond had been a wedding videographer for years. She took up the camera and recorded NMs work. She had never seen an autopsy before and was fascinated. Fortunately she held most of her questions until the event was over.

NM began explaining what he was planning. He realized there was little time but wanted to be as thorough as possible. This video might be of use to others besides the town folk of West Falls. Since communications with the outside world seemed to be suspended, no one in town knew how big the invasion was.

NM had always hoped to someday see an alien up close and personal, maybe even talk to one. But this was okay with NM. One question had been answered and a bunch of new ones were on their way. "Now we know we are not alone in the universe," he said absently. "Now we find out a little something about you," he said to the body as he began.

"For the record we are making a video of this autopsy and an audio recording as a backup. I am NM Roswell and I will be doing the autopsy. I am not a medical examiner. I am trained as an astrophysicist although I have observed two autopsies. I have also watched several videos of autopsies. I realize this isn't much training but I will do my best.

"The subject I will autopsy is a Yrartz, an alien that landed Thursday evening or Friday morning during what we thought was a meteor shower. The Yrartz have identified themselves to us and this is how we know their name.

"Today's date is October the tenth, 2015. It is a Saturday. With me in the room is our videographer, Shirley Richmond. Angie Hammond is a retired nurse and she will be assisting with the autopsy. There are four other observers, Bill Webster our military leader and …Huh? Let it be known the other observers do not wish to be identified by name.

"The first thing I notice as I look over the body is the smell. These Yrartz smell very bad. This is not a subjective thought. I am not the only one who feels this way." To Shirley he said, "Could you pan the crowd."

The intense smell arising from the Yrartz overpowered even the toughest of the bystanders. NM himself choked and gagged but he bravely began work. Angie Hammond had been a nurse for many years before moving to West Falls. She had some experience with autopsies so she stepped in to help him. She wisely dipped her face mask in perfume before putting it on.

"What in the universe makes Yrartz smell so bad?" NM asked her, smiling. "You don't have to answer that." He went back to observing the body before him.

"The body appears to be of an average size Yrartz. As with all of them this one has armor. The armor seems to be made of some type of composite material, it is green in color. Is that forest green or what? I guess it doesn't matter. The armor is a dark green. The armor protects the body but only extends to the neck. The shape is conical with the point at the top but instead of a point the head sticks out of the cone.

"The head sustained a gunshot wound that appears to be the reason for the Yrartz demise. The left arm is missing at the shoulder and this injury also seems to have been caused by a gunshot. I do not see any other injuries beside these two."

NM moved slowly around the table. He turned the body over trying to find a way to remove the armor. "I do not see how they get into their armor. The entire unit seems to be of one piece with no latches, zippers or any other method of attachment."

He turned the body over several times trying to determine how to remove the armor. Finally NM noticed a fissure near the bottom of the cone. "I finally see what appears to be the location where the body armor is joined. It looks as if the unit has very close tolerances. I am trying to figure out how it is held together." He peered under the armor, his face blushed as he felt like he was looking up a woman's skirt.

NM was going to take a saw to the armor when he decided to try one last thing. He gripped the armor on either side of the fissure and pulled. To his surprise and everyone else's the armor came apart relatively easily. "The Yrartz armor apparently is merely pushed together. It comes apart simply by pulling in opposite directions."

Shirley zoomed in on the Yrartz body, moving from head to foot trying to show as much detail as possible. "This Yrartz has what appears to be a body suit of some sort. It is grayish green in color and I see a zipper running down the middle. The suit runs from the neck to just below the knee and it has long sleeves." NM pulled the zipper all the way down and began removing it from the body.

"Now as I observe the body I see it is covered in green skin, mottled green skin, that seems much like ours. I have surgical gloves on but I can feel the skin is still warm as this Yrartz has only been dead for a few minutes, less than thirty minutes.

"The mottling on the skin is not well pronounced. It is just a shading in the skin I believe. The skin also seems to be as smooth as ours and nearly hairless. At a guess I think they have similar tolerances to us such as to heat, cold and air quality.

"I will be cutting open the body and removing the heart, liver and brain if it has these organs and I can identify them. As I said earlier the body sustained a gunshot wound to the head. The brain undoubtedly is damaged, however, I will try to preserve as much of it as possible. We will preserve the organs by placing them in containers and putting the containers in a large freezer.

"The Yrartz looks very thin by our standards. The legs have a metallic structure that appears to be support for them. The legs are quite thin and perhaps cannot hold the body up. We have noticed that the Yrartz move on wheels rather than walking as we do. However this specimen has no wheels attached to its supports.

"Make a note of that. We should ask the men who recovered the body if they saw any wheels that might have been attached at one time." NM took a breath. "Moving on we observe that the body appears to be less than a meter long. Does anyone have a tape measure?"

"Now so far I have not been able to identify any differences that would indicate whether this specimen is male or female." NM examined the lower parts closely. "Hmmm," he hummed as he searched. He stood up straight. "Seriously I do not see anything that conclusively tells me this is male or female. This is astounding. Perhaps astonishing is a better word."

The good doctor picked up a magnifying glass and continued looking, shaking his head. Standing straight up again he scratched his head. "Wow! This truly is unbelievable." Silence in the room. "Wait," he leaned closer once more, a big smile crossed his face. "There's the little thing." Turning to Shirley he said, "It's a boy."

"Hey I just realized something. I know this is the only body we examined so far, however this one has what appear to be horns on his head. From what Tom said some Yrartz seem to have round ears. This isn't scientific but perhaps the one we are examining is a male and could be identified by the horns and the eared ones are females." No one argued the point.

Dr. Roswell continued on with his examination having Shirley zoom in on each organ as he identified and removed them. She also took particular care with any points of interest NM expressed. They found the heart, the liver and the brain all of which were smaller than an adult humans would be. The organs were roughly the size of a human ten-year-olds.

"It appears as though the Yrartz are similar to us in many ways. They breathe oxygen, they bleed like we do, they need to eat. But they seem to need protein far more than we do. From the contents of this Yrartz' stomach protein was all he ate.

"From all the reports I have heard the Yrartz only are interested in protein. Further they ignore all other types of food. They are not particular what form the protein comes in either.

"Now, I have removed the brain and as I said earlier there was a head wound. The brain was severely damaged. We weighed it and it is several grams lighter than it should be judging from a size comparison with humans. The brain was the only major organ that sustained any damage."

Dr. Roswell placed the brain in a plastic container and snapped the lid on. "Here put this in the freezer with the other organs." Turning back to the body, "Well the Yrartz have red blood like ours but green skin."

Off camera someone asked, "Why do you think they have green skin doctor?"

"Chlorophyll I suppose," NM grinned.

"Maybe you start to mold after a while in space," someone else laughed.

"NM what do you want to do with the rest of the body?"

"I'm tempted to put the whole thing in the freezer but I don't believe there is enough room."

"Doc, I got room in my freezer. The one in my garage is empty. We could put it in there."
"Let's do it."

"Hey you don't think the rest of them will come looking for the body do you? You know like in some of them alien invaders movies?"

"No Joe," NM reassured him. "I think they probably made a cursory search of the area and gave up. I did not see any tracking device on the body or his equipment. I believe he was just another soldier and he fell at the wrong place at the wrong time."

Four men picked up the body and headed for Joe's place. The Yrartz had not done any damage to the electrical grid so the power was still on in West Falls. Joe's freezer would be the temporary storage for this alien invader.

# Chapter 18

The Shell Lake Institute of Astrophysics was like a firehouse when the alarm sounds. It seemed everyone was interested in getting to the meteorite impact area. Several of the professors began planning a fieldtrip for early Monday morning. Every student signed up to go along.

Doctors Blair Westby and Colby Strum were colleagues of Doctor Roswell. They were desperately trying to get hold of

NM. He was right in the impact area according to their best information.

They both thought how spectacular the sights he must have seen. What they didn't realize was that NMs cabin was nestled in amongst the trees of the forest. Since the meteor shower wasn't expected to be something special Doctor Roswell hadn't bothered to go outside. He didn't see anything.

Kaitlyn Holmen and her husband Matt were graduate students at the Institute of Astrophysics. She was studying astrobiology. Kaitlyn was fascinated by the serious study of something that doesn't exist. Most of her professors said the same about Bible studies. But she knew that God was real. She wasn't so certain about aliens.

They had been married just eighteen months and already both of them wondered why. At first there had been frequent hot passion and angry fights. Soon the passion ceased and eventually so did the fights. Now the pair no longer shared a bed or slept in the same room. Sometimes he didn't come home at all.

Husband Matt wanted to go to the impact area now, before anyone else got there. He and some friends were hoping to make a discovery prior to the fieldtrip on Monday. Such a find would put them at the top of the class at least for a time.

Kaitlyn argued against going. She felt it would cause more trouble than it was worth with their professors. "They are already planning a fieldtrip. Why do we have to get there first?" she asked.

"Because we can and should. We could discover something special and get our names in some prestigious scientific magazine." He heard all the arguments before and was getting tired of her always trying to stop him. Well this time he would go with or without her.

Jared Barnes, Kara Sanborn, Amery Rhinelander and Carter Wentworth planned to go with the Holmen's. All were graduate students at the Institute. They all shared Matt's enthusiasm for the chance at such a huge discovery.

Since Matt and Kaitlyn had the only vehicle large enough to transport them all they took it. "I'll drive," Matt said as the six of them headed for the parking lot.

"You're so excited about this I'm not sure you should," Kaitlyn said. *Am I the only one who is worried about this road trip?*

"Oh come on Kate," Matt said. "Share the excitement with me. You act like you don't want to go. What's wrong?"

"I don't know. I just have a bad feeling about this. I think we should wait until the fieldtrip."

Jared spoke up, "Hey Kat get with the program. This will be fun and it may even be profitable. We just might find something valuable. Whether we do or not at least we get away from here for a little while."

Kaitlyn scanned their faces and realized she was the only apprehensive one. They all had on their happy/excited faces. She felt like she was being sucked into a black hole or something. She recently read that book about an alien fungus that came from outer space and killed everything on the planet. Sure it was fiction but what if they really found something like that?

Bob, Tom and Nate got out of their beds and headed for the church kitchen. The aroma of a noon meal was flowing to every corner of the basement, assaulting their noses like a culinary temptress. Nate took the lead as expected.

"What is that that smells so good?" Nate asked.

"Whatever it is it isn't your cooking," Bob said.

"Yeah and thank God for that," Nate agreed, nodding his head.

When they entered the dining area each man took a tray and stepped up to the counter. One of the ladies in the kitchen handed Nate a bowl of potatoes and one of meat. "Here take these to your table," she told him. "And make sure you share with the rest."

"Oh I will, I will," he promised.

The cook handed Tom a bowl of beans and one of salad. He took the bowls and thanked the cook.

Kelly came in just as the boys were finishing up. "Did you guys leave any for me?"

"Oh sure sis. I think there's a half a roll and maybe a carrot or two."

She placed her arm on Nate's shoulder and leaned in, face to face with him. "Really nice of you to think of me big brother."

"Is that a crack about my weight?" Nate asked with a hurt look on his face.

"Only if you want it to be," she said. Kelly sat down and started dishing up potatoes and gravy. "This looks good. Is there meat and vegetables here too?"

The boys passed everything her way. They decided to stay and wait for Kelly to eat before seeking out Bill Webster. The men would ask for an assignment when they saw him.

"So what are you guys planning," she asked.

"We don't know what Bill has in mind," Tom answered.

"I hope it's something good," Nate said rubbing his hands together.

"Like what?" Bob asked.

"Oh I don't know but I hope it's exciting and ah maybe useful too."

Joe came into the dining area. He walked over to the group. "Hi guys."

"Hello Joe," Tom said.

"Say Bill wants to see you guys right away."

"What's up Joe? You know what he wants?"

"No Tom I don't, but he has some mission for you. He wants all four of you," Joe told them.

"Me too?" Kelly asked surprised. She quickly stuffed the rest of her food in her mouth and stood up grabbing her coat.

"Bill's over at the machine shop," Joe said.


Bill had taken over Ted Hawkins shop including the office. The place looked like a typical tractor and farm machinery repair facility. There were tractors in various states of repair both in the building and outside in the yard. There were machine parts strewn about and even a few in some kind of order on shelves.

The place had seen some form of white paint on walls and ceiling at a time in distant memory. The windows were partly painted, partly dirty. There were tools neatly placed in racks and tool chests. Ted was a stickler for taking proper care of tools. The tools seemed oddly out of tune with the soiled disarray.

The group went to the office. The room was big enough for a couple of beat up filing cabinets and an equally marred desk. The disarray continued in here with papers and parts lying about. It was a stark, no frills room. The only accomodation to comfort was a lumpy couch, an ancient fan of dubious reliability and a nearly new adjustable office chair.

Bill looked up from his work as the foursome approached. "Oh good you're all here." He motioned them to some chairs and the couch. "Take a seat. I have a mission I need to discuss with you all."

He waited for them to get comfortable. Nate, Kelly and Bob took the couch. Tom chose a chair that faith said would hold him up. They all looked to Bill and waited for him to proceed.

"Well I'm glad you all came. I have a mission for the four of you that is dangerous and may very well fail." He paused to let that sink in. "Before anyone asks I'll tell you what I want."

"You all know we have had virtually no contact with the outside since yesterday morning. With the exception of a few minutes early this morning the cell phones have been out. The land lines are down too. For some reason the Yrartz have left the power alone but TV reception and internet are down. We all have those bundled together so we know why those are out.

"You found the bridge over Telemark Creek is down. We have no other road out of town. We are surrounded on three sides by the Bibon. The Yrartz hold the north and the road out. We don't know if they have us completely surrounded or not.

"What I need you to do, if you are willing, is to discover the truth of the matter. Are we surrounded or not? Can we get out through the swamp? Have the Yrartz taken over the entire country and maybe the world or is this an isolated invasion?" Bill sat back and waited for a response.

Tom began, "The first question that comes to my mind is why us?" The others nodded in agreement.

"Well at least you started with an easy one. You four are the youngest adults in town. Therefore I believe you are in the best shape and most able to succeed in this mission."

"Okay so where would you like us to try? What direction?" Tom asked.

"First I'd like to know if you agree to go on this mission."
"I don't speak for anyone but myself," Tom said. "Yes I will go."
"I'm with my brother," Bob added.

"I'm in," Kelly said and looked at her brother.

*I'm running out of candy bars so it's either go or?* "Sure I'm in. I go where they go," Nate gestured.

"Good I was hoping you would say that. But keep in mind this isn't going to be a picnic. You could all die. We don't know what is happening in the rest of the world." Bill paused to let that sink in. "As to where I want you to go," he stood up and pushed a map across the desk. Leaning over it he began to outline his plan.

"I think the obvious first choice is northwest. See here where the Bibon has a short arm extending up and kind of surrounds Earl Stinnett's place?" Each of them looked at the map where Bill was pointing. "Now this is a fairly short distance across here. On the other side is forest road 1210. That is by far the closest road to West Falls that might not already be taken over by the Yrartz.

"Now the only other sensible choice is southeast. But if you go that way you have to cross a creek and more than twice as much of the swamp. I've been in there and it's a tough go and I was in it during cold weather when much of the Bibon was frozen. Even then it was a heck of trek."

"Yes Bill I have been in there too," Tom said. "I agree it isn't my first choice. It is extremely wet and full of hummocks. We would quickly exhaust ourselves trying to go thru that."

"We all been up here through at least part of this area," Bob pointed at the map. "It has its wet spots too but I think we can get across."

"Right, we tracked a wounded deer in there once. I forgot that. Good call Bob."

"Was that the big one horned buck we trailed in the rain that time?" Nate asked.

"Yep," the brothers said in unison.

"So you guys know this area then?" Bill asked.

"Well I wouldn't exactly say we know it, but we have been in the area. We have an idea what to expect and what to look for," Tom answered.

"Have you gone all the way to 1210?"

"No we haven't. But we got close. We zigzagged across the swamp several times. I'm certain it's passible even this time of year."

"Okay that's settled. You go northwest. Now what do you guys need in the way of supplies? We don't know how long you will be out there," Bill said.

"I think we could make out with two days' supply of food and water." Tom looked at the others. "What do you think?"

"Sounds good to me," Bob said.

*Let's see I need twenty candy bars each day so two days would be...* "Nate?"

"Huh? Oh sure two day's worth."

"What about weapons? You guys aren't going to want to carry a double-barrel shotgun through the swamp."

"What did you have in mind Bill?" Tom asked.

A smile crossed Bills face. "I went rummaging around in Ted's house. It seems he has some, how do I put it, special weapons. He stored them in a gun safe at his place."

"Gun safe? You mean gun cabinet, right?" Tom asked.

"No I mean gun safe. Yes he had a gun cabinet where he kept his sporting guns. But he also had a safe. It was hidden in his garage."

"What kind of guns are they? We know he had an M-16 and a Tommy gun. Is that what you are talking about?"

"Nope. Gordon and I found the safe, opened it and found these," Bill said as he pulled two Heckler and Koch MP-5s out of a desk drawer. With a big smile on his face Bill announced, "These are MP-5s. I think they are the sf A-3 version which means they are semi-automatic.

"I want you to take these with you. They are short enough to be much more convenient then a shotgun and these are 9mm so you can carry a lot of ammo. And it seems our Mr. Hawkins had several cases of 9mm. I'm not sure if he was expecting an invasion or what?"

Bob reached out to take one of the MP-5s and Tom slapped his hand. "Don't touch it until you know how to use it."

Ignoring his brother he turned to Nate, "Hey man you were talking about a machinegun. Well these are machineguns, well at least semi-automatics anyway."

Nate stood up and moved closer to the desk, careful not to touch the weapons. His eyes got big. "Wow these are cool. Just what we need to take out those little green buggers."

"Guys hang on a moment," Tom said to them. Turning to Bill he continued, "I think Bill has more to show us."

Bill had the floor again. "As a matter of fact I do have more. Ted had some very interesting items in his safe that I don't believe he wanted just everyone to know about. I think it would be best if we don't let people know about them either."

Having said that Bill placed several hand grenades on the desk. He bent down and picked up some more objects, put them next to the grenades. By the time he was done the guys were in awe of Mr. Ted Hawkins.

There were smoke grenades, parachute flares and an assortment of fireworks. There were semi-automatic handguns. Flash-bangs, a small amount of C-4 and some old-fashioned dynamite also cluttered the desk.

"Do you guys think you can use these?" Bill asked, considerable sarcasm in his voice.

"I do believe we might find a use for these items," Tom agreed.

"Can I have a grenade?" Nate asked.

"NO!" Tom and Kelly said in unison. Nate looked hurt.

"It's for your own good," Bob assured him. "They're afraid you will accidently eat it." Nathan swatted his pal.


The foursome found backpacks and even some web gear to carry the equipment in. They helped each other pack and adjust the gear. They checked to make sure things didn't rattle or make noise.

"Tom what else do we need to bring?" Bob asked.

"More candy bars," Nate suggested.

"What's your favorite candy bar Nate?"

"Milkyway. I think you must have Milkyways to sustain life."

"Nate may have the right idea there. Except instead of candy we should take some energy bars, something like that." Tom began searching through the leftover pile. Kelly joined him and they soon found the box they were looking for.

"Here," Kelly handed out the energy bars.

"Everyone make sure you have plenty of ammo. We can live for a couple of days without water and a week without food if we have to. But we won't live ten minutes if we run out of ammunition in a firefight with these goobers." Tom was ready to go but nervous at finding himself in charge of this group. He was responsible for the welfare of all of them as well as the success of the mission. He believed if they failed the town was doomed.


Bill decided to have Tom's unit leave with as little fanfare as possible. He believed some of the town's folk would panic if they saw the group leave. Others might demand to go with.

Still others might object to the weapons leaving. These were the best guns in town.

Bob took his truck and went to the home he and his brother shared. He had the guns and equipment Bill had given them hidden in the bed. He put the truck in the garage to conceal everything.

Next Kelly and Tom walked over to the house acting as if they were just on a romantic stroll through town. They tried to appear as nonchalant as possible. No one really noticed them except for neighbors who merely gave a friendly greeting.

Finally Nathan arrived on his bicycle. The tires were nearly flat and the bike groaned from the weight but he made it. His legs were screaming at him. He hadn't done that much walking and bike riding in a long time and he was feeling the soreness deep down.

Bob and Tom were almost ready and Kelly was loading magazines. She tossed a couple empties at Nate. "Here load these and be quick big brother. Tom wants us out of here within the hour."

"Okay sis. But you don't have to throw things at me. Say Bob do you have any candy around here?"

"No and you really don't need it. We do have some energy bars though. Want some?"

"No thanks."

"Nathan?"

"Yeah bro?"

"You going to wear that," Tom asked pointing to the T-shirt he had on.

"I planned on it, why?"

"Oh I don't know. You know I'm all for a T-shirt that says 'Jesus is the answer to all your problems.' However a white T-shirt, no matter whose face is on it, is probably not the right attire for sneaking through the woods. Could you put on some of your camo gear please?"

"Sure Tom. I'll do it right now."

"You dumb cluck," Bob said as he punched Nate's shoulder.

"Ouch, you don't have to be mean about it," Nate whined. He took off that shirt and put on a different one.

"What color is that?" Bob asked.

"It's eggplant," Nathan answered. He was proud of the fact that he knew the names of even the less common colors.

"That's eggplant?" Bob questioned. "I thought eggplant was purple. That shirt is black."

"Burnt eggplant," Nate replied. He grabbed his camo jacket and put it on to allay any further trouble.

"Tom how are we going to get out of here without being seen?" Kelly asked.

"I have a plan."

"Care to enlighten us?"

"Well Kelly, we will go out in pairs in different directions. That way no one sees us all together.

"I think people will believe we are just going out to patrol the town. That at least is my hope and plan. You and Nate go out the back door and down Pine Street straight towards the Washburn's house. Bob and I will go to The Rose and act as if we are checking that establishment out.

"We won't spend much time there but we will make it look good. Then we head to NMs cabin and past that into the woods. We can walk the path between NMs and the Washburn's."

"What happens if Sarona comes out and asks us what we are doing?" Kelly asked.

"Tell her the truth and ask her not to tell anyone," Tom shrugged. "What else can we do?"

They all agreed to Tom's plan. But Kelly had one more thing. "Say you think we should say a prayer before we go? This is a pretty dangerous mission after all."

Tom smiled. "You know that's a very good suggestion." He bowed his head and the others followed suit. "Lord Jesus we ask you to protect us as we go out and try to find a way to escape these enemies. Help us to find the right path and guide us on our mission. Amen." Everyone added their amens.

Kelly and Nate started out first even though they had the shortest distance to go. They left by the back door and between the houses to Pine Street. The brothers waited ten minutes and exited by the front door. They walked down Cedar Street to The Rose and checked it from the outside.

No one bothered Bob and Tom. They saw no one either. Kelly and Nate were not so lucky. Three people saw them and stopped to talk to them. The siblings tried to act normal and give out no useful information. They were brief without being rude.

Bob and Tom made it through the woods to the rendezvous point first. There was a good stand of hemlock with their feathery, deep green needles. But in October the trees had many yellow needles ready to fall. They stood under one large hemlock tree. This area was mostly hemlock, tamarack and birch fading into cedar in the swamp.

The four linked up in these woods at the edge of the swamp behind Gordon and Sarona's house. "Okay everyone take a last look at each others equipment before we go. Make sure you have what you need and everything is secure. We don't want any more noise than absolutely necessary," Tom said.

Kelly checked Nathan's pack and shifted things around a bit. Nate was looking at Bob's pack while he checked his brother's equipment. Tom moved Kelly's rig and pulled the straps tight.

"Everyone ready?" Tom asked. "Okay let's go." He started off into the Bibon. The team headed north by northwest, Tom leading the way with Kelly right behind. Next came Nate and finally at the rear Bob.

# Chapter 19

The old game trail behind Gordon's house led across the swamp from one point of solid ground to another. It left the swamp near forest road 1210 and continued on through the forest. The trail was an ancient one first used by animals, later by man.

It never was much of a path, only a few inches wide at the widest. But it was the best way across this section of the Bibon. Few people knew of it and fewer still used it but it would be valuable today.

Bob, Tom and Nate had all been on the trail a time or two. They knew where it was and where it went and that was about all. In a dry year you wouldn't get your feet wet. In a wet year you could drown. It was a middle year so they expected to get wet feet as they moved along the path.

In addition to being the leader of the team Tom felt he should take point as they moved through the swamp. His eyes were constantly on the move checking everything. Any movement brought a halt to the column while he peered into the brush trying to determine what caused the movement.

Minds were on high alert and all eyes were wide open. Nervous fingers were on every trigger ready to go into combat mode. Well almost every trigger. Nate had his on his second candy bar of the mission.

When they first entered the swamp the trees were mostly cedar and spaced far enough to allow easy travel. It was perpetually dark under these but enough light filtered through so they could move safely without fear of tripping over roots. The cedars gave way to tag alders and other small brush. These grew closer together and made movement more difficult.

The small brush gave way to a mixture of grasses and even smaller brush. The sky was visible and therefore more light was available. In this area the team was exposed. Tom disliked this and decided to detour around the more open areas. He figured they could afford the slight delay it would cost them.

Tom backtracked into the cedars again then turned straight north. They stayed in these trees until he saw something ahead. He stopped and waved the rest to stop and get down. Resting on his knees he waited until he was sure that everyone had stopped and were in defensive positions.

Peering around a tree he saw two Yrartz. They seemed to be guarding something but Tom couldn't make out what. He turned and crab walked back to the others.

"What is it?" Bob whispered.

Tom held his finger to his lips indicating they should keep quiet. He motioned them to move farther back. They followed him and when he felt they were out of earshot he stopped.

"What is it?" Bob asked again.

"I'm not sure. I saw two Yrartz and they seemed to be guarding something. I couldn't tell what is was. I think Bob and I should go around and approach it from the side, find out what is so important."

"Good idea," Nate said.

"Except for the part where I go with," Bob added.

"No, that's a good idea too," Nate insisted.

"Do you have a guess as to what it is?" Kelly asked.

"I'm not sure. I have an idea but, well here goes. I think they may be guarding some of their ships."

"Spaceships. Really?"

"Not sure and since we don't know what the ships look like who knows," Tom shrugged. "Doesn't matter right now. What does matter is they are in our path and we need to find out what it is and why it's important. We need to find out how many Yrartz are there and whether we should attack them or not."

"I really don't think we should attack them," Nate offered.

Tom ignored that comment. "What do these ships, if that's what they are, look like?" Kelly asked.

"Well like I said I'm not certain. I think they look like a large ball with a stick stuck out the back or the front. Whichever it is."

"So they look like a lollipop?" Nate asked.

"Leave it to my brother to think of food."
"No they are lying horizontal and I think they are a kind of dirty grayish-brown."

"So more like a lollipop that fell in the dirt?"

"Okay so Bob are you ready to go?" Tom was anxious to find out what the things were and continue the mission. They dropped their packs so they could travel more quickly taking only what they needed.

Bob and Tom moved off in the direction of the Yrartz. "Tom, should we split up?"

"No, we stick together. That way if one of us gets into trouble the other can help. We don't know how many Yrartz are here or exactly where they are. I figure the more eyes we have looking out the better."

"Then why didn't we all come? Why didn't you have Nate and Kelly come too?"

"Because if you and I get in a bind they can either rescue us or go back to town. Or they could continue the mission. If it comes to it we may distract the Yrartz so Kelly and Nate can get through.

"Any way we can complete the mission will do. We need to find out what is going on and whether we are alone in this."

"Okay I understand. So let's go."

Once again Tom led the way with Bob following. The area was white cedar scattered among tall grasses and the occasional tag alder. There were some islands in the swamp with birch and hemlock and even a few white pine.

The Yrartz were guarding several acres of flattened grass. Some of the objects had slammed into cedars knocking them down as well and opening up more space. There were dozens, perhaps hundreds of the metallic things.

Tom crept up close to the edge of the flattened grass. He lay down partly behind a tree. Bob joined him there. The brothers watched for several minutes without moving. They saw no aliens only the ships.

After checking all around Tom pulled out a pair of binoculars. He zeroed in on one object and then another and another. The ships, for now he was sure that's what they were, seemed to be of two different sizes but otherwise the same.

Handing the binocs to Bob he said, "Check it out. I'm sure they are ships. Some are larger. See that one over there. I think some bring just one or two Yrartz. Others bring a whole troop or some equipment."

Bob looked at some of the ships. "I think you're right. It looks like there are hundreds of them or at least twenty."

Tom smiled grimly, "I'm pretty sure there are more than twenty. Anyway we need to move. If these are ships and we're sure they are, there have to be more than just those two aliens guarding them."

Tom got up into a half crouch and moved off to the left. Bob followed. They went only a few feet before Tom dropped and Bob did the same. The two Yrartz were rolling toward them. The brothers weren't sure if they had been seen.

Yrartz 713 and his partner 1001 had been on guard duty since arriving on earth. It was dull, boring work that allowed the thoughts to wander when the feet couldn't. It was the same mind numbing duty throughout the universe. One craved a change, a little excitement, a little action. Anything to break up the tedious routine.

The pair were rolling along on what seemed their ten-millionth trip around the perimeter. As usual they were talking and not paying attention to anything. They went past Bob and Tom without a second glance and continued on.

Relief flooded the brothers. They were certain they had been blown but the two Yrartz seemed to take no notice of them. Even so they stayed down until the aliens were well past.

"Those two are the same ones I saw before," Tom said.

"How do know?"

"The one has a tear in his armor up near the right shoulder."

Tom slowly got up and motioned for his brother to do the same. The pair moved off directly away from the landing site. When a safe distance they headed back to Kelly and Nate.

"You ever see that trailer for *Giant Cats?*" Nate asked his sister.

"No Nate I never have. You know I don't watch those kind of movies," *unless I'm with Tom.*

"Yeah I know. But anyway it goes like this; *Giant Cats from Outer Space. They're friendly until they get hungry. Then they're very friendly.*"

She looked at him oddly. "So what does that have to do with this?"

"I think the Yrartz are like that," he paused. "Well except for the friendly part."

That caused Kelly to roll her eyes at him. "Shush!" she said. "I hear something moving in the brush." The duo listened intently, guns up and ready. "There," Kelly pointed as she eased her gun down. "It's Tom and Bob."

Relief swept over Nathan. "I gotta pee. Be right back."

Bob and Tom walked up to Kelly. "Hey where's Nate going?" Bob asked.

"He needs some alone time," Kelly answered. "So what's up there?"

"We were right. It is a landing zone. There are dozens, maybe hundreds of ships"

Nate came rumbling back pulling up his zipper. "So what do they look like? Can we drive one?"

"They look like a fuzzy lollipop, like Tom said. And no you can't drive one. You are about the same size as the smaller ships. You couldn't even get in one."

Nate's face saddened. He harbored dreams of flying a Yrartz ship and possibly using it to attack them. Now those dreams were shattered on the cold hard rocks of reality.

Clouds moved in threatening rain. The air cooled some as well. Now the already dark swamp took on an ominous feel. The day shifted from okay to serious paranoia. Every rock, every tree, every bush taking on an eerie cast.

Commander 1881 was tasked with the attack on West Falls. He decided to come in from the back, the south west end of town. His scouts quickly nixed that idea when they told him of the pond behind and next to The Rose.

"We can't attack from where I wanted to on the south west. So we attack from the northwest. This will work better anyway since it is close to our base and our ships.

"Now all you unit commanders gather round. I have your assignments marked on the map." 1881 continued giving out orders to the Yrartz leaders in preparation for the imminent assault.

# Chapter 20

The intrepid foursome crouched behind some trees looking across the landing zone. All was quiet when suddenly a loud rumbling sound emanated from close by.

"Nate, was that your stomach? Man you gotta find a way to control that thing. It's making so much noise I can't hear anything else."

"Shush!" Tom whisper-yelled. "You guys keep it down. I can't hear anything but your yapping."

"It's not us," Bob protested. "It's Nate's stomach."

"Shut up!" Kelly added, whispering intently.

Nathan had been lying on the ground too long. He desperately needed to move and stretch. Now with both Kelly and Tom mad at him and Bob he just wanted to get a little distance between them.

Nathan stood up. "Yowww! Eeeeee!" Yrartz 713 howled. He had never seen so large a person before. He thought the swamp was rising up to engulf him. Nate almost lost his water.

713 turned and sped away as fast as his wheels would take him. His head was turned back so he could watch the thing. He went screaming and suddenly disappeared.

Yrartz 1001 was looking in a different direction. Startled, he saw what his partner had seen. He started screaming only a second after 713. He too turned and followed 713 in a headlong dash. When he got to the place where his partner vanished he fell into the same hole and disappeared.

"Did you guys see that? That was awesome," Nathan said laughing. "They were coming up behind us and all the sudden they ran away and disappeared."

"We saw most of it," Tom said as he ran past Nate. He stopped just shy of the place the Yrartz fell in. The others gathered on either side. They all peered down at what looked to be just a large puddle.

"What is it Tom?"

"Looks like a sink hole. There are places in the swamp up here where there isn't any solid ground. You step there and you go right down through the roots of the trees. Usually you don't come back up. The tree roots close over the hole. You won't find a way up and out of that."

"Man it sucks to be them," Bob said. Turning to Nathan he put out his hand. "Way to go bro. You found a sink hole and got rid of two Yrartz all at one time."

Nate shook his hand. "You know what I think? I think Yrartz are proof God has a sense of humor."

Tom said nothing, he reached his arm around Kelly and pulled her close. She leaned her head on his shoulder. They stood there looking at the hole in the swamp, their faces emotionless masks.

"Hey, maybe the shortest distance between two points isn't a straight line. Might be a sinkhole," Nate suggested.

"Dude, you might be right," Bob said. Kelly rolled her eyes in disbelief that this was her brother. Tom just shook his head.

"Well at least I didn't wet myself," Nathan commented.

They all turned from the hole. "I read somewhere that a man needs to drink at least 125 ounces of water and all fluids a day to stay healthy," Bob said.

"Really? What is that in dog years?" Nate asked.

Pastor Gordon Washburn had a feeling, an inkling. He found Bill Webster walking the perimeter near the command post. "What are you doing out here preacher?"

"Well I had this feeling something was going to happen today. I'm not going to cower in the church while my friends, my parishioners are out here fighting for our lives. I have to be here side by side with everyone else."

"Of all the preachers I've met in my life I think I would rather have you by my side over any of the rest." Bill walked along a while then stopped. "What is it you think is going to happen? What does your inkling warn you of?"

Pastor Gordon thought a moment. "I'm not really sure. It just seems as if something is out of place. I can't put my finger on it, can't quite see it clearly.

"I woke up this morning with an uneasy sense that something was wrong. It seems to be getting worse as the day goes on. I feel like I need to do something but it just isn't forming in my mind. You ever get that?"

"Sometimes," Bill agreed. "But I run a bar and grill. When I get an uneasy feeling something was missed or wrong I figure I forgot to buy enough beer or peanuts."

Bill put a hand on Gordon's shoulder. "Why don't you go home and see your wife and kids. Stay there for a while. Maybe it will ease your mind and let you think more clearly."

"Maybe you're right. I think that's just what I will do."

Bob and Nate walked into the landing zone together. "I think the Yrartz ships look more like a Q-tip than a lollipop," Bob said. "Except for the color."

Nathan agreed. "A giant Q-tip, a giant dirty Q-tip."

Kelly and Tom were together on the other side of the zone. "I don't see any more of the aliens. Do you think there were only those two?"

"I don't know Kelly. I hope so. We could spend a little time looking things over here and maybe find a way to destroy or at least damage some of these ships.

"It might help to know a bit more about the Yrartz too. Looking through the ships could give us some clues. Just maybe we could help end this invasion and get things back to normal around here."

She looked at him quizzically. "You really think this place will ever be normal again?"

He gave her a wry smile. "No I guess you're right. There is no way things will ever go back to the way they were."

The two pairs walked toward each other. As they came close Tom could hear Bob and Nate arguing but he couldn't make out what they were saying.

"Tom is it Emily Dickinson or Emily Davidson?" Bob asked.

"Davidson." He thought a moment. "You're talking about the old lady that lives down the road right?"

"What was that about?" Kelly asked.

"Haven't a clue."


Commander 1881 had his final meeting with the unit commanders before the attack. They were set up in a field south of Earl's Road. The Yrartz were lined up along the edge of the swamp checking equipment and getting ready.

There was the nervous chatter of an army preparing for battle. Some of the Yrartz worked silently. Some had to talk to hide their nerves. Many worried that they had forgotten something important, some one thing that they would need suddenly. They would go down their mental checklist one more time.

Over four hundred Yrartz would participate in this battle. The plan was to move through the swamp and hit West Falls from the back. Another group was waiting along Tamarack Road ready to pounce on the town from the north.

That unit numbered just three hundred. However they had reserves up at Telemark Creek and at Granny Hayward's over on Hawthorne Road. The Hawthorne Road unit doubled as reserves for Commander 1881s group. Both reserve units numbered around two hundred and fifty.

All the Yrartz units were on high alert. They all had to be ready to move at any time. The key was 1881s attack. If it was successful the units to the north were supposed to attack. The Hawthorne Road reserves were to move up into position to back the northern assault. If all went well the Yrartz would take the town and be able to eat the residents at their leisure.

Meeting over, the Yrartz commanders started moving their troops into the swamp. The point unit moved to the front and waited for the signal to begin the assault.


Pastor Gordon started to take Bill's advice and head home but a thought stopped him. He found Bill again. "Bill I think I need some assistance. I think what has been bothering me is a noise I heard early this morning when I went outside with the dog. Old Jeff started barking like he always does. Usually he quiets down and goes to do his business.

"But this morning he stopped barking and started growling. He did that for a couple of minutes and then all the sudden he turned tail and ran back to the house. He stayed on the porch and wouldn't go to the bathroom or anything. He acted as if something bad was out there."

"So you think there might be some Yrartz lurking around your place?" Bill asked.

"Maybe or it could have just been a bear again," Gordon said. "But I guess I want to go check it out. Maybe bring a couple of the guys and search out back of the house."

This brought an unexpected response from Bill. "John you are in charge. I have to go with pastor to check out his place." Bill turned toward some of the men lingering at the berm. "I need three or four of you guys right now. Carl Vue, Ed, Slim, you guys come with me."

Looking at Pastor Gordon he said, "Come on. I just sent Tom, Bob, Nate and Kelly into the swamp right there. We have to go and see if the Yrartz are already there." Bill jumped into a pickup truck and started the engine. Gordon didn't waste any time climbing in. The rest of the guys jumped into the back and hung on for dear life.

Bill pushed the truck to its max not obeying speed limits or any other traffic law. He was worried about the unit he had sent out and he was worried about pastor's wife and kids. Gordon Washburn worried only about his family. He hardly heard what Bill had said.

"Can this thing go any faster?" Gordon asked. "We need to get there ten minutes ago."

"I'm giving you all she's got," Bill replied. He didn't bother looking at Pastor Gordon. He knew what he would see. He desperately wanted everyone to be alright. Like pastor he was praying too.

"Pastor you gave a sermon once, something about the more I get to know you the less I hate you. The more I understand you the less I want to harm you. Somehow I don't think that applies in this case."

Gordon didn't answer. He jumped out of the truck before Bill had it fully stopped. Sarona had looked out the living room window just as the vehicle came roaring up the driveway. She knew immediately something was wrong.

Their dog Jeff started barking the moment he heard the truck. Sarona opened the front door as Gordon ran toward the house. Jeff rushed out the opening and barked at everyone before running around to the back of the house.

"What is it?" Sarona asked fearfully. "What's going on?"

Gordon stopped in front of her and reached for her. "We think the Yrartz may be coming here. I heard noises earlier this morning and Jeff was acting odd. We think they may attack the town someplace close so I came to get you and the kids out of here."

He stopped talking long enough to catch his breath. "Did you see Bob, Tom, Nate and or Kelly within the last hour or so?" Bill asked.

"No I didn't, but Jeff put up a ferocious fit of barking about then. Why would I have seen those kids?"

"Bill sent them on a mission into the Bibon. They should have come through here close to our house but they may have been trying to stay hidden," Gordon explained.

Suddenly Jeff squealed from the back of the house and came running back around. "Gather up some clothes for all of us. I'll round up the kids." Sarona didn't wait for any further instructions. She went immediately back inside and raced from room to room picking up clothes and other necessary items.

Bill said, "We will go around back and see what's up." Waving the men over he added, "The Yrartz won't get to anyone. We will guard the house until you are clear."

With that Bill and the rest of the guys went toward the back of the house. They almost made it. Slim was the first to see a Yrartz but Carl was quicker on the draw.

One of the Yrartz was poorly hidden in the trees at the edge of the lawn. Carl shot him twice while Slim added another round. Ed saw another alien nearby and cut loose too.

Bill stopped where he was and peered intently into the woods. His eyes got big. What he saw wasn't what he was hoping for. "Men! Start retreating. There are all kinds of them in the woods. Ed you go alert Gordon and Sarona and help them get everybody out now!"

The Yrartz commanders realizing the element of surprise was gone began yelling at their troops to move forward. They came out of woods and swamp from three different sides. The aliens moved slowly now that they knew how effective the humans were at defending themselves.

The foursome heard the gunshots and wondered what was happening so near. But they continued checking the ships and looking for ways to sabotage or destroy them. Tom smashed the butt of his gun against the glass bubble over the pilot's seat but it didn't break. The bubble was also the door to the ship. Soon he discovered he could push the bubble back far enough to break the hinges.

Nathan quickly found he could not fit in any of the ships but he could get far enough to sort of sit in the pilots chair. He broke as many as he could. "They are going to be very uncomfortable when next they fly somewhere," he said in answer to Bob's quizzical look.

Most of the Yrartz ships were of the smaller size. They had either one or two seats. The ships with a single seat had a cargo space directly behind the pilot's chair. The two seaters had chairs inline, pilot in front copilot behind him.

Tom entered one of the large ships. "Hey Tom, you sure you should be in there?" Bob asked nervously. "These guys may come back at any time."

"If you mean the two that fell into the sink hole I don't think we have to worry about them."

"I was thinking of the rest of the invasion force."

"Come on in Bob. It's unlikely you will ever get a better look at an alien ship." Kelly took Tom up on his invitation.

"Wow! These are ten times as big," Kelly said when she entered the ship.

"Yep and I think these are the main troop ships. They may also carry cargo, whatever supplies they have." Tom examined the controls. "I think if we damaged or destroyed these bigger ships the aliens wouldn't be able to leave. These must be able to haul at least ten Yrartz plus the crew."

"I think you're right, but why would you want them to stay? I thought we were trying to get rid of them."

"We are Kelly. But if they can't leave they may be more interested in communicating with us and maybe even have real negotiations. It could help us by demoralizing them too."

Bob entered the big ship and looked around. "This is more what I expected aliens to have. How many do you suppose will fit in here?"

"I'm thinking ten plus a two Yrartz crew," Tom answered.

"The outside looks like all plastic and metal. Inside it looks like a cramped camper," Bob said. "This thing here looks like a minifridge." He tried the handle but it would not budge.

"Bob leave that alone. These things might have some kind of a self-destruct device in them," Tom suggested.

"Whoa bro, you really think so?" Nate asked as he too entered the ship.

All four had to stoop to get in the ship. None of them could stand up straight. The floor was metal with a nonstick substance on the surface. Most of the walls had storage cabinets attached so that there were few blank spaces.

"Guys, maybe one of us should get out of the ship and pay attention to the surroundings. One of the Yrartz may come looking for the missing guards." Tom continued, "Besides there really isn't enough room for all of us."

"The little ships look like dirty Q-tips. This one looks similar only bigger and longer," Nate said as he backed out the door.

# Chapter 21

Pastor Gordon rushed his children out the door and into his car. "You guys wait here. Don't get out of the car. Your mom or I will be back to drive you to the church." With that he went back in the house to help his wife. He knew there was a battle taking place just outside and he wanted to get everyone safely away.

"Fall back men," Bill advised. "We can't hold off this many aliens." Bill looked around to see if the pastor and his wife were outside yet.

Slim, Carl and Ed were firing at the Yrartz as fast as they popped into sight. The trio weren't killing very many but they were scaring a lot of them. Even so the aliens kept coming and the men kept retreating.

Bill finally saw Gordon and Sarona leaving the house. "Get to the truck men and be quick about it." He went running for the vehicle, the other three right behind him.

Sarona had her car running and Bill started the truck. "Where's Jeff?" the younger boy, Brad, asked.

She looked around the car and the yard. Sarona could hear barking. "He's still in the house. Gordy Jeff is in the house."

Gordon unhooked his seatbelt. "I'll go get him," he said as he exited the auto.

"Hurry honey," Sarona encouraged. Gordon ran to the porch and took the steps two at a time. Sarona gasped. Yrartz were coming around the left corner of the house. She looked to the right and they were coming around that corner too.

She took off her seatbelt and got out of the car. Sarona stood next to the vehicle a worried look on her face as she rubbed her hands together. She was silently praying Gordon would hurry up and come out.

"What's the hold up?" Bill shouted.

"Gordy went back inside to get the dog."

Bill already had the truck turned around headed back to town. Now he had to wait. "Guys, get ready to shoot. Pastor is still in the house."

"You hear all that shooting?" Bob asked.

"Yes I do and I think we should get moving," Kelly said. "Tom, don't you think we should get out of here, now!"

He was still trying to damage as many Yrartz ships as he could. Tom looked up as Kelly and Bob approached. He cocked his ear and listened to the sounds of battle.

"You know I think you guys are right. It sounds like the fight is going on near Pastor's place. That really isn't so far from us.

"Where's Nathan? Either of you seen him lately?"

"I think he went into the woods to relieve himself," Bob said.

"About how long ago was that?" Tom asked. "Doesn't matter. Bob go find him now. Kelly and I will go to the northern end of the LZ and see if there are any more Yrartz up there. You come as quickly as you can and meet us there."

Bob said okay and ran to find Nate. Kelly and Tom picked up their packs and headed north. There was no going in a straight line because there were so many ships spread out in no particular order.

Bob found Nathan almost immediately. He grabbed Nate's sleeve and pulled. "Come on Nate. The Yrartz are attacking somewhere. We think it is close to Pastor Gordon's house."

"Oh wow! If they are that close some of them may come here. We better go now," he said as he reached for his pack and shotgun. Nate straightened up to see Bob gazing off in the direction of the shooting. His pack fell off and he had to fix a strap.

Bob touched his shoulder. "Nate we gotta go buddy. Come on." Nate was still fixing his strap. "Nate!"

He looked first at Bob then in the direction Bob was looking. "Oh my," He said as he grabbed his pack. "You're right, we gotta go. Lead the way."

Bob pushed Nathan in front of him. "You get going. I will catch up."

"No Bob. I'm with you."

"Go! I will slow them down for a while. You find Kelly and Tom. I will be alright. I don't want to be a hero so I will be right behind you. Now go," Bob said as he pushed him again.

Yrartz were in sight now and coming in ever larger numbers. Bob watched them for a few seconds when he realized they weren't coming from the south and they weren't shooting either. These Yrartz were coming in from the east and seemed to be coming right at them. They were clearly headed for the LZ.

Bob swiveled around to check on Nate's progress and saw that he was almost out of sight. He decided not to wait any longer. There were way too many Yrartz and they were coming way too fast.

He did his best to stay out of sight of the aliens. Bob figured why let them know where we are or even that we were here in the first place. They might realize it when they tried to fly their ships but by then maybe the unit would be away and gone.

His hopes were quickly dashed as he heard shooting up ahead. Bob started running as fast as he could and soon came in sight of Nate defending himself. He was shooting at a group of Yrartz at point-blank range.

Bob immediately began engaging the enemy as well. He heard something behind him and whirled around and almost pulled the trigger. "Don't shoot it's me," Tom hollered.

"Sorry brother."

"Nate you get going. Kelly is just over there. Grab her and go as fast as you can."

"Where to?" Nate asked.

"Try for Earl's place. If we get there we can hold them off. We will have a better chance to defend ourselves there than here. Now get going." Tom fired off a burst taking out several aliens.

Nathan moved as quickly as he could. Kelly was waiting for him when he rounded the last ship. She didn't ask what was happening. She just started walking fast. She didn't plan on getting caught out in the open again.

"We're heading for Earl's," Kelly said by way of explanation.

"I know. Tom told us. I sure hope they get moving soon too." Nate took a few steps before saying, "I'm sorry I move so slowly. I guess maybe I should lose some weight and get back in shape."

Kelly couldn't remember a time when Nathan was in shape. *Must have been before I was born* she thought. "Well you can start to get in shape today. Come on, let's go." She led off again hoping Nate would keep up. It was more than half, maybe three quarters of a mile to Earl's and half of that was through swamp. Slow going for sure even for someone in good shape.

Tom yelled, "Get moving. Run brother run. I'm right behind you."

Bob started off at a trot, firing as he went. His shots mostly missing. Tom ran with him but stopped periodically to shoot more accurately. He did hit several of the Yrartz and even killed a few. But running and stopping to shoot while still breathing heavily did not make for accuracy either.

The aliens kept pouring into the LZ. Most of them seemed to stay in static positions or move among the ships with no intention of pursuing the brothers. They had other ideas in mind.

These were 1881s reinforcements. Their purpose was to prepare to fill in gaps in the attacking force or flank the enemy. Each small unit would do whichever seemed most useful. Attacking a small unit of the enemy that was trying to escape was not their mission.


Yrartz were moving around both sides of the house. Bill and his men started shooting with extreme prejudice. The bodies began piling up when they all heard an agonizing scream from within the house. Jeff the dog ran out the front door followed by an ever increasing flood of aliens.

Sarona screamed and started for the house. Bill and Carl caught her and dragged her back. "Gordon's still in there," she screamed again, one hand reaching out as if she could pull him from the danger.

Bill took her by both arms and held her out in front of him. "He is gone. Gordon is gone. We have to get out of here now." She shook her head in disagreement as he spoke, tears flowing freely down her cheeks. In her mind she knew it was true but her heart told her otherwise.

"Carl, the keys are in the truck. You take that. I will take Mrs. Washburn and her kids in her car." Carl needed no further explanation. He ran to the truck and jumped in. Making sure Ed and Slim were in the back he started it up and shifted into drive.

Bill dragged Sarona to the car and helped her get in. He slammed the door and didn't wait for her to put on the seatbelt. Rushing around to the driver's side he kicked the first Yrartz to arrive in the head sending him sprawling. He got in the car as several other aliens surrounded it.

Sarona screamed again and the children were crying, yelling for their daddy. Bill started the engine and dropped it in reverse backing over some Yrartz as he spun the wheel. Now there was screaming outside the car as well as the aliens were mangled under the tires.

Bill put it in drive and stepped on the gas. The automobile lurched forward and picked up speed. He drove over several more aliens without swerving or trying to avoid them. Carl had the truck right beside Bill keeping pace as the two vehicles headed toward the center of town horns honking. They wanted to alert the entire town.

People came running out of their houses wondering what was going on. Bill stopped on Pine Street at the first intersection and opened his door. He got out and stood beside the car and waited until a crowd gathered.

Carl took the truck up to the command post. He did not wait for orders from Bill. He knew they needed everybody who could shoot to come down to the northwest end of town. This was the fight they had expected.

"What's going on," someone shouted.

Bill held up his hands for quiet. "The aliens attacked us at Pastor Gordon's house. He didn't make it." The crowd went silent at that. "We need everyone to get their guns and prepare to fight. The town is in danger. We all are in danger. We need to set up a barrier and defend it right here, right now. Go! Get your weapons."

The people gathered around Bill turned and scattered to their homes. They knew what they needed to do. They had been preparing for this all day. Several people moved their cars and trucks into position on Oak Avenue. They blocked the road from north of Pine Street to south of Cedar. The town was now effectively cut into two parts.

Carl left Ed and Slim with Bill. They did their best to comfort Sarona as Bill began directing the defense. He had the first people to arrive with weapons set up facing west on Pine. He put the next group on Cedar also facing west.

"Ma'am I don't know what to say. I lost my wife a few…"

"You watch my kids. I'm going to kill me some little green men," Sarona said as she got out of the car. She had a .40 semiautomatic in her purse which she pulled out and tucked in her pants. She then picked up Gordon's deer rifle and checked to make sure it was loaded. She grabbed an extra box of shells and turned.

Ed and Slim watched dumbstruck as Sarona marched purposefully toward the barricade of automobiles. The determined look on her face kept others out of her path. Even Bill didn't try to stop her from setting up at the front line.

She placed the rifle carefully on the hood of a car. Sarona then put the extra ammunition box on the car next to the rifle. She took up the rifle in both hands and looked through the telescope. She adjusted the position of her arms for greater comfort and accuracy.

The Yrartz success at the Washburn's emboldened them. They marched up Pine Street shoulder to shoulder believing that final victory was in their grasp. They were the superior race and were about to prove it.

Success in one battle does not always translate into ultimate victory. The Yrartz moved up Pine and as soon as the first ones were in sight Sarona released the safety, aimed and fired.

Before the aliens dead body hit the blacktop she fired again. Then the rest of the town opened up.

The town's folk did not fire in panic. They controlled their shots in a manner that would do a drill sergeant proud. Yrartz after Yrartz fell to the ground dead or screaming in agony. Within seconds victory turned to rout. Pastor Gordon was a beloved friend of all in the town and anger, not fear motivated the people.

General 1881 told his unit commanders to fall back. There was simply no point in continuing the attack. The enemy was well armed and well-disciplined and ready. He would have to attack at a different place, at a different time. The element of surprise was lost early on and a prepared enemy was a very dangerous enemy.

The Yrartz fled into the swamp. Only a few troops stopped to help their wounded comrades. Many of them caught bullets in the back.

The people of West Falls stood up and walked around the barricade. Firing as they went they followed the Yrartz shooting into them. Sarona led the assault with Bill close behind. In all twenty-some people pushed the Yrartz out of town.

When the last of the aliens had retreated into the swamp Sarona went back to her house. "Sarona I'm asking you not to go in there," Bill pleaded. "You won't like what you find, if you find anything at all."

Without a word Sarona went up the steps and into the house. The front door had been torn off its hinges and lay against the side of the porch. The interior of Gordon and Sarona's home was a shambles. It was hard to say if the Yrartz purposely trashed the place or were just that clumsy.

The house Sarona now looked upon was missing most of it's curtains. Windows were broken, plates and cups littered the kitchen floor. The table was on its side, one leg torn off. The pictures in the hallway were down and smashed. The TV was gone.

Bill entered behind her and gazed over the carnage. He had never seen such a thoroughly ransacked home. He was about to say something in apology for not protecting her husband and her home. But he noticed something else.

Then she saw the blood stains on the floor. It was human blood and not much of it. The aliens consumed the good pastor and left very little trace. Knowing without a doubt, Sarona lost control. She dropped to the floor and began sobbing uncontrollably.

Bill motioned for two of the men to finish clearing the house of aliens. Then he went to her and knelt down beside her. He put one arm gently around her shoulder and wisely said nothing. He simply held her there on the floor.

When the men came back they silently mouthed that the place was clear. Bill nodded by way of a thank you. The pair continued on outside without a word. They knew they couldn't do any more for Sarona.

Bob acted as rear guard once the foursome linked up again. Tom took the lead with Kelly close behind. Nathan was huffing and puffing but keeping pace just the same. He had no desire to be an alien appetizer.

Tom's original plan was to go straight to Earl's place. But the Yrartz were coming in from the east, the direction he wanted to go. "We have to go north a ways," he told Kelly. "The enemy are thick over that way. I just hope we can get around them."

"I'm not worried," Kelly lied. "I know you will find a way and get us safely through."

"I hope your confidence in me is well founded," he said.

The farther north they went the more Yrartz seemed to be in front and to the side of them. Tom had to stop the unit several times and let aliens pass. He was thinking of turning back when at last he saw an opening in the wave of enemy units. The only problem was the opening was to the west.

# Chapter 22

Things calmed down in West Falls for a time. Bill did his best to comfort Sarona but she kept wailing for some little while. What quieted her was the simple fact that her children needed her now more than ever. So she stopped crying, washed her face and went out to find them.

Bill, with advice from some prominent citizens, decided to abandon part of the west end of town. He chose to move the automotive barricade they had at Oak Avenue one block up to Elm Avenue. This put Tom and Bob's house just outside the front line. It also meant that nearly half the town was no-mans land now.

The people were welcome to go to their homes outside the boundaries any time they wanted. But they all knew what risks they were taking. Many decided to move semi-permanently into the church or some friends place.

Bill suddenly found it easy to man the lines. No one balked at being assigned duty any time of day or night. The attack on the Washburn's was enough to bring the whole town together and strengthen their collective resolve. It made his job somewhat easier but that did not lessen the feeling that he had failed Pastor Gordon.

He further believed the Hayward's and the Minong's were dead. He had no way to communicate with them to confirm or dissolve this belief. Bill knew in his heart he had lost those kids too.


Matt, Kaitlyn and the others from the Shell Lake Institute drove down Cumberland Road and stopped a hundred meters short of the bridge at Telemark Creek. They pulled off the road into an old logging road and went as far as they could up the road. "I think we should go into the woods here," Jared said. "The GPS indicates the primary meteorite field should be just over there," he pointed.

"Okay everyone out. Let's go see what we can find." Matt pulled the keys out of the ignition and grabbed his backpack. Reluctantly Kaitlyn followed his lead.

Jared was already walking toward the woods. Holding the GPS in one hand he pushed some limbs out of the way with the other. He didn't bother checking to see if the rest were behind him.

Carter rushed to catch up with Jared. Matt was right with him. Amery and Kara walked together and Kaitlyn brought up the rear. The atmosphere within the group was festive. For all but Kaitlyn this was a special adventure.

The woods became thicker as they moved deeper in. Jared was brought up short when he arrived at Telemark Creek. Matt bumped into him and nearly knocked them both into the creek.

"What do we do now?" Jared asked.

"The GPS is pointing across the creek?" Matt questioned.

"Yes, it's showing the best impact area is about two hundred meters or so that way," he said pointing.

"What's happening?" Carter asked.

"Ah Jared says the GPS points across the creek and maybe another two hundred meters or so," Matt informed him.

The girls caught up with them. Kaitlyn had closed ranks with the other two once they got deeper into the woods. She did not want to be alone in the forest. Even though the sun was high overhead it was still dark, perhaps threatening in the woods.

"What's up?" Amery asked.

"We have a creek in front of us and the GPS shows we have to keep going straight ahead," Carter answered.

"Is there a bridge or ford or something?" Kara asked.

"We don't know for sure," he answered.

"Well let's go," Matt said and started off along the waterway looking for a way across.

Tom sat under the black spruce waiting. He hoped to find a dry and easy way across this section of swamp. But while looking he had to keep out of sight of the Yrartz. They seemed to be everywhere, at least everywhere he looked lately.

Since the way to Earl's farm was temporarily blocked he decided to take his team west to Forest Road 1210 and try to complete the mission. If they could get to the road perhaps they could find a way out of the area and get help.

Tom waved the others forward. Each one carefully dropped down near a tree or thick brush. They had a good spot here in a cluster of spruce. But the area directly in front of them was fairly open. It would expose them for several minutes as they moved through it.

"Tom," Bob grabbed his brother's arm. Pointing with his other hand he said, "See over there? That looks like a game trail. It looks dry and wide enough to walk on without making too much noise."

He moved the binoculars over to the trail Bob pointed out. Tom scanned back and forth along every inch of the path that he could see. "I think you're right. Okay everybody, let's go."

With Tom leading the way they moved quickly through the open section and once again found themselves in forest. The spruce and cedar slowly began to give way to ash, maple and elm. The ground seemed to be rising rapidly in this direction.

Suddenly Tom stopped and crouched down. The others did the same. They watched as he scanned the area ahead of them. He turned and said, "Guys we've found the road. We must have crossed the swamp without realizing it. Apparently it's drier than I thought."

The four of them stood up and slowly, quietly walked forward. Even though all of them wore camouflage clothing they didn't want to make any sudden movement that might alert the enemy. Tom stopped at the edge of the trees. The rest came up and stopped too. Everyone scanned the road in both directions. Now was not the time to take chances.

Under Bill's direction the residents of West Falls began stringing lights out to all points on the perimeter of their defensive positions. Since the electricity was still coming to town they decided to put it to good use. But they found a couple of generators and hooked them into the lines just in case.

The Yrartz hadn't proved to be especially intelligent so far. This encouraged Bill and his officers. But they were not about to underestimate these extraterrestrials either. After all they did manage to fly across millions of miles of space and land here. Something humans had yet to accomplish.

"Bill we are almost done setting up the lights. Carl has his people moving cars, trucks and tractors into position. The barricade should be complete soon."

"Thanks John. I still think there is more we can do."

"You're still bothered by Tom and his gang aren't you?"

"Yes. I was the one sent them out. I'm responsible for their deaths," Bill mused. "I can't bring them back. You know John, command is not an easy thing. Sometimes you send people out knowing that at least some of them will not make it back."

John put his hand on Bill's shoulder. He could add nothing to that so he wisely kept his mouth shut. A moment later he dropped his hand, turned and went back to his duties.

*Does he know how much we respect him? Does he know how much we need him?* John prayed for his leader then. He asked God to give Bill strength and guidance and help him forgive himself for the losses.

Bob, Tom, Kelly and Nathan weren't the only ones Bill was grieving for. He felt he had lost the cream of the town's fighters. But he had also lost the town's encourager and spiritual leader. Losing Gordon Washburn hurt like nothing else ever had before.

Bill also felt the loss of Earl, the Seeley's and Ted Hawkins. The deputy was the man who should be in charge of the town's defenses. Even though he died before Bill took over he still felt at least partly responsible for his death.

He was resolved not to lose another person. Bill would do whatever he needed to do to ensure the safety of everyone in town. The lights and barricades were part of that. New patrol schedules and pairings would help too.

After the fight at the Washburn's things quieted down. The aliens had not probed anywhere or attempted any further attacks. Bill couldn't help but wonder whether this was the lull before the storm. What were they planning and where would they attack again? When? How many?

All these thoughts went through his mind as he considered what to do next. This brought him back to the people he had lost. Circular thinking. He had to get out of this line of reasoning and get the job done. Bill shook his head as if to send the negative thoughts fleeing.

"Commander 1881, you are relieved of command. Your army will be given to another and you are hereby demoted to lieutenant." The Supreme Commander had made his decision. "In answer to everyone's unasked question I will take over command of the next battle. It is time I show you gentle Yrartz how a real warrior commands."

The Supreme Commander's arrogance grated on the nerves of the generals. They had no choice but to follow his lead. He was the Supreme Commander. It was their heritage, their beliefs. Their whole lives they obeyed without question. It was what a Yrartz did, what a Yrartz always did.

Blind faith or blind obedience was the accepted rule for this race of aliens. There were no resistance movements in the Yrartz universe. You did your job. You did what you were told to do. There was only one path.

The Supreme Commander began to outline his strategy. "I want the reserve units brought here." He slapped his pointer down on the map. The Yrartz had not perfected the flat screen computer monitor or holographic imaging.

"Sir I have been trying to call Deputy Hawkins for the last hour and I get no response."

"Well he usually calls in on Saturday night, doesn't he?" the Sherriff asked his dispatcher.

"Yes sir, but he always has his radio with him within earshot. We are always able to get in touch with him."

"Well I wouldn't worry about it. West Falls is a sleepy little town. Nothing ever happens there beyond a fender bender or game law violation. I'm sure everything is alright.

"If we don't hear from him tonight I'll send Fifield over there to check things out," the Sherriff said dismissing the dispatcher.

Sara Hudson was concerned as she walked back to her station. Ted Hawkins always answered his radio immediately when called. He took this job very seriously. On Saturdays, his call in day, he was especially diligent.

The Sherriff opened the drawer he had slammed shut when Sara knocked on his door. He pulled the paper out and leaned back in his chair. He always wanted a boat like this and now it looked as if it would happen.

Sara decided to call Deputy Fifield on his cell phone. She hadn't been ordered not to call him but she didn't want to do so publicly over the radio. The Sherriff might get angry or even take that as insubordination.

"Brad, could you watch the lines for a couple minutes, please? I have to make a phone call," she said.

She went into the women's washroom and called Deputy Fifield. Sara dialed his number. "Hello, Cliff?"

"Hello, Sara? That is you right?"

"Yes, it is."

"What can I do for you?" *and why are you calling me on your cell phone instead of the dispatch radio?*

"Have you been over near West Falls lately?" She asked.

"No not really. Closest I got was Highway 63. Why, what happened?"

"Well nothing as far as I know." Sara wondered if she should tell him or not. "We haven't heard from Ted Hawkins today and I tried to call him earlier and he didn't answer."

"Hmmm, that's not like Ted."

"That's what I thought," Sara agreed. "But the Sherriff says don't worry about it. He said he would send you to look into it if we don't hear from him tonight."

"Huh, Sherriff's got his mind on that new boat he plans on buying. Big discount this time of year. He's been saving up for it for a long time. He probably wasn't listening to anything you said."

"That's kind of what I thought too. He was looking at me but seeing the boat."

"Hey Sara, tell you what, I will swing on by there this evening on my way home. If you hear from Ted before that call and let me know."

"Okay and thanks Cliff."

# Chapter 23

Matt found a large log that had fallen across the creek and led the group over it. With Jared giving him advice on direction he continued moving through the woods. "Are you sure this is the right area?"

"I'm reasonably certain," Jared replied.

"What does that mean?" Carter asked. "Are you sure you're using that thing right?"

"Of course I am," Jared said clearly offended.

"Let me see that," Matt said as he pulled the GPS unit from Jared's hands.

"Wait a second. You loser, you been heading us in the wrong direction."

"No I haven't," Jared protested. He came alongside Matt and looked at the device.

Carter nosed in between them for a better look. "Would you look at that. Our primo navigator has us on a wild goose chase," he said.

"He's right," Matt confirmed. "You been taking us west when we should have gone south." Turning he started off on a new heading.

Jared just stood there embarrassed and upset. "What happened?" Kara asked him.

"I had us going the wrong way. Sorry."

"Ah don't sweat it. Matt is perfectly capable of getting us just as lost as you are." She smirked at him and followed the leaders.

"Tom, what's that?" Kelly asked as she pointed toward something in the road to the south.

"I don't know but I think we should check it out very carefully." He led off motioning for the others to follow. Kelly stayed close.

"What's your second favorite candy bar?"

"Snickers. They are a diet candy bar," Nathan told him.

"How so?" Bob wondered aloud.

"They have peanuts. Less sugar, so diet candy bar."

"Guys!" Tom loud whispered to them. "Keep a close watch out."

"What is it?" Kelly asked.

"It looks like a Forest Service truck," he answered without turning around. His eyes were scanning the brush and trees on both sides of the road. Tom was worried now. The truck appeared abandoned.

Bob and Nate became quiet and serious. They too scanned the road edges looking into the woods. They had fingers on the triggers of their weapons, safeties off.

Tom held up his hand to stop them. He motioned that he would go alone to check out the truck. They were to stay put but alert, ready to fight or run.

He approached the vehicle slowly checking out everything. Tom found what he was afraid he would find. There was blood on the ground near the open front door. When he got even with the truck he noticed blood on the seat too.

He turned and put his finger to his lips telling everyone to keep quiet. Tom saw something in front of the truck. He moved slowly up to it and identified it as the remains of a large wolf. He was surprised to note the head was gone but otherwise the animal was intact.

Not seeing any evidence that Yrartz were currently in the area he waved the others forward. Kelly stopped at the door and looked in then looked at Tom. "He's dead isn't he?"

"I'm afraid so," he replied.

"What the heck? Why do you suppose they left part of a wolf?" Bob wondered aloud.

"Probably because they had something they liked better," Nate said pointing to the truck. Bob nodded in agreement.

Tom walked back to Kelly still standing beside the vehicle. He put his arm around her. She looked at him. "I wonder who he was."

"I don't know but I guess this answers a question we had. Now I think it's clear West Falls isn't alone in this invasion."

Kelly peered into his eyes. "You think the whole world is under attack? You think these Yrartz have taken over the earth?"

"I can't say for sure but it doesn't look good for us. You would think that if a Forest Service worker disappeared someone would come looking for him," Tom said.

Frowning Kelly said, "I suppose you're right." She looked around them. "So what do we do now?"

"We go back and report to Bill and the residents of West Falls. Then I guess we get ready for one heck of a fight." Tom turned to the brothers. "Guys let's get going. We should get off this road and try to get to Earl's place before dark."


"I'm giving some serious thought to attacking the Yrartz," Bill told the men on his war council. Eyebrows raised and a murmur went through those assembled. One man even shook his head in disagreement.

"I know you all probably think that's nuts. Maybe it is but sitting around here waiting gets old fast. If we attack them it puts them off guard and we may even score a major victory." The more he talked the more it sounded like Bill was trying to convince himself rather than anybody else.

He looked at each of them individually. "Anyone care to comment?"

"I think it's a good idea Bill, but I think we should wait until Tom's group returns."

"I don't know that we have much time. And we don't know if they are still alive or not. We have no way to communicate with them." *And I wish I had never sent them out. I just have to hope and pray they are still alive, that they got through before the aliens arrived.*

"Bill let's be positive and assume they got through. They aren't coming back until tomorrow, right?" Carl asked.

"That's true. Now what's the point you are making?" Bill asked.

"Well if they did survive, and I believe they did, we should wait until they come back. I mean we really don't have a pressing need to assault the aliens. Unless someone saw them massing for attack again I think it best we wait and see. Give Tom and his group a chance."

"I see your point," Bill said. "If we wait and they make it back we will have needed intel. The only problem as I see it is the enemy making a new fight.

"My argument for an attack is simply this; if the Yrartz attack they do it in their own time. However if we attack, we do it in our own good time. We start it we decide when and where and how many of us we need to make a successful assault. We go from being a defensive unit to taking the fight to them."

"I have no problem with that," John agreed. "However I feel as Carl does. We can wait another day I think. I really believe we have to. What if we make our attack and accidently involve Tom and his bunch? Suppose they are coming back and get caught in the middle? What if their failure in their first assault makes them call in greater reinforcements? Or what if we attack at the exact place they are massing for an all out charge against us?"

"John and Carl I wanted to hear opinions. These are good arguments in favor of waiting." Bill turned his attention to the two that hadn't voiced a preference. "What about you two? What do you say?"

NM spoke up. "I don't believe we have enough strength to make a decent attack force. I think we should be content to wait for help. That said, I realize the whole world might be under assault at this time.

"If the Yrartz have taken the rest of us then we can expect no help. Conversely if this is all there are of them, well someone will come and help us. In that case we would only get some of our people killed or wounded needlessly.

"Since we don't yet know the truth I think we should wait. Postponing the attack one day will be good. We have a good defensive position and enough people to defend it. Let's save our strength. If we need to start a fight later we will."

"Okay I've heard enough. I will bow to the majority. We wait until Tom's unit returns or until we are certain they are gone. In the mean time get all your people ready for an assault. We will attack with everything at our disposal.

"I need you lieutenants to inventory your weapons, ammo and other supplies. I also want to know how many effectives each of you has. I need to know numbers and I need it now. Okay dismissed."


"Hey everybody! I found a road," Matt told the group.

Carter came up beside him. "Any idea which one it is?"

"No, but it has to be on our map. Jared where's the map?"

Jared pulled the map from his back pocket and began opening it. Matt stepped toward him and grabbed the map tearing a corner. Without comment he opened it the rest of the way and began checking it over.

Carter and Jared looked on. "Here, I think this is the road we are on. See there is the tee in the road. Here it is on the map."

"Yep that looks like it. According to the map this road is 1210 and it is just a loop," Carter said.

"True and the GPS says this is the area where the greatest concentration of meteorites fell," Jared added.

"You as good at interpreting data as you are at reading a GPS?" Matt sneered.

The girls wisely stayed out of the conversation. They let the boys fight their own fights. None of them had been looking at either the GPS or the map and had nothing to contribute anyway.

"I say we go this way," Matt pointed south along 1210. Without waiting for a reply he took the left fork and started walking down the road. Carter shrugged and started after him. The others followed.

Tom was doing a final check of the forest Service truck and surrounding area before heading back. Kelly stayed close. She was more than worried and did not want to be here any longer.

"Hey Tom," Nate called quietly, almost a whisper.

Tom looked in his direction a questioning frown on his face. Nathan motioned vigorously for him to come quickly. "What is it?" he asked as he approached.

Pointing, Nate said, "Look over there. It's a Yrartz and he's all alone. See you can see deep into that pine plantation and all the way to that sign post. There aren't any more of them things around."

"Okay?"

"Well see I figure I will go and sneak up on it and capture me a Yrartz." Smiling he looked at Tom. "What do you think?"

Before Tom or Bob could answer he added, "See I could sneak up behind him. I walk pretty quietly in the woods. Ask Bob." Standing behind Nate, Bob vigorously shook his head no.

Reaching out his hand and touching Nate on the shoulder Tom asked, "What happens if he sees you? What if he turns around?"

"I'll hide behind a tree," Nathan beamed proudly that he had come up with the answer on his own.

Looking at the trees in the plantation, then looking back at him, Tom said, "Ah Nate, maybe you better let me or Bob do it. Those trees are kind of thin."

"You saying I'm fat?"

"No, I'm saying the trees are skinny."

"Oh, right."

Before anyone could do anything about the Yrartz he disappeared into the swamp at the far end of the plantation. Tom decided it was time to go. They had no real idea just how many of the aliens were out there and he did not want to fight them here and now.

The Supreme Yrartz Commander decided to wait for the next attack on the town of West Falls. He felt he and his unit commanders needed a little time to organize. He didn't want another disaster such as earlier.

He had most of his reserve troop's bivouac in the landing zone. Many of the Yrartz chose to sleep in the ships. They felt much safer that way.

The various unit commanders sent scouts out all around the LZ and the northern end of West Falls. They had guards out in all directions. Patrols were moving up and down all the roads in the general area too.

The alien horde were taking no chances that they might be hit with a surprise attack. Every precaution was taken, every possible move was made. They did everything but build a wall.


Bill had doubled his guards. He was taking no chances either. He walked the perimeter all afternoon and planned to be out there all night. His people would stay awake and alert and he would see to it personally.

Some of the town's folk were getting a little tired of him. They started feeling another leader, maybe a local born one, would do a better job. Several had begun to grumble aloud against him. The attack at the Washburn's house was frequently mentioned.

Some of the people were more than happy to follow his every instruction. They thought of the fight at the Washburn's as a successful defense of the town and rout of the enemy. They volunteered for duty. They helped build the barricades and helped with anything that needed doing.

He was feeling the strain of command. Bill thought about quitting the leadership role but he saw no reasonable alternative. He would not abandon his duties and he wouldn't hand things over to an incompetent.

"Matt my feet are beginning to hurt," Kara complained. "Can we stop for a minute?"

"Aw are you girls going to slow us down again?" Matt was getting sick of them. They spent more time complaining than anything else. He felt like he was back in middle school again. He dearly wished he had said no to the girls and maybe Jared too. "If you all can't keep up…" He left the rest unspoken.

Kaitlyn was about to say something when Carter opened his mouth. "Matt, we probably should take a break. We've been walking for two hours and some of it hasn't been the best terrain. We've been in swamp and forest, uphill and down."

"You going to wimp out on me too?" Matt sneered.

"No!" he said a little too loudly. I just think we should hold up and rest a bit. This isn't a race. We don't have to keep up the pace. Nobody's going to beat us to the meteorites."

"How do you know?" Matt looked at the women and at Jared. He realized he needed to let them rest or he would have a mutiny on his hands.

"Okay, let's take five. You all stay here for a few minutes. I'm going to that curve in the road and see what's beyond it. I'll be back in a couple." He turned to Carter. "You want to come with me?"

Carter nodded affirmative. "I'll come too," Kaitlyn said.

Surprised Matt acknowledged his wife with a gesture. Shifting his pack he said, "Okay let's go."

When they were out of hearing range Kara complained, "He's just plain mean. It's like he's a drill sergeant and we're the troops. I didn't join the Army when I came on this expedition."

"Ah don't worry about it honey. He'll get his someday," Amery said.

Jared kept silent. He had had enough of Matt's command too. He would have just turned and left if it wasn't for the girls. He did not want to leave them alone out here in the wilderness. Besides he was still hoping Kara would finally notice him.

# Chapter 24

The intrepid foursome were walking single file in the ditch on the east side of 1210. They stayed close to the woods preferring rough terrain near good cover to exposing themselves on the open road. It was slower going and occasionally wet too. However, it was so much safer no one complained.

Tom was leading them to the place where there was a tee in the road. He intended to go right or east when they got there. This would take them closer to Earl's farm and what they all hoped was safety. They would hold up at the farm before going back to town tomorrow.

None of the gang wanted to encounter Yrartz in the dark of night. It was already late afternoon and they still had a mile and a half to go. Some of that was in the Bibon. Tom figured it best to get through that in daylight.

Clouds were thickening so it would be dark early. All four realized this and moved faster. There was enough of a breeze to cover most of the noise they made.

The Yrartz patrol was moving along Forest Road 1210. They would make a sweep of the road and the forest to the west. The mission was very clear. Find and destroy any threats they encountered. Take no prisoners. Eat any people you find on the spot and don't bring any snacks home.

The patrol was travelling light carrying no supplies. They had not eaten since early morning and the unit commander felt this would help keep the men alert. They were hungry and hungry troops tended to stay on edge longer and fight better.

They reached 1210 only a few minutes ago and had stopped to take a breather. Moving through the swamp had tired them. Rest and a water break would give the troops back their edge.

The commander sent two Yrartz in each direction to watch for enemies. They were his eyes and ears while the unit rested. The military called them LP-Ops, listening posts-observation posts.

The LP-OP troops would join up with the unit when they went past. The other LP-OP would catch up and act as rear guard. It was standard operating procedure for all ground troops in the universe.

One pair of Yrartz had just settled into their position when they noticed movement a few meters to their front. "How many do you see?"

"More than one for sure. Call the commander."

"Six this is LP one, over."

"This is six, report."

"We have movement to our front. At least two humans, perhaps more."

"LP one have the enemy spotted you? Over."

"Negative commander. They have not seen us."
"Can you get out of there without being seen?"

"I think so sir."

"Then move out. Get back here as soon as you can." He turned to his sergeants. "Put your men in ambush formation. We have unfriendlies on their way to this location. Make sure your men are aware an LP-OP is coming in. Don't shoot them."

The Yrartz sergeants began rapidly moving their troops into ambush positions. Unlike a human army ambush this one was set up so as to stun the enemy not kill them. They would have to be much closer to their target.

Since the aliens had no idea which side of the road the humans would come down they had to set up on both sides. If one of their own was hit it would not be fatal. It would stun, it would hurt and it might anger but it wouldn't kill.

Matt came around the bend in the road and saw yet another bend. "Well at least we know what's around the corner," Matt chuckled.

"What do you think we should do? Go into the woods or stay on this road?" Carter asked.

"I think we should go back to the others and go home. Wait for the fieldtrip on Monday," Kaitlyn said.

Ignoring her Matt said, "I think we have to go into the woods and look around. Chances are we will find a tree or two that are burned. We might even find a meteorite. It's pretty clear we aren't going to find any on this road."

Kaitlyn grabbed Matt's sleeve. "Matt why don't we wait until the fieldtrip? We could still be the first to find something important. Why not wait until we have the whole class out here? Then you can show off your finds."

"Kaitlyn let go of me. What is wrong with you? We came here for adventure and discovery. We will find something new and it just may be worth some cash.

"Now if you don't want to come with Carter and me fine. Just go back to the others. We are going on. We will find something fantastic, something special that will change our lives."

Matt took a few more steps. "What's that putrid odor?" he asked wrinkling his nose. An unbearable stench washed over them.

"Smells like a sewer," Carter said.

"No it's worse than that. You think someone is illegally dumping some nasty chemicals around here somewhere?" Matt said.

Tom stopped suddenly. He wasn't exactly sure why but he had a feeling. Something seemed out of place, out of kilter. He took a slow 360 examining every tree, rock and tuft of grass.

"What is it Tom?" Kelly asked. "You see something?" She looked all around too but saw nothing out of the ordinary.

"I don't see anything unusual. It's just a feeling, kind of like the ones you get sometimes. You know what I mean?"

"Yes I know what you mean. I'm not getting that kind of feeling now though."

"Well Kelly I don't know what to make of it. I thought I heard something a minute ago but I don't hear it now." Tom's eyes grew big. He pushed Kelly down and motioned the brothers to drop where they were.

Peering around a tree Tom pointed. "See over there?" Kelly looked and didn't see anything at first. "Next to that stump. There is at least one Yrartz, wait I think I see two."

"I see them too. Yep there are two. I don't see any more. What do you suppose they are doing?" Kelly asked.

"I'm not sure but I think they are an early warning system. In the army they call it an LP-OP, listening post- observation post. Armies use them to give a warning that the enemy is getting close. I learned that from one of my uncles who was in the army. Plus I played some X-Box games."

"Do you think they saw us?"

"Hold on," Tom said. "I think they are moving out." They watched as the two aliens picked up and started through the brush. Tom and Kelly kept them in sight until a curve in the road swallowed them.

"You guys get ready to move fast."

"What's up bro?" Bob asked.

"Kelly and I saw a couple of Yrartz over there by that cluster of spruce. I think they were on the lookout for any one that happens down this road."

"Where do you think they are going now?" Nate asked.

"Good question," Tom said. "I have no idea where they are going but I think we should follow them and find out." With that the four started after the aliens. They moved cautiously keeping the enemy in sight at all times.

Matt was watching the edge of the road hoping to find a clue as to where the meteorites fell. He was so intense he didn't notice anything unusual about the bushes alongside the road. It wasn't until they started moving that he noticed anything at all.

"Ouch! What the heck is this?" Matt yelled. Several more tasers hit him then and he fell to the ground yelling.

Carter came running over. "What's going on?" he shouted as the first dart hit him. "Ouch, what are these things?" He stopped and did a one-eighty and stopped again. The Yrartz were coming out of the swamp on the side he had just come from.

Kaitlyn came running too. "What's going on?" she asked as a dart narrowly missed her cheek. A second dart bounced off her shoe.

"Stop!" Carter yelled. "Go back. I don't know what these things are but clearly they don't like us." He tried to go to Matt's aid again but more darts flew his direction, one hitting his hand. He pulled it loose and tossed it at the nearest alien.

Kaitlyn stood still, frozen, unable to move. "Go," Carter urged her again. He gave up on trying to help Matt. He grabbed the girl by her arm and started pulling her along the road. "Come on, let's go."

Matt screamed as the first Yrartz bit into him. Kaitlyn screamed in terror. "Let me go. I have to help him."

Carter kept his grip on Kaitlyn. Looking back at Matt he couldn't believe his eyes. These things, whatever they were had begun eating Matt. Others were coming toward them as fast as they could go.

"You hear that?" Bob asked.

"Sounds like someone is shouting," Tom said.

"We should check it out," Kelly suggested. "They sound like they are in trouble. The Yrartz we saw must have friends."

"I don't hear anything," Nate said.

Just then they heard a blood curdling scream from somewhere up the road. "I heard that," Nathan said.

"We have to help them Tom," Kelly urged.

"We don't know what we're getting into," was Tom's only comment.

Nate nodded. "He's right. We don't know how many of them are out there. We don't know what weapons they have. They might have tanks, rocket launchers, nuclear bombs…" his voice trailed off as he realized what he was saying.

"Doesn't matter. Everybody check your weapons. Make sure you are fully loaded. Make sure your other equipment doesn't rattle. Let's go," Tom commanded as he started off at a trot.

Kelly put a few more rounds in her rifle. She swung her pack onto her back and took off after Tom.

Bob wasn't about to let his brother out of sight. He slung his backpack on his back and ran. He checked his weapons on the run. He figured the MP-5s would come in handy today.

Nate checked that he had sufficient candy bars then started off. He remembered to look at his rifle as he jogged. Then he turned around and went back for his pack.

Matt no longer moved or made a sound. Kaitlyn just stared, unable to either look away or move. Carter gave up trying to talk to her. He pushed her in front of him hoping at some point she would come back to reality.

Jared came around the curve at a run. "What's happening? Is someone hurt?" He stopped and looked at Carter and Kaitlyn. "Where's Matt?" When he got no answer he brushed past them and stopped again.

*Is that Matt? And what are those things?* He thought. "What, what's going on and what are those," Jared pointed. "Where did they come from and what are they doing to Matt? That is Matt?"

"Yes that is Matt and we have no idea what those things are. Matt's dead and those things are responsible for it. Now let's get out of here before they get another of us," Carter answered.

"We can' just leave him there," Kaitlyn screamed.

"We don't have a choice. Whatever those are they are intent on killing and apparently, eating us." Carter turned to go and grabbed Kaitlyn again. She tried shaking him off but this time he held on.

Eight Yrartz were coming toward them as fast as they could go. The first ones were almost close enough to get the trio with their tasers. They already fired a few to help judge distance.

"Jared you see those darts they are shooting?" Carter asked.

"Yes. What are they?"

"The aliens or whatever they are, are getting too close. Let's move." Carter pushed Kaitlyn again. Looking at Jared he added, "They are some kind of taser. That's what they hit Matt with and I got hit too. The one that hit me stung a little. But four or five of them hit Matt and he went down hard. He started screaming and the aliens went over to him and started biting him."

"Kaitlyn's right. Shouldn't we do something?"

"Jared, do you have a weapon?" He shook his head no. "I don't either. Let's keep going. We grab the girls and get back to the car and get the heck out of here."

"Do you have the keys to Matt's car?" Jared asked.

"No I don't. Kaitlyn do you have keys to your car?" Carter asked her.

"Yes, in my purse in the car."

"We locked the car didn't we?" Jared asked.

"We did," Carter answered. "Ouch!" he said. "I just got hit by one of them darts."

Jared pulled out the dart and threw it back at the advancing aliens. He grabbed Kaitlyn's other arm and helped pull her along.

Tom saw the Yrartz going after the three people up ahead. Without waiting for the others he started running at the aliens. Suddenly he let out a yell and pulled the trigger on his MP-5.

At the sound of shouting and gunfire Jared, Kaitlyn and Carter turned and looked behind them. They all stopped and stood staring at the men and woman with the guns. "Where did they come from?" Carter asked.

Bob ran up and joined Tom running and firing in unison. Yrartz were scattering into the woods trying to escape the onslaught. Kelly and Nate added their guns to the mix.

The four slowed to a fast walk as they approached the dead body. What was left of Matt wasn't worth trying to bury. The aliens had stripped most of the flesh from his bones. The remains were an unrecognizable mess.

Without stopping Tom put his gun on safe, jumped over the corpse and ran to the three people up ahead. Bob was right beside him and Kelly and Nate just behind.

"Who are you?" Tom and Carter asked simultaneously.

"I'm Tom and this is my brother Bob." Pointing, he added, "That's Kelly and Nate. We are from West Falls. Who are you?"

"I'm Jared, this is Kaitlyn and Carter. We are from the Shell Lake Institute of Astrophysics. We came here hoping to find meteorites."

"You won't find any meteorites. You might stumble on some alien spaceships," Tom told them. "Come on let's get moving. We are under attack by these aliens," he continued as they walked.

Kaitlyn fell into Bob's arms weeping. He looked at his friends with an expression that said what am I supposed to do now? Not knowing what else to do he put his arms around her and held her a moment. Then he started leading her away from the alien infested area.

"They call themselves Yrartz from the planet Yrartz," Tom informed them.

Jared and Carter looked at him strangely. Tom answered the unasked question. "When we first ran into them they had this speech they gave. They said they were Yrartz from the planet Yrartz and we shouldn't be afraid. That they were going to take over our planet.

"We quickly learned they meant business. So now whenever we come across them again we shoot first and ask questions later. It saves time and human lives."

"So what you're saying is that the meteor shower we thought we saw was actually alien spaceships full of hungry Yrartz?" Carter asked.

"Yep," Nathan answered. Looking back at Matt's remains he added, "Boy, they don't need a best used by date on their food."

"You hear that?" Bill asked the people guarding the barricade. A smile crossed his face morphing into a grin and then laughter.

John rushed over to him. "What's wrong? What happened?"

"Did you hear the gunfire?"

"Yes, what was that all about? Who was shooting? It didn't sound like it came from over here or anywhere on our perimeter." *And why were you laughing* John wanted to ask. *Has our commander finally snapped?*

"Those guns were the MP-5s I gave Tom and his unit. I'm sure of it. You know what that means? It means that at least two of them are still alive. Maybe all four made it."

A sobering thought brought a frown. "They were shooting. That means they were or are under attack." Bill threw up his hands. "Well there's nothing we can do about it now. But it means they survived the attack on the Washburn's home."

John finally realized what that meant. "So there is a good chance they will complete their mission. They may come home and give us a report and just maybe it will be good news."

Bill put his hands on John's shoulders and smiled. "Now you're looking at it optimistically. They will get back and they will have good news. You can bet on it."

# Chapter 25

Tom, Kelly and Nate continued the fast walk. Carter and Jared kept pace as best they could. Bob and Kaitlyn, still holding each other fell behind a little. They all came around the end of the curve and suddenly they stopped.

Tom turned to the others, "Are they with you?"

"Yes. That's Amery and Kara."

"What happened?" Kara asked. "Where's Matt?"

"It's a long story. We have to get moving," Carter said.

"You haven't been gone long enough for a long story," Amery said. "Tell us."

Carter grabbed her arm and pulled her along. "Ouch, what's your problem? Let go of me." She didn't know what was going on but she noticed the guns the strangers had and the look in their eyes. Amery decided to keep quiet and wait for answers.

Tom and Kelly led the way again. Bob went to Kaitlyn and put his arm around her to comfort her. She put her arms around him and held tightly, sobbing. They awkwardly walked that way. Nate stayed behind the group as rear guard.

"How did you get here?" Tom asked.

"We drove up from Shell Lake in Kaitlyn and Matt's Suburban. They have the only car we could all fit in," Carter said.

"I don't see a vehicle. Where did you leave it?"

"I don't know where we are now. I'm not sure where the car is anymore."

"The GPS indicates it is over there," Jared said pointing toward the northeast. "It says we are about a mile from the car. We crossed a creek to get here and I'm not exactly sure where we crossed. I don't think anyone put a waypoint in."

"Okay," Tom said. "You have the keys?"

"No, Matt had them. But Kaitlyn said she has a set in her purse. That's locked in the Suburban."

"So we smash a window and get the keys and we all get out of here alive," Carter suggested.

"We can't go," Kelly told them. "We are on a mission for our town. We have to get back and tell them what has happened."

"Yes it's important that we get back." Tom stopped at the intersection. "We have to let our people know that this is a small, localized invasion and that help is on the way. You all can go and tell the authorities about what you saw and have them send help." Looking right then left he shrugged, "Which way?"

"We came from the right. We hit this road about thirty meters that way," Jared indicated.

NSA senior analyst Bret (not his real name) noticed the report from the low level scanner operator. He noticed that the operator had over stepped his position by checking further into the transmission than he should have. However he was willing to let that pass simply because of the unusual nature of the situation.

Bret immediately sent a report on to his superior, following it up with a phone call a few hours later.

"Sir I sent you a report on an unusual signal we found emanating just above the earth and seemingly sent to a swamp in northern Wisconsin."

"Yes I have it right here."

"Well sir I just wanted to follow it up and make sure you received it. I was also wondering if you had any questions that I could answer."

"Thank you for the follow up. I am analyzing the report and discussing it with my colleagues. Good day." The superior hung up and Bret never heard any more about the incident.

Tom went left, moving rapidly. "Hey, wait a minute," Jared caught Tom by the arm. "We came from that way."

"I know. You told me. Do you want to lead the Yrartz back to your car or would you prefer getting away clean?"

"Oh," was all Jared had to say.

Tom led the group two hundred meters along 1210 then turned north into the woods. He kept up a good pace and got them to Telemark Creek in short order. They began looking for a way across and soon came to the log that they used earlier.

"This is it," Jared told them.

"Okay," Tom said. "This is where we part company." Looking at them he pulled a handgun from its holster. "Do any of you have experience with firearms?"

"Yes I do," Carter said.

"So do I, and I target practiced with several different handguns," Amery told them.

"Good. So I'm going to give you this gun." Tom held it out, not knowing which he should give it to. Amery took it and pulled the slide part way back to check it was loaded. Tom nodded approval.

"I'm afraid it's all we can spare. We have a ways to go through alien infested territory. We don't know how long it will be before you can convince authorities to come help and we have to get back to town. You understand?"

Amery and Jared nodded yes. Carter stepped forward and began shaking hands with first Tom, then the others. The group from the Institute thanked the West Falls group for saving their lives and helping them escape. They promised to try and get help as soon as they could.

"You know not everybody would have helped us. Those Yrartz things didn't know you were there and neither did we. You could have just gone the other way and minded your own business. We would never have known," Jared said.

"No we couldn't just go our own way," Nathan contradicted. "We are Christians and we're Americans and we're humans. Humans just couldn't let another human be eaten by these things. Americans help oppressed people and defend the weak and defenseless. Christians, well we just love on you and share and care."

Kelly was as proud of her big brother as she had ever been. Jared thanked everyone again. There were a few tears shed as they parted company.

Jared led the group with Amery right behind him. She had the holster strapped to her waist but preferred to keep the gun in hand. She reasoned it was better that way since she could more quickly dispatch any aliens they ran into.

Kaitlyn did not move and Kara came to her. "Come on Kaitlyn. We gotta go."

"No. I'm staying with them," she indicated the West Falls group. "I have nothing to go back to. No reason to go back."

Kara gave her a hug. "Okay, we'll see you soon." She followed the others across the creek.

"Good luck," Kaitlyn called after them. She took Bob's hand as they began their trek toward town.


Deputy Fifield drove his cruiser down Cumberland Road only vaguely aware of his surroundings. His mind was on Ted Hawkins and what had become of him. First he had the odd call from dispatcher Sara Hudson. Moments ago the sheriff called and also asked him to check on Ted.

"What's going on?" Cliff said aloud to himself. Too late he noticed something odd about the road ahead. Cliff slammed on the brakes and the vehicle slewed side to side. He literally stood on the brake pedal and yanked the wheel around in an attempt to keep the car straight on the road and stop in time.

The cruiser slowed rapidly and stayed near the center of the road. Instead of plunging off the bridge and into Telemark Creek the car stopped just as the front wheels rolled over the edge. Cliff threw the vehicle into reverse and hit the gas hoping to back away from the hole. But there wasn't enough traction for the front wheels to push it up and out.

Heart thumping in his chest Cliff climbed carefully out of the car and back on solid ground. Scratching his head at what just happened he looked back at the hole that was a bridge a few days ago. It looked to him as if someone had blown it up.

*What happened here? Who blew it up? And why?* Cliff pulled his gun from the holster. Right now the who was what he was most concerned about. The what was obvious and the why didn't matter at the moment.

Cliff didn't see or hear anyone. He decided to stay with the vehicle for now. The first thing to do was call the office and let them know his car was unusable and what happened to the Telemark Creek Bridge. After that he would take a walk around the immediate area and see if there were any clues.

"Dispatch this is deputy Fifield calling in. Over."

"Go ahead deputy."

While he was updating them on the situation Cliff heard an odd noise. He looked through the windshield then remembered the car was hanging over the creek. He looked to his left and saw some little green men.

"What the...?" Cliff wondered what these things were. To him they looked like some sort of robot. "Who are you?" he asked.

In answer three of the Yrartz fired taser darts at him. The first one hit Cliffs gun and bounced off harmlessly. The second glanced off his deputies' badge. But the third struck him in the arm up near his shoulder.

Deputy Fifield pulled the dart out before the full voltage hit. It hurt but it didn't make his arm go numb. He dropped the mike and had the presence of mind to kick the closest Yrartz out of the way and slam his door shut. Several more darts bounced off the door.

Clifford Fifield wasn't the oldest or youngest deputy in the county. He wasn't the smartest or the dumbest either. He may not have been the quickest but he was smart and quick enough to grab the shotgun and extra shells and slide across the seat. He jumped out the passenger side door and aimed the shotgun at the Yrartz.

"Don't move or I'll shoot," he shouted.

Once again he was answered by darts. Cliff ducked behind the cruiser cocking the shotgun. The darts flew harmlessly over his head. He came back up and fired the shotgun in the general direction of the aliens. One rolled backwards and one lost his head or most of it. The rest milled about momentarily stunned into inaction.

Cliff could see he was outnumbered and sort of outgunned. He decided his best bet was to clear out of the area fast. He had no idea how quickly these things could move but they were short and he was six feet, two inches. He figured his long legs would get him away without too much trouble.

The radio crackled to life. "Dispatch calling Deputy Fifield. Over." The aliens fired off dozens of darts at the car in answer to the dispatchers call. Cliff took off running as fast as he could. He stopped once to turn and shoot one shot to discourage any Yrartz that might try to follow him.

Jared and Amery took turns leading the group. The forest was growing darker by the minute as clouds thickened overhead and the wind picked up. The trees seemed to come alive with menace. Kara did something she never would have otherwise, she took Jared's hand.

Amery stumbled and fell heavily against a tree. "Ouch, why the heck did we have to come through all this mess?"

Carter helped her to her feet. "Are you okay?" he asked, checking her over.

"Define okay?" she snarled as she yanked her arm out of his hand.

"She seems okay to me," Jared said sarcasm dripping from his lips. "Let's move before it rains," he added as he took the lead. Kara still held his hand and even gripped it more firmly.

The West Falls four plus one watched as the Shell Lake group crossed the log and disappeared into the woods. Then they began the trek back to the forest road. "It looks like rain," Nate said as he tripped over a stump and went down face first.

Tom and Kelly helped him up. "Are you alright?" Kelly asked with concern.

Nathan began checking here and there on his body. He looked up at her with a smile on his face. "I'm fine and so are my candy bars."

"Whoa what a relief," Bob said wiping his forehead. "Thank God one of your Snickers didn't shatter."

"I know bro," Nate said. Kelly rolled her eyes. Tom rolled his eyes. They took each others hands and started off again. Kaitlyn tightened her grip on Bob's arm but didn't know what to make of the verbal exchange.

When they approached the road they hunkered down and watched. It was better to be careful than sorry. They did not know how many of the Yrartz were still in the area or if more had come in to search for them.

They waited a full ten minutes and saw nothing out of the ordinary. The first few sprinkles fell as they got up and began moving along the road. Tom felt it was safe enough to travel on the gravel and they would make better time.

Jared and Kara came to the old logging road first. They stopped to wait for Amery and Carter. The clouds were spitting tiny beads of water just enough to be annoying. It was more than a mist but not quite a sprinkle. But the clouds promised further developments.

"Come on, let's move a little faster," Jared urged.

"Blow it out your…" Amery let it drop. She was hurting from her earlier fall. The spider webs and tree branches grabbing at her hair didn't help either. She had had enough of this part of Wisconsin and its charms.

They spotted the Suburban up ahead and everyone began to move a little faster. They all wanted the comfort and dubious safety of the vehicle. With one broken window it would be a cold and possibly wet ride to civilization but it was one they all would gladly endure.

Jared began looking for a likely rock to smash the window. "What are you doing?" Amery asked.

"Looking for a rock to bust the window with."

"Stand back," she said and tapped the window with the handgun she held. The glass cracked with jagged spider webs. She hit it again and the glass shattered putting most of the window on the floor and seat.

"Well that was easy," Carter observed. He reached in and unlocked the door. He pulled it open and retrieved Kaitlyn's purse.

"You going to open it?" Amery asked as she snatched it out of his hands. She didn't know what his problem was but she wanted to get out of there as soon as possible. She found the keys, tossed the purse in the car and went round to the driver's side. Without a word she opened the door and climbed in behind the wheel. As she slammed the door shut she yelled, "You guys going to come with or stay here and be alien food?"

The other three rushed to get in the car. They had no intention of becoming Yrartz supper. Amery didn't ask if everyone had their seatbelts on. She started the car, threw it into reverse and jammed the gas pedal.

# Chapter 26

Deputy Clifford Fifield ran as fast as he could for half a mile then slowed to a fast walk. He reached down to his belt and realized he had forgotten his handheld radio. "Well it don't matter. When I don't answer the radio they'll send someone to investigate."

Secure in the knowledge that someone would soon come he slowed to an easy stride. He had quickly outdistanced the aliens or robots or whatever they were. But the more he thought about it the more he decided he had to get in touch with the sheriff's office soonest. He didn't want someone else stumbling into these things.

"What is happening?" the lieutenant asked.

"The radio is speaking," one of troops said.

The lieutenant was wise enough to realize he had to do something about the radio or more humans would come. "Give me the mike," he commanded.

Sara Hudson was just about to send a couple more deputies to find out what became of Cliff. The radio crackled to life. "Cliff is that you?"

In his best imitation of a human voice the lieutenant answered. "This is Cliff."

"Oh thank God. I thought I lost you too," Sara said with relief. "What's happening out there?"

"Everything is well."

"I thought you said something about the bridge."
"No the bridge is fine."

"What about Ted? Have you found him yet?" Sara asked anxiously.

Thinking quickly the lieutenant said, "Yes I found out where Ted is. He went on a hunting trip with some friends."

"Oh? How do you know that?"

"He left a note on his door. He will be back Monday."

"Cliff are you feeling okay?"

"Yes, I am well. Why do you ask?"

"You sound different. Do you have a cold or allergies?" Sara asked with concern.

*Which is the right answer* the lieutenant wondered. "I have allergies."

"Oh that's too bad. Cliff you should take something for that. You don't sound good at all."

"I will take something for it as soon as I get home," he answered.

"Okay. Keep me informed if anything happens."

"I believe I fooled her," the lieutenant announced as he put the mike back.


"Amery!" Kara shouted.

"What?"

"There's aliens in back of us," Jared shouted.

"Well it's too bad for them," She said as she pressed her foot down harder on the gas pedal. Some of the Yrartz jumped out of the way. There were several thumps as the car went over the rest.

Amery spun the wheel over and hit the brakes. She shifted into drive and hit the gas again. The suburban strained and coughed at the sudden abuse. Just as it seemed the engine would quit it caught and the big rig lurched forward.

Yrartz fired darts at the retreating vehicle and two of them went in the smashed window. Both darts hit Carter in the head and caused him to jump then slump.

"Are you okay?" Amery asked.

"Bluhblubb," Carter answered, his mouth and jaw going numb.

Looking in the rear view mirror Amery asked, "Could one of you check on him please?"

Deputy Fifield knew the road he was on was crooked. It followed every turn in the creek. He decided to try a shortcut. He knew the direction of the highway and that the creek wasn't all that big. He believed he could jump across it most anywhere. He figured he could get to the highway before anyone else got here.

The aliens stopped chasing him almost immediately. He felt safe enough here as long as they didn't have some sort of ground transportation. He believed if they did they would have used it already. With that in mind he stepped off the road and into the woods on his shortcut.

Amery pulled over as soon as she felt it was safe to do so. Jared had checked on Carter and reported that he was still breathing normally. But Amery wasn't satisfied. She had to check him herself.

"Do you think it's a good idea to stop so soon?" Jared asked.

"I think this is just the place for you to get out and walk," She glared at him. Jared decided to keep his mouth shut for the duration of the journey home.

Once satisfied Carter was okay, Amery started the car and pulled back onto the road. "Guys who do you think we should report this to? I mean should we go to the sheriff's office or should we just go back to the institute and tell our professors?"

"I think we should do both," Kara answered. "I think we should go back to Shell Lake and then call the Sheriff. Somehow we have to convince our professors. We don't want them coming in contact with the Yrartz like we did."

"Good point," Amery said. She was wishing she hadn't made the statement about Matt finally getting his just reward. Thinking about it made her feel sick inside, sick and guilty.

The Supreme Commander ordered all troops on high alert. He did not know what was going on but he sent his officers to find out. The reports coming in were universally bad.

It seems a small group of humans had surrounded a patrol on 1210 and wiped them out. Another group ran over some of his men. And yet another man shot several of his best troops and got away clean.

"Officers I want all of you out there with your troops. We are losing too many to the enemy. Retreat if you have to but only as a last resort. I believe in you and I know you can deliver victory to me. Now go," he sent them off hoping he had inspired them.

Tom thought he heard the sound of a car engine. He said a silent prayer for the kids from Shell Lake. He was hoping they would get help very soon and this war would be over. He wanted to be able to go home and not have to worry about aliens.

Kelly didn't like the Yrartz and wanted them gone. But right now she was glad they had come. It seemed Tom was paying more attention to her than he ever had before. She decided they were going to stay together after this whether he liked it or not.

Bob felt protective of Kaitlyn. He wasn't sure what she wanted or what to do for her. But he was happy to have someone to fuss over. It helped him forget his own worries. He began to think of Kaitlyn as someone he could spend time with.

Kaitlyn was mostly numb. She and Matt hadn't been getting along well for some time now. They had even talked about a divorce. Clearly there had been problems but she had never wished him dead. She never wanted to see him killed in such an awful way. The tears began again.

Nate was worried about his candy bars. He had been eating them way too fast and didn't think he had enough to last till morning. The can of beans he carried in his backpack were just not an acceptable substitute.

"Hey I smell something funny," Jared said. "Smells like something burning."

"Me too," Kara affirmed.

"Look! There's smoke coming from the engine compartment and what's that thumping noise?" Amery asked.

As if to answer her the engine coughed a couple times and died. Amery had to use all her strength to keep the car on the road when the power steering failed. She brought the vehicle to a stop at the edge of the road and everyone jumped out.

Clifford Fifield heard the car approach and stop. He heard the doors slam shut and realized someone had gotten out. Why he didn't know and didn't care. He turned back toward the road and started running, thinking he could get a ride if he got there fast enough.

Amery stood looking at the smoking Suburban. "Well what do we do now?" she asked no one in particular.

Jared went to the front of the vehicle and opened the hood. Two of the Yrartz they ran over were still stuck in the engine compartment. He noticed that something dark and oily was dripping from the engine. Oil? Maybe.

"Does oil smoke like that when it gets hot?" he asked.

Carter had been helped from the car but was now standing without help. "I think oil smokes a lot when it gets overheated," he offered. "I'm no mechanic but I heard oil puts out black smoke when it burns."

"What's that noise?" Kara said. Before anyone could answer she shushed them. "It's coming from the brush over there."

Amery brought her gun up ready to fire. Jared found a tire iron from somewhere and stood next to her. Kara and Carter ducked behind the car hoping the other two could take care of the threat.

Deputy Fifield came out of the brush. "Don't shoot!" he called when he saw the gun in Amery's hand.

Amery lowered the gun. "Who are you and what are you doing here?"

"I'm a county sheriff's deputy, Cliff Fifield," he answered. Under normal circumstances he would have offered to shake hands. But this was far from normal and everyone was on edge. "Who are you and what happened to your car?"

"We're students from the Shell Lake Institute of Astrophysics. We came to look for meteorites," Jared told him. "We found out they weren't meteorites they were alien spacecraft. We ran over some Yrartz and they killed our engine."

At the name Cliff's eyebrows raised. "What did you call them?"

"Yrartz. The people that helped us said that is what they call themselves."

"The people that helped you? Where are they?"

Jared quickly updated Cliff on what had happened to them and a little about the aliens. The deputy told them of his own encounter. "Don't worry about it. When I don't call in they will send someone out to find me. Meanwhile we should get out of here. By now these Yrartz of yours have seen the smoke and are probably on their way."

"He's right," Jared agreed. "Let's go."

The five of them took off at a fast walk. Cliff figured to stay on the road instead of taking the shortcut. He saw the clothes the students were wearing and believed they would have a hard time in the woods and swamp.


The Yrartz officer in charge of protecting the approaches to West Falls had seen the smoke on Cumberland Road. He immediately sent a patrol to investigate. He was worried they might soon come under attack. He wanted to have firsthand knowledge of what was smoking and what was out there beyond.

The patrol leader took point on the road and led his unit quickly to the wrecked Suburban. They managed to stop the engine from smoking then searched the vehicle and surrounding area and found nothing. They extracted the two unfortunate Yrartz from the engine compartment and brought them back to base.

The unit leader had four troops stay in the brush near the car in hopes that the humans would return. He took the rest of the patrol and went down the logging road the astrophysics students had taken. They found several more aliens. Some were dead but some were only injured.

The patrol leader sent word back to base for more help in bringing out the wounded and the bodies. While they waited they moved the wounded out to Cumberland Road. The medic assigned to the patrol did what he could for them.


Tom and Kelly led the way through the swamp. They moved quickly fearing they might not get to Earl's farm before dark. The swamp was thick with cedar, spruce and tamarack. The trees and the brush in between made travel difficult.

Tom worried that they wouldn't get anywhere near the farm in daylight. He frequently had to go back and push Kaitlyn and Bob to go faster. It seemed the two of them were walking in a fog. Nate was finally moving along more quickly.

"I don't know what to do about them," Tom complained. "I understand that Kaitlyn is hurting. But the way her husband died, wouldn't you think she would want to get out of here and get away from those things?"

"I would," Kelly answered. "But I'm not her. I don't know how she is feeling or what she is thinking. Just go easy on her, okay Tom?"

"I will as long as we don't have aliens attacking us."

The NSA began calling up assets and notifying the right people. The monumental wheels of the federal government began slowly turning. Things were happening and agencies across the nation came to life and knowledge.

Satellites were redirected. Troops began deployment. Equipment moved rapidly into position. Hundreds, perhaps thousands of people went to work on the problem and possible solutions. Scenarios were developed, rewritten, redesigned. Every idea was given at least a little of the light of day. Nothing could be overlooked.

The information gathering process left more questions than answers. People in the higher pay grades pondered what to do and why. The President had to be briefed and hard data given.

First strike aircraft and helicopters swarmed the skies like angry hornets. Details, particulars, facts had to be discovered. Data was fed to computers and human analysts. Someone with the big picture had to make a decision.

Just as Tom and Kelly thought they would get safely and quietly to Earl's house gunfire erupted. Both of them dropped to the ground and began a 360 search. Kelly saw Bob first. She nudged his arm. "Tom look. Bob and Kaitlyn are coming at a run. We better go."

"Yep," was all Tom said. He stood up and pushed Kelly ahead of him. "You lead off. I'm going to wait for Bob and find out what happened."

Nate came running by first and didn't stop for a chat. He kept going trying to move fast enough to catch Kelly. He almost did before they made it to Earl's Road with Kaitlyn right behind him.

"What happened Bob?" Tom asked.

"Somehow some of them little green guys got between us and Nate. I had to shoot my way past them. A couple of their taser darts hit my clothes but none of them penetrated to the skin. I had Kaitlyn ahead of me so she wouldn't get hit."

Tom took aim and shot two quick ones at the enemy. "You catch up to Nate and Kelly. I'll hold them here for a minute."

Bob didn't argue. He headed off at a fast, ground eating trot. Kelly and Kaitlyn were crossing the road when he caught up to them. "Boy am I glad to see you're okay," Nate said.

"Me too," Bob replied.

The two men ran across the road together and joined the girls in the ditch on the other side. Kelly had binoculars out and was scoping the house. "What is it sis?" Nate asked.

"Get down," Kelly hissed at him. "I don't like the feel of this."

"You see any Yrartz?" Bob asked.

"Not yet but I think they are there. Ever get that feeling something is there but you can't see it?"

Tom came running across the road. "What's going on? Why aren't you guys moving?"

"Kelly thinks something is wrong," Nathan answered.

Tom looked at her questioningly. "No I can't see any of them. It's just a feeling, like when they jumped me in the swamp last night."

"The same feeling or a similar feeling?" he asked.

"The same feeling, exactly the same," Kelly said.

"Good enough for me. We take to the cornfield." Tom got up in a crouch and ran north along the ditch. Once he was past the first few rows of corn he turned and went into the cornfield. The others followed closely.

Tom thought it better to stay out of sight. Rougher going maybe but easier to remain hidden. They had escaped the Yrartz for the moment and he hoped to keep it that way.

He planned on using the house but now he decided to avoid it. The barn was too big to effectively defend. They were short one gun and now had an extra person to hide so Tom chose the shed north of the barn instead. It held a few pieces of machinery and a large number of bales of straw for bedding.

The shed Tom wanted to use was about twenty feet by thirty feet. It had one large door on the west end and two man doors one on the south near the big door. The other was on the north at the east end of the building. It was this door he decided to use. It faced away from the house, the road and the barn.

Earl's shed was an all wood affair with wood framed windows and an ancient wooden overhead door. The dirt floor gave it that musty odor common to old barns, sheds and root cellars. The old farmer had some people come in a few years back to shore up and straighten the place. It was a sturdy if aging building.

The walls had at some distant time past, been painted red on the outside. He had never bothered painting the inside walls.

The boards were dry and weathered. The cracks between them were big enough to see through.

Given enough time Tom would have preferred to wait for dark. But he didn't believe they would be safe that long. He felt they needed to get under cover in some defensible structure. The shed seemed to fit their needs best.

Bob was sitting just inside the cornfield about fifty feet from Tom, Kelly and Kaitlyn. Nate was about fifty feet the other side. They were security. Tom would dash across the open space to the shed first. Kelly would follow if the Yrartz sounded no alarms or made no moves. Then it would be Kaitlyn's turn.

"You ready," Tom asked.

"Yes," Kelly leaned toward him and they kissed. "Be careful," she admonished.

"I will," he answered and with that he was gone. Tom ran as fast as he could across the grass to the shed. He flattened himself against the wall and waited, watching Kelly for any sign or signal.

Kelly checked both right and left. Neither her brother nor Bob made any indication that the aliens had seen or heard anything. She checked once more and gave Tom a thumbs up sign.

Tom turned and grasped the door handle. He gave it a turn and then pushed. Nothing happened. *What the…*He tried again with the same result. He stepped to the window and looked into the murky interior of the shed. He couldn't see anything.

He checked the window to see if he might open that from outside. Tom tried pushing up on it but the window didn't budge. He tapped it lightly to try and jar it loose. Nothing. Kelly made a motion and mouthed *hurry up.*

Tom didn't need encouragement to hurry. He wanted to get in the shed and out of sight as soon as possible. They should be safe once inside. At least they would have a defensible position.

He tried the door once more and it seemed to give just a little. He put his weight into it and shoved hard. If it moved at all he couldn't tell. Kelly ran out of the cornfield and flattened against the wall. Kaitlyn followed closely unwilling to be alone.

"Try again. I'll help."

Together they pushed and the door moved ever so slightly. Silently shaking out his fingers, Tom counted one, two and they shoved again. This time the door opened enough for Kelly to slide through.

She so wanted to flip on the light switch so she could see everything. Instead Kelly flicked on her penlight. She immediately saw the problem. Evidently Earl had pushed a large cabinet up against the door at some time in the past. Whether he did so to hold the door shut or to make more room in the shed was anyone's guess.

Kelly pushed the cabinet and found she wasn't strong enough to move it by herself. Tom tried to squeeze through the opening and couldn't quite make it. He shoved against the door and managed to gain another couple inches, sufficient to let him pass.

Kaitlyn slipped in behind Tom and found a place in a corner. She backed up against the wall and slid down, seating herself on the cold dirt floor. Silently she began to sob.

Once inside Tom stuck his head and arm out and motioned for Nate to come over. The large man motored as best he could. With Tom and Kelly pushing from inside and Nate from outside they got the door all the way open.

Bob moved up to the spot Kaitlyn, Kelly and Tom had recently vacated. When given the signal he sprinted across the open ground and didn't stop until well inside the shed. Nate shut the door and put a two by four under the knob for greater security.

Tom and Kelly were looking out the small windows in the large overhead door. Now they could see several Yrartz milling about the house and driveway. Two even walked over to the barn, spent a little time in there and returned.

"Man I wish we had some way to communicate with Bill," Tom groused.

"We could send up smoke signals," Nate offered.

"I'll bet you don't even know how to send smoke signals or how to read them either," Bob said.

"Maybe not but I bet my granddad could," Nate retorted.

"If he was even here," Bob added.

"If he was still alive I'll bet he could," Nate said.

"And I'll bet my dad could beat your dad at checkers," Tom said getting into the fray.

"Nate, you, Bob and Tom are just like identical twins," Kelly told him.

Nate was about to reply when he realized what she said. He frowned, "Kelly that's not even possible." Bob nodded and Tom just snickered at the absurdity.

# Chapter 27

Bill had most of the town of West Falls on alert. He was taking no chances. He firmly believed the Yrartz would attack during the late hours of the afternoon, perhaps at dusk. If that didn't happen then he was sure they would attack at night or just before dawn. He really had no idea when they would attack but he was certain it would be soon.

John was concerned for Bill. Ever since the fight at the Washburn's he had been acting paranoid. It seemed he was seeing aliens coming from everywhere. But the evidence showed them only to the north. None had been seen south of town.

Now with much of the citizenry up and ready John was worried that most of them would be dozing when the attack actually happened. He had already approached Bill and asked that at least half of them be allowed to take a break. But Bill said no, that they needed to be ready.

John learned to take orders in his years in the army. So he would obey Bill's wishes. However when he could he would give people a chance to eat and sleep so they were refreshed when an attack came.

Currently every positon had two or three people in it. John made sure Bill was busy with strategic planning before he walked around the perimeter. He told the people that at least one of them had to be on alert at all times. Then he told them the others should rest, sleep if possible and eat. He tried to stress the importance that food and rest would play in the upcoming battle.

Deputy Fifield led the group into the woods alongside the road. "We had better stay under cover. I don't know what kind of vehicles the aliens have. Did you see anything like tanks or armored cars? Any big guns, cannons?"

Carter looked at him funny. "Ah, no we didn't see anything like that. All we saw were these darts that I think were wireless tasers and they all had something in their other hands too."

"I think the other weapon was a laser. That's what it looked like to me," Jared said.

Cliff looked at the girls expecting something. "We didn't see much," Amery said. "We weren't there when they attacked and killed Matt. We were up the road around a curve and couldn't see anything.

"The only Yrartz we saw were the ones I ran over on the logging road. I really didn't pay any attention to what weapons they had."

Feeling she had to say something Kara added, "I didn't see any guns or tanks or anything like that either."

Cliff let that sink in. "So they have some kind of spacecraft that they landed in but they don't have any ground vehicles?" he asked no one in particular. "That doesn't seem logical. I mean why would aliens travel millions of miles and land here with no way to travel a few thousand more? Why would they come here without tactical vehicles?"

"Honestly deputy, we really hadn't thought about it until now." Jared continued, "But now that you mention it that doesn't make sense. All I can tell you is we haven't seen or heard anything like armored vehicles."

"I'm not sure if that's a relief or makes things scarier."

"What do you mean?" Carter asked.

"Well if you haven't seen any tanks and such then are they keeping them in reserve or did they just forget to bring them on this invasion?"

"Are you being a little sarcastic?" Jared asked.

"Not at all," Cliff said. "Do they have armor? We don't know. If they do where is it and why haven't they used it? If they don't have any then what kind of invasion force is this? I mean, you invade a planet you bring your best stuff, right?"

Cliff's argument was sound however it made the four students uneasy. Now they had something big to worry about. Before they only had a small invasion force with pathetic weapons. Now that force could be hiding nasty WMDs.

Did the Yrartz have chemical or biological weapons? Did they have nuclear capabilities? Did they have planet killer lasers on spacecraft just waiting to see how this war went?

These same questions had been floating through Bill's thoughts lately. The what ifs had been taking a toll on his mind. Those questions kept him awake as if he needed anything else to do that for him.

But Bill had come to the conclusion that these particular aliens either didn't have heavy weapons or choose not to use them. That brought up a whole new series of questions. If you had big guns why didn't you use them? If you didn't have any big guns, why not?

Bill kept these questions to himself. He did not want to add worry any of the defenders of West Falls any more than they already had. Combat leaders often keep things from the troops and he was certainly no exception.

Carl Vue was put in command of the southern barricade. He had proven his abilities and Bill had faith in him. The West falls commander did not expect an attack from the south but he still wanted one of his best men in charge down there. He could better focus on the north and the aliens he knew were gathered there.

Within the dubious security of Earl's shed the group of five began rearranging things. They couldn't move the Case H or any of the other machinery without making too much noise. But there were a number of objects they could place against the doors or make a barricade of.

Tom and Bob moved a heavy workbench up against the man door. Kelly rolled several tires against the overhead door. They wouldn't stop the door from opening but they would give the gang something to hide behind.

Nathan joined in, candy bar in hand. He picked up a metal truck tire rim and set it near a door. He looked at that and then at the others and realized he should be doing more. He stuffed the last of the candy into his mouth and went to help Bob with a cabinet.

Tom pulled several straw bales over to the center of the shed. "What are you doing Tom?" Nate asked. Bob looked at it and wondered the same thing.

"I'm building a fallback position," he answered. "See the Yrartz weapons are short range and not powerful enough to penetrate these bales. If they get in here we will try to defend ourselves from in here."

"I thought we were planning to run if they come," Bob said.

"We will run if we can't defend this shed. But if only a few of them attack we stay and fight."

"Okay, I can see that. Sounds like good strategy," Bob agreed. He went to the pile of straw bales and picked two up. Nate followed his lead. Soon they had what appeared to be a viable defensive position.

"I hate to ask this question but since the Yrartz have lasers won't they be able to start these very dry straw bales on fire?" Kaitlyn asked. Those were the first words from her since she parted company with her fellow students.

Tom felt really stupid. "She's right," he admitted. He immediately began removing the bales and switching them with material they had at the overhead door.

Before anyone asked, "Lets move the bales to the door and the tires and other stuff into our fallback position. That way if the bales start on fire we can escape through the back door while they are stopped. It will be a good diversion."

Everyone, even Kaitlyn pitched in to help. They formed a chain to make it go faster. The fallback position quickly took shape again. Tom decided to keep the wall of straw bales low and wide for greater surface area. More flames he reasoned.

With that done the five went back to work on covering windows and blocking doors. The only door left open was the one they came in by. The rest had everything and anything piled against them.

Yrartz 1307 was assigned guard duty again. He had been on guard duty since landing on earth. He was happy to be on watch out here at this farm house. It was easy and relaxing. No one bothered you, not even the generals. But he still wanted to get into the fray.

He knew the enemy were dangerous and deadly. But this was his chance to prove himself and he didn't want it to slip away. So he walked his route carefully and kept his eyes open.

One of 1307s friends found a pair of binoculars in the farmhouse and he gave them to him. Every now and then he would put them up to his eyes and scan the area all around. So it was he thought he saw something up at that old shed, just a

348

flash of movement. Not enough to be sure but enough to make him curious.

From then on he checked the shed frequently. He began to notice little things. Like the windows seemed darker than they had been. He believed he even saw a person's face, a human face, at one of them.

1307 determined to check it out once his duty was over. He would take some of his friends along and look inside the shed. If there were humans in it he would be a hero for finding them plus he and his friends might get a quick snack.


Darkness descended on the swamp adding to the spooky feeling. Halloween was a few weeks away but things often went bump in the night near West Falls. Mostly they were Yrartz that got lost or were afraid of the dark. In fact many of the aliens were afraid of the dark and so they tended to huddle around the spacecraft in the LZ.

The Supreme Commander was in his tent trying to sort out the best way to attack the town. He had already figured on launching the first wave at high noon local time. He believed that was the best time for an assault because the people would be eating lunch. He had no idea his timepiece was set to Pacific Time.

One other issue kept the Commander up at night; food or rather lack thereof. The Yrartz had seriously depleted their food stocks on the voyage to earth. Something had to be done within the next couple of days or he would find himself at the mercy of over a thousand hungry aliens.

To that end the Commander had sent out special units to forage for food. So far they had returned with a sheep, five whitetail deer, two dogs, a goat, three coyotes, an unlucky moose and seventy-five rabbits. That was enough to feed maybe a hundred and fifty troops one meal.

That was the main reason the Yrartz kept trying to take the town. The Supreme Commander felt the residents of West Falls could feed his people for at least a week. It wasn't just the humans. There were dogs and cats and maybe some other animals.

One of the Yrartz food foraging units was traveling south on Cumberland Road a little after dusk. The point alien called a halt and motioned his lieutenant forward. "Sir I think I heard someone talking in the woods over there," he pointed.

Without a word the lieutenant took two men and went forward. They stopped at the edge of the road and listened. They all thought they heard something too but they also smelled smoke.

The lieutenant immediately moved his troops on down the road at a fast clip. He believed the woods were on fire and they needed to get out of there to avoid being burned alive. The entire unit clustered together and went rapidly toward the LZ.

Clifford Fifield saw the Yrartz leave but did not comprehend their reason for going. He was concerned they might come back and so had the students pack up and move again. It was a precaution that he felt was warranted in light of the type of enemy they were.

Much to his surprise none of the students complained about moving again. They picked up quietly and trudged farther on into the woods. Clifford wasn't certain he could find his way out of the woods but he figured he would eventually get back to some road. All he had to do was walk in a straight line long enough and he knew he would hit some kind of road.

None of the students thought to bring matches or any kind of fire starter. But Cliff never went into the woods without a cigarette lighter. He didn't smoke but found plenty of other uses for the lighter. This night a fire would cheer up the kids and keep them warm. He believed it was worth the risk.

Walking along a game trail the deputy found some pieces of birch bark. Carter asked, "What are you doing?"

"I'm picking up bark. Birch bark starts on fire easily even when wet and will help us get a good fire going once we are a safe distance from the road," Cliff answered.

Carter began picking up bark too. He also grabbed small sticks and branches. He had no idea how much wood it took to keep a fire going all night.

When deputy Fifield felt they were far enough he called a halt. "We will camp here for the night. I don't understand why no one has come looking for me yet but there isn't anything I can do about it tonight."

Clifford kicked leaves and forest debris out of a circle he planned for the fire. Then he started building a teepee out of the birch bark and small sticks near the center of the circle. Carter contributed his material.

The students gathered more branches and bark. Cliff broke off larger chunks from the blowdown he had located. The blowdown was the primary reason he chose the site. It would give them plenty of wood for the fire.

Once the fire was going one person was put in charge of feeding it. Clifford directed two of the young people to try and sleep while one kept watch. He decided to walk out away from the site and listen for any sign of the aliens.

"We have to make our inner sanctum as solid as we can," Tom told them. "The walls of this shed have lots of holes. We can't have any light escaping. So if anyone uses a flashlight or lighter you must do it in the fallback position. Everyone understand?" Everyone did.

Tom went around the perimeter of the inner room to check for any sign of light. He hoped he had stressed the importance of light discipline. If the enemy saw anything up here they would come and they just might succeed in killing them this time.

October in northern Wisconsin can be cold, especially at night. They couldn't build a fire inside the building and no one brought any blankets. The gang had to use what was available to keep them warm.

Fortunately Earl kept everything. Tom found a large quantity of old style gunny sacks. He placed several layers of these down on the floor in the fallback position. Bob helped him as he brought more sacks to use as blankets and pillows. By the time they were done they had a remarkably comfortable bed.

When the inner room was finally ready it was dark outside. Tom took the first watch as the others tried to sleep. Kelly was tired but unable to nod off so she joined Tom. They both peered out the small windows on the overhead door.

"You should try to get some sleep," Tom suggested.

"I can't sleep."

They could hear Bob and Nate talking. "Fighting Yrartz is like fighting zombies except these are real and zombies are fiction.

"Yeah and Yrartz smell worse," Nate added. "If we have to make a run for it we can tell if they are close. We will smell them in the dark just as easily as in daylight."

"True enough."

"Apparently you aren't the only one who can't sleep," Tom said. "I should go tell them to be quiet and get some rest."

"Oh Tom, leave them be. They probably are talking because they're too scared to sleep. Talking takes their minds off the danger and they probably will fall asleep eventually."

"You're probably right," Tom agreed. He straightened up suddenly and stared out the window.

Kelly sensed it more than saw him. "What is it?" she asked anxiously.

"I thought I saw something. Maybe a couple Yrartz or maybe not. Could have been a deer or some other animal."

An eerie silence surrounded them. There were no natural sounds from animals or even the wind. It was so quiet they could hear the blood squirting through their veins.

In the absence of all else, fear came. It engulfed and overwhelmed them. Fear embedded itself deep in their minds, a swirling darkness that chills. The fear seemed to push down on them all, stifling creeping in.

Kaitlyn heard Tom say he thought he saw something. She couldn't sleep any more than anyone else could. She stood up to better see and hear Tom and Kelly.

"There they are," Kelly pointed. "I see three, no four at least."

"Keep quiet. They don't know we're here and they might just bypass us," Tom said hopefully. The aliens or animals or whatever they saw were coming straight for the shed but they were moving slowly as if to sneak up without being seen or heard.

Staring into the darkness Tom finally made a positive identification. "False alarm. They are deer not aliens." Kelly went to check on Kaitlyn and reassure her.

Bob and Nate were still talking. "My sister is about the only single girl in town. She's my sister so I can't date her and your brother likes her so you can't date her. There are real disadvantages to living in a small town."

"Miss Grace is single," Bob pointed out.

"You're a sick puppy. She's old enough to be your grandma. She used to babysit us."

"True but she is single."

"Well your grandmother is single too. But I ain't gonna date her either." Nathan got up and went over to where Tom was.

He had temporarily grown tired of Bob but their conversation had made him think.

"Hey Nate. What's up?" Tom asked.

"I just been thinking."

"What's on your mind?" Tom asked.

"Are we friends because of my sister?"

"What do you mean?"

"I know you think my sister is hot."

"Yes she is gorgeous. She's the most beautiful woman I've ever seen."

"I know you like her. Is that why we're friends?" Nate asked again.

"Dude we've been friends since I was four and you and Bob were two years old. She wasn't even born yet. How could she be a factor in our friendship? What four year old thinks about girls?"

"Maybe a precocious one?" Nate answered.

"Do you even know what that means?" Tom asked.

"Use it in a sentence."

"Listen Nate, we are friends because we have been forever. We met at Miss Grace Whitefeathers daycare. We played together as kids. We love each other like brothers. We like to do many of the same things like hunt and fish and play football."

"And eat. Well at least I do."

"Yeah that's why you weigh, I mean that's why you're…"

"You saying I'm fat?"

"Yep."

"I'm not fat. I'm vertically challenged. That's covered by the Americans with Disabilities Act I think."

"You're not vertically challenged. You're six feet tall."

"Okay I'm horizontally challenged. I'm sure that's covered by the ADA."

"I'm not sure if overeating is covered by the ADA."

"I don't overeat. I'm just eating for the future. Never know when we might run out of food, especially with the Yrartz around."

# Chapter 28

Yrartz 1307 finally got off guard duty. He quickly rounded up some of his friends. "I think there are humans in that building over there," he pointed.

One of his friends asked, "What makes you think so?"

"I've been watching it all night and I noticed some things. It looks like someone is covering the windows. Before that I thought I saw a human face in one of the windows. Plus it's the perfect place to spy on us from."

"Well you go right ahead and check things out. If you find anything let me know and I'll come help kill them." Yawning he added, "Now I'm tired and I'm going to bed." He left 1307 and the other two Yrartz.

"What about you guys? You with me?" 1307 asked.

"Yes sure we're with you," they both affirmed.

"Okay here's my idea." 1307 went into the details of his plan. He told them it was fool proof. There really was no danger and there was the potential for great reward. The others swallowed his argument without question.


Bill finally forced himself to take a break. He went inside Ted Hawkins shop and found a comfortable place in the office. Seconds after he sat down he fell asleep. He needed this more than anything right then.

John came in with reports from each sector. Upon finding Bill asleep he backed out of the office quietly a smile crossing his face. Good, the boss is sleeping.

John assumed command for the moment. He checked everything Bill would have checked. He made sure everyone was ready for an attack if such should come. He made the rounds to keep up morale and assure himself all was in place.

"I read that book Cervantes Inferno once."

"Nate, Cervantes wrote Don Quixote. Don't you mean Dante's Inferno?"

Nate nodded, "Could be."

"Hey I saw the movie," Bob interjected. "Wasn't that the one where the skyscraper in New York is on fire?"

"You're thinking of the Towering…"

"Everyone shut up," Kelly hissed. "I hear something." She was looking through a knothole. "Oh," she cried as she jumped back.

Tom turned to her. "What just happened?"

Kelly hushed him with a finger to her lips. He moved quietly across the shed to her side and sat down. "I almost got hit in the eye by a laser," she whispered.

"They're probing the shed, trying to see if anyone's in here. They've lost a bunch of troops and don't want to attack without some good intel." Tom looked for a crack in the shed walls that he could see through. He carefully put his eye to the opening just as a Yrartz rolled past. It spooked him, he jumped. He had to smile at himself for being startled by a shadow.

Kaitlyn had been quietly watching all this. She had a worried look on her face, the look of terror. Soon she began to sob. Bob didn't know what to do as he sat beside her and held her.

Suddenly a laser shone through the gloom. A straw bale began smoking, the smell penetrating to every corner. Smoke poured out then a flame flared up from the bale.

Nate scrambled to cover the fire with a gunny sack. Tom prepared to shoot at any Yrartz that got close. Kaitlyn screamed and jumped up shouting, "We're all going to die."

Bob grabbed Kaitlyn in a bear hug and stifled any further noises. He held her tightly and put one hand over her mouth. He was trying to force her to sit down again when Kelly raced over and slapped him in the face.

Still struggling with Kaitlyn he looked at Kelly with a dumb expression. "What did you slap me for?"

"You were closer," Kelly replied.


Outside the Yrartz were getting agitated. They were sure they heard noises, human voices inside the shed. 1307 was ecstatic! Now he knew for certain he had humans trapped. He could see a big promotion for himself and maybe a medal. He would be seen as a huge hero.

1307 motioned for his buddies to move to the sides. They would flank the enemy and make lunch of them. It was all so easy. Everything was falling into place.

"Where's Tom?" Kelly asked as she headed back to her place by the door. When no one answered she asked again a little louder. "Anyone know where Tom is?"

Bob shrugged his shoulders. Kaitlyn still had her mouth covered by Bob's hand. Nathan looked around the room before answering, "He was just here."

"I know that mister obvious." Kelly was frustrated. Kaitlyn had made noise and given them away. Nate was making useless comments and now Tom had gone missing. "If that chicken sh…pup ran I'm going to live long enough to catch him and…" She let that drop unsaid.

There was a thud as of something blunt hitting something semi-soft. Then a heavier thud. Kelly looked out the knothole she almost got zapped at. She had just enough time to see Tom swing and hit another Yrartz and watch it drop as he ran for the last one.

The second of 1307s friends had turned and was rolling for his life when Tom's swing caught him on the back of the head.

The third Yrartz went down on the third hit. Tom batted a thousand.

Kelly ran out of the shed and into Tom's arms. He let go of the axe he had used. "What were you thinking?" she demanded as she threw her arms around him. Before he could answer she planted a kiss on his lips. "You saved us."

When Tom could breathe again he said, "No, I only allowed us some time. We made too much noise. The Yrartz surely heard all this commotion. They're going to come and investigate."

Smiling at him and still holding his arm she said, "Well we better get moving then."

Tom and Kelly went back inside the shed. "Okay everyone start packing up. We have to move now."

"Why Tom? What's happened? I thought you killed those Yrartz."

"Unfortunately Bob I'm not sure if I killed them or not. I didn't check the bodies. Doesn't matter. We made too much noise. The Yrartz are sure to send more troops up here to investigate.

"When they find their dead or wounded comrades they will come after us. We have a few minutes to get out of here unseen. So let's stop the chatter and get ready. Nate, you keep an eye out the door. Make sure our escape route is still open."

Nathan moved out the door and positioned himself in the cornfield. He had a good view of the house and barn. He could see well enough to make out most of the area around the shed.

Kaitlyn had calmed down and was doing her part to prepare for the move. Bob helped her into a heavier coat and gave her a small backpack. He put on his gear and picked up his rifle. "We're ready."

"Good," Tom said. Turning, "Kelly?"

"I'm ready. Let's go."

Once more Tom led the way out the door. When he came up beside Nate he asked, "You see anything?"

"The deers," Nate pointed into the cornfield.

"The deer," Tom corrected.

"Huh?"

"Deer is both singular and plural."

"Yeah, that's what I said. Deers, plural. There was more than one of them," Nate said exasperated.

Tom gave up and rolled his eyes. He moved past Nathan, Kelly following close behind. Nate took the middle this time. Bob and Kaitlyn shared the rear guard.

The aliens in and near Earl Stinnett's house had indeed heard the scuffle up at the shed. The first response from the leaders was to set up a defensive perimeter. They made sure the troops were surrounding the house and covering every compass point.

They held positons for several minutes allowing the five humans to escape. When the leaders finally decided to check out the commotion they had heard the people were gone. Tom had eased his group silently into the swamp leaving the Yrartz wondering where they went.

"Get patrols out now," the Yrartz commander yelled or squeaked. "I want to know who they are and how many. I want them here and whole. I will personally interrogate them. Now move!"

The area around Earl's place became a hornet's nest of activity. Aliens were running into each other trying to get ready and form up units. Unit commanders were shouting orders and countermanding other orders. Confusion reigned.

It was thirty minutes before the first patrol left. They headed straight west, the opposite direction of the shed. The patrol commander had no intention of coming across the humans that had been in the building. He did not want a fight and he did not care if he lost an easy promotion.

Tom had run his people down the rows of corn and into the woods near his archery deer stand. He kept everyone moving as fast as he could. He wanted to be out of the cornfield, through the woods and into the swamp before the aliens could begin pursuit.

Running through the corn wasn't a problem. The rows were clearly defined even in the dark. But when they entered the woods branches hit them in the face and trees blocked their path. They kept going faster than prudent anyway.

At first they could hear the sounds of major activity at the farm. But soon all sound was lost except what they made. The only noises were their foot falls and the brushing of their clothes against the trees and bushes. There was no need to push anyone. They all wanted to get away as quickly and quietly as possible.

Once in the swamp Tom slowed his pace. He stopped and made sure everyone was still together. The last thing he wanted was to lose someone now. The swamp was much darker than the woods or cornfield and therefore easier to get lost in.

Fear kept Nathan moving, kept him with the rest of the group. It also made him want to talk. Every time he became nervous he talked incessantly, usually saying whatever came to mind first.

He dropped back to Bob and Kaitlyn. "Ever read a book where it says someone swept into the room?"

Bob's eyebrows knitted. *What has this got to do with anything?* "Ah, yes I have."

"Makes you wonder, did they use a broom? What does swept into the room mean?"

"Not sure but I know normal people don't say things like that," Bob replied.

"Writer's must be very odd ducks," Nate said.

"Yep, I think so although I've never met one."

Kaitlyn took all this in then leaned toward Bob and whispered in his ear. "So go ahead and say it," Bob urged her.

"What?" Nate asked.

Kaitlyn wouldn't say what was on her mind. "She says you are kind of weird."

"Hey, weird is good sometimes, as long as you aren't trying to get a date."

Tom was waiting for them. "You guys know we are fleeing from the alien's right?"

Bob protested, "He started it. He came back and talked to me first."

Tom shook his head at his brother's excuse. He turned to Nate. "Sometimes I wonder where your brain is."

"I'm told it's inside my head. But that's still unproven," Nathan answered seriously.

"I'll have to take a flashlight and look in your ear sometime," Bob said.

"Yeah or up my nose."

# Chapter 29

There is a super-secret government agency known as the Security Deposit Corporation or SDC. Its name is not secret. Its mission is.

Many people believe the Security Deposit Corporation ensures those who return bottles and cans get their deposit back. Others think the SDC insures the security deposits renters give their landlords. Yet others think it may have something to do with banks.

The Security Deposit Corporation was created after an incident in New Mexico. In 1959, after much discussion at the highest levels of government and the scientific community, the new agency was formed. Most of the people involved in the dialogue were not ultimately part of the agency or even knew of its existence.

The SDC was charged with finding, securing and removal of alien artifacts. The real purpose of the agency was simply to gather and preserve these pieces of extraterrestrial materials and beings. The idea was to put the items in a safe place and make them available to persons allowed to study the items.

Area 51 was part of the Security Deposit Corporations plans. The place was set up as a false front. The agency leaked information that led people to believe it was where these alien artifacts were kept. Area 51 is perhaps the best counterfeit base ever created by the US government. Only two US Presidents ever knew the truth about the SDC or Area 51.

The true location of the SDCs main facilities remains secret. Most of the people working for the agency don't know where it is based. The scientists and engineers that study extraterrestrial artifacts and aliens do so by use of computers and other electronic means. They do not actually touch the items and are not allowed in the presence of them.

We believe the Security Deposit Corporations primary base is located approximately here. All evidence suggests that is the true venue. It is one of three sites maintained by the SDC. The others are over there and not so far away.

Somewhere deep in an SDC vault is an alien ship that landed on Mount St Helens. In that same vault is the body of an alien that until now had remained unnamed. The Yrartz was the first to arrive and the first to die though not by human hands.

The first Yrartz came to the Security Deposit Corporations facility in pieces. Robots dissected it so that now it is in many more pieces. Tests done on the body confirmed what scientists believed.

Yrartz patrols found no trails linking Tom's group to the shed. They found no trails at all. None of the unit leaders really wanted to encounter an enemy that could do such damage as these humans seemed able to. This particular band of people were especially volatile.

No amount of bellowing or cajoling by the Supreme Commander could get the troops to find Tom's unit. Most of the leaders felt if the Commander wanted them that badly he should lead the element. They did their best to assure him they were doing everything in their power to capture these enemies.

Any evidence brought in by the patrols was quickly and quietly confiscated and destroyed. Talk of findings were suppressed. The higher Yrartz commanders kept all of it from their leader.

There was mutinous talk among the generals. They now believed this invasion was a total failure and the only prudent move was to pack up and leave. It was with this thought in mind that they began preparations. Secretly units were sent back to the LZ to check out and repair ships for imminent departure.

The generals fed the Supreme Commander whatever information would make him happy. Under no circumstances would they tell him the truth. They planned to move troops back and forth around the area so that if the Commander ordered them to attack West Falls it would appear they were complying. The only wrinkle in their plan was the odd enthusiastic patriot.

All was quiet in West Falls. Bill Webster was still sound asleep. Most of the town's residents were sleeping also. John made sure an adequate number of guards were at their posts to defend the place or at least sound the alarm.

He set up roving patrols of which he was one. The patrols went along the perimeter and made sure guards were alert. They also patrolled across the town itself to capture any aliens that snuck through the lines. So far none had.

John believed what Bill said about an attack. He too felt it was imminent. He was planning to get everyone up before dawn and man every position with at least three people. This would be a big surprise for any Yrartz that assaulted the town.

The gang of five did not know if any Yrartz were still at Grandma Hayward's farm. They suspected some were left behind to guard the place. Tom stopped the group just short of the barnyard fence.

"Okay everybody. Listen up. We have to approach the buildings carefully. There may still be aliens around but even if there aren't we don't want to make a lot of noise. We want to avoid both domestic livestock and wildlife. We don't want any animals making noise. All of you understand that." Pep talk over Tom said, "Let's move out."

The group had not encountered any Yrartz on their way to Grandma's farm. Now they had to be extra cautious. They had made good their escape and no one wanted to screw that up.

Tom motioned for Nate to stay at the fence. He sent Bob and his stick on companion to the north past the house to watch up there. Kelly came with him as he slowly moved on the house.

To Tom it seemed every board on the porch groaned in protest as he stepped lightly across it. The screen door was no help either. It made more than enough screeching noise as he opened it. He had to push hard on the kitchen door to get it open.

When Tom had the door open about six inches he encountered resistance. Sticking his head through the opening he smelled and saw two dead Yrartz blocking the door. He shoved harder and managed to get through.

After a careful check of the kitchen Tom waved Kelly in. She would stand guard and cover his back. As she came in she noticed the smell and the Yrartz. She helped him move the bodies enough so they could open the door wide.

The pair cleared the house using penlights to help find their way. They did not want to turn on any lights and risk alerting the aliens. Once the place was secure they motioned Nate in and waited for Bob and Kaitlyn to make a reconnaissance of the barnyard and the out buildings except the barn. Tom felt three or four of them should check out that structure since it was the largest.

"What's that smell?" Nate asked as he entered.

Kelly answered, "Two Yrartz died in the kitchen. I'm surprised you didn't know them by their odor."

"They don't smell as bad when they've been dead a while. I swear Yrartz are the only things I know of that smell worse when they're alive than when they're dead."

"You know big brother I think you're right," Kelly agreed. "Say big bro help me carry these things out. No need for us to gag on the smell of dead aliens."

Kelly and Nate took the bodies out while Tom tried to clean up some of the mess. Chairs and tables were overturned from the fight. There were books and dishes on the floor. There were other dead aliens in the house too.

Bob and Kaitlyn joined the rest in the kitchen. "I think we should set up a watch," Bob suggested.

"I agree. Who wants the first turn?" Tom asked.

Bob said, "Kaitlyn and I will do the first watch. She can't sleep and I'm not feeling tired right now either."

"Okay that's settled. Nate can you take second? Kelly third? I will bring up the dawn watch." Noticing something he asked, "You look confused Nathan. What is it?"

"I'll take the second watch but what time does it start? It's midnight already."

Tom said, "Good point. Bob and Kaitlyn take from now till two. Nate, two till four. Kelly and I will take the dawn watch together. That way one of us can start breakfast. Granny always has something good in the fridge. There are probably still eggs and milk in there."

Nate's eyes lit up. "I am hungry. Maybe I should take the first watch."

"No Nate. I know what you're thinking. But you do your time outside where you can see aliens before they get close to the rest of us and not here in the kitchen."

Nathan was about to start pouting when Kelly stepped over and gave him a hug. She said, "Hey big brother, since you don't start your watch till two you can have something to eat now." She smiled warmly as she went to the refrigerator and opened it. She leaned in and looked for something Nate would like to snack on.

For the first time since the invasion began, West Falls and the area around it was relatively quiet. The only serious activity was in the Yrartz LZ. Mechanics there were doing their best to repair damaged ships. Refueling began in earnest and the troops in the area gathered belongings in preparation.

The generals ordered everything be kept in strictest secret. No one outside the LZ was to have any knowledge of the goings on there. But as with any military organization leaks occurred. More troops seemed to be drifting in with every hour that passed.

The primary objective of the generals was to prepare the ships for launch while keeping the Supreme Commander and most of his staff from finding out about the LZ. So far that was working. But with all the Yrartz moving in it would soon become impossible to hide.

General 441 was commander of the elite Yellow Yrartz. The Yellows were like the Navy Seals, Army Rangers and Delta Force but in an unimaginative and less deadly sort of way. Fear was not a factor, unless something scared them. They would go where no Yrartz had gone before and possibly stay there.

441 was charged with perimeter security. The generals needed his elite force to stop the influx and turn it back. The Yellows set up all around the LZ and held the line letting no one in. They began moving nonessential personnel out of the LZ as well. They checked everyone in the zone to make sure they had a reason to be there.

Only mechanics, their helpers and their officers were allowed to stay. Still some Yrartz managed to find ways to remain in the LZ. They took up tools and made as if to work on the ships. At least a dozen of them were good enough actors to hide in the open this way. In the process they did more harm than good.

Granny's house was old and porous so she kept a roll of plastic and a bundle of wood laths to use to cover the windows. Tom used some of these items and went from window to window tacking up blankets to keep the light from being seen outside. Even with this precaution he would only allow low wattage lamps to be used.

Bob and Kaitlyn were outside watching for aliens and checking Tom's work. They let him know if any light could be seen from the windows. She stood close and checked for leaks. He stood well back from the house and listened for approaching Yrartz.

The pair made a good team, each doing their duty. Bob's closeness seemed to calm Kaitlyn down and greatly relieve her fears. He felt protective and this heightened his resolve to survive and keep her safe. The combination made them both better, stronger.

Nate got his snack. Kelly cooked up some grilled cheese for the three of them. She ate one, Tom ate two and Nathan ate the other five. Satisfied, he went to one of the bedrooms and fell onto the bed. He was snoring within seconds.

Kelly washed the dishes while Tom finished with the windows. They sat down on the couch and fell into each other's arms. "There's a verse in the Bible," Tom said. "Psalm 4:8. *'In peace I will both lie down and sleep, for You alone, O Lord make me dwell in safety."* They went to sleep with smiles on their faces, not thinking about the danger outside.

Bill's alarm woke him at 3:56 AM. He couldn't believe he slept through the night. He bounded out of bed and threw on some clothes. He rushed to get to the front lines and prepare his troops for battle.

The military commander of the town of West Falls, Wisconsin still firmly believed an attack was imminent. He would have everyone up, awake and alert. Bill expected the Yrartz to come at dawn, the usual time of a surprise attack. But this would be no surprise to the humans.

Bill found John at the barricade on Cumberland Road. "Why did you let me sleep so long?" he demanded. Then without waiting for an explanation, "Is everyone up and ready? Are all posts manned? Have you heard anything from the outside? From Tom and his unit?"

"Whoa, slow down Bill. Hey buddy you need to let me answer some of those questions before you go on to the next ones."

"Sorry," Bill apologized. "I'm a little wired today. We may be under attack at any time and I want us to have a chance at survival."

"I understand Bill. Now to answer some of your questions, yes everyone is up and alert. I made sure all posts are manned by at least two or three people. I checked to make sure everyone has plenty of ammunition and other supplies.

"Somewhat against your orders I had everyone take a nap last night. I did it in shifts so we had fifty percent alert at all times. And I made sure no one disturbed you so you could get plenty of sleep. You need to be one hundred percent today and that means you get some sleep."

John paused then went on, "Now is there anything else you have a question about?"

Bill looked at his second in command. "Wow you did a great job. Maybe you should lead this group instead."

"No. You are the elected commander and you have the experience. I am a behind the scenes man and always want to be."

"As you wish. Now there are some things I need to know. Did anyone see any movement by the aliens last night?"

"Negative."

"Did you hear from Tom's unit or any other person from the outside?"

"Again, negative."

"Okay so we are on our own as far as we know. So let's get ready for the assault. We have just about three hours before sunrise." Bill thought a moment. "Are the cooks in the kitchen? Do we have breakfast set up?"

"Yes sir. I made sure they had everything ready and I started sending small groups to breakfast about ten minutes ago. One out of three people at a time and they have to wait until that person returns before the next one goes. We should have everyone through by five thirty, quarter to six."

"Good, good. Well it seems you have everything in hand so let's go have breakfast and we can discuss strategy."

General 441 and the Yrartz Yellows had removed all unnecessary personnel from the LZ. They clamped down hard and even finally found the fakers and kicked them out. Unfortunately a few legitimate mechanics were sent away also and had to find their commanders in order to get back in.

The Supreme Commander went about his routine completely unaware of what was going on in the LZ. He had no idea the patrols he wanted sent out were uselessly beating the bush in the opposite direction from any threat. He was blissfully ignorant that all his troops had been pulled back from the borders of West Falls and that the generals had no intention of attacking the town.

The Yrartz generals began a meeting at four AM where they were trying to decide what to do about the Supreme Commander. If they openly mutinied they would have to either jail the Commander or kill him. Both possibilities left problems that must also be overcome.

If they jailed him what to do with him afterward? If they took his life what would stop lesser officers from doing the same to them? Which action would cause the least trouble for the generals?

General 441 had gained his position as commander of the elite forces because of his abilities. One of those attributes included thinking outside the box. Therefore when he spoke everyone listened.

"GentleYrartz I believe we have an option you have not yet considered." 441 paused and scanned the faces around the table. "We do not have to be held responsible for any harm that might befall the Supreme Commander." He let that sink in.

"How is this possible?" one of the generals asked.

"Simply let the humans kill him."

There was a rumbling at the table. "So you think the humans will just come in here at our request and kill the Supreme Commander?" General 533 scoffed.

"No general. I have an easy and foolproof plan. We simply tell the Supreme Commander we want him to accompany us on a tour of the front lines. We can get him close and one of my loyal unit commanders will hit him from cover. No one, not even any of you will know who did it. Then we blame it on the humans and all of us are free of any culpability."

"Except what if your loyal commander talks or worse blackmails us?"

"Not to worry. I will deal with my unit commander. He will not talk. He will not get the chance."

The generals were satisfied. The plan was put into effect. The Supreme Commander would soon be gone and so would the Yrartz. They would leave the earth as soon as the Commander was dealt with. There were many smug smiles around the table.

# Chapter 30

The lead elements of the SDC were pushing through the darkness. The unit commander had possibilities running overtime in his brain. He knew very little about what he was coming up against. He knew what the terrain looked like and where the buildings, roads and woods were. He had knowledge of some of the people in West Falls. What he did not have is knowledge of these aliens.

The sum total of the information available to him was that aliens had invaded a small town, West Falls, Wisconsin. There was no information about what the aliens looked like or how many there were. There was nothing on what type or how many weapons they had. No one knew what affect human-made weapons might have on the aliens either.

The unit commander was a major, at least for this mission. He commanded an elite team of two hundred men and women plus support units. His operation was backed up by the equivalent of two battalions of special forces. They included Green Berets, SEALs, US Army Rangers and various black ops units.

The operation was run by the SDC major and everyone was directed to obey his orders. He met with all the unit commanders and informed them of his plans and what their individual roles would be. Questions were asked and many of them were answered.

But everyone knew the major and the SDC were in charge. Many of the unit commanders were frustrated by the lack of information about the Security Deposit Corporation and its members. They speculated on what these people were actually doing and what they would do with the aliens if they acquired them.

Part of the mystery surrounding the SDC units was the fact that all their equipment and personnel arrived on site in vans and tarp covered flatbeds. The only people anyone saw were a few truck drivers and the major. None of them wore unit or rank insignia and all of them sported sunglasses of the mirror shades variety. The one other distinction between these people and everyone else was they all wore old-style jungle fatigues.

It was clear from the beginning that the SDC was manned by no nonsense individuals. As soon as they landed on the outskirts of West Falls they jumped from the vehicles and set up a perimeter. Within thirty minutes the town and surrounding area was enclosed by a high voltage electric fence. Within another thirty the two hundred SDC personnel had put high intensity arc lights along the fence line. Automatically fired machineguns were placed every one hundred meters, the guns set to fire on any humans or aliens that tried to escape.

Once all these measures were in place the SDC personnel awaited the order to flip the switch on the lights, electrify the fence and activate the machineguns. There was always the chance someone would stumble onto the fence before the soldiers were ready. But they were stationed all along the perimeter to keep such an event from happening.

Deputy Clifford Fifield woke the students at a little after four in the morning. He felt they should all be up and ready to move before daylight. He wanted to get them safely away from the West Falls area in case the Yrartz expanded their territory and he needed to alert the sheriff's department.

They had nothing to eat and nothing to drink. None of them had slept very well on the cold hard ground. They all looked terrible and felt worse. Even Cliff was feeling renewed pains in his back as he tried to get the fire going again.

Most of the blowdown they camped near had been burned during the night. But Clifford was able to find enough wood to get a decent blaze started. He found some birch bark and made a funnel-like cup in which to boil water.

Carter asked him, "How are you going to boil water in that? It will just burn up."

"Actually as long as there is water in it the bark won't burn. My grandfather taught me how to make one of these when I was a boy. He said an old Indian showed him how.

"We would go hunting with just a knife and gun. We would make one of these cups and boil water, add a few cedar leaves and have a hot tea full of vitamin C. Grandpa knew how to survive in the wilds without all the paraphernalia most guys think they need these days."

Carter was fascinated by the skills Cliff was displaying. He had never before seen a fire started without lighter fluid or at least paper. He had no idea one could cook with birch bark. He would have died of starvation or thirst on his own in the woods.

Deputy Fifield made a birch cup for each of the kids and boiled a tea for them. He kept the fire going while they sat back and enjoyed their drink. When everyone was ready he put out the fire and led off down a game trail.

Tom woke to find his left arm numb. Kelly's head was resting on it. He pulled his arm out carefully so as not to wake her. Just as he successfully did so Nathan came stumbling inside and announced loudly that it was their turn to watch.

Kelly came awake to the sound of her brother's voice. To Tom she was the most beautiful woman he had ever seen as she rubbed her hands through her hair. She yawned and stretched as she stood up. Sleepily she said, "Good morning."

Tom stood beside her. "Good morning beautiful," he said to her. Kelly looked at him letting her eyes search his face carefully as if something she lost could be found there. She smiled and kissed him, their lips lingering maybe a little too long.

Nathan turned away muttering something about them getting a room. He stepped into the kitchen and looked for coffee. Picking up the carafe he saw it was empty. He took it and started making a new pot.

Tom came in the kitchen and said, "I'm going outside to watch. You and Kelly want to get breakfast going?"

"You bet I, ah, we do. I'll bring you some coffee when it's ready."

"Good enough." Tom put on his coat and took up his rifle. He opened the front door and went out swiftly so as to keep the disturbance to a minimum. He waited on the porch a few minutes breathing in the sharp morning air and letting his eyes get accustomed to the darkness.

He moved off the porch and began his rounds going first to the back of the house. Walking through the grass he could see the faint trail Nate had left in the frost on the lawn. Tom followed the trail past the house and stopped under a large oak tree in the back yard. He stood there a few minutes then went around the opposite side of the house and back into the barnyard.

Tom planned to go into the barn and check it to make sure no unwanted visitors lurked there. But just as he started walking he heard the front door open. He stopped and turned around as Kelly came outside. He waited for her to bring him the steaming cup of coffee she held in her hand.

When she came close he reached for the cup and Kelly pulled it away from him. "No this is mine," she said unable to keep a straight face. Tom didn't fall for the joke but kept his hand out stretched. Smiling, she carefully put the cup in his gloved hand.

"Thank you. Did you get some coffee too?"

"Not yet. I figured you needed it more than I did. I'm going to go back inside and cook up some eggs and ham I found. I'll eat quick and come out here to relieve you as soon as I can."

Tom kissed her and said, "No worries. Take your time and eat plenty. We don't know when we will get a chance to eat again."

"Good point," she said and headed toward the house. Kelly turned to wave at him from the porch but he had already gone inside the barn.

When she got back to the kitchen Nate was sitting at the table eating. "Did you leave anything for me?"

"Believe it or not sis' I did." Nathan talked while he ate and did not look up at her. "I even made toast."

Kelly squeezed his shoulder as she passed him on her way to the stove. There was still some ham in one pan but there were no eggs in the other one. One piece of toast sat warmly in the toaster.

She started cracking eggs into the fry pan while humming to herself. Kelly heard the chair scrape on the wood floor. She turned as Nate got up. "I'm going to take a nap now. Wake me when you guys want to go back to town."

Kelly answered, "Okay, I will." She went back to her cooking. The eggs were just starting to cook. She pulled the piece of toast out and put two pieces of bread in and pushed down on the handle. She buttered the warm toast and began eating as the eggs and ham sizzled.

Tom wanted to turn the lights on in the barn but chose not to. He did not want to alert any Yrartz that might be close enough to see. Instead he closed the big door and used his flashlight to peer into the corners and dark spaces. He climbed the ladder to the mow and looked around up there. None of the aliens they had seen seemed to be able to or interested in climbing.

He stayed up in the mow and shined the light down on all the corners of the first floor again. Tom knew he could see more from above than from ground level. But all his searching came up empty. He found no Yrartz in the barn.

Tom began a systematic search of the outbuildings next. Walking between buildings he kept a sharp look out for aliens in the surrounding fields. He stopped several times thinking he saw something out there. But everything he checked turned out to be bushes and farm equipment, no Yrartz.

Kelly finished eating by the time Tom was checking the old chicken coop. She left the eggs out and turned down the heat under the ham. She put fresh pieces of bread in the toaster then put on her coat and headed out the door.

She saw Tom as he left the coop and walked to meet him. "All's quiet," he told her.

"Good. Maybe we can get to town without another fight," Kelly said, relief in her voice.

"I sure hope so. It seems we been running and hiding forever." He looked around again. "Well we know those kids from the institute will get somebody out here. It shouldn't take them too long. In fact we should be getting help within the next several hours I would think."

"I certainly hope so. I never wanted to be in a sci-fi horror movie."

"I agree. I don't ever want to see another alien in person or on TV or movies or anywhere else." Tom reached down and kissed her. "I'm going to get some breakfast."

"I left the eggs out and some ham in the pan."

"Thanks. I won't be long." He turned and walked away.

Kelly wanted to follow him into the house and stay there with him but she knew she had to keep watch. She was more afraid than she cared to admit even to herself. She stood up straight and forced herself to move out beyond the buildings.

Tom went inside promising himself he would only eat a little and then rejoin Kelly. He hated to leave her alone. He knew she could take care of herself but he felt better when he was by her side. He was fairly confident there were no Yrartz anywhere near. But the little guys were short and green. They might hide anyplace and there certainly were plenty of spots to hide in.

The pasture behind the barn appeared empty. So Kelly took a hike out into the middle of it thinking it would bolster her courage. She was close to center between the road to the east and the swamp to the west. The barn was north and the woods were south.

Suddenly Kelly had an uneasy feeling she was being watched. She did not want to run for fear the watcher would run after her. Instead she slowly backed toward the barn. It took all her nerve to keep from turning and running headlong back to the house.

She was only a few yards into her retreat when she saw them. They were coming out of the woods on the east side of Hawthorne Road. They were going straight west and if they didn't see her they would enter the swamp and soon be gone from sight.

Kelly stopped and stood still, barely breathing. She slowly crouched down trying to hide in the tall grass. She silently prayed Tom would not come out now and walk right into this.

She did not count them but she knew there were too many for the five of them. Worse, if they had to defend themselves others would come to the sound of gunfire. They would quickly be overrun.

The Yrartz patrol leader continued on across the field intent on getting back to the LZ. He wasn't sure what was up but one of his buddies radioed him and told him a lot of activity was going on. He should get back as soon as possible. No problem, he wanted out of here too.

Tom left the house and started walking toward the barn. He thought about calling out to Kelly but decided against it. There was a chance the aliens were in the area and he didn't need them attacking now. They were too close to getting back to town and he did not want another fight.

Kelly watched as the patrol crossed the pasture and entered the swamp. She started counting the aliens and discovered there were twenty in the group. That was way too many for their gang to handle. She crouched down lower after counting them.

Tom was searching for Kelly and getting a little worried. She wasn't in the barnyard or behind the house. He was certain she wouldn't be in the barn and probably not in any of the outbuildings either. He didn't see her out in the pasture west of the yard or on the driveway. There was only one other place to look.

He started walking fast alongside the barn. Kelly had to be behind the barn somewhere. Tom felt that something was wrong. She would have made the rounds and been within sight by now. He picked up the pace.

When Tom was nearly at the end of the barn he saw Kelly in the grass. First he thought she was hurt. She was low down as if something was wrong with her. But then it dawned on him she was hiding from something. He ran then.

Kelly whirled around at the sound of Tom running toward her. She half expected to see an alien and her gun came up. Tom skidded to a stop hands up, "Don't shoot! It's just me."

The gun lowered as Kelly came to her feet. Tom rushed to her and she threw her arms around him. "Man am I glad to see you," he said.

She sobbed in his arms as relief washed over her. He didn't immediately understand why she was crying. Through the sobs she told him, "I saw them." She held him tighter. "I was afraid." She pulled her head back and looked at him. "I was all alone and there were twenty of them but they didn't see me."

"Thank God they didn't." Tom held her and kissed the tears from her eyes. "I'm here now. You're safe." He spoke too soon.

There was one alien trailing behind the rest of the patrol. He was rear guard and had stopped to take a leak. He was rushing to catch up when he saw the Earthlings out standing in the field.

He started yelling into his radio for help. The squealing he made alerted every Yrartz in the area. Dozens of aliens began looking for this new threat as the patrol leader realized one of his men was making the call. He immediately turned and led his group back to the field to try and find the missing man.

The generals dropped their plans to eliminate the Supreme Commander. They started issuing orders for the troops to form up and begin searching for the source of this threat. Within moments hundreds of aliens were moving in skirmish lines in all four directions away from the LZ.

# Chapter 31

"Shoot!" Tom exclaimed. "That Yrartz saw or heard us," he pointed.

"That's the same path where I saw the others. There were twenty of them," she repeated. Fear transformed her. Kelly had been brave in the face of the enemy up to now. But something finally got to her and she fell apart.

Tom could see the terror in her eyes. He grabbed her arm, "Come on. Let's go. We have to get back to the others and get out of here." He pulled her along as quickly as he could. Kelly turned to stone, unable to move on her own.

Tom thought about slapping her face as he had seen in many a movie. Instead he slung his rifle and took hold of both of Kelly's shoulders. He shook her hard enough to knock some of the fear out of her. "Kelly get hold of yourself. We have to get out of here."

Kelly's eyes focused on him then. She shook her head yes and turned toward the house. Tom pulled and pushed her along trying to hurry her up. She finally came out of it and started running, the terror still gripping  her heart.

The Yrartz patrol leader caught up to his man and started asking questions. The poor alien was so afraid he couldn't speak so he just pointed in the direction of the humans. The patrol moved up the hill toward Granny's farm buildings.

On the run the leader called in the situation. Soon dozens of aliens were on their way to the scene. They descended on the farmhouse from three directions and soon closed in on the fourth as well.

It seemed every Yrartz wanted to get in on a chance to harm some humans again and perhaps get a bite to eat. They had been defeated in recent battles and wanted to get some back. This looked like an easy fight with only two people in sight.

The patrol updated as they went forward. They were hot on the heels of Tom and Kelly and hoped to catch them. The humans were running and showing no intention of turning to fight. It was the kind of battle the Yrartz preferred.

Tom and Kelly ran into the barnyard as Kaitlyn came out onto the porch. She was smiling and holding a steaming cup of coffee. The smile vanished and she dropped the cup spilling coffee across the boards.

"What happened?" she cried.

"The Yrartz spotted us. They are coming in numbers," Tom explained on the fly. "We have to get everyone and get out of here."

Kaitlyn pointed toward the barn. "Bob's in the barn. We can't leave without him."

Tom whirled around as the first aliens entered the barnyard. He fired his rifle from the hip completely missing all the enemy. But he jacked another shell in and shot one Yrartz in the head. Then he put the MP-5 on semi and started shooting for real.

Kelly pulled up her rifle and fired round after round. Kaitlyn had a shotgun Bob found in Granny's house. She shot all three shells and reloaded as she started down the porch steps. She started to run.

"Kaitlyn get back. Where are you going?" Tom shouted.

"I'm going to find Bob. I lost my husband. I'm not losing Bob too," she answered defiantly.

Nate opened the front door. He didn't ask any questions he just lifted his shotgun and started taking out Yrartz. He kept up a steady fire that allowed Tom to reload the MP-5 and shoot down the advancing hordes.

"Nate fall back inside the house and check out the rear windows. They may be coming at us from all directions by now." Tom looked at Kelly and nodded. "Inside and keep up a steady fire out this way. Kaitlyn and I will rescue Bob from the barn."

Kaitlyn ran toward the open barn door. As she got close an alien fired a taser dart at her. She fired the shotgun as she slid on her knees in a great impression of a quarterback sliding on the field to avoid being tackled.

Tom ran up beside her and helped her to her feet as he unloaded the MP-5 at some Yrartz. Together they ran into the barn and turned to look outside. They heard gunfire from the back of the barn.

Bob was in the haymow firing through the open door up there. He turned and waved at them, "Hey how's it going out front?"

"We're in trouble Bob. We best all try to get back to the house and form up. If we are together we have a chance. Spilt up like this we are done for sure."

"Okay Tom. I'll be right down." Bob slung his gun over his shoulder and grabbed hold of a rope that hung from a badly rusted pulley in the mow. He swung out over the open and slid down the rope landing on his feet. He let go of the rope and slid the gun into his hands ready for the fight.

"Good thing I kept my gloves on. That would have hurt," he said as he moved by Tom. Kaitlyn put her arms around him and they embraced briefly. "Let's go."

Tom let Bob go first while he laid down covering fire. Kelly was shooting from a window in the house. Kaitlyn helped with a few well-placed shots of her own then followed Bob out the door.

Tom reloaded just as he hit the open door running. Bob stopped at the bottom of the porch steps to let Kaitlyn get past him. Kelly kept up her shooting switching to another gun when one emptied out. She had two shotguns and two rifles with her.

The dead Yrartz were piling up around the barnyard. Finally they began to fall back as unit commanders called retreat. Clearly they needed to formulate another plan.

Shots could be heard from the back of the house as Nathan got into the fray. He was shooting a rifle taking his time and making shots count. The enemy were closing in on the house but he still had room.

Kaitlyn opened the front door of Granny's house and held it for Bob. He ran through and went to the window in the kitchen. Tom got to the door and pushed Kaitlyn in then stumbled in after her. Taking a knee he fired at the retreating Yrartz.

"Kelly, you go back and see if your brother needs help. Kaitlyn go to the first bedroom and watch out to the west. Bob go to the kitchen door and see if any of them are out there." Tom stood up and kicked the door shut with his foot. He moved to the window Kelly had been using and looked out while checking the guns she left behind.

Kelly was back in seconds. "There are lots of them out back advancing on the house. Nate's in control for now but we aren't going to be able to escape out that way."

They heard glass breaking. Tom and Kelly turned toward the kitchen, questioning looks on their faces. Bob answered their unspoken question. "There are a bunch of them out here too." He used the butt of his rifle to clean out the rest of the glass from the window. "I kind of wish this door had a smaller window," he commented.

Kaitlyn stepped backwards out into the hall. "There's a lot of them out this way too," she said and went back into the bedroom. She found a comfortable seat on the bed and watched out the window.

With any chance of escape gone, Tom had to come up with a new plan. The Yrartz had them surrounded and were closing in. It looked like their whole army was here.

He checked his ammunition and got a shock. In the fight in the barnyard he had used the last of the 9mm. Tom only had the magazine in the gun left. "Hey Bob, do you have any ammo left for the MP-5s?"

Bob fiddled around with his pack keeping one eye on the aliens outside. "I have just what's in my gun. The rest of the mags are empty."

"Me too. We are going to have to use our deer rifles."

"Ah Tom, that is significantly reducing our firepower," Bob said dryly.

"Yep," Tom replied. "Soon we are going to be throwing stones at them."

"Problem is we don't have any stones in the house." Bob added, "Granny always has bullets in the place somewhere."

"In the cabinet. But I already checked there. She took all the ten gauge which is alright since she has the gun too. There are some twelve gauge and a few .30-'06. The rest are .22. I'm not sure if we can kill them with that."

"We will have to be more accurate is all," Bob suggested. "Heck we shot some of them when we were running from here last time."

"True, but when we were rescuing Granny we left them behind. We don't know if we actually killed any of them."

Bob gave that some thought. "You are right but I did shoot at them and they did fall. So I know I hit them. We know their armor isn't that great and we can shoot through it. They don't have helmets on so we can shoot them in the head. We have a couple twenty-two pistols and at least two rifles. We can hold them off for a while," *maybe.*

Tom was looking through the cabinet again. He pulled out several boxes. "Well Granny was well stocked with rim fire ammo. She has three five-hundred round boxes and some fifty round boxes plus some loose stuff up here."

"Good. And you know Granny always had a few in her underwear drawer and probably some in one or more of her coats."

"You're right brother. She always has twenty-two ammo stuffed everywhere. But we don't have enough guns to go around so we better start using them now and save the big gun ammo for when it gets serious."

Tom went and found the rim fire guns. He loaded a pistol and gave it to Nathan. He gave the other pistol to Kelly. He took the rifles and handed one to Bob and kept the other for himself.

The brothers would use the rifles but Tom told Nate and Kelly to use whichever gun they were comfortable with. He also told them the reason they were using the smaller caliber guns. That didn't help morale amongst the trapped humans.

Bill heard the intense shooting and rightly deduced it was Tom and his group. He wished he knew what was going on and what he could do to help. But with no communications and no intel he could do nothing but listen to the gunbattle.

That did not stop him from doing his best to keep the town from danger. He immediately made certain everyone was up and alert, ready for whatever came. He had John and the rest of the leadership checking on ammo and medical supplies. He made sure the people had food and water close by so they did not have to leave their posts.

Some of the barricades were strengthened. Roving reserve units kept moving between outposts to confuse the enemy and make them think there were more people than there really were. The people unable to fight were moved to the auto repair shop just behind the farm machine shop. Bill had done, was doing everything he could to stop the Yrartz from overrunning West Falls.

There was some excitement in the Yrartz camp. The Supreme Commander had given orders for a change in the plan of attack on Granny Hayward's farm buildings. The generals for once approved of what he had decided. They immediately began preparations.

The mood in the alien lines was one of anticipation and exhilaration. The Yrartz were electrified when rumors of the new plan spread like wildfire through the ranks. Gone were thoughts of a difficult battle ahead. Instead the troops could see victory in this fight.

Smiles crossed every face as the generals put the new plan into place. Units moved in readiness, changing positions with other units. The cordon enclosing the farm drew closer and closer. Troops crept in behind the barn and entered it from the back. Everyone was ready.

# Chapter 32

Kelly and Bob traded places so she could be in the kitchen and closer to Tom. Kaitlyn spent much of her time with Bob but went between the others making sure they were awake and had everything they needed. She had the least weapons training of them all so she was the gofer. She had just returned to the bedroom when they heard an odd sound.

"Oh no!" Tom said loud enough for everyone to hear. Bob and Kaitlyn came from the bedroom.

From the kitchen Kelly asked, "What is it?"

Bob looked out the big window. "It looks like something out of a fifties sci-fi movie." Kaitlyn moved next to him and held his arm, leaning in.

Kelly came in and looked out the window. Nate walked down the hall. "What's everyone doing in here? What are you all staring at?" he asked. Then he looked out the window too. "Oh my."

"What do you think it is Tom?" Kelly asked.

"I don't know but I think it isn't good news. It looks like some kind of giant laser maybe. Whatever it is everybody back to your stations but be ready to move at a moments notice."

Nate stopped by the kitchen on his way to the back bedroom. He needed to replenish his food supplies and grabbed a bottle of water to wash it all down with. He resumed his place and found everything as he left it.

Bob went into the first bedroom and peered out the window. He noticed some of the aliens had moved closer to the house. They were behind good cover so he couldn't do much about them.

When Kelly checked out the kitchen window she saw several Yrartz trying to sneak up behind a tree close in. She shot one of them in the arm and the other squealed and ran away leaving the first one. Kelly emptied her pistol at the alien missing every shot with the short gun. The wounded Yrartz crawled toward a low spot in the yard.

The aliens had one weapon they had yet to use on this planet. They rolled it up alongside the barn keeping just out of effective twenty-two range. The weapon was mounted on a carriage with six wheels. It was driven by one Yrartz while two more stood on a platform at the back.

The gunner and his assistant prepared to aim and fire the weapon. As soon as the driver halted the vehicle they went into action. The gunner aimed at the house and fired.

Tom's worst fear was realized. The weapon was real and relatively powerful. The front door of Granny's farmhouse burst into flames. The alien gunner shut it down and prepared to hit another target.

"Quick get some water on that fire!" Tom shouted. Kelly was already filling a pitcher. She grabbed other containers and kept up a steady barrage of water.

Kaitlyn rushed into the kitchen and picked up some pans. She ran into the bathroom and filled the pans in the tub. Bob came and dropped a steel bucket in the tub, took the full pans and ran back to the fire.

Before the fire was completely out the Yrartz fired again. Bob narrowly missed getting scalded as the wall between the front door and the living room window blew out. The fire quickly spread around the hole and reignited the door.

"Bob are you alright?" Tom asked as he dropped down beside his brother. Bob assured him he was fine. Jumping back up he shouted, "Kelly and Kaitlyn, put together some food and any ammo you find. Be quick about it." He threw his backpack at them.

He sent Bob back to his position while the girls packed. When they were ready Tom gave them covering fire so they could cross the opening. "You get back to Bob. When I'm ready I'll signal you."

"Where do you expect us to go?" Kelly asked breathlessly. "We're completely surrounded."

"Just get to the bedroom. I'll think of something by then."

Without any further questions the two women went to work. Kelly gathered all the ammunition she could find no matter what caliber. Kaitlyn stuffed crackers, cheese and trail mix into Tom's pack.

Instead of waiting for Tom's covering fire Kelly pushed Kaitlyn across the open spot and followed her. They ran to the bedroom and joined Bob. Tom fired a few fast shots at the Yrartz out front and headed back shouting to Nate to come too.

As soon as Nate entered the room Tom shouted, "Follow me." He stepped out the broken window and ran to the wooden fence just a few feet from the house. He stood up and fired the last of the 9mm rounds at the Yrartz that were crouching behind the fence. The bullets missed most of the aliens there but sent them all scurrying away.

Tom dropped the empty MP-5 and raised his deer rifle. He turned toward the alien laser and shot the gunner out of his seat. While Kelly joined him at the fence he shot at the assistant gunner.

Nathan took a three step run at the window and leaped. While Kaitlyn and Bob tried to get him unstuck Tom ran toward the barn. Kelly kept up covering fire and moved along behind him.

Bob and Kaitlyn managed to pull Nate back into the room. "Maybe you guys should go. I'll stay and fight to the last bullet."

"Kaitlyn go," Bob told her. "I will find a way to get him through that window."

Kaitlyn kissed Bob on the lips and told him, "You come right behind me. Don't make me come back for you." With that she grabbed a pack and jumped out the window. Hitting the ground running, she quickly made it to the fence.

The front of the house was engulfed in flames and smoke was leaking under the bedroom door. Both men began coughing. They could feel the heat through the walls. The whole house would soon go up.

Without warning Nathan picked up Bob and tossed him out the window. He threw all the guns out too. Then not waiting for anything Nate launched his considerable bulk at the offending window. This time he tucked and rolled through like a giant bowling ball landing on his bottom.

Bob had just enough time to get out of the way. He picked up his rifle and a shotgun. He handed the shotgun to Nate and turned toward the fence. He grabbed two handguns off the ground then took up a position next to Kaitlyn.

Nathan shook his head to clear it then struggled to his feet. He slung the shotgun over his shoulder and picked up a twenty-two rifle. Instead of going to the fence for cover he strode forward through the smoke from the burning house.

Granny's house was a typical wood frame structure. It was old and dry and so it went up in flames quickly. Nate ignored the heat and smoke walking and firing the little rifle as he went.

Tom was crouched next to the open barn door. He was reloading the semi-auto twenty-two he had as he noticed something moving through the smoke. He turned in time to see Nate striding toward him as if there were no aliens near.

The big man held the rifle in one hand and a pistol in the other. He went through the barn door shooting any alien he saw. When the pistol emptied he stuck it in his waistband and reloaded the rifle. Tom stood up and joined Nate inside the barn.

The pair shot at anything that moved. Kelly soon came into the barn also. She took up a position next to the open door shooting any moving thing that wasn't human that the boys missed. She knew she was running out of ammo but she kept up a steady fire.

She held her fire and pointed the gun toward the sky when she saw Kaitlyn and Bob coming her way. They ran into the barn without stopping for a chat. They stopped just behind Tom and Nate and scanned the interior of the barn for aliens.

The Yrartz were trying to get the laser moved so they could burn the barn down. The fight had escalated for them and now it was all about killing the pesky humans. The fact that they were edible no longer crossed their minds. They just wanted these humans dead without losing any more of their own.

Bob went up the ladder into the loft followed by Kaitlyn. They began the task of making sure there were no live aliens up there. They searched the whole thing and found only one Yrartz cowering in a corner near the open haymow door.

He squealed when he noticed them looking at him. The little alien jumped up and rolled out the open door crashing to the ground outside. His squealing turned to whimpering.


Outside the Yrartz were gathering around the giant laser trying to move it away from the barn. They needed some distance so they could burn the place down without causing any harm to themselves. One of them had tried to restart the engine but failed so now they were stuck with pushing the machine to a safe area.

A dozen or so of the aliens repeatedly fired taser darts at the barn in a vain attempt to hit one of the humans inside. Most of the darts fell harmlessly to the ground. Very few even flew far enough to hit the building. The one thing they did do was alert the people inside that they were trying to move the laser.

"Hey everybody!" Nathan shouted as he pointed to the windows on the west side of the barn. "The Yrartz are trying to move the laser."

Tom shouted, "Kelly hold the door and keep an eye out for any aliens out to the east. I'm going to help Nate get rid of those over there," he pointed.

Kelly positioned herself next to the open barn door. She had a pistol, a rifle and a shotgun all loaded and ready. She closed the door halfway to give her some extra cover.

"Bob," Tom yelled looking up. "You and Kaitlyn watch the back while we try to destroy the laser."

"Will do brother," Bob yelled back. He put Kaitlyn on one side of the open door and positioned himself on the other. They immediately began engaging the aliens outside. Because of the limited range of the Yrartz weapons the pair were safe enough shooting out the door. The enemy scurried away to hide a safe distance from the barn.

Nate and Tom started smashing out windows and taking shots at the aliens near the laser. They hit a few but many bullets merely bounced off pieces of the machinery. It was frustrating and dangerous work. Some of the Yrartz snuck along the barn wall under the windows and shot taser darts into the openings.

"Tom this ain't gonna work. There are too many of them and now they are shooting darts in the windows. Sooner or later one or both of us is gonna get hit," Nathan yelled while reloading.

"It's worse than that," Tom said. "They got the engine running on that thing and one of them is driving it away. I can't seem to hit him."

"Great!" Nate said as he stood and shot at where he hoped the driver was.

Tom moved over beside Nathan. "Shoot at those things on that box. I think they might be the controls. At least we can try and disable the darn thing."

"Okay." Nate shot every round out of his gun and stopped to reload again. "I think we're in trouble."

"Hate to say it but I think you're right."

Before Nathan could reply the Yrartz driver turned the laser around so it was aimed at the barn. The machine wasn't far enough away that the men couldn't hit it with rifle fire but it was long range for a twenty-two. It was iffy hitting anyone on the unit. The aliens had a shield in back near the controls to protect the shooters. Only a ricochet could wound or kill the green guys.

"We're in deep trouble!" Tom shouted loud enough for everyone in the barn to hear. Kelly looked over at him. Kaitlyn and Bob peeked down from the mow, questioning looks on their faces.

Tom stepped out toward the middle of the barn so everyone could see him. Talking loudly he said, "The Yrartz have moved the laser and are getting it ready to fire on us. Be ready to move."

"Move where?" Kelly asked.

"I don't know but we can't stay here if they start shooting that thing at the barn. This place will go up a lot faster than the house did." As if to accentuate Tom's words the front wall of the house crashed in sending sparks and heat waves billowing.

Tom looked out the east windows. "We all make a run for the old 33"
"The what?" Nate asked. Kelly, Kaitlyn and Bob all had the same question on their tongues.

Tom pointed. "The old red tractor out there. We run for that. When everyone is there we run for the road."
"What are we going to do then, stick our thumbs out?" Nate asked.

The Yrartz gunner fired into the roof of the barn burning a hole through the shingles and boards and into the hay. There was a whooshing sound as the hay caught fire. Kaitlyn screamed and Bob shouted for her to get down the ladder.

Nathan fired the last of his bullets and turned for the front door. "Kelly go with him," Tom yelled. "Hurry!" he called to Kaitlyn and Bob. They needed no urging.

Kaitlyn climbed as fast as she could, missed the last rung and tripped. Tom caught her and kept her from falling. Bob stuck his legs on the outer edge of the ladder and slid down.

Tom grabbed his arm and Kaitlyn's arm and hurried them out the door. Nate and Kelly were at the tractor and they looked back as they heard the trio approach. Fear etched their faces.

Tom asked, "What is it?"

Nate waved his arm out in the direction of the road. "That," was all he said. It wasn't necessary to explain. A hundred Yrartz were in a skirmish line coming toward them. The five humans had no bullets for the deer rifles and no shells for the shotguns. They were down to rim fire guns and ammo.

"Well it looks sort of hopeless doesn't it?" Nate said. He handed the pistol he had to Kaitlyn. "Here." She took the gun wondering what he did that for. He took off his coat and dropped it to the ground.

"What are you doing?" Kelly asked, worried.

Tom stepped up beside him and grabbed hold of his arm. "What's going on Nate?" he asked. "What are you planning?"

Nate looked at him, shrugged off his hand and saying nothing started forward. He stepped slowly at first then began jogging. Finally he burst into what for him was a full out sprint roaring wildly as he went.

To everyone's surprise, including Nathan's the Yrartz line faltered then broke. The little aliens started running away in all directions. It looked like a classic rout of an entire army.

# Chapter 33

Eight Humvees came roaring down the road toward the Yrartz skirmish line. The little green line fragmented as soon as the first vehicle came over the hill. Aliens scattered in every direction trying to avoid the convoy. Screaming, squealing and an occasional thump could be heard as they fled.

The shooting started shortly after the line collapsed. The guns mounted on the Humvees came to life as the Rangers in them spotted targets. What aliens didn't get hit by bullets were run over by the big trucks.

Four of the vehicles came roaring down Granny's driveway their guns spitting fire like dragons at any alien thing that moved. One Humvee stopped on the hill just before the farm road and concentrated fire to the north of the barnyard. The other three went on past and turned into the field mowing down fences and Yrartz in the process.

The sickly sweet smell of diesel fumes slammed into their noses as a new invasion began. This time it was the U.S.

military led by elements of the SDC. The situation had turned from hopeless and helpless to safe and secure in just seconds.

Nathan nearly fell over when he saw the first Humvee. Relief left him startled and light headed. He had never seen anything so welcome as the Ranger unit now taking control of the farm. He dropped to his knees and set his weapon down. He folded his hands, bowed his head and said thank you to God.

Tom, Kelly, Bob and Kaitlyn stood up and cheered. "Guys drop your weapons. We don't want our own army to shoot us," Tom suggested. He looked toward the sky and said a thank you to God as well.

The first three vehicles into Granny's yard fanned out and took up positions near the buildings. The men in them continued shooting at the retreating aliens even as they exited the machines. On foot the rangers formed a skirmish line of their own.

The last Humvee stopped next to the grateful humans. The driver's door opened and the soldier asked, "You all alright?"

"Yes sir," Nate saluted as he stepped forward.

Tom asked, "How about the town? Are some of you going there?"

"Yes sir. We have units travelling into West Falls even as we speak. They should be arriving about now.

"You all can stay here or go to town and join your friends there. Whichever you want. We will mop up here and secure the area. We already have the entire West Falls area as well as the farms and swamp surrounded. We believe we have the threat contained."

"Thank you sirs," Tom said as the soldier closed his door. Everyone behind him said their thanks too.

Tom reached down and picked up his weapons. He believed they were out of danger now but felt better having a gun in his hands. There was always the chance some of the Yrartz might escape.

Bill was at the barricade on Cumberland Road waiting and watching. "What is that sound?" John asked.

"I don't know for certain," Bill answered. "It sounds to me like trucks, big trucks and a bunch of them." The pair watched the road in expectation. Soon they were joined by many of the town's people all asking about and wondering what they were hearing.

Suddenly the first truck came over the hill and a huge grin brightened Bill's face. "What is it?" someone asked. "The aliens got a new fighting machine?"

Bill slapped John on the arm. "It's the cavalry man. It's the cavalry." He started laughing. The incredible relief he felt made him double over with uncontrollable laughter.

The SDC units were the first to arrive in West Falls. Their Humvees roared up to the barricade and fanned out along the line. Their guns trained on the people manning the roadblock.

The captain in charge of the lead elements of the SDC force spoke into the microphone he held. The loudspeakers belted out, "Put down your weapons immediately! I will only ask once. Put down your weapons immediately. My men will commence firing on you unless you surrender immediately."

Bill's laughter ceased. He jumped to his feet leaving his rifle on the ground. "Everybody drop your weapons now! Drop your weapons now!" He went slowly along the line using his voice and hands urging everyone to drop their guns. He knocked the gun out of one man's hand when he didn't immediately comply. He realized these soldiers meant what they said.

Slowly, one by one, the men and women on the barricades let go of their guns. Many, dazed expressions on their faces, raised their hands in the air in surrender. None of them seemed to understand just why they needed to give up their weapons.

Two of the SDC Humvees began pushing the cars in the roadblock out of the way. As soon as there was room other trucks moved into the town. Bigger trucks came in and troops dropped off the back and began moving the town's people out of the way. Others began collecting the weapons and putting them in the other trucks.

Bill tried to step up to the man he thought was commanding these units. But as he got close troops stopped him with their rifles pointed at his chest. "Hey what the heck is going on? All I want to do is talk to the commander of your unit. I'm the guy in charge of the town."

The unit's leader looked over at Bill. "Check him for weapons. Let him come to me."

One of the soldiers frisked Bill none too gently and then let him pass. He walked over to the leader. Before he could say anything the man started, "Since we don't know what these aliens look like, you and all your people will be placed in protective custody. We will determine your status and then decide what to do with you.

"I suggest if you really are human that you comply with all our requests. We do not want to kill any innocents or damage any buildings or equipment unnecessarily. Please keep your people under control. Now if you will excuse me I have orders to give and details to take care of."

Once again before Bill could say anything one of the troops took him by his shoulders and turned him. He pushed him toward the line of soldiers. His first thought was to turn and slap the man but he did not have a gun and the soldier did.

Tom and Kelly hugged as if they would never see each other again. They looked at the farm buildings as the barn crashed to the ground in a shower of sparks and flame. "Wow am I glad those boys came when they did," he said as he held her close.

Kelly looked up at his face, smiled and nodded. She leaned her head into his chest feeling the warmth of his body. She had no words at this moment, only relief that they had all survived. Tears came then, tears of joy and relief as she went limp in his arms.

The wind whipped around and brought the pungent odor with. "Wow, that's nasty," Bob commented. Kaitlyn wrinkled her nose but said nothing. She held him close, happy that it was all over. The smell no longer bothered her now. She was safe in his arms.

"You know I don't think they smell as bad after they're dead. I walked past one I killed a couple hours ago. It wasn't as bad," Nathan said. He shook his head. "There ain't no way around it. Yrartz stink."

"Well let's get to town and see how they fared," Tom suggested as he turned Kelly in that direction. Holding hands the pair started walking along the driveway toward Hawthorne Road. The others fell in behind them.

When they reached the road they turned toward West Falls. They walked slowly, exhausted from the previous days and nights with very little sleep. The fighting and running had taken its toll so they walked in silence for a time.

Nate stepped up next to Bob and Kaitlyn and kept pace with them. "You think they will ever write a book or make a movie about this?" he asked.

"Naw," Bob said. "The government is gonna cover it all up. They'll swear us to secrecy. Probably detain us on some remote island somewhere and we will never be heard from again."

Tom smiled at that. But Bob's words had a ring of truth to them and it gnawed at the edges of his mind. He began to think about what the soldiers would do with the alien bodies and ships. What would they do with their group and the residents of West Falls? Surely they would all be put in some kind of quarantine for a time. They would assume there were alien bacteria or other organisms that came with the aliens.

Nathan couldn't let it go. "If they do write a book or make a movie what do you think they will call it?"

Bob shrugged. Nate continued, "Maybe they'll call it *The Day the Earth Smelled Bad.*"

"Or maybe they'll call it *Invasion of the Body Odor,*" Bob added.

"I know, *Dawn of the Dead Smell,*" Nathan beamed.

At the edge of the woods Tom stopped and turned for one last look at Granny's farm. The house and barn were piles of burning boards. The rest of the buildings were still intact. A tanker truck had moved in without siren and some men were spraying water on the ruins of the barn. Soon all that was left were some blackened, smoldering boards.

Bob looked at Tom and asked, "Where is Granny going to live now?"

"Probably with us," he said without thinking on it. "Well let's get moving." Tom turned for town again as Kelly put her head on his shoulder and held his arm in both her hands. She was hoping the two of them would get married and have a place of their own and Granny could live with Bob.


The residents of West Falls were disarmed and herded into the church parking lot. The SDC personnel had searched each house and moved, in some cases forced, everyone outside. Then they pushed them toward the church.

Now the soldiers were separating the people into smaller groups. A GP-medium tent had been erected beside the church and each person was taken into the tent to be processed. They were asked the common questions such as name, occupation and exactly which house they lived in. Then began the less common inquiries.

Bill was in the first group brought in and questioned because he seemed to be the leader of the town. "Okay Mister Webster, are you an alien come to invade the earth?"

"Huh?"

"Why did you invade our planet? What exactly are you doing here?"

His first thought was *I'm being interviewed by an idiot.* "I live here. I have a bar, The Yellow Rose. I've been living here for many years."

"Sure you have. What do you serve at your bar? Worms? Blood sucking alien bacteria? Come on, what's the plan?"

"I don't serve any of those things. I serve booze and beer and normal human food."

"So you admit you're an alien."

"What? No! I didn't say that."

"What's the normal human food? Humans made into alien dinners? You chop up the locals to feed your friends?"

"No, no, I—we—I just have a bar that serves food and drinks. Nothing special about it." Bill was frustrated and upset. This interview was not going well. "The aliens are out there," he indicated with a sweep of his hand.

The interview at the next table wasn't going any better. John suddenly jumped up and knocked his chair over as he did so. He slammed his fists on the table shouting, "I am not an alien. I'm a normal human being. I'm an American. Stop treating me like I'm some sort of little green alien monster. Those things are real and they're out there. You need to grab your guns and go after them, kill them."

At a nod from the captain, two soldiers took John by the arms and led him out the back door of the tent. Bill had the uneasy feeling he might never see his friend and aide again. Fear crept up his throat and made it difficult to talk or even to breathe. *What are these people going to do with us? Do they really think we are the aliens? What are they going to do with this town? Will word ever get out? Will the world ever know what happened here?*

A truck load of Rangers drove by and the men in the back waved at them. Tom and Kelly waved back smiling and happy to be safe again. The truck headed down Earl's Road. A Humvee passed them going toward town. Two wounded soldiers were laid out in back.

One of the soldiers had been tased and attacked. He had several bites on his leg. The wound had been bandaged but blood could be seen on his torn pants leg. He appeared to be in a lot of pain.

The other soldier had been hit several times by lasers. His uniform caught on fire and he had burns on his left side from his knee nearly to his armpit. He had been given morphine and wasn't feeling the pain.

A third truck rolled up next to the group and a dozen SDC personnel got out. They quickly surrounded the five warriors. The leader of the unit shouted, "Drop your weapons immediately or we will shoot."

Nate dropped his gun as if it suddenly was fiery hot. Tom started to speak but closed his mouth when four guns pointed at him. He dropped his guns. Kelly's were already on the ground and both Bob and Kaitlyn were setting theirs down too. Not sure what else to do everyone raised their hands.

Another truck roared up beside them. "Get in the truck," the leader commanded.

"Where are you taking us?" Kaitlyn asked and began to cry. Bob moved up beside her and took her hand. He helped her into the vehicle and sat next to her. The others followed them into the truck.

"Hey guys," a voice said from the dark interior. "I see they got you too."

"Is that you Deputy Fifield?" Tom asked as he took a seat opposite Bob and Kaitlyn.

"Sure is. Oh and I ran into these friends of yours. Carter, Amery, Jared and Kara are here too. We got rounded up as we were walking along Cumberland. They haven't told us anything about where we're going or what they plan to do with us," Clifford Fifield said.

Tom looked at him and asked, "What do you think they will do with us?"

"I got some ideas. They'll quarantine us for sure. I figure they'll test us to make sure we don't have any alien diseases or anything like that. Probably check to make sure we are all humans and not aliens. They will interrogate us to find out what happened here and then I expect they'll let us go after three or four weeks."

"You really think that they will keep us locked up for four weeks?" Kelly asked.

"I surely think so. They have to quarantine us. Who knows what we may have contracted from them little greenies?"

"I'm more than a little worried that they threatened us and made us give up our weapons," Tom said.

"Yeah that bothered me too," Clifford admitted. "But I guess there isn't much we can do about it now."

Kaitlyn quietly sobbed in Bob's arms. Tom and Kelly held each other as they searched the faces of the rest. Jared, Kara, Amery and Carter acknowledged them with a nod. Deputy Fifield and Nathan began conversing in low voices.

The ride in the back of the truck was rough and loud. Military trucks aren't known for comfort, especially in the back. The driver of this truck seemed to be in a great hurry and didn't much care who got tossed about in the bed of the vehicle.

To make matters worse there was no canvas flap over the back. The cold wind blew into the truck making everyone even more miserable. The wind picked up any dust that might be lying about on the surface of the road and threw that in as well.

"It's cold," Kara complained. Amery nodded her head in agreement and others mumbled something similar.

"Well at least we can see where we've been," Nate said.

"You're right Nate. And look at where we are going," Tom pointed. "This is Earl's Road. They are taking us to Earl's place."

"You're right," the deputy agreed. "Why do you suppose they are doing that?" No one had an answer.

"I hear something, like a loud engine. A train or?" Bob didn't finish the thought.

"Helicopters!" Tom exclaimed. "They must be planning on taking us out of here on those."

"I sure hope that's the plan," Clifford Fifield said. His expression showed doubt and worry.

"What else could they be doing with helicopters?" Nathan asked.


The entire population of West Falls was put in quarantine (read that: made prisoners) until it could be determined who was alien and who was not. The Security Deposit Corporation troops hastily set up an eight foot high, chain link fence to keep them in. Soon requests for bathrooms, shelter, food and water were presented. The troops largely ignored these.

The captain in charge had the soldiers bring in four portable toilets. Pallets of bottled water were also brought in. The people were allowed free use of the toilets but the soldiers distributed the water one bottle at a time. They required each person must open the bottle and drink at least a couple of ounces.

This was a test. The SDC personnel observed each person drink to see if they did it in an unusual way or with an odd body part. They hoped to determine if there were any aliens in the crowd.

A second GP-medium was erected in the church parking lot. After receiving water the town's people were led to the first tent for interrogation. Then they were sent to the second tent where food was served. When they were done eating the people were escorted to the church sanctuary and held under guard until transportation was arranged.

When Bill entered the sanctuary he was one of the first there. He saw John already seated near the front. He rushed up to greet him. Holding out his hand to shake John's he said, "Man am I glad to see you here. I thought they might decide you really were an alien and take you someplace to be dissected or something."

"No they must have figured I wasn't one of them. But they sure gave me a hard time." John smiled as he took Bill's hand. "What do think they will do with us?"

"Well I don't really know for sure, but I overheard some soldiers say something about quarantine. I'm sure they will do that but after I don't know. We can ask but I get the feeling they will only tell us what they want us to know and only when they feel we need to know it."

"I get the same impression. This bunch doesn't seem too friendly and they sure aren't chatty."

"You got that right John." Bill looked out over the folks that were in the sanctuary. "The place is filling up. I think we should go and mingle with the people, assure them that everything is going to be alright."

John looked at him with eyebrows raised. "You really believe that?"

"I don't know what to believe," Bill replied. "But I don't think it will help if we let them know that. I think we should do our best to reassure them. No sense in scaring anyone."

"Okay Bill. I will talk to the folks and try to make them believe it will be fine. I will do my best."

# Chapter 34

The trucks stopped in the pasture next to Earl's house. SDC troops appeared behind the vehicle and ordered everyone out.

They surrounded them and motioned for them to move into the pasture.

One soldier, an officer came up to them. "I'm Lieutenant Jefferson," he said with a friendly smile. "Welcome to the four-oh-seven field hospital. We will check each of you out to see if those little green boogers did anything to you."

He held up his hands. "I know, you never got close to them or they never touched you. But we don't know what they are capable of so we are going to do thorough tests on each of you to make sure you are okay. This way please.

They walked along with the lieutenant as he talked. "We start with questions about what you saw and where you encountered the aliens. We will move on to medical checkups. Then you will be quarantined for a short period of time. Do any of you need anything, food or water?"

"He needs food," Bob said jerking his thumb in Nate's direction. Nate merely nodded affirmatively.

Each person was handed a water bottle and shown into a tent. There they were led to the mess line and served some lunch. As soon as they were done eating they were led individually to the interrogation area.

Tom's appetite was off so he was the first finished. He sat down at the table and the man behind it began. "Are you human?"

"Huh?"

"Simple question. Are you human?"

"Yes."

"Did you encounter aliens in the past few days?"
"Yes."

"Did you touch them or were you bitten? Did you make any physical contact with them?"
"No."

The questions went on. Were you sprayed with anything? Were you captured by the alien's? Did they do any experiments on you? Did you see them land? What kind of weapons do they have? How effective are their weapons? What was their purpose in coming here? Did they inject anything into you? Did they hypnotize you? Are you now or have you ever worked for the aliens? Are you being controlled by them?

When they were done with the questioning they were taken to the barn. The animals had been removed and the building had been cleaned and disinfected. Sterile opaque sheets covered the walls and ceiling and were used to create separate rooms.

Tom was led into one of these rooms and told to disrobe. "Why?" he asked.

"You are going to be examined for alien diseases and infections."

He started taking off his shirt. "Are you going to stay and watch?"

"Yes. We need to make sure there are no parasites clinging to your body."

"What you really mean is you're still not sure if we are aliens or not."


The people of West Falls were herded into trucks ten at a time. They were driven to Earl's farm where they waited in the back of the trucks for their turn to enter the medical building. Bill was taken in the first group after Tom's group had gone through.

When each person had been poked and prodded, x-rayed and blood taken they were placed in the waiting area. When all ten in the group were done they were taken outside and led to a helicopter. They were loaded up and, still under guard, they were flown to the nearest military airfield.

Tom's group were the first to fly out. They would be closely followed by Bill's group. When enough of the groups arrived at the airfield they would be put on a plane and taken to another location.

Things went smoothly until the group John was leading came through. "We demand our rights as American citizens," he shouted at the guards.

The captain in charge came over to address John and his group. "You are all being quarantined for twenty-one days to determine if you have any dangerous diseases or other problems from the aliens. After the quarantine period you will be given your rights if it is determined that you are indeed American citizens and not some alien filth.

"Now form a line starting here or I will have you all accidently shot for disobeying orders. Is that clear?"

John and the others immediately formed up. To them, the captain did not appear to be especially patient. He did, however appear to be prepared to follow through on his promises/threats. Whatever rebellion John and his group thought of starting died quickly and never came out again.

It took 48 hours for all of West Fall's residents to arrive at their new temporary home. Granny Hayward, NM Roswell, Deputy Fifield and the kids from the Shell Lake Institute were added in. Altogether there were just one hundred and twenty-three souls. Fred and June Seeley, Pastor Gordon and Deputy Hawkins were gone. Of The Cajun, Bills cook at The Rose, nothing was ever found.

The people of West Falls were not told where they were or much about how long they would be there. Later they would find out they landed in the little island country of San Socorro. They were confined to area 52, a small island in the San Socorro chain.

Upon arrival in area 52 the people were subjected to an intense indoctrination. They were told to forget everything they had seen or heard regarding the Yrartz invasion. They were each required to sign a form stating that they would never utter a single word about what they saw or heard.

The entire town would be relocated. Most of the former residents chose to remain in San Socorro.

Granny Hayward was given a farm not far from where her old one had been. She lived there a few more years and died in 2018. She passed away peacefully in bed clutching a newer version of the double-barrel shotgun she used against the Yrartz.

Tom and Kelly, Bob and Kaitlyn returned to Wisconsin as well. Tom and Kelly were married shortly after returning and lived near Granny's farm. Bob and Kaitlyn were married a year later and still live in Ashland.

NM Roswell went home and was reunited with his wife Corona. Deputy Fifield and Nathan Minong were among those who chose to stay in San Socorro. Bill Webster moved to Louisiana and looked up some of The Cajun's relatives. There was an unsubstantiated rumor The Cajun escaped the Yrartz and was living somewhere in the swamps southwest of New Orleans.

The Security Deposit Corporation was thorough. Every shred of evidence of an alien invasion was vacuumed up and moved to a secure storage facility. Nothing was left to chance, nothing was left behind.

The units that aided the SDC were broken up and individuals were reassigned. Everyone was sworn to secrecy under threat of severe penalty. No one was ever to speak of anything done, heard or seen at that area in that state.

SDC personnel went over every square millimeter of the entire area where West Falls once stood. The ground was removed to a depth of four centimeters. Water samples were taken from the swamp, the pond and nearby creeks. Every tree and rock was taken. The buildings were turned to dust or taken if there was evidence aliens had been in them.

The LZ was photographed every way possible with every type of camera available including satellites. Every ship and alien body was packaged and removed. Holes were drilled and core samples taken. Metal detectors went over the area. Radar, sonar and other devices were used. In short everything the SDC could do to remove all traces of the Yrartz and the battles was done.

When they were finished the area resembled what it must have looked like when Adam West first arrived. There were no roads, no buildings, no tracks of anything but animals. Trees, grass and brush thrived where once streets and businesses existed.

Local citizens were told there had been an accident in the place where a town once was. They were told the less said the better. When a brave one asked they were told the problem was chemical in nature and was contained. There were few survivors and they would not want to talk about it. Best to leave them alone and stay out of the area altogether.

The last unmarked SDC truck left the area just twenty days after the incident began. Locals were left scratching their heads and wondering exactly what had really gone on there. Many rumors were started. Some died quickly, others went on for a while but none actually came close to the truth.

It was possible some Security Deposit Corporation personnel began most or all of the rumors.

# The End

## Postscript:

There in the darker regions of the swamp lay a motionless, lifeless female Yrartz. It's belly bloated oddly, almost as if pregnant with twins. The dog coyote trotted around it in ever diminishing circles. He stopped and sniffed from several feet downwind.

The things odor was powerful, pungent. The kind of odor that emanates from something long dead. Just the sort of putrid smell the coyote loved. Suddenly his ears perked up, he whirled around and flew off away like his tail was on fire.

The big grey alpha male watched all this from the hummock he was hiding in. If a wolf could smile then he did. On an ordinary day he would have leapt on the dog coyote and ate his fill. Food was food. But there was something better waiting.

Slowly the wolf rose to his feet. He took his time stretching and yawning. He moved cautiously forward picking his way thru the swamp. He did not mind getting his feet wet but preferred not to.

He stopped over the dead Yrartz and watched a while. The wolf was in no hurry since he had eaten well only two days before. He carefully sniffed the carcass then sniffed the wind. Seemed like rain or snow was on its way soon.

The alpha male looked at his next meal with satisfaction. He did not have to run it down or stalk and kill it. The thing was already several days dead judging by the smell. This pleased the wolf. The meat would be soft making it easy on the old canine's dull, loose teeth.

He bent down to take his first bite. The taser stunned him and rendered the wolf immobile. As his eyes closed he saw the "dead" Yrartz standing over him.

+